To my cousin Gladys :.
I hope you enjoy my first novel!

THROUGH HIS
EYES ONLY

A NOVEL

Jack Seville

Jack Seville

PROSPECT
PRESS

Sistersville, WV
New York, NY

Copyright © 2001 by Jack Seville

All rights reserved. No part of this book may be reproduced or transmitted in any form or by any means, electronic, mechanical, photocopying, or otherwise, without the permission of the Author and the Publisher.

Published by Prospect Press
609 Main Street
Sistersville, West Virginia 26175

Library of Congress Catalog Number: 00-136219

ISBN: 1-892668-28-9

Manufactured in the United States of America

First Edition

10 9 8 7 6 5 4 3 2 1

JACK J. SEVILLE, JR., D.D.

Hi Gladys,

Your Mom asked me to send you a copy of my novel — published last summer. Hope you enjoy it. Hope you are doing well.

Love,

Jack

To my beloved Fanny Lee who has journeyed with me through the years and given me courage at every turn along the way.

THROUGH HIS EYES ONLY

A NOVEL

Chapter 1
PENNSYLVANIA STATION

By this time in Lark's life, he'd seen many like her. She was the kind of woman who brought on a sweat, just from looking at her. One had to be careful how he watched her, it could be embarrassing. Lark was careful but comprehensive in his analysis.

She had high cheekbones, and a soft figure flowing like water inside her dress touching here and there the shores of hems and seams. She gave the appearance of fragility, vulnerability, and yet some strange strength, all in one glance. But glance she didn't. She seemed unaware of Lark's eyes moving around her form like an architect scanning a blueprint.

He sat on the bench awaiting the call of the train to Lancaster, transfixed by her physical appeal. He always played a mental game when presented with such beauty, trying to make a list of all the quirks and eccentricities about a woman which would quickly turn him off: she was already deeply and madly in love with a man more powerful than he; she was colder in bed than an Alaskan glacier; she was actually stupid; asking her the time of day would reveal her inability to read a digital dial or her inadequacy to engage in even the most minimal of conversations; she was very sick; she had an incurable form of venereal disease; her voice was like that of a trapped owl in broad daylight.

1

He noted that, as he engaged in this amusing game, she shifted from foot to foot and glanced outside, from time to time. Rain was falling softly on each passerby, and people seemed to be passing silently between one another, barely peeping around the edges of their umbrellas. Puddles were forming in sidewalks and splashes several inches high cascaded when plodding and careless shoes encountered their depths. Once or twice, he noted that men glanced in her direction as they walked past the station window. Most just went by, unaware that she paid them the compliment of noticing their wet bodies negotiating the sidewalks of New York City.

Inside, Pennsylvania Station was crowded with rush hour crowds pushing and shoving to catch their trains. And there, in the midst of all that activity, it seemed as though only Lark and this stranger existed. Once he thought he almost saw her glance in his direction. He was glad their eyes had not locked, however. Her apparent ignorance of his ogling afforded him more time to gather details.

Red hair, natural. Slightly freckled face suggesting a chronic condition which exceeded the length of any summer. Atlantic City? Dark green eyes behind those garish sunglasses, he guessed. Couldn't really tell unless she chose to drop the shades and walk his way. Five six, without heels. Trod as she was, she nearly equaled his height.

Moving down her frame, he estimated a very neat thirty-four inch bust heaved slowly up and down in a most relaxed manner, to no apparent rhythm. Her waist was trim. Perhaps altered by any one of numerous tummy tuck devices available on the market? Hips nicely rounded toward the rear, so as to form one of those classic heart-shaped derrières men love. Her long limbs seemed restless in their panty-hosed presence in the ninety-two degree heat.

He sought words to codify her face. Simply stunning, came to mind. So accommodating. She seemed to give him all the time in the world to sit and stare at her. He guessed she was about ten years his junior. But who can tell anymore?

Lark was positive she was younger than he. He knew for certain no woman his age would stand there and be visually undressed by a man as old as he without turning to stare him down or to give him one of those renowned feminist smiles. He couldn't count how many of that type of women had turned him off in the past ten years. He had grown up in a culture and time when young men claimed that God gave women to men to look at. Suddenly, the feminists, with whom he identified on so many political issues, were demanding that no one's body should be subjected to such long-distance fondling.

There they were: two people in Manhattan, among thousands of people. His momentary fixation upon her presence, not unlike similar events everywhere in the world everyday, made it seem to him as though they were nearly alone. He thought about it. Men and women move into and out of one another's presences like fish in an aquarium. He wondered if fish had memory? Were they trapped in a self-consciousness which was precisely limited to the present? Lark fancied them so. If not, he surmised, they would bash themselves against the walls of this world's aquaria and be done with the singular and unalterable boredom of meeting and passing the very same fish all their lives.

Without warning, her head slowly turned and the dusk-mirrored lenses stared in Lark's direction. He was caught. Her feet moved decisively in his direction. He noted that her hips swayed gently as she approached him.

"Pardon me," she said in a voice as soft as the late spring rain outside, and as sexy as any movie star he'd ever fallen in love with in his youth. "Do you know what time it is?"

During Lark's hesitation, he found himself wondering how a woman like this made judgments about men like himself? He quickly thought of a number of snappy responses like 'it's time you and I had a drink and got to know one another better,' or 'it's time for you to grow up and know how much you can agitate a man,' or 'it's time you and I got down and dirty,' or 'it's time for you to wake up and smell the coffee, girl, you're absolutely

3

beautiful.' In that moment, sitting and staring up at her, Lark was simply unable to answer.

She waited patiently for a response. Lark experienced an awkward little-boy-like feeling in the presence of this beautiful woman. He made a mental note to conquer this bad habit before more women suddenly walked out of his fantasies and started asking him questions.

"It's almost four," he replied after lifting his arm to glance at his new watch to be sure.

She never took her eyes from his face. "Thanks." She smiled. She just stood there, close enough to embrace, albeit awkwardly, as he was still seated.

Lark could smell her. Her perfume, deodorant together with faint traces of shower soap she'd obviously used earlier in the day. All were delicately mixed with sweat and bodily secretions accumulated over the day, until she was one glorious musky hip-wide redolence before him. He rose to meet her eyes.

She just stood there, smiling right through Lark, it seemed.

"What's your rush?" he heard himself ask her.

"I beg your pardon?" she responded. Her teeth were perfect, he noted. And her lips looked as though, beneath the pastel shade of gloss she had painted across them, they could simply spread out and cover one's face once the petting began. Her lips looked to him like they could, with just a gentle tug, lift wallpaper from a wall. He'd always been attracted to women with full lips.

"Nothing," he fumbled forth a response. He was making an absolute fool of himself. Here before him stood a positively gorgeous creature of God staring him right in his eyes, and he was only able to come up with two- syllable conversation starters. Lark was incapable of thinking.

"Are you going to Lancaster tonight?" she asked.

"Why—yes," he hesitated.

"Great, so am I," she said enthusiastically.

Lark was on his feet now. He could not help but wonder why this young woman thought it was good they were going to the same destination. It really couldn't be that good for him. What does a man do with his wife and three kids when the 609 pulls in at 8:45 p.m. and he alights with a luscious nubile female on his arm, he wondered.

Silence surrounded them as they gazed into one another's eyes. She seemed to be looking at something not quite attached to Lark, but close enough to claim kinship. He looked at her, he imagined, the way any middle-aged male in this country looks at a really beautiful young woman—with lust so evident Lucifer drools.

What was she looking at? Women have a different way of sizing up men, Lark knew. They start with the eyes. Then they quickly scan how a man is dressed. Shoes interest them, for some weird reason. Lark wondered if his shoes had any shine left on them, after trudging around this big island all day long. Then, it's the hands. Lark had heard that the hands were of interest either because of the grooming of the nails or the length of the fingers were of some prurient interest. He was aware that women also like to watch men walk. If men pass the test, they're usually home free, he'd been taught.

"Perhaps we can have supper together?" he ventured as her eyes moved to his hands.

"Why not?" she quickly responded as her eyes swiftly raised to meet his.

"I've always enjoyed meals on wheels," he quipped in his best imitation of Johnny Carson.

She barely smiled, and that worried him immensely. He'd always been suspicious of people who couldn't at least be polite enough to fake a laugh at someone's attempt at humor.

Having grown up in Western Maryland, Lark would always be self-conscious about his Appalachian roots. He'd grown up in the 1940s, when folk often found humor wherever they could glean it, yet thought it impolite to laugh at anyone who was being serious, making a fool of himself. Jerry Lewis was not that popular in Western Maryland. Obviously, he'd grown up somewhere else.

"Seriously, would you entertain the thought of having dinner with me tonight?" he recovered. "I've always felt that meals are best eaten with another."

"You think too much," she confidently confided.

"What?" He was astonished.

"You think too much," she repeated. "You're probably one of those intellectual types I always seem to run into on these trips."

"Maybe so," he mumbled sheepishly.

"Do you teach at Franklin and Marshall?" she wanted to know.

"No," he retorted. "But, I graduated from there in 1956."

"That so?" she mused to herself aloud. "I knew it. Where did you do your graduate work?" she wanted to know.

"Look, is this a pre-dinner interview?" he asked her, deftly shifting the attention back to her and away from his past. "Do you want to see my resume?" he continued with a slight smile on his face, daring humor once more. "Perhaps you could call some of my references before we meet in the dining car?"

Without a smile, she said simply, "My, my, aren't we testy."

An awkward and mysterious silence emerged between them. Then, her face softened.

"Forget it," she said now in her movie star voice. "I'm sorry I insulted you."

"You didn't! It's just that I'm not used to—" he couldn't finish.

"You're used to picking up women. That's obvious," she flattered him.

"Let me finish, please," he begged. He really wasn't that skilled with women.

"Okay. It's your nickel," she replied with a twinkle in her eye.

Her attempt at humor did not go unnoticed by Lark. This woman was bright. She was beginning to intrigue him more than most he'd met. She was more than just casually or socially intelligent, he sensed. He was certain she was adept at the game in which they engaged. She'd done this many times before, he thought. Flirtatious and brilliant, a dangerous combination in any woman, Lark mused.

"I was going to say that I've never been quizzed quite so rigorously by one whom I've invited to dine with me on a three-hour train trip," he offered.

"I'm not just anyone," she coyly replied.

"What does that mean?" he asked.

"I saw you staring a hole right through me as I stood over there, minding my own business a few moments ago," she said with a smile. "I couldn't take it any longer without trying to find out what you're made of."

He was caught. "And, what do you think?"

"I'm not sure," she said with only the slightest hesitation. "There's something about you, and I don't mean the fact that you're married and trying to act as though you aren't."

"How do you know I'm married?" Lark never wore a wedding band.

"You all are," was her only response.

"Oh, now I suppose I'm going to get the ninety-five cent feminist lecture on how helpless we males are without some woman to take care of us?"

Almost as if totally disinterested, she said, "Look, let's forget it for now. We've got three hours on a train coming up, and we can continue this in the dining car or wherever you'd like. I've got to go powder my nose."

Lark last heard his mother use that phrase when he was a little boy. Somehow he felt a kinship with that lad at this moment.

She turned without waiting for any word from him and walked quickly toward the ladies room. Her backside had that nice easygoing Southern swing to it—seeming to move at a different rhythm than her feet. Funny, he thought, as he watched her, how this woman had afforded him the opportunity to look at her from every angle except down. He had the sense she'd let him look at her anyway he wanted, as long as it was on her terms.

Suddenly, he had the need to relieve himself. He walked toward the men's room. Once inside, he noticed his immediate environment. They never seemed to clean these places, he mused. By the end of any day, men's restrooms have that peculiar male mixture of odors: sweat, urine, women's bodies, men's secretions, and tobacco, all rolled into one very heavy smell.

What does a woman see in a man, he wondered, as he leaned against the wall and watched himself do what men have done for millions of years since they learned to walk upright. With a slight shaking of his appendage, he deftly placed it inside his pants, where it would obviously rest until summoned to action again.

Relieving one's self is not a particularly philosophical action. Yet Lark found himself in an academic mood as he completed his task by yanking the zipper up. He disliked urinals. He thought them to be ridiculous inventions. Pretending to be one-size-fits-all, except for the ones recently placed closer to the floor for boys or very short men, urinals have their easily recognizable faults. Splashguards and rinky-dink deodorizers, neither of which are very functional. Lark often was more than a little embarrassed by telltale spots down his trouser legs.

What's needed, he thought at one time, are some type of umbrellas. He even had sketched his device on a note pad at a meeting one time. No one ever asked him what he was drawing, thankfully. Eventually, he gave up. Not because he didn't think it could be done. He feared someone would steal his idea and patent it as the latest tool for bringing women to complete sexual satisfaction during intercourse. Just another good intention gone awry.

Hence, Lark deduced to simply stand farther from the urinals when relieving himself. The thought that such a tactic offered only diminishing returns had not grazed the periphery of his mind. He had to admit, albeit only to himself, that such a strategy for keeping relatively dry reminded him of certain male adolescent games played in vacant building lots on moonlit nights in Western Maryland. But, that too would be a subject best left alone by a man in his profession.

Trying different angles of approach to urinals wasn't always the best solution. Especially when the restroom was crowded. Perhaps the things could be built upon moveable tracks or installed at a slightly reclining angle from the wall, he once thought. Such inventions, flexible enough to adjust according to height, weight, projectability, and age, would give all men something much more challenging and stimulating to read upon restroom walls than the usual trite fare. The directions, printed in such litigious times, would most likely challenge even Rhodes scholars.

As he turned away from the urinal, he heard the sound of the automatic flush. Now, there's an invention that gives all mankind hope, he thought. Future restroom historians will inform their readers that it was the 20th century that created this ingenious manner of saving water at the same time humanity was straining to lift thousands of pounds of flesh and steel toward the moon. An electric eye stealthily watches an unsuspecting variety of penises pass their waters and disappear, waiting to notice the larger shadow disappear from view so it can release its waters in a never-ending attempt at the illusion of cleanliness.

Lark was reminded of his younger son's discovery of the automatic urinal-flushing device. He had permitted his sons to go to the restroom together alone in O'Hare Airport only a few years before. One trip into that labyrinth unchaperoned, and his son's life was changed forever. Lark's older son came hurtling from the restroom, yelling, "Dad, come see what Saul is doing."

When Lark entered the men's restroom, he spied his younger son running gaily back and forth in front of the urinals as fast as he could. He was so utterly delighted to learn that he could make them all flush simply by passing so closely to them, he almost fell in.

Lark recalled that sight as he stood at the wash basin. He laughed to himself as he held his hand beneath the waters which, like those in the urinal, were controlled by another electric eye beam. Out comes the water. Dispensed like the grace of God to opened upheld hands.

The water was cold. Not a hint of a water heater cooking somewhere in the bowels of Pennsylvania Station. Lark looked around for a soap dispenser which might still have something to deliver to a dusty traveler. No luck. Ignoring the unheeded omen, he placed his hands beneath the spigot again and water coursed through his fingers and across his wrist.

Removing his hands, he looked for a paper towel dispenser. Nothing. Just a ready row of electronic blow dryers. None of the five attached to the wall at slightly varying angles functioned properly.

So, Lark did his best imitation of a New York City traffic cop at rush hour to dry his hands. Men walked in and out of the facility as he swung his arms in all directions in a frantic effort to remove the water droplets from his skin. People in New York City are used to kooks. Hence, no one paid any attention.

During one of his last swings of his right arm Lark's watch deftly left his wrist. It proceeded in orbit across the room, until it landed and careened across the floor, having narrowly missed an older man's spectacles in its descent toward the corner stall. As the older man ducked, he turned his head and followed the path of the Seiko as it bounced off of the floor, slammed into a wall, and slid under the last stall which was closed.

Lark gingerly walked across the room and attempted to open the door to the stall. Knowing that locked men's restroom stalls do not necessarily mean they are occupied, Lark did the sensible thing. He knocked on the door. "Pardon me. I believe my watch just slid under your door."

No response. He knocked again.

"I beg your pardon. I was drying my hands and my watch came off my arm and slid under your door. Could I have it back, please? I'm awfully sorry if I disturbed or frightened you."

By this time, almost every man in the restroom had stopped whatever it was they were doing so they could watch the drama unfold. Lark was only vaguely aware he was the center of attention. He was feeling sillier than usual, but he wanted to expedite this transaction, retrieve his watch, and get the heck out of there.

10

Lark, curious now, got down on his hands and knees and peered under the door. That's when he saw four feet, shoe heels and toes facing his glance and looking very tentative. As he stared at this revelation, a hand extended from somewhere above, its middle finger gesturing toward the top of the door. He'd seen this gesture many times before. The hand then moved menacingly close to his nose. Lark took note of several things about the hand and arm to which it was attached. It was gnarled from hard work. The arm was particularly tan and muscular. Upon the wrist was a very familiar Seiko.

"Screw off, buddy," came a voice from within the cavernous stall which undoubtedly belonged with the hand and arm. It was said with such force that now everybody in the room took note. "What do you think this is, a Borgia orgy?"

Lark didn't answer. He felt warm and rubescent as he quickly got off his knees, wiped his trousers with his still-damp hands, and announced to anyone in the room who was still interested, "Not there! Now, where could it have gone to?" He left the restroom in Pennsylvania Station with one last longing farewell glance toward the stall that now imprisoned his former trophy. It silently ticked upon one very muscular left arm.

As Lark exited the restroom, he heard his train being called. He glanced around but did not see her, whoever she was. Then he rushed, like everyone else in the station, toward his appointed platform and the trip home.

Chapter 2
JOURNEY HOME

Train 609 to Newark, Trenton, Philadelphia, Lancaster, Harrisburg and points West was being announced as Lark scrambled through Pennsylvania Station toward the entrance to the platform. "All aboard" cried the loud speaking system which must have been installed by the same sound engineers as those who placed soundtracks on National Geographic educational films. Lark didn't notice his newfound interest anywhere in his rushed descent to the train they called "The Broadway Limited."

Once aboard, he scanned the car and found two vacant seats in which he could spread out and enjoy the nearly four hour trip to Lancaster. He did not see the woman in his car. But, with numerous passenger cars, several sleeping pullmans, and a dining car, there were lots of places where folks could find privacy, if they sought it.

Lark preferred to be near the dining car, for he always went to it for supper on these trips. There was something special about dining cars. He decided he'd sit through the first thirty minutes or so of the trip, then amble back to the dining car and see what the chefs had prepared for rail bound gourmets.

Amtrak, famous for its slow starts, crawled out of New York City that late afternoon. Were one used to the sound of the

12

rail junctures beneath the wheels, he might catch the slow, steady, rhythm indicating the soundness of the vehicle carrying its occupants on a journey to an unknown destination. The train started its course up into the sunlight from beneath the station, and wriggled its way toward the Hudson River and all that lay beyond it—"all points West."

Soon the 609 was descending again toward the part of this trip which Lark disliked the most. Into the tunnel that traversed the bottom of the Hudson River slid the long, silver-colored invention carrying its unsuspecting travelers into sudden darkness. The onboard lights flickered while the train, tortoiselike, crossed beneath the flowing water. Lark was always glad when the train arose in New Jersey, coming out of the tunnel like a snake shedding its skin. This day was no exception.

Once they were back above ground in the late afternoon sun, Lark decided to do what he liked second-best on train rides. He opened his briefcase and pulled out the book he was reading by Tom Robbins. He loved Robbin's writing and wished he could write half as well. Robbins, to Lark, was capable of taking the most unusual and inanimate objects as subjects for his novels. By the time the reader ended a Robbins novel, he would likely believe anything possible. At least, that's the way Lark read Robbins.

He chuckled aloud as he began to settle into one of Robbins' chapters. He glanced around to see if anyone noticed. In this story a young girl with unusually large thumbs adopts the life of a cowgirl at a dude ranch in the Dakotas and becomes involved in trying to save whooping cranes, as well as meets some of the strangest Native Americans ever portrayed by a novelist.

Lark had long before decided it was useless to try to identify with any characters in a Robbins novel. Nobody else in the world could be like anybody depicted by Tom Robbins. Sissy Hankshaw was genetically deformed. Her only real ability in life was to catch the sight of a driver of a passing car at any speed simply by extending her thumb! From there on, every other character in Robbins' story is less believable by being even more unique.

As the train began to move faster, Lark momentarily looked up from his book to note that people were stirring a bit. Unconsciously, he looked down at his right arm, only to be reminded that his Seiko now adorned another's arm.

Lark leaned toward the passenger across the aisle.

"Pardon me, do you know what time it is?"

The man didn't stir. He was wearing a headset of some type and reading *Playboy*. No use disturbing this genius, Lark thought to himself. So, he got up and walked toward the rear of the car. That's when he saw her. She had been there the whole time, on the same car. Asleep, in the very last seat, curled like a kitten, she was dead to the world.

Lark surmised that her problem was no doubt some kind of drug use. No one could sleep that soundly on a train, not even in a Pullman.

He quietly walked by her and moved through the double door, across the connecting platform, and through the doors to the dining car. No use skipping his favorite experience on a train. He'd have dinner alone. He'd done it many times before.

The dining car was empty except for a couple of waiters. He decided upon a table halfway back, to the left. He sat on the far side of the table, so as to position himself to have a view of the door through which he had just passed. The waiter approached his table.

"May I help you, sir?"

"Yes. I'd like to see the evening menu, please," Lark responded. He pondered this stilted conversation between himself and the waiter he'd never met before. There is still some civility left in this world, he thought.

"I'm sorry, sir. We're not serving dinner until six."

Lark hesitated to ask the waiter what time it was. He didn't want the waiter to think odd of him, dressed as he was, with no wrist watch. So he decided, during the short silence between them, to question this kind of policy schedule.

"If you don't serve supper until six o'clock, what do folks like myself do who are only going as far as Lancaster?" Lark inquired.

14

"Eat fast."

Lark laughed. It was obvious that the waiter was not joking, however.

"Furthermore, it is dinner that we serve, sir."

"What?"

"Dinner, sir. Not, what did you call it? Supper?"

This guy's pulling my leg, thought Lark, but nothing about his demeanor had changed. Lark had taken this trip many times and never run into a waiter like this one. He operated strictly by the book. Must be new at it, he thought.

"Okay, what kind of service can a person get at this time of day?"

"I can serve you something to drink, sir."

"Fine. What do you have?"

"We have the finest coffee from Columbia, the most delicious tea from Beijing, and an unusually delicate hot chocolate from the Netherlands."

Lark laughed out loud this time.

The waiter didn't. "Is there something wrong sir?" he wanted to know.

Either this man was the greatest "straight man" Lark had ever met, or he was putting Lark on something terrible.

"I was hoping you'd have some nice beer from Allentown," Lark said calmly.

"We do not serve alcoholic beverages until—"

"I know, let me guess—six o'clock," Lark said. He was annoyed at this waiter's lack of humor.

The waiter smiled for the first time. Lark knew it, the waiter had been putting him on.

"Right," was all the waiter said in response and stood at attention, awaiting Lark's order.

"I'll have some of that hot chocolate, I suppose," Lark said, resigning himself to his fate. "I'm boycotting Columbian coffee, and I never like tea, no matter where it comes from."

The waiter did not flinch. He stood there, waited, and stared at Lark for what seemed an eternity. Lark wondered if the waiter were having a seizure of some kind. Lark wondered if he had offended the man. He couldn't tell, from the waiter's demeanor.

"You suppose?" the waiter asked.

"Oh, that's it. I want some hot chocolate. I'm absolutely sure," Lark almost yelled.

The waiter turned on his heels and went slowly toward the kitchen. By this time, Lark was very glad to see the waiter's backside as he hurriedly fled the scene. The silence afforded him time to cool down a bit and reflect upon this strange encounter. Lark just wasn't sure what to make of the man.

As Lark sat there, considering his fate, he noticed the clock upon the wall of the moving train car about three tables forward and to his left. He arose and walked toward it. As he leaned over the table to peer at the clock, the doors to the dining car opened abruptly and a very familiar voice proclaimed, "There you are! I'd recognize that rump anywhere."

It was John. He was a black clergyman Lark had known and trusted for many years. They were colleagues. They had just been together in New York, attending the planning session for the next peace demonstration, set for Washington, DC. Lark had left the meeting early to pursue his favorite thing to do in New York City—walk the streets and note the people of various cultures all clamoring to make a living in the nation's largest city. Lark and John hadn't seen one another in a few hours.

"How's it going old buddy?" John asked.

"Okay, but I hope you're not in here for dinner."

"As a matter of fact, I am. Why?" replied John.

"You'll be happy to learn that they have some new policy on the old 609. They don't serve dinner until six." Lark said in his best imitation of the black waiter whom John would soon have the pleasure of meeting.

"So, what are you doing here then?" John asked.

One of the things Lark had learned about friends is how easily they can see through the masks most of us wear. No stranger to the ways of the world, John had suddenly found himself hanging between marriages. He washed up upon the rocky shores of

16

marital discord only a few months before, simply due to his forgetfulness, he claimed. He had forgotten to tell his wife that he had been a candidate for a denominational job and had accepted the invitation to serve. The new job would require them to move from Lancaster to New York. She read it in the *Intelligencer Journal* before John had had the time to inform her. She understood this oversight for what it was: a sign that something very basic was missing in their life together, communication.

Lark often wondered what was missing in his marriage. He had long given up looking for it in Fran. There was some kind of void, he knew. He could sense it in the loneliness he often felt, even when he was with Fran. He could not escape the pain of it, even in their most intimate moments. He guessed that was why so many women intrigued him as he journeyed through life. He and John had talked about this nearly a year before as they travelled to New York together for a meeting.

"Well, you know, a woman should never take a man for granted. That's what washed up my first marriage with Carolyn," John said.

"What do you mean?"

"It's like this. She isn't there to meet you when you get home. You have to get a taxi or bus from the train station or airport. Next, she isn't awake when you get home. Hell, you might die in a terrible crash, and she wouldn't even know it 'til the next morning."

John had laughed out loud in that full-bodied way which was all his own whenever he launched into his philosophy on marriage. Lark often thought of these conversations over the years they had known one another. Lark was convinced that nothing John ever described came close to explaining what his experience was with Fran. Or, did it? All Lark knew was that he felt guilty about looking at women. He blamed this, somehow, on his marriage. Maybe Fran was taking him for granted. Sometimes, he actually believed he'd found evidence of her neglect.

Fran always had a way of not really listening to him. "Selective listening," he called it. Her attention was always given

17

to someone else—anyone else. Lark would come home excited about some project or meeting. He could hardly wait to share it with her. She'd sit on their sofa, mending a garment or folding the wash and simply say, "Uh huh. Go on," while he gushed. And, Lark would go on, feeling more like Hamlet than King Henry VIII.

Lark, from time to time, had tested his theory with her. In the middle of sentences, he'd slip a totally unrelated subject or some unintelligible phrase into their conversation. Once, he even used Greek, a language he spoke fluently, and she said, "Uh Huh. Go on."

Maybe it was the suit John always seemed to wear. Or perhaps it was the fact that they found themselves meeting again in the dining car on the Broadway Limited (where so many of their best conversations were held). Lark wasn't sure what had triggered all of this instant introspection. In a split second, it was all there in his mind again, as though it were happening just as he and John ambled toward his table.

"You seem to be in deep thought, old buddy."

"Who? Me?" Lark retorted, as they pulled their chairs across from one another.

John glanced around the swiftly moving dining car, surveying its obvious vacuity. "Yes, you."

"I'm just trying to learn what time it is. I lost my watch this afternoon, and I'm lost without it."

John shot Lark a knowing glance. "Who is she?" he asked bluntly.

How is it friends are so aware of what's going on right behind the masks, and spouses never have a clue? It's a mystery, thought Lark.

"I don't know what you mean," Lark almost shouted, defensively.

"Uh huh. Go on." John said quietly.

Lark was about to tell him of his latest encounter when the waiter appeared with his hot chocolate. As the man bent over to place the hot chocolate on the table, John reached upward and gave the waiter a high five.

"How's it hangin', bro?" John inquired. The two black men immediately launched into a most animated conversation that Lark positively could not decipher. Their laughter and ease with one another suggested once more to Lark that racism would be all but impossible to squelch in the human spirit. There is no mistaking the common bonds of skin tone and experience of race in any culture. There is no substitute for that common ground. Perhaps this is the way things are meant to be. The "melting pot" simply boils up a hopeless stew of unmet expectations and despair. Blood is much thicker than social theory. Lark simply sat and watched the two men enjoy one another's company.

Suddenly, as though the waiter became aware of the exclusion which was taking place, he stood straight, looked Lark in the eyes, and asked, "Will there be anything else, sir?"

It was an unbelievable change in demeanor, and it almost caught both John and Lark off guard. They glanced around the dining car quickly to ascertain if some railroad official had wandered into the car, taking notes on this waiter's performance.

"Yes," Lark said, "where can I learn that language you guys were talkin'? It might help me when I visit the sixth ward," Lark chuckled to himself.

The waiter didn't laugh; neither did John. Lark guessed humor depended upon where one grew up in America. When it was obvious the waiter was still awaiting a response to his question, Lark mustered the most serious voice he could find at the moment and replied, "No, thank you."

The waiter turned so his back faced Lark, slapped John's palm and said something indistinguishable, and scurried from the table.

"Okay, what were you two guys saying about me?" Lark asked of John.

"He said to me 'Your honkey friend here has that lean and hungry look, but it ain't supper he's lookin' fo'.'" John said, grinning.

"Give it up, John. I know he didn't say that. He was not badass enough!"

19

"Say what? You done gone and learned street talk, boy? I'm impressed. Man, you sho don't need your servant John no more—does you?" By the time he got to the last word, both men were rolling with laughter. And both men knew that any chance of serious discussion on this trip was lost. They'd settle for some hot chocolate and professional bullshit. Both of them were really good at the latter.

Chapter 3
HOME
AT LAST

The 609 slowed as it approached Lancaster. People began to gather their things to disembark. Lark retrieved his briefcase from beneath the sleeper seat, in which he had drifted off after John's conversation made him drowsy, and strolled toward the front of the car. He nearly fell over as she slid from her seat in front of him.

"We seem to keep bumping into one another," she said as she stared into Lark's baby-blue eyes.

"I guess if we're going to keep meeting like this, we ought to get to know more about one another," he flirted with a boyish grin.

"That would be nice." She smiled at him.

Lark's heart seemed to skip a beat. He wondered what to say next. They stood, looking at one another for what seemed like a year.

"I guess so," he said again.

She turned from him and swayed toward the exit. He followed her as though he were magnetized. The train slowed to a standstill as they reached the door to the passenger platform. Once they were inside the station, he lost sight of her once more. Lark was looking for Fran.

He glanced around the station, but Fran was no where to be seen. He wished he could see her immediately so his game would end. This was a game he played mentally, and Fran was a key player who never knew. How did Fran compare with what's her name? When he was sure that Fran was better looking and far more intelligent, the memory of chance acquaintances could be erased. Whenever he was certain that Fran and the other woman were evenly matched, his senses were heightened to a pitch not quite describable in words. He could only feel it.

Lark was always extremely uneasy whenever the person facing him in such encounters moved across his memories of Fran like the moon eclipsing sunlight. He felt that what he had just experienced was somewhere between a lunar and solar eclipse. But Lark found these games to be amusing, at times. It was humorous to him how often he indulged in it. Yet no one was ever aware he was playing at comparing his wife with most other women in the world he knew. He sometimes called it Who's The Winner? Double Jeopardy was the name he reserved for comparisons between twins and Fran.

The game had not been amusing this time. This woman, whoever she was, had already gotten to a level of attraction no one else had attained with him, and he was not sure why. All he knew at the moment was that he felt strangely certain Fran might lose. Deep inside, this thought worried him more than he'd admit.

This was unexpected. Fran had lately failed to be there when Lark arrived. He sauntered down the step which led from the train station in Lancaster. The early summer evening aromas of Lancaster were a noxious concoction of cigar factories, stockyards, and Armstrong Cork Company products which, when mixed with the humidity of the city, seemed to seep into every possible sense. When Lark first moved to Lancaster, the smog of the city in summer cooked his eyes until they were a nice light orange and pink. Now, the smog simply confronted him with its hazy uncertainty and its irrefutable stench of home. He rarely blinked a tear these days.

The taxis waited like cows in a feedlot outside the train barn. He walked slowly to where a checkered cab was pulling to the curb and got in when it stopped rolling. The cabby was listening intently to the Phillies, who were losing yet another game. It was only the first inning. True Phillies fans knew in their hearts, ever since 1964, that the Phils were only good once every generation. For one brief year, they would climb atop the National League, beat up the team from the upstart American League in the World Series, then sink into oblivion until the next unsuspecting generation of fans would come of age. Then, not unlike the Loch Ness Monster, they would arise and frighten every other team into line behind them.

Richie Ashburn was giving the play-by-play and relating the names of players in the field. "Steve Carlton is throwing tonight, fans. He's going for win number eight. Old lefty looks like he has his stuff tonight." Ashburn droned on while adroitly failing to mention that old lefty had already been touched for two home runs, and the Phillies were down 4-0.

The cabby turned the radio down just long enough to take directions. "Where to, pal?"

"709 North Lime," Lark replied.

"Hell." snorted the cabby, as he reached for the meter. This would be a short ride: a low fare. He turned the radio back up and put the car into gear.

"Well, Luzinski sure misjudged that routine pop fly to left, fans," Ashburn reported with an edge to his voice. It must be really hot and humid at Veterans' Stadium, Lark thought to himself. "Dawson is standing on third base and Lefty's in trouble here," Ashburn noted with ever so slight a trace of sarcasm.

"Those Phillies sure know how to lose," Lark said, trying to strike up a conversation with the cabby.

"Yeah," the driver responded, "Ashburn can't say a whole hellavu lot about it, but my opinion is that he must be steamin' watching Luzinski play. Hell, Richie was an All Star outfielder who could outrun almost any ball hit beyond the infield in his day. Luzinski can't catch a cold out there! He couldn't hold Richie's jock!"

Lark laughed as the cabby glanced into his rear-view mirror. They rode the last two blocks in silence. When the cab turned onto Lime Street, the cabby spoke anew. "Here you are, buddy. You could have walked faster."

The meter read two dollars. Guiltily, Lark handed the man a five dollar bill. The cabby looked at it and then slowly raised his eyes to meet Lark's. There was a mixture of awe and terrorless guile that met Lark in that glance. For what seemed like an eon, the two men simply stared at one another.

"Keep it," Lark said. He could have sworn there was a slight smirk on the face of the cabby as the cab sped off up North Lime Street toward the train station. How do cab drivers learn such intimidation, Lark wondered?

As Lark turned from the street to face his house, he said aloud, "Thank God Almighty, I am home at last!" Lark was to go to Washington again in a few weeks. Not for 'jobs and freedom' this time, but to protest the war which dragged on in Vietnam. He genuinely wished his country would bring the soldiers home. He saw no reason for American blood to be shed in such a place. It was not a popular view in his parish, but, it was one this son of World War Two soldiers took, nevertheless.

Chapter 4
REUNION

Once inside the house, Lark gradually reacquainted himself with all the familiar odors of family: dog, leftovers, sticky substances in odd places, and just the faintest of hints of Fran's perfume. Nothing seemed out of place. The kids' toys were in their usual places—everywhere. As Lark strolled down the long hallway through the dining room and toward the kitchen, nothing seemed amiss.

Whenever the *House Beautiful* magazines picture homes, everything seems so orderly. Lark thought that if he ever entered his house and it presented itself in such a manner, he'd check the photos on the walls. Men have been known to wander into the wrong abodes, from time to time. Especially into row homes.

This evening, nothing seemed out of place because everything was out of place. He checked the refrigerator out of habit. It was a role he had picked up watching his dad return home from work each evening. Lark knew what would be in the refrigerator: three pitchers of Kool-Aid, a slightly used loaf of white bread, and, all kinds of Tupperware. Lark mused whether that stuff actually bred in cold, dark places. He gently closed the door. There never was a beer there. It was a principle with Fran, and he accepted it.

Fran had been reared in a typical all-American dysfunctional alcoholic home. She was determined to avoid all of the pain associated with her upbringing in West Virginia. Her plan was to simply forbid any alcohol in their home. Fran never really forgot what it was like to deal with an adult male who drank too much. For that matter, neither had Lark. That's why their uneasy truce was forged not consciously, but solidly. Lark always understood her fear of the fruit of the vine. He, too, had seen its destruction of family.

Fran and Lark had groped for each other across a vast wilderness of paranoid uncertainty and pain throughout their marriage. They had met on a blind date. When Lark asked her to marry him two years later, Fran didn't actually perceive the invitation as a "ticket to ride," but as one more possibility to disclaim her attractiveness as a woman.

"You don't know what love is," she said to him that first night he dared profess his love to her. Over the years, Lark had become accustomed to rebuffs of his emotional disclosures to Fran. It was not that much different than those he'd witnessed between his own mother and father as a child. He wanted more. But, because he really didn't have the courage to ask for it, he rarely received more. And, since he was used to failure, he merely accepted it. Perhaps it was their combination of low self-esteem and meager expectations, which led them to gradually become soul mates in a marriage bereft of emotional support for either one.

After an on again/off again romance and courtship, they married. Like two lost souls, they swore their devotion to one another until "death doth us part." What neither realized was that it might be impossible for those already emotionally departed from this life to make such a promise.

They were brave. They were courageous. And they were absolutely unprepared for the pain they would bring to one another and those they brought into the world. They left their homes when they were but babes and declared that, come what may, they would always be faithful to one another alone.

Lark was startled out of his review of history by the sound of the carport door suddenly opening. Fran soon appeared, dressed in a sack dress, sweaty, hair a mess, and a sleepy child in each arm.

"Hello," she said quietly. "Help me with the children."

Lark nodded. He walked out the door to the carport where their cooling white Rambler wagon stood to rest for the night. In the back seat, sound asleep, was the eldest. Lark opened the door and gently removed the boy from the plastic seat covers, to which his sweaty body slightly adhered. He barely paid attention as he reached his slender arms around his father's neck and snuggled close to his father's chest for the ride to his bedroom.

"Hey, partner, where you guys been?" Lark whispered as he carried the boy upstairs.

"Long's Park," he muttered. And, with these few words, his breath revealed that they had also been to a pizza parlor and the concession stand at the park for more than one frosty drink. As they made their ascent, Lark thought there is always a special harmony between a firstborn father and his firstborn son.

All three Wilson kids shared the same expansive bedroom on the second floor. This bedroom could have served as half a bowling alley with three lanes, if located just five blocks North or South on Lime Street. Fran and Lark liked this arrangement for their children. They could say good night to all three children at the same time. They wouldn't have to bear the argument somewhere down the road that they treated one better than the other. Their children would begin life in a more socialized context and eliminate the view that any one of them was the center of the universe. Such rationalizations for the arrangement seemed to fit Fran and Lark at the time. They both knew the children would outgrow this dormitory lifestyle soon. But, for now, it was perfect: two boys and a girl in one cavernous bedroom.

"We'll take our baths tomorrow morning," Fran was quietly explaining to one of the children as Lark carried his son into the room.

"Good night, all," Lark said, placing the lad in his bed.

"Daddy!" Lark's daughter was suddenly aware of his presence in the darkened room. She sat straight up, rubbed her baby-blue eyes, and giggled aloud. "I didn't see you in the park." Her tone of voice seemed to indicate that she had expected him.

"I was there," Lark said rather meekly.

"You were?"

Lark was in trouble. This was a game she always played with her father. He could make up some of the biggest whoppers in history. She'd pretend to buy them through the prologue, and, just as he entered the climax, she'd look at him, smile that smile that turned to a knowing giggle, and end with an "Oh, Daddy."

"I was on stage," Lark continued with the game.

"Which one were you?" she slyly inquired.

"I was," Lark paused as he thought of what to say, "the biggest."

"You were Droopy?" his daughter exclaimed with delight.

Lark now knew they had seen Disney characters on stage. That was all the information he needed to continue his part of the game. She gave him just enough information to go on. He was off and running.

"Yep! It was tough to sing and dance in that hot costume tonight. But they knew I could do it because they'd heard of all the plays I'd been in when I went to elementary school at Woodland Way. So, when they called me this afternoon in New York, I caught an early train and came right to Long's Park to get ready."

By this time, Fran was becoming uneasy with the game. She gave Lark one of her best "let's not get the children all riled up" looks as Lark continued to elaborate.

"I had a little trouble with the feet, I mean, paws. They were kind of clammy. But, once I got through rehearsal, I knew I could do it. Piece of cake."

"Did you see us, Daddy," his daughter quietly asked.

"Honey lamb, I sure did!"

This part was easy. They were still wearing their clothes. Lark simply went on to describe how he had spotted them as he came on stage and peered through the oversized eyes of the Droopy costume. He explained that he knew where they were the whole time he was on stage. They were getting to an important part of this ruse, and Lark knew he had to be careful. He began to back off, and his daughter somehow sensed where they were in the game plan.

"Why didn't you come out to us, like Mickey did," she asked matter of factly.

"Well," he paused anew, "I didn't want you to know it was I."

She knew she had him. He knew it, too. So, he tried to win this time by resorting to that time honored trick of diversion which has worked for centuries with children in a state of near sleep.

"We'll talk about this tomorrow, sweetheart, Okay? Why don't you close those big blue eyes of yours and dream of old Droopy tonight?" Lark bent to kiss her on the cheek.

She gave him a quick peck on the cheek and whispered in his ear, "Sing me Droopy's song."

Lark's heart raced. She was really good at this. But, he tried one more diversion.

"Not anymore tonight, honey. Your brothers are sleepy." This diversion, if successful, afforded Lark the opportunity to learn the song from Fran who, by this point, was standing in the doorway, staring angrily in Lark's direction.

"No we're not," piped up their youngest son. There was no way Lark could ever fool this little one. He was so intelligent he could do multiplication tables by memory up to the tens by the time he was three years old. Lark was in big trouble. He had counted on the boys being out of this conversation, and they had waited until just the right time to enter it.

"Yes, you are, son," Lark said sternly.

"You're a big fat liar, Dad," he protested.

Fran, frozen and framed by the hallway light, groaned audibly in the doorway. Lark knew the meaning of this sound. The air of the room was suddenly more tense and still. Through sleepy eyes, all three children now were sitting up in the beds, anxiously awaiting their father's response to the youngest son's latest assault upon his father.

"I beg your pardon," Lark said firmly.

"You weren't at the park, and you know it," the boy shouted.

"How do you know?" Lark asked quietly.

"Because my dad wouldn't wear that stupid Droopy suit," the boy said, as he stood up in his bed.

Lark knew he had only one chance of getting out of this. The mixture of defiance and disappointment which met him in his youngest son's glance could not be ignored. Lark walked to the bed. The child jumped into his father's arms and squeezed his father as tightly as his little body would permit.

"Dads do stupid things sometimes," Lark whispered to the child, as he kissed him good night. That was what the child wanted. Just a little extra attention along with a private explanation. He'd keep the secret. He might even repeat it some year down the way.

Lark's daughter looked at him as though she had buyer's remorse. The oldest child lay back in his bed and summarized the game for all to hear by saying, "They sure do!"

Fran and Lark left the room in silence.

Fran joined Lark in the spacious living room on the first floor, just beneath the children's bedroom.

"I'm sorry I forgot your were coming home tonight. Did you wait long?"

"No," he answered. "It was obvious you weren't there to pick me up, so I caught a cab."

"You what?"

"I caught a cab."

"Why? Couldn't you walk? Don't you need the exercise?" she went on like a courthouse lawyer. Fran never concealed her jealousy of Lark's freedom to travel. She fancied herself imprisoned by motherhood. She never fully grasped that he would gladly have changed places with her if she could have supported a family of five.

They were so good at hurting one another. It came from being adult children of alcoholic fathers. Their childhood had plotted a course for their lives: Fran was great at shifting blame; Lark was great at accepting responsibility. So, suddenly, he felt guilty for catching a cab, and he felt very tired.

"Look, I'm tired. Could we just drop this part of our reunion?"

"Suit yourself," she replied.

They sat in silence and stared at the *Mary Tyler Moore* Show. Ted, the ever pompous wanna-be anchorman was working a scheme to become a star. Mary was being an air head. Lou was trying his best to get through the night without succumbing to a nightmarish binge at the corner pub. Lark quietly identified with Lou for a moment. He had no idea why Fran even watched the show.

When it was time to go to bed, nothing more had been said between them. Such were the games they played.

"Well, I've had it. I think I'll go up and take a shower."

"Call me when you're through," she said.

"Okay," Lark replied dutifully.

"And, Rack," she said, using his high school nickname, "I've got a bit of a headache this evening. I'll be up after I take something for it."

"Uh huh," was his only response. He turned, went through the glass doors, and marched up the stairs.

Chapter 5
Doc

It had been a rather lengthy day, even for Doc, by the time he reached the fourth floor of Lancaster General. He was walking down the East hallway to room 472 to see a patient who desperately needed his assistance. He'd had precious little rest in between the sixteen persons he administered to in his office and the five he was seeing this evening at Lancaster General.

But this is why he had struggled so hard after being discharged from the Navy in 1948. Franklin and Marshall had been a blast for him after the tedium of military service. Following World War II, the school was flooded with GIs like himself who were taking full advantage of Congress's generosity toward those who had saved this nation from the fascists. Although Doc had never been out of the country during the war, he had served his country, nevertheless. He had served four years as a radio technician, servicing the field radios which linked patrols to one another in combat. With each radio came a story. Doc liked to think that he was right there, on the battle front, with the radio he was repairing.

When he was discharged, his college education, paid for by Uncle Sam, enabled him to take those steps toward his lifelong dream of becoming a dentist. Upon graduation from Franklin and Marshall in 1948, he entered dental college at the University of Pennsylvania in Philadelphia. He excelled there as he had at F&M—first in his class. Doc couldn't have been happier to return to his native city, Lancaster, to set up his practice.

With his wife—high school sweetheart Millie—and their three children, Doc began his practice rather inconspicuously in their home, using the front two rooms of their row house as his office and treatment room. Millie served as receptionist and secretary/bookkeeper for the enterprising young dentist.

Business was so good over the years that Doc eventually relocated his office to a suite of rooms in Eden, a suburb of the city. Once there, his fortunes improved, and his stature in St. Andrew Church rose to the level of wise elder long before his years matched the title. By the time Lark came to serve as pastor, Doc Willard had been practicing dentistry in Eden for over a decade.

This night, Doc was seeing his last patient at Lancaster General for the purpose of preparing the dear woman for surgery, which was to be performed at seven the following morning. Doc's preparation method involved a practice of relaxation hypnosis which he had learned over the years through working with patients who could not take anesthetics due to allergies. Doc was very good at this and was in much demand, once word spread through the medical community that he possessed the skill. There were even times when he accompanied patients into the operating room. His presence in such cases was invaluable to the surgeons as well as the patients.

"Hello," Doc said as he entered the room.

The woman looked up at him with relief as she barely recognized who was speaking to her. "You took your sweet old time getting here, Doc," she said with a twinkle in her eye. "Do you think, after you get me through this operation, you could talk me into playing the piano again?"

"Now, Mrs. Larrabee, I think it would be wise if we took one thing at a time. Don't you?"

"I suppose you're right, Doc. But, it was worth a try."

Doc chuckled along with her. They were relaxed with one another. Although Doc had only met her once before, he'd done his homework on her, with the help of her chart. She lived alone. She was eighty-seven years old. She faced a double mastectomy and had a one-in-four chance of surviving for a year, as she had advanced cancer. She had never had surgery in her life. She was depressed. She was frightened. She was willing to talk with anyone about tomorrow. Doc was available.

They talked for half an hour. He learned that she had been a school teacher in Quarryville, in southern Lancaster County. Her parents had been Mennonite farmers, native to the area. She had married a salesman, had three children, and had been a widow for seventeen years. Doc listened appreciatively as the woman talked about everything except what faced her in less than twelve hours.

When a lull in the conversation presented itself, Doc said, "Is there anything I can do for you?"

"My, my, Doc. You've done it," was the old woman's reply.

"I have?"

"Yes, I know I'll sleep better tonight."

"Good," Doc replied. "I'll bring my homework in on time tomorrow."

The woman, totally immersed in her past exclaimed, "You'd better, sonny, or you'll stay after school with me."

Doc quickly left the room like a little boy who had been spared with his life. The old woman was asleep before Doc got to the elevator. Doc thought to himself about the ease with which he had handled this patient. She would be more relaxed for surgery, and thus her prospects had improved. Doc was happy he could play a role in making it so for her.

Before he left the hospital, he ducked into a phone booth and dialed a number in Harrisburg.

"Hello?" the voice at the other end said crisply.

"Are we set?" Doc asked.

"All systems are go," the voice replied. "Our subject made contact today, and things are looking good."

"All right, I'll check with you later," Doc quietly responded.

"Good," was the reply; and, the line went dead.

Doc hummed one of his favorite hymns, *Onward Christian Soldiers,* as he left the building and walked briskly to his car which was parked in the Duke Street parking lot.

Chapter 6

FRIDAY MORNING

This was going to be a busy day. Lark knew that before he arose at seven and rushed to prepare breakfast for the children, a task he dearly loved to perform. The kids weren't too hard to please in the mornings. They wanted Dad to either make pancakes or French toast. Lark could do either in his sleep.

Fran had competently prepared all the ingredients and had them labeled in the refrigerator. The orange juice was ready. All Lark had to do was ascertain which fare would receive the majority vote for the morning.

"What'll it be from Dad's breakfast nook?" he asked three very sleepy heads which rested in various positions upon their pillows. "Pancakes," was the unanimous choice. Lark dashed downstairs and began the procedure after heating the griddle pan to just the right temperature, so that bubbles of water danced across it.

By the time Lark had made ten pancakes, the children arrived in the kitchen and took their places at the redwood picnic table which served as kitchen table in the Wilson household. The children were generally quiet at breakfast time, and this made the task of getting a family of five moving in the mornings relatively easy. This Friday morning was no exception. Within fifteen minutes, morning prayers had been uttered and breakfast had been consumed. All three were back upstairs, getting ready for their busy day of play in what summer remained before school began.

Fran quietly entered the kitchen from the back stairway of the home, poured herself a cup of coffee, and sat at the table. "Do you have any pancakes left?" she wanted to know.

"I saved you the best two," Lark replied. He went to the oven and retrieved two very large pancakes and set them before his wife.

"They smell good this morning," she said. She poured syrup over them and began to cut them into eight pieces, a habit of hers. "How'd you sleep, Lark?" she asked.

"Fine."

"What's on your schedule today?" she inquired.

"After I go through the mail from this week and get Jane started on the bulletin, I have to type my sermon and do my first run through this afternoon. Then, I will go to the Y, and I'll check in at the hospitals to see any patients we might have there.

"This evening?"

"Nothing."

"How about tomorrow?"

"Just practice my sermon. I'll be able to take the day off. Maybe we can do something."

"That would be nice," she said, smiling as she sipped her coffee.

Lark was in his office by nine. Jane, the church secretary, was already there. She had arranged all of the mail on his desk so as to facilitate his review of it, from most important to the least. On busy days, Lark simply tossed the bottom third of such mail into the waste basket with barely a glance. Business, keenly aware of the small church market but seemingly oblivious to their hectic pace, had an endless penchant for third-class and fourth-class advertising. Lark avoided this as much as he did shopping trips to the mall with his family.

By ten, he had read the important mail and organized his day on paper. Now he was ready to dictate a few letters to Jane, give her the Sunday bulletin information, and then get to the really important part of the day—his sermon for Sunday.

Jane was a very efficient secretary. She had grown up in Lancaster County and possessed the work ethic of most of the early settlers of the area. She was a no-nonsense kind of person who didn't waste time or energy on personal matters when she was at work in the office. She once nearly missed the fact that her husband had become desperately ill at his job when she refused to talk to her daughter, who had called her with the news. Lark found her to be extremely competent and a person of the highest integrity when it came to confidentiality. Every time he worked with her, he was glad she had decided to become his secretary after he had fired the one inherited from his predecessor.

"Good morning," she said as he entered the church office.

"Good morning," Lark said, fully knowing that this was as much bantering as she would tolerate on a Friday morning. There was a lot of work to get done before her quitting time at three. The bulletin had to be run off on the hand-cranked mimeograph machine after last minute instruction from the pastor. Personal notes might need to be typed to various liturgical assistants. The flowers needed to be ordered. And, because Lark had been gone most of the week, correspondence had to be completed. So, he got right to the point with her. She smiled, several times he noted, in the midst of the flurry of dictation and instruction he gave her. He recounted most of the events which took place in New York during his sojourn. He left out one experience. She would not have appreciated the time the retelling would take, nor the subject matter. Lark finished with Jane and returned to his desk to type Sunday's sermon.

Lark had been reading Oregon Senator Mark Hatfield's book, *Conflict and Conscience*. Lark had met the senator in January and was tremendously impressed with his prophetic stance regarding the nation's needs. But, he only got his autographed copy of Hatfield's book in recent weeks. He decided to use the senator's book title as the title for the sermon. He reviewed the outline of it, which was based upon St. Paul's comment in his letter to the Romans about his personal struggle with wanting to do the right thing, but being unable to accomplish it.

Lark looked at his phrasing and edited some of it so as to give the words the emphasis he felt the sermon needed in order to affect thinking in the church about the nation's struggle in Vietnam. But he wasn't satisfied when he was finished. The sermon didn't seem to touch him. Lark knew enough about preaching to know that if the sermon didn't touch him, his delivery of it on Sunday morning wouldn't touch anyone else.

By noon, Lark knew he had a dilemma on his hands. His text from Romans and Mark Hatfield's book on our nation's struggles were not coming together as he had perceived they might. He'd start over. This was not new to him. It often happened. He sometimes wondered if this were a sign of some preaching anxiety or lack of commitment to ministry. Some Sunday's he found himself unsure of how to phrase something right up to the moment it needed to be said.

He knew what to do in order to get through the writer's block with which the hour brought. He would go to the Y and play some basketball with the noon crowd. Then, later this afternoon, it would come together for him. He just wasn't ready.

Two hours later, after playing so hard he nearly exhausted himself and visiting one patient at St. Joseph's Hospital across town, Lark sat down to his typewriter to start anew on Sunday's sermon. If only people knew how difficult this task was for him, Lark thought, they'd not be so critical of his efforts.

In the midst of game four of the noon basketball competition, the sermon began to take shape. Lark was dribbling down the right side of the court when Teddy, a young black man Lark had gotten to know through the Y Men's Basketball League, shouted from the sidelines, "Do it to him, Lark. Burn him!"

With a quick shift of the ball from his right hand to his left, Lark made a swift diagonal cut to the left corner of the floor. With the greatest of ease, he lifted his frame into the air, while his back was still turned to the basket, twisted, and softly sent the ball on its way through the hoop. Teddy clapped with glee and shouted, "Way to go, man. You did it to him again."

Lark glanced at the face of the older man who had been guarding him. Bill was a salesman who Lark liked a great deal. He had played for Bill's team one year during league play. As Lark was backing into his defensive position, the older man ran toward him, face reddened by physical exertion and embarrassment.

"Save it for the sixth ward, hot dog," Bill said, as he brushed by Lark.

Lark turned to Bill and asked, "What did you say?" just as the ball came over his right shoulder into Bill's hand for an easy lay up against the glass. Now Lark's face was red. Teddy was chuckling on the sidelines as Lark ran past him on offense.

"Letting an old man beat you like that—shame, shame," Teddy said, as Lark passed. That's when the sermon took shape. Lark knew that it had to deal with the personal struggle St. Paul talked about with the Romans.

> *I don't understand myself at all...*
> *I know perfectly well...*
> *But, I can't help myself...*
> *Now, if I am doing what I don't want to, it is*
>   *plain where the trouble is...*
> *I love to do God's will...*
> *But there is something else deep within me...*
>   *that is at war with my mind...*

Lark found those phrases of St. Paul's so inviting, he had to rewrite the sermon. He pulled Ross Snyder's book *Becoming Human* from his library shelf. He had read this several times and knew there was a quote in it he had to use. Soon, the sermon was coming to life on paper before him. Within an hour, he had the outline and most of the manuscript typed.

St. Paul's letter to the Romans reveals the basic human situation. We all know it to be true when we are honest about ourselves and face our lives in the light of Christ. Ross Snyder has written: "You were not born for the purpose of obeying someone else, or being a branded member in a herd. "You were born to become a unique, particular expression of human being. And you are the only one who can make something of your life on earth."

"You had nothing to say about where and when you were born, of what parents. And all your life, world events and situations not of your own making set conditions in which you must make your way. But you remain in charge of your decisions and what you intend to mean to those events. That is where the conflict—the inner conflict—begins." And, if Dr. Snyder were to reflect with us upon his comments in those paragraphs, he would agree. For, after saying what we don't have control over, he tells us we do have charge of our lives in the decisions we make. That's like the old saw about two guys who were discussing their roles in marriage and the one says to the other, 'I make all the big decisions in our home, and my wife makes all the little ones— like, she decides what colors the walls will be in our home, what school the kids will attend, what friends we'll have for dinner, where we are going for vacation. I decide how high the national budget can go, how we'll extricate ourselves from Vietnam, and who the Democrats will run for President this year.' It is true that individual uniqueness is a fundamental characteristic of life. And, it is true that God has made us basically free to make decisions which do affect and chart the course of our lives. And, that is where the inevitable base of human conflict rests: within our everyday lives and the necessity we face to chart our course through life. Dr. Albert Outler, renowned psychologist from SMU, has written:

41

"There was never a generation since Cain
and Abel as free to do their own thing as this one;
and, none less joyous in their freedom."

The phone's ringing stirred Lark from his intent to finish the sermon by supper. Jane was not in the office to intercept. Lark picked up the receiver and said, "St. Andrew Church."

"Really? I must have the wrong number," returned a slightly familiar voice.

There was an uneasy silence. Lark had received crank calls. He wanted to know who this was before he said much more.

"I beg your pardon," he politely responded.

"You don't know who this is, do you?"

"No, you sound familiar, though. Give me a hint."

"Do you know what time it is?"

He saw her clearly: a vision in Pennsylvania Station and again on the train. He was intrigued.

"Hello, are you there?" she asked.

"Yes. How may I help you. I don't even know your name."

"My, my, aren't we formal? I thought traveling with a lady on a train would change all of that."

"We didn't exactly travel together, as I recall," Lark said stiffly.

"Oh really? You were on a different train last night, then? That was your twin brother I saw?"

Lark had to laugh. "No, that's not exactly what I meant," he said. He began to feel a bit nervous about talking in such a way over the church's phone with a woman he barely knew.

"Anyway," she continued, "I hear you are involved in planning Lancaster's preparation for the peace rally in Washington next month, and I thought I'd call you to tell you I'd like to go along." She was very smooth and relaxed. She was evidently enjoying this conversation. Lark was beginning to ease into it with her. She still hadn't mentioned her name. And, she obviously knew his.

"That would be nice. We leave at half past five in the morning on August 5. The busses will be lined up in front of Hartman Hall on College Avenue. But I'm sure you know where that is. Right?"

"Of course," was her only reply.

"Then, who shall I tell my companions is going to be part of our frolic?"

"My name is Jennifer," she said, hardly hesitating. "Jennifer Brooks."

"And you're lecturing at Franklin and Marshall?"

Now, there was a slight pause. "Yes," she said. "English Literature."

"My name is Lark Wilson. But I suppose you know that already!"

She laughed easily. "No, I just dial numbers at random and talk to total strangers all the time. It's the in thing in the Big Apple."

They both laughed. Lark liked her, and he thought she had more than a simply professional interest in him. They were equally adept at flirting. Or, was there a chemistry between them that neither fully recognized?

"Is there anything else I can do to help you get ready?" she wanted to know.

Lark hesitated. He wanted to see her again and to get to know her better. He had only the faintest awareness his attraction to her could lead to complications. He had always handled this unspoken bit of mayhem between the sexes before. He was confident he could again.

"Well," he hesitated, "there is a local coordinating committee meeting next Thursday evening at seven thirty. It'll be at the All Saints Episcopal Church. You're welcome to attend."

"You don't need any other assistance?"

What was it about this woman, he mused. He felt flattered by all of her attention. "No, I don't believe there is," he responded.

"Okay, it's a date. See you." She hung up.

His heart was racing and a sweat broke out upon his forehead. He found it difficult to return to the sermon. He wanted to finish it, but every time he tried to work, his mind wandered to a vision of the woman who had just called him. By five o'clock, he had still not gotten the sermon done, so he simply packed up his notes and typewriter and carried them to his home across the parking lot. He'd finish the sermon early Saturday, before anyone arose for the day's activities. Having done this before, Lark knew he could do it again.

Within a minute, he was in the kitchen. The usual cast of characters were there: two boys, a girl, and a slightly frazzled spouse. It was Fran who looked in his direction when he pushed the sticky door open.

"Hello," she said with a smile.

"Hi! How's my favorite family?"

"We're all fine," said Walt, the oldest. "I want to show you what I painted in the park today, Daddy. I know you'll like it," he exclaimed. He held up yet another wrinkled piece of paper upon which he had carefully finger painted something which undoubtedly would grace their refrigerator door until the next art class.

Lark mumbled some words of appreciation and hoped his son wouldn't ask him to identify it.

"Do you know who it is, Daddy?"

"Of course," Lark lied once more to his child. It worked. Nothing more was said. The boy beamed at his father, and each gave the other a knowing smile. By this time their daughter Leigh Ann was telling her mother that she hoped they'd have baked macaroni for supper. It was her favorite dish, and she could eat it every day of her life, she explained.

Saul, the youngest, was preoccupied with the tropical fish tank which stood in the corner of the kitchen. His little hands were tracing the course of the fish and he was singing to them as they made their rounds.

Lark walked over to him and bent down beside him on his knees. "They're beautiful, aren't they?" he asked politely.

"Uh huh," the lad said, and continued to sing to them. Lark noted that Saul sang them a lullaby which he'd sung to him at night.

"Are they getting ready for bed?" Lark wanted to know.

"No," Saul replied, "they're just lonely."

Lark gave his son a hug and kissed him on the top of his head. Lark loved his children. These tender moments with them, re-entering their lives after a full day of school or play, were some of the best times of his life. Each of them was a unique child of God, thought Lark, as he stepped over to the sink and gave Fran a squeeze from behind. He snuggled into her neck and whispered, "I love you." Fran was too busy brushing carrots to respond. Fran was always busy. She often seemed embarrassed by Lark's attention to her in front of the children. Lark was rarely sure what to do when Fran didn't respond to his affection. Mood swings were not his forte.

"Well," Lark said, recovering from his latest icy encounter with Fran, "anyone want to go to the lake tomorrow?"

"Oh yes, Daddy," Leigh Ann shouted with joy. The boys agreed. It was a great idea. They talked of fishing, swimming, and canoeing. All three started to arrange their schedules and hence, an argument began between them as to what would be done first, second, third, and so forth. Fran continued brushing the carrots. Staying clear of the fray was her forte.

Lark saw the opportunity to leave the room and place his typewriter and papers in the study, where he could get at them first thing in the morning. Tonight they would eat supper, go for a walk, and continue dreaming and planning for the trip to Harrisburg and Italian Lake the next day. That ought to take care of this evening, thought Lark, as he washed his hands and prepared to help with the evening meal.

By six o'clock, everyone was gathered at the kitchen table. Saul said, "Why don't we eat outside?" Their yard was tiny. It was surrounded by a fence, and trees and bushes, all affording them some privacy from the church parking lot which encroached upon the parsonage from the East, North and South. The weather

45

was great. The meal simple. Fran glanced at Lark as if to ask what he thought.

"I think it's a great idea," said Lark. "Let's do it."

So, as they had done so many times before on a summer evening, they simply picked up everything, including the table and benches, and carried them into the yard. They would dine outside.

Chapter 7
MIND OVER MIND

Human beings have always believed it possible for one person to influence the thinking and behavior of another. All kinds of means to that end have been practiced throughout recorded human history, but perhaps none quite as mysterious as hypnotism. In truth, some have believed such powers to be nothing short of miraculous. How close such events really come to the intervention of the supernatural upon the natural, however, depends upon the self-assurance of the hypnotist, the receptivity of the client, and, sometimes, the gullibility of the onlookers.

Mass hypnotism played a key role in ancient Roman revelry. Ancient Greece had its oracle at Delphi and Dodona. Moses was even accused by Pharaoh's magicians of engaging in some kind of hypnotic sorcery with serpents. Dances to incessant rhythms and cadences often played a major role in mass hypnotism. European traditions from the middle ages onward recounted strange hypnotic dancing by large groups of people which had disastrous consequences.

Doc thought of all of this history as he stood outside St. Andrew Church on Friday evening, listening to the steady drum beat emanating from the teen dance taking place in the basement. The pastor had been a friend to the teens and children of the neighborhood. He had persuaded the consistory to spend nearly five-hundred dollars to establish a Friday night hangout for the teens of the inner city who were not welcome at the local YWCA dances. It was not unusual to find over one-hundred kids in the fellowship hall of St. Andrew Church on a Friday evening, chaperoned by young adult members of the church whom Lark had recruited.

Doc didn't see his pastor, at first. Lark sat with his back to the lone tree in the parsonage yard and stared away into the distance. The dance would soon end. It was near nine o'clock. Doc hadn't seen a light in Lark's study and decided to walk on through the parking lot, minding his own thoughts about modern dance, noise and its possible affects upon teenagers.

Most summer Friday evenings, Lark would sit in the back yard and listen while the two-hour dance ensued. Sometimes, he would walk across the parking lot and sit in his office, waiting for the teenager who needed help solving a particular problem. Whether it was an abusive parent, a broken love affair, or plain advice about human sexuality, Lark was a good listener, and the kids grew to trust his wisdom. It was rare that Lark actually went downstairs to the dance itself. On occasion, some teen would become hard to handle, due to drugs or alcohol. Lark would then be called down to the basement by one of the chaperons. He had yet to meet a teenager he couldn't handle.

Suddenly Lark saw Doc walking through the parking lot between the house and the church building.

Lark called to him. "Hi, Doc!"

"Oh, I didn't see you there, Lark. How's it going tonight?"

"Fine. No problems."

"Oh, I wouldn't say that," Doc stopped and leaned against the fence of the yard.

"What do you mean?" inquired Lark.

"In the land of my ancestors, only seven centuries ago, such constant rhythm and noise was enough to send hundreds of children those kids' age into convulsions and spasms."

"You don't say," Lark was always interested in this man's grasp of history.

"They danced from Erfurt to Arnstadt—twelve miles, mind you—where they all collapsed completely, some dying on that very spot. None of the rest ever recovered." Doc chuckled.

"That was certainly an anomaly, Doc," Lark said, knowing Doc was ready to talk about this subject and relate it somehow to the teen dance at St. Andrew Church.

"Not on your life," Doc was just getting started. "In 1278, a mad dance began by over two-hundred people as they were crossing a bridge in Utrecht. The bridge collapsed beneath them, plunging them all into the river where every one of them drowned."

"Well, there's not that much water in all of Lancaster County," Lark said, amused now at Doc's animation as he talked. "You know any more stories about dancing, Doc?"

"I'm not talking about dancing, pastor," Doc said, changing his tone a bit. "I'm talking about mass hysteria—mass hypnotism."

"I see," Lark said as he sensed Doc was about to recount another story.

"The worse case on record took place in 1374, I believe," Doc continued. "In, of all places, Aix-la-Chapelle."

"Is that in France?" Lark inquired.

"Heavens no," Doc was quick to respond. "Seems all my stories come from Germany. Anyway, it was in July. I guess they were celebrating something. They began to dance in the streets. Their frenzy grew to fantastic proportions. They whirled wildly night and day—kind of like those dance-a-thons we had after World War Two. Only these people didn't dance quietly in one another's arms. Some screamed as they danced. Some seemed to foam at the mouth. Some collapsed from exhaustion—just like those kids in our church basement will do some night if they don't turn that music down—and, some died as result of beating their heads against stone walls."

"Doc, this sounds weird," Lark said.

"Word spread about the dancing in Utrecht," Doc continued. "Soon, troops of dancers, together with wild musicians, were coming from all directions. It was kind of like a moving Woodstock." Doc chuckled again.

"Go on, Doc," Lark begged. This was truly interesting.

"Well, from what I recall, the Church in those days didn't promote this sort of thing like we seem to today," Doc said seriously. "Soon the Church was endeavoring to stop the dancing by use of the ancient practice of exorcism. The Church believed these people were possessed by demons."

"Are there any historical records of this action that you are aware of?" Lark wanted to know.

"I believe there is for I recall reading that the Church announced it had been successful in its exorcism. But, in spite of the Church, the dancing went on. At its height it had spread to Cologne, Strassburg, and that home of my ancestors, Metz. I believe the Netherlands was also infected."

"How did it end?" Lark asked.

"I don't recall. I guess it just petered out."

"Do you recall how long it lasted?"

"Just a year or so, I think," said Doc. "People left their shops, homes, families. And, many died."

"And, you think modern rock and roll might find its antecedent in this German history? I doubt if Elvis or the Beatles would agree. Do you think Dick Clark knows about this?"

Doc didn't laugh. He just stared at his pastor.

"What do you think of this weather?" Lark asked, sensing a change in subject was needed. "Isn't it great?"

"Couldn't be better here in God's country," Doc said as a smile crossed his face.

"Of course, it'll be a lot cooler after the dance," Lark smiled in return.

"Seriously, pastor, I don't see how those kids can take it," Doc said. "At the least, they'll all be deaf in thirty years. If I were younger, I'd take up auditory science. This nation's going to need it!"

Fran came into the yard. She and Lark had already put the children to bed. They had resisted very little, for they knew they had a big day coming on Saturday.

50

"Hello," she said. Doc nodded in return. "Would you like something to drink?"

Fran, ever the hostess with the parishioners, thought Lark. He didn't want to spend the rest of this evening listening to Doc expound, but he didn't show it to either of them.

"How about it, Doc? Fran has made some great sassafras tea. It's really good iced. Almost tastes like root beer," Lark said with feigned enthusiasm.

"Sassafras, huh. Did you know that stuff might be carcinogenic?" Doc questioned.

"No," was Fran's reply. her face revealed concern, for she had been making it all summer for the children. They loved it. Fran would never knowingly do a thing to place her children in harm's way.

Lark noticed her unease. Truth be told, he was also unnerved by the latest bit of information from Doc. "Hell, Doc," he said confidently, "if we're going to avoid things which might be carcinogenic, we wouldn't eat, drink, or breathe."

Doc laughed along with Lark. Fran simply stood, waiting for an answer.

"Okay," Doc replied. "We'll do as Luther advised; 'Love God and sin bravely!' I'll have some of that tea."

"So will I, Fran," Lark replied.

Fran returned to the kitchen to prepare the drinks, while the two men continued to spar with one another. Both men were highly intelligent, and each respected the other. Like so many men equally matched in wit, their conversations went a mile wide and one inch deep as each searched for the other's weakness.

Hence, when Fran returned to the yard, Doc was still leaning against the fence while Lark remained seated, only turned enough toward Doc to hold a civilized conversation.

"Come in and sit a spell," Fran said to Doc.

Lark always felt Fran made these polite gestures to unexpected visitors to the parsonages in which they lived simply to be friendly and to model the role of the pastor's wife. Many a time, when Lark desperately needed to be alone or to spend some time with her, Fran would manage to fill that time with a neighbor or parishioner. God sent company to their homes. Fran, in an effort to take the role to new heights, ever obliged and eagerly served them.

Doc hesitated. Then he replied, "I can't stay very long," as he walked toward the gate which opened at his touch and permitted his entry to the yard. Fran unfolded a lawn chair which stood, with three others, against the wall near the kitchen door. Soon, Doc was seated, sipping his iced tea.

"This is mighty fine tea," he said as he smacked his lips.

"Thank you," Fran replied. "How's Millie this evening?" Fran and Millie had become close friends since the Wilsons came to Lancaster. They often chatted on the phone during the week. They were seen sipping coffee after every service on Sunday. Fran and Millie found a sanctuary in one another's company where they could discuss children, family, and even their faith. Doc knew and respected this even though he, like Lark, often resented intrusions into his family life.

"Oh, she's fine. She's packing some vegetables for the winter. I always try to stay out of her way when she's doing that," Doc replied.

"She's going to teach me someday," Fran said.

Lark sat, quietly listening and wondering why Doc had driven into the city on this hot Friday evening to stop by the church.

"How do you put up with all that noise every Friday night?" Doc asked Fran.

"I don't pay any attention to it," Fran replied. She meant it. She could shut out just about anything, if she put her mind to doing so. In her childhood, she had learned to close out the world around her. It was a survival mechanism which served her well as a mother, wife, and adult, thought Lark.

"And, the children," Doc went on, "how about the children?"

"Summer is difficult," Fran replied. "But, it was difficult before we had the Friday night dance."

The music from the church basement was being played with a frenzy by some rock group known as Iron Butterfly. The guitars were screaming and the bass drum was beating like a human heart which had become uncontrollably erratic. Lark could visualize the teenagers swinging back and forth to the rhythms.

"I suppose your neighbors still haven't adjusted to this, either," Doc said to Lark in particular, for he knew that Lark had several run-ins with senior citizens in the neighborhood who complained the music was too loud and that the teenagers were a menace most other evenings, as well. The teens, once they got used to gathering on Fridays, often gathered in small groups in the parking lot during weekday evenings, just to shoot the breeze. Although there were suspicions that some drug dealing was taking place, Lark had never really witnessed anything. So, he couldn't say.

"Like the songwriter says, Doc, 'they're not listening still,'" Lark said dryly. Lark knew that Doc would have no clue as to his reference to one of the kid's favorite songs about the artist Vincent Van Gogh.

"I tell you," Doc went on, "this generation scares the living daylights out of me. They are anti-military, anti-education, anti-art, and anti-family. Who knows, they might someday embody the anti-Christ!"

"Oh, they're just being kids," Fran said thoughtfully.

"Perhaps they've got good reasons for their behavior," Lark added. "Just think how many of their heroes have been gunned down in the past ten years."

"Oh, come on," Doc retorted, knowing he had finally engaged Lark, "you're trying to say that those teenie boppers in the church basement felt something for JFK and RFK? Hells bells, most of them weren't even five years old when JFK was assassinated."

"You know children are influenced for life by what happens during their formative years," Lark said with more emphasis. "They weren't asleep the past ten years."

"Don't tell me you believe in Jesuit theories on personality development?" Doc said with a chuckle.

"No, as a matter of fact, I believe in the Biblical theory on personality development, Doc."

Doc knew by Lark's voice that he had gotten somewhere beneath his pastor's skin. He continued, "And, what theory is that?"

"The sins of the fathers are visited unto the children of the third and fourth generation," Lark stopped. He knew this conversation was going where almost every conversation with Doc led, lately. It was headed toward his clash with Doc over Vietnam.

In the silence that ensued Fran asked, "Would either of you like a refill?"

"No, thank you, Fran," Doc replied. "What time is it?"

"It's almost ten," Fran replied.

"I'd best be going," Doc said.

Lark got up, and Doc did also. They shook hands, and Lark thanked Doc for stopping by while continuing to wonder what this member of the consistory wanted to accomplish by his visit.

As Doc turned to go, he said quietly, "How was New York?"

Ah, there it is, thought Lark. What could he say without getting into it with this leader of the church? Lark thought for a few seconds before replying, "Hot, really hot."

Doc laughed at that one. He knew he would have to be more specific to draw Lark out. Turning to face Lark in the walkway beside the house Doc asked as politely as Lark had ever heard him speak, "and your demonstration in Washington, is it going to come off well?"

"What do you really want to know about it?" Lark said, a clear note of agitation in his voice. "Do you want to know how long I'll be gone? Do you want to know how many are going? Do you want to know why I am insisting upon going?"

Doc could tell his pastor was nearing the edge of his patience, but he quietly pressed on, "All of the above."

"We don't have time tonight, Doc. I'll give a full report next month at consistory. Okay?" Lark tried to sound much more open and conciliatory. It seemed to work.

"I'll look forward to it," Doc said jovially. "Thanks again for your hospitality." He was into his car and out of the driveway before Lark reached the kitchen door.

"You two really don't like each other," Fran said to her husband as they carried the glasses into the kitchen.

"Why do you say that?" Lark asked. As a pastor, he truly endeavored to like all of the members of the church. He had learned that ministering to people required that one somehow get past the usual barriers to interpersonal relationships which so often are based upon likes and dislikes. He had heard himself say something like this so often that he actually began to believe that he could conquer his feelings toward those who reacted to him in negative ways.

"You're not hiding your feelings very well," Fran said quietly. She always recognized his body language and tone of voice. Lark knew her feelings for Millie, Doc's wife, were so strong, she wished they could all get along well.

"There's just something about him, Fran. I can't put my finger on it. I've always been able to get along with parishioners who held different views. Hell, look how I got along with some of those rednecks in our last parish."

"They weren't rich," Fran said.

Lark thought about that comment for a moment. Maybe that was it. He always held that those who were wealthy were not much different than he. Circumstances which had not come his way had come their way; that was the only difference. They married into wealth. They inherited it. Some even, like Doc, had worked hard to earn it.

"Maybe you're right," Lark said thoughtfully. But, once he said it aloud, he could then argue the opposite point. He didn't. He was too weary. The dance was breaking up. He would go to the church in a few moments and help clean up the fellowship hall. He just wanted to get that done, then settle down for the evening.

"What's the matter?" Fran asked.

"What do you mean?"

"You don't seem to be yourself this evening. You're giving in too easily," she said.

He thought about her comment. He was preoccupied. He had been thinking of Jennifer's call earlier in the day. He had been thinking of her reddish hair, her perfumed, curvaceous body, her Halston dress, and her voice. In fact, he was having trouble thinking for very long about anyone or anything else.

"I'm fine," he said. "I'll be back in a couple of minutes." He went out the kitchen door and walked across the parking lot toward the church building. A young couple embraced beneath the steps leading to Lark's office. When they saw him approach, they each said, "Evenin' Rev" and resumed kissing and petting. Lark thought back to his teen years and the summer evenings filled with grabbing and groping all sizes and shapes of teenage girls. A man's life is never that simple, he thought to himself.

For one brief moment, he was back in the school yard with Barbara, the first girl he had ever kissed. The moon was full. She looked anxiously into his eyes as he moved toward her face and kissed her on the mouth. She flung her arms around his neck and held the position so tightly, he wondered if he'd ever find release. He kissed her again, and she responded more heavily. His heart skipped a beat. He felt something he'd never felt before. He felt comfortable with this young lady who was holding onto him as though he were a life raft in a sea gone wild around her.

"Hi, Rev," said a familiar voice. He nearly stumbled into a girl as he climbed the steps.

"Hey, Sue," he replied casually. "How did it go tonight?"

"Just great! There's not much to clean up tonight. The kids helped us."

"I'm glad to hear that," Lark said as he opened the door. "Thanks for everything!"

"Sure, Rev, no problem," the young woman said. She began to walk to her car. He heard the young couple beneath the stairs say goodnight to Sue as he closed the door behind him.

When he reached the fellowship hall, Deb and Ron were just completing the task of cleaning the popcorn maker. The signs which read "The Place," the title for the Friday night gathering that the neighborhood kids had picked the year before, had all been tucked away in a cupboard for another week. The soft drink cans were all in a neatly tied bag in the corner of the kitchen. Deb looked up as he entered the kitchen.

"How's it going, Rev?" she asked.

"It's going," he said with a smile.

"We had a good group of kids tonight," Ron said. "If they would be like this every week, we'd never have any complaints."

"Oh, I doubt that," Lark replied. They all laughed knowingly.

"You look washed out tonight, Rev. Tough week?" Deb inquired.

"Oh, I went to New York to plan the peace demonstration for Washington next month. Those meetings and train trips always take a lot out of me."

"I hope everything is coming along all right," Ron said. "Deb and I are looking forward to going with you. My parents aren't looking forward to dealing with the boys." Deb and Ron had two pre-schoolers. Ron's parents, who were also members of the church, were always ready to care for their grandsons, but only too eager to give them back when their son and daughter-in-law came for them.

"Everything looks good," Lark said. "It'll be the largest peace demonstration this nation has ever seen."

Deb, Ron, and Lark were all children of parents who had fought in World War Two. Their friendship was based on personal knowledge of the hardships and sacrifices that came with war. They couldn't accept the politics which led this country's involvement in Vietnam. They were very cynical about the promise of Lyndon Johnson that this nation could produce "both guns and butter." They all knew young men who had been drafted and sent to Vietnam during the Nixon presidency who did not come back alive. They knew there were some who never would be sent back. This was a war like none of them had ever witnessed. It was a war in which the poor, the minorities, and the under class were being drafted; and the college educated, well-to-do, and influential were staying home. What was even worse, they shared the suspicion that this war was being fought primarily to put a lid on the unrest the nation had experienced since JFK's assassination. They could not bring themselves to support it. And, when the shooting, bombing, and killings started on U.S. streets and college campuses because of the war, these three people, and the many who felt as they did, were determined to bring it to an end. Even if the majority of the people Lark served at St. Andrew did not agree, Lark knew Ron and Deb did. He felt comfortable with these parishioners, and they with him. They never made the mistake of thinking they represented the majority opinion at St. Andrew Church, however.

"Well, I guess we can wrap this up for the night, then," Lark said.

"Yep, let's call it a night," Deb said enthusiastically.

"I really appreciate all the hard work you two give us in this program," Lark said as they walked upstairs toward the exit.

"We love doing it, Rev," Ron said. "We hope someone will care for our boys when they're teens and we're too old and crotchety to twist." They laughed.

"Good night," Lark said as they walked arm-in-arm toward their car.

"See you Sunday, Rev," Deb called over her shoulder.

Fran was sitting in the living room, watching TV and drinking more tea. He sat down in the rocking love seat next to her and watched the solution to a mystery by Perry Mason with her. This show was Fran's favorite. He dared not ask her the plot or sequence of events prior to his arrival. He'd simply have to wait to see what unraveled.

When it was over, Fran got up and turned the set off. She walked toward the love seat, bent over, and kissed Lark hard upon his lips. "I'm going to take a bath," she said with a glance that told him this was an invitation.

"I'll be up in a minute," he said. And he was.

Chapter 8

SATURDAY
MORNING

Lark was up at six in the morning. He savored these early mornings, before anyone arose on Saturdays. These were the times he wrote best. Perhaps it was because he knew Fran would care for the children's needs when they arose and nothing would happen much before nine. Perhaps it was simply because everything would start happening at nine. He wasn't sure. All he knew was that he could count on this time being his, and he made the most of it.

He glanced through parts of the Sunday sermon he had written the day before. They looked good. Not too much polish, and those pages would be ready. But something was bothering him. He knew that people of the parish were aware of his absence this week, and they would expect him to reference it in his sermon. He couldn't think of a way to do it, at first. He found himself just sitting before the typewriter, waiting for inspiration to come and tap him on the shoulder. Instead, it was Fran who tapped him lightly upon the shoulder.

"Here's some coffee," she said. She bent and kissed him on the cheek. He hadn't even heard her arise and stir in the kitchen. He was really deep in thought.

The coffee was excellent. It awakened his senses and his mind. As he leaned back and sipped the cup of steaming morning beverage, a thought occurred to him. He remembered something which Senator Hatfield had written in his book. He got up and walked to the bookshelf. There was the book, its white cover reinforcing the title in red print. Walking back to his desk, he began to page through the book, looking for the quote he wanted.

Suddenly, there on page forty-seven were the paragraphs Lark would reference. He would weave them into his message in a manner to which he was accustomed. He would mention the peace demonstration planning, then use Senator Hatfield's own words to justify the need to be involved in such an enterprise.

We must look at our country, to examine the values that are guiding our culture, and ask whether they are true to God's will and purpose. If not, they must be challenged with a prophetic word, and Christians must witness to the need for national repentance... As Christians, our basic responsibility is to express the values and truths that we have acquired through our faith.

Further, we must attempt to implant them within the lives of others. Therefore, one of the urgent avenues for personal action is to influence public attitudes and values. Public opinion drove a president out of office in 1968; the attitudes of the people in our democracy can change the course of our country.

So we must be diligent and responsible in the expression of our views regarding the state of our nation. We must attempt to mold public attitudes so they will become attuned to God's purposes... When we look at the state of our nation, how should we react? What should our attitude be toward a people who are absorbed by materialism, controlled by greed, and motivated by the pursuit of selfish and corporate gain, with little regard to the value and quality of human life? How should we judge the way our nation uses its resources?

Lark continued to type the sermon which was now beginning to come to life upon the page in front of him. At such moments, Lark could understand the concepts of divine inspiration, even if he'd never admit the fact to another soul. He continued with another quote from the senator.

> When we conclude that our nation is not following
> God's way, then we must speak out. That must be
> part of our witness. And, that is where each of us
> can take personal responsibility...

Lark typed on, preparing to explain to the people he believed God had called him to serve, and that the forthcoming peace demonstration beckoned to all of them for support. As he typed these words, he knew that there were those in the congregation who would take offense. He sought soft but steady ways to communicate his faith in God's word, which he thought, negated what the nation was pursuing in Vietnam. He knew that Doc would be especially vigilant during this sermon, for he had made his position very clear in past consistory meetings. One family in the church had already lost a son in the war. They would be torn by their deep allegiance to their son's memory and their utter disdain for the nation's leaders who had called their son to die so far from Lancaster.

Finally, as was Lark's way of writing a sermon, he focused on the text from the Old Testament. He would appeal to it in his closing paragraphs. He would trust that God's word would be communicated and that the people would understand. He needed to demonstrate that their pastor was not just engaged in a political diatribe against the present administration in Washington, but was faithfully attempting to apply Scripture to contemporary life in America. In closing he typed:

> Ancient Israel experienced the same struggle our
> country has today. In their quest for security in
> their world, they were encouraged by their leaders
> and tempted to trust in their military power. Hosea,

from the words we read this morning, warned them prophetically against this fallacy; "because you have trusted in your chariots and in the multitude of your warriors, therefore the tumult of war shall arise among your people."

Lark decided to conclude the sermon as he had finished many such prophetic performances in the past. He would simply recite words well known in the church since the first century; "Let him who has ears hear what the Spirit says to the church. Amen."

He sat back and surveyed his sermon. Usually, they were four to five pages long, single spaced, when in complete manuscript form. The manuscript, as he was taught in homiletics class, was but a platform. As sermon, it was but the foundation. Preaching is an art form. As such, what happens during the sermon is really a combination of content, context, and emotional response on the part of the hearer. Many times before, Lark had adjusted a sermon's manuscript to fit what he witnessed before him in the pews as he preached. It took some getting used to as a preacher, but it was absolutely essential to the craft.

"When it comes right down to it, preaching is communication of faith," he once explained to an elderly woman who asked him how he viewed the sermon. "And communication is a two-way street. Therefore, the preacher had best be alert as to how what he says is being received by the congregation."

John had once explained to Lark that people in black churches understood this better than people in white churches. Black preachers in particular understood it, according to John. Lark, never sure that this might not just be another of those myths regarding the difference between the races, nevertheless listened eagerly to John.

"You white preachers are too mental. Your people expect that of you but don't really respond to it on a level that's helpful to preaching," John said one day, as they sat having a cup of coffee in Lark's study at St. Andrew. "Listen to Dr. King's preaching. He waits, almost seems to pause too long. He uses multiple metaphors. To white ears, it almost sounds as though Martin is not sure what to say. But, he's waiting for the nibble. And, in the black church, that nibble sounds like this—'yeah, right on. Uh huh, that's right. Amen.'"

Lark thought he understood. John was telling him that the congregation's response, on an emotional level, was vital to communicating the gospel. Unless he could assure himself that people were listening with that "inner ear," as John called it, Lark would never feel secure in the pulpit.

"You don't always listen for affirmation, Lark," John continued. "You need to know when people aren't buying what you're selling, as much as otherwise. So, be open to hearing the feedback."

Lark scrutinized his sermons after that conversation with John for clues as to how he was progressing in this art. He often wrote footnotes to himself in the margins and at the bottoms of the manuscript pages to remind himself of the need to take his time and wait. This sermon looked good. He would go with it as it was.

Glancing at the clock, he noted it was eight-thirty. He could hear the children stirring upstairs, and he knew Fran would soon be getting them ready for their big day. He decided to have another cup of coffee. Getting up from his desk, he noticed a slight throb to his jaw. Thinking little of it, he sauntered out to the kitchen to fetch a cup of coffee and glance at the morning newspaper. Perhaps he would have time to get through the scores and news he wanted to read before they packed the car to drive to Harrisburg and Italian Lake.

As he sat down at the picnic table and waited for his children's arrival, his jaw thumped, and suddenly, a tremendous pain crossed over his face. Then, as mysteriously as it had come, it was gone. Lark thought he might have a bit of neuralgia. Perhaps it was the night air of the evening before; there had been a slight chill to it around ten.

Soon, the children were seated around him, each of them excitedly talking about the day ahead. Not many of the arguments centered upon their schedule the night before had been settled. But, somehow, it was all easier to face at the beginning of the day.

As Lark took a sip of coffee a feeling not unlike that of being hit in the face with a baseball crushed his upper jaw. He winced. It didn't subside. It throbbed for a good five minutes. An instinctual need to suck on his upper teeth overtook him. As he did, the pain began to diminish, at last.

Fran, standing by the sink eyeing his sudden change of demeanor asked, "What's wrong, Lark?"

"I had a pain," he replied.

The children went on, talking about the day before them, as Fran studied Lark's face. "Are you all right?" she asked.

"I don't know," he said honestly. Having never been subjected to this kind of sensation in his life, he really wasn't sure what was happening.

Suddenly, as if triggered by the talking, there it was again. Like labor pains, he thought to himself, each time, it came a little fiercer than previously. Each time it lasted longer. This time if felt as though it would not cease.

"Perhaps I ought to give Doc a call," Lark said.

"You want me to?" Fran kindly inquired.

"That would be helpful," Lark said with a grimace.

The children still had not noticed that their trip to Harrisburg might be in jeopardy. They ate their breakfast and talked as fast as they could about how they were going to spend the day.

When Fran returned, she quietly informed Lark that Doc could see him if he went to the office right away. It just so happened that Doc had a free hour on this Saturday morning. When Lark got up from the picnic table, Walt asked, "Where are you going, Daddy?"

"Your father has to go see Doc Willard right away," Fran explained.

The children stopped their talking. Each of them looked at their father with concern.

"Is Daddy going to get a tooth pulled?" asked Walt.

Poor child, thought Lark. By the time he was six years old, Walt had experienced no less than eleven extractions. As far as he knew, that was all dentists did to people.

"No," assured Fran. "Daddy just has a toothache. He'll be fine."

That said, the children went back to finishing their breakfast. Fran sipped her coffee nervously, wondering if this would end their plans for the day. Lark hurried out to the car, while his jaw thumped now with each step he took.

Lark arrived at Doc's office fifteen minutes later. The Saturday morning traffic into the city was beginning to build, but Lark managed, even with what was now clearly recognizable as one nasty toothache. But, as Lark turned the car into Doc's parking lot the throbbing in his face and jaw ceased as it had begun, suddenly.

The receptionist smiled as Lark entered the office. No one was waiting, but Lark could hear the high pitch of a dental drill coming from somewhere deep in the office. He could also hear Doc's incessant babbling, which he liked to do whenever he had a patient in a chair. Many parishioners had complained to Lark that Doc always talked to them when they could not answer. Some of them truly resented his behavior. Lark had witnessed it with his own children. And Lark had concluded that this was a nervous habit on Doc's part.

Lark couldn't understand what Doc was talking about with his patient. Whatever it was, though, he was really excited about it. The drilling ceased. Within seconds, Doc was standing in the doorway.

"What's the matter?" he asked.

"Not sure, really, Doc," Lark replied. "My jaw hurt like hell, until I drove into the parking lot just now."

Doc laughed knowingly. "Patients often tell me that. We understood it at dental school as the overwhelming power of anxiety." He chuckled to himself.

"What does that mean?" Lark asked seriously.

"Simple," Doc went on. "Your jaw still hurts. But the sight of the office or dentist sets in motion a series of denials based upon anxiety, which causes the patient to believe the pain has disappeared." He laughed this time. "It's that simple. I see it all the time."

Lark was not comforted, but he followed Doc into one of the patient rooms and climbed into the dental chair. Soon, he was reclining and staring into three bright lights while Doc, leaning over his body, was saying; "Open wide. Uh huh, looks angry. Haven't seen one this sick in a while. Boy, this will take time, I think. Did you see the paper this morning? They got an article in there about the peace march." Doc probed with a metal pick, and Lark's facial nerve jumped in response. "Yep, it says they expect quite a crowd. They won't even know if you're there or not, pastor."

Doc backed away as Lark's chair automatically came forward into an upright position. The pain was beginning to come back, ever so slightly.

"I'm not going to be able to handle that this morning. There's a lot of swelling around the gum line, and I suspect there is considerable puss around the root. It wouldn't even make sense to x-ray it this morning."

Lark sat and listened as Doc outlined the procedure he prescribed. "I'll give you some antibiotic patches. They're like little tea bags. You just keep this up against your gum for the rest of today. They have a numbing medication in them, as well. So, I doubt if you'll notice the pain much, unless you bite down on that side. Just be careful."

"What about tomorrow, Doc?" Lark asked.

"Oh, I think you'll feel somewhat better by morning. You'll be able to preach. Just be careful what you eat. Then, be back here on Monday at eight sharp, so we can take some pictures and make sure this is what I think it is."

"You don't sound sure, Doc."

"Well, there's so much swelling, I can't be certain. I've seen popcorn cause this, and my first impression can be wrong. I don't want to say for sure until I can get some x-rays."

"Well, that's a relief, Doc," Lark confided. "We have big plans for today. We're going up to Harrisburg, to Italian Lake."

"Uh huh, nice day for it."

"The kids will be glad to hear that we can still go."

"Just be careful. Don't forget that you have a pretty sick tooth there. We'll try to save it for you, but, you've got to be careful for the next couple of days. Okay?"

"Sure, I'll be careful," Lark said.

Lark left with a small package of the pain relievers and antibiotics Doc had prescribed. He was feeling better already, and, he was glad that his family could go on with their plans for the day.

As he backed away from the front of the office, Lark noted there were no cars in the parking lot. Lark wasn't sure why this fact seemed so important. All Lark knew was that it was a beautiful morning. Within an hour, he'd be driving the family to Harrisburg for a day of fun.

Chapter 9
THE LAKE

When every member of the family was into the station wagon Lark and Fran had bought six years and 126,767 miles before, Lark made one more tour around the car for its final visual inspection. This was something Lark had learned in drivers' education in high school. It had saved his life once. Today, it simply confirmed that the rubber boat, picnic basket, various beach towels, plastic floating devices, three kids, and their mother were all in the car. This time, everything fit snugly into the "back in the back," as the kids called the area behind the rear seat of the station wagon.

This six cylinder family wagon had seen better days. It was rusting in several spots around the fender wells, and its water pump and power steering motor made noises as the car started. Warming up, it emitted a high-pitched scream. The car burned some oil and always started, even when warm, with a generous offering of smoke from the tailpipe which only a month before had hung by a thread, until Lark reattached the pipe to its hanger bolt with some heavy duty wire.

They drove out of the carport, and headed north toward the highway. The traffic was really beginning to jam up in the city. It was ten-thirty, and the trip to Harrisburg would take approximately one hour. And, depending upon the city traffic in the state capitol, it would take another twenty minutes to get to a parking space at Italian Lake. Lark and Fran discussed that the first thing they would do upon their arrival would be to look for a picnic table and then have lunch. This fit the children's agenda perfectly; they loved picnics.

As they rounded the ramp connecting Highway 72 to Highway 230, Lark thought he felt an odd bumping sensation in one of the front tires. How could he have missed something, he thought? Once upon the highway, the car performed as best it could, so Lark dismissed the sensation. Soon, they were zipping along the highway, along with thousands of other people; the traffic was heavy on both sides of the three lane highway.

The children were occupied in the rear seat of the wagon. Each had brought something along for amusement during the ride while Lark and Fran sat silently, taking in the passing scenery. Lark's toothache had subsided considerably. He was beginning to feel more like a normal person.

"What are you thinking about?" he inquired of Fran.

"Nothing," was always her reply. Lark wondered if that were true. Could it be that she simply never had a thought? Or, was it simply that she revealed to no one, especially her husband, her innermost ruminations. All Lark knew was that he had never been successful in getting her to talk about herself.

"Would you like to listen to the radio?" he asked quietly.

"Uh huh."

The station wagon hummed along the highway, nearly like it did when newly purchased. The radio crackled on at Lark's twist of the knob. There were so many radio stations in the area that sometimes it was difficult to tune into only one on the dial. Lark located a Harrisburg station the family found entertaining. The morning disk jockey always made the children laugh. Fortunately, he was commanding his post this Saturday morning. When the children heard his voice, they squealed with delight from the back seat.

69

"Now, ladies and gentlemen," the announcer was saying, "you have to go out by the Colonial Park Shopping Center to see this sight. I have never seen anything like it. The trailer hauling Skippy the Whale has overturned and there is water all over the highway. Skippy is just lying there alongside the highway flipping on his side. So when you go out there, be sure to take a glass of water to throw on Skippy, to keep him alive until they can hoist him into another tanker."

Lark and Fran were rolling with laughter in the front seat. The children were all giggling, except Saul. Lark peered into the rear-view mirror to see Saul beginning to cry. His little body heaved with empathy for Skippy the Whale.

"The announcer's only making a joke, Saul," Lark assured.

His sister and brother also sought to convince him that it was all make believe. Fran turned to ask if the children would like to go to the shopping center, just to make sure. Saul was the first to assent, and this seemed to settle him down. So, they resumed listening to the announcer's inane babbling.

Soon, the usual Saturday morning weather report and local news replaced the announcer's fun for the morning. Commercials blared into the car, proclaiming the virtues of this department store over that one, one car over another, and on and on. For several minutes, nothing was aired regarding Skippy.

It was Saul who spoke from the rear seat during the lull. "Should we take some water, Dad?" he asked directly into the mirror. Lark could see that his younger son was now in on the joke. There was no mistaking that twinkle in his eyes.

"I guess we ought to," Lark replied. "We'll get some at a filling station before we get to Colonial Park." That was all which needed to be said. The rest of the trip, the children talked about how they were going to throw water on Skippy the Whale when they got to the shopping center. The announcer had come back on air and curiously, he never mentioned Skippy again. No doubt children all over the Harrisburg area had reacted as Saul had and the station had received angry calls from parents who had other things to do besides driving through the city in search of an overturned tanker truck and a roadside attraction unlike any other in America this day. Lark was aware that the announcer had often gone too far with his jokes, and his job had been on the line many times.

It was nearly eleven-thirty when they made their way into Harrisburg. The children watched a jet plane lift into the air to the west of the highway. Their planned detour to Colonial Park would take at least forty-five minutes extra time. But, by this point in the trip, everyone in the car was anxious for the diversion.

Pulling into a nondescript filling station which had a basic color scheme of blue and yellow, but no doubt had passed through the hands of many different aspiring oil men since it was built, Lark asked if anyone had to go to the rest room. Everybody did. So, after pulling up to blue and yellow pump, everyone jumped out of the car. As he filled the tank, he watched his wife and daughter trudge to the ladies' room, one a miniature of the other, moving like confident gazelles toward their destination. Fran's walk was almost model-like. Leigh Ann's gait mimicked her mother's. The boys waited for their father to finish his task, and once complete, all three walked into the station.

"Good morning," said the attendant. "That's three dollars."

"Do you have any cups?" Lark asked the attendant, as he paid for the gas.

Before the attendant could answer, Lark's older son said; "We're going to pour some water on Skippy the Whale."

The attendant muttered something under his breath and then looked quizzically at Lark. The boy continued, "We heard on the radio that there was an accident. Skippy is lying by the side of the road."

Lark could tell by this time that the attendant had been listening to a different radio station this morning and was totally baffled by what he was hearing.

"Where did you say that whale is?" he inquired.

The youngest child replied; "He's at the Colonial Park Shopping Center."

"Why, that's right up the road a mile or so," said the attendant. He winked at Lark. "You'll find big cups in the rest room, over there," he pointed.

The two boys scampered for the rest room with Lark in pursuit. They found the cups, which were very small, three ounces, at best.

"These won't hold much water, boys," Lark said. "But if each of us carries one, it'll help Skippy."

All held a small cup of water in hand as Lark drove the car away from the filling station and onto the roadway. Several blocks passed before they reached Colonial Park Shopping Center, the city's very first center of its type, located in one of Harrisburg's important suburbs. Outside of the usual Saturday morning traffic, there was no sign of the extraordinary event reported on the radio only fifty minutes before. They drove about a half mile past the shopping center, when they came upon what appeared to be a gigantic traffic jam. The cars were not moving in either direction. Silence overtook the Wilsons as they sat, waiting to move ahead.

After fidgeting for a few minutes, Lark put the transmission in park and stepped outside the car. The children wanted to know where he was going. Lark assured them he was going to walk ahead to see if he could spy Skippy along the side of the road. After walking several car lengths, Lark looked into one of the waiting vehicles and asked the driver, "What's the hold up?"

"Don't know," was the response. "I heard there was a whale truck overturned up here a ways."

Lark looked into the car. Four very quiet, anxious-looking children with paper cups full of water sat in the back seat. Two older women sat in the front seat, beside the driver. Each was holding a paper cup. "Where's your water?" Lark asked the driver.

"Ran out of cups," was his reply. "And if this traffic doesn't move soon, I'll be out of gas!"

"How long you been tied up here?" Lark asked.

"About fifteen minutes. Haven't moved a god-damned inch in fifteen minutes."

"Hush," the woman in the center of the front seat said.

"Well, it's true," the driver snapped.

Lark walked back to the car. Once inside, he took his cup of water from Fran and informed the family that the traffic tie-up was due to Skippy the Whale. As he sat there, behind the wheel of his motionless automobile, surrounded by thousands of persons trapped as he was, he thought of a statement one of his practical theology professors said in class on a very dark and dreary Lancaster morning: "The problem with life is that most people stumble into their future, instead of planning for it." Somehow, those words seemed very apropos.

One hour later, after they ate their lunches in the car, drank the water they had garnered for Skippy the Whale, and driven quietly by the corner where the whale was supposed to be, they were on their way toward Italian Lake. The children were a bit fussy, hot, and confused. Each of them muttered what could be considered defamatory remarks about the radio announcer.

Fran sat quietly beside Lark as he managed to find a parking space near the lake. He'd been unable to chew every nail from his fingers, which usually offered some relief from tension. He was becoming more conscious of his aching jaw as the day progressed. She sensed his uneasiness and reached across the front seat, taking his hand in hers.

"It's been a good day." She looked into his furtive eyes. His quietness always signaled the need for reassurance. This was one of his needs she always seemed keyed into, and he had surmised that this was due to her maternal instinct. This day had not only upset the children, he once again felt inadequate as a father. Having given in to Fran's impulse, no doubt spurred by her dislike of water sports and her fear for her children whenever they ventured forth in a boat, Lark had virtually ruined the day for everyone, he felt. When would he be able to head these moments off, he wondered to himself, as Fran withdrew her hand and they all exited the vehicle.

"Dad," said Walt, "I'll get the boat." He was big enough to handle it by himself and took great pride in doing so each time they visited a lake. Fran took Leigh Ann and Saul's hands and began to walk toward the lake. Lark grabbed the air pump and mattresses from the rear deck of the station wagon and trudged behind his family. As he watched them walk ahead, he noted how each of the children's heads moved up and down like cartoon characters' as they walked. No doubt animated by the potential adventure before them, each child's body strained and jumped toward the lake as they walked. Meanwhile, Fran's normally erect and noble walk now had an ever-so-slight awkwardness to it. She was always tentative about this part of family life. She had once confided to Lark, in an unguarded moment, that she feared something happening to her children more than anything else in the world, more, even, than his death. While this might seem admirable to those who espouse the virtues of motherhood, Lark felt cheated by his wife's confession. On the scale of things, he felt he was now no longer number one.

Once in the rubber raft, the children waited for their father to do something with them in the water. Fran never did; she always positioned herself nearby with a look of horror upon her face until the children were safely out of the water. It was Lark who got into the thick of it with the children.

Once used to the temperature himself, Lark dove under the water and swam toward their raft with his forearms and hands joined in an arc above his head. From a distance, this maneuver created the appearance of a very small dorsal fin. "Shark," they shouted as the hands moved menacingly toward their little seagoing craft. Then, the fin would slip under the water, only to come up beneath their raft so as to tip it. The children loved this game and never grew tired of it, as Lark did. They would kick and scream and make such a fuss, that often people nearby became concerned. This afternoon at Italian Lake was no exception.

At one point, as Lark tread water to get some rest after a foray toward the children's raft, he saw Fran talking with a young man on shore. He was tanned and healthy-looking. Lark surmised he was a lifeguard who had possibly responded to the screams of the children. Then, after what looked like reassurance offered by Fran, the young man turned and walked away. Lark went on with his play with the children.

Later that afternoon, after an absolutely great day of rubber rafting, sun bathing, snack food, and sunburn, the Wilsons again packed into the wagon and headed north along the river toward their favorite ice cream spot on Peter's Mountain. This final snack of the day would suffice for supper, since about all they had done that day was eat. Nobody argued. It had been a good day; Fran was right about that. Lark had redeemed the earlier disappointments created by his jaw and Skippy the Whale, both of which had threatened to undo the day's promise.

"I saw you talking to the lifeguard at the lake," Lark said to Fran as they drove up Peter's Mountain toward Sharkey's Ice Cream House.

"Oh, that was not a lifeguard," Fran explained. "He was a reporter."

"What?"

"A reporter," she continued. "He said he worked for the *Patriot* and was there with a friend when he noticed us."

"Oh," Lark was both flattered and mystified by the thought that some reporter who worked in a city forty miles from where they lived would recognize them.

"He said he had met you last year at an ecumenical luncheon."

"What did he want?" Lark asked.

"At first, I thought he just wanted to say hello to you."

"At first?" Lark knew she was pondering the conversation with the reporter for some reason, but she was not forthcoming with her thoughts.

"Well, yes," she went on. "He seemed a bit nervous. It wasn't clear to me what he wanted, beyond just saying hello."

"Did he say anything else?" Lark asked, intrigued now.

"He asked me when we'd be home tonight."

"Why did he want to know that?"

75

"He said he wanted to talk with you about the peace march. He had heard you were leading the Lancaster contingent, and he wanted to interview you about it."

"That's interesting," Lark said. He wondered how anyone working for the *Patriot* would know of his role in the forthcoming march. "Maybe the denominational office gave out a list of leaders," he said. Fran said nothing. Lark would have to await the telephone call to learn more about the young man.

"Anybody want to listen to the radio?" Lark asked, as they drove toward Lancaster after sharing five different flavors of ice cream: strawberry, peach, chocolate, vanilla, and licorice. Saul was the adventurous one.

One very sleepy voice responded, "Yeah." Lark reached for the dial and got the volume up just in time to hear the end of the local news. The announcer was giving details regarding the gigantic hoax played upon area residents by the station's disk jockey earlier in the day. Pennsylvania State Police judged the traffic jam to have involved over one thousand cars. The tie-up lasted more than several hours, the newscaster added. The disk jockey had been roundly reprimanded for his behavior, and there was even a recorded apology from the errant radio personality himself.

"Neither this station, nor its management or sponsors, are responsible for today's misfortunes near the Colonial Park Shopping Center. I take full responsibility for my actions, and I want you all to know that I acted alone, on impulse, this morning when I reported the fictitious whale incident. I never dreamed so many children would coerce their parents into trying to save that whale. To tell the truth, I thought most kids watched television on Saturdays (the disk jockey chuckled) and only their parents would hear my story and get a laugh out of it. Please accept my apology for any inconvenience this adolescent prank might have caused anyone in our listening area."

The Wilsons listened to this familiar voice grovel. The children, eventually losing interest in the news, fell asleep in the rear seat, each leaning upon another.

"How about that," Fran said quietly. "He plays a practical joke, discovers a market, and watches his ratings soar. No wonder he can be so magnanimous!"

That about sums it up, thought Lark. Fran saw the whole picture and summarized it in two sentences. Her economy with words made him envious. She would have made a great preacher, as she was an excellent teacher.

It was nearly ten when they pulled into the carport. Lark and Fran decided to simply leave everything in the car until Sunday afternoon. They gathered up the children and carried them to the bedroom. Once there, they undressed them, took each to the bathroom, and prepared them for bed.

Lark knelt beside each tousled head and whispered a prayer of thanks for the fun God had given them this day. Each one hugged their dad and whispered good night. As Lark and Fran were quietly leaving the bedroom, it was Saul who said aloud; "I wonder where Skippy is tonight?" There were soft chuckles all around.

Lark and Fran were still laughing to themselves as they crawled into bed at eleven. Fran rolled near Lark, embraced him, and whispered, "I love you, Daddy." Lark, already half-asleep, assured her that he loved her, too. All grew quiet in the Wilson household as the cicadas sang outside the bedroom windows so softly, they could barely be discerned above the slow-moving traffic below.

Chapter 10
THE LORD'S DAY

It felt like someone was pushing against his jaw with a sharp pointy stick. The pain was unrelenting, determined to move him. Lark was awakened by it at 2:30, and he got up to fetch some relief.

As he walked down the stairs, the pain thumped in his head with each tread. Quietly, he went to the kitchen, turning on lights as he careened toward the cabinet which held headache remedies. Each jab of pain reminded him that something had to be done about this soon.

As he reached for the pain reliever Doc had told him he might need before Monday, he was reminded of the early hours he'd spent with Fran when she was pregnant with Walt. It seemed she got up every night for months with pains of one kind or another. She just couldn't get comfortable: she was big, she was hot, she was just plain anxious to get birth over with and begin being a mother. Lark just wanted to get this pain in his jaw fixed and go on being a pastor.

He took two tablets and turned the faucet on to get some cold water. Switching the light off, he ambled into his study to read through the sermon he had finished the morning before. It looked fine. It would be a good one; he knew which ones were and which ones were not. Most preachers knew, he suspected.

The room was very quiet at this hour of the morning. The entire house nestled in darkness, and the street outside was dark except for the corner streetlight which winked at him through the gently rustling trees nearby. Lark couldn't remember being in this room at this hour since they had moved to Lancaster. He made a mental note to himself that this would be an ideal time to write: no telephones, no visitors, no children, no wife to interrupt him.

It was then that he thought of Jennifer. Between the pain and the fun of the day with his family, Jennifer had not once crossed his mind. Now, alone in his study in the middle of the night, he thought of her. He closed his eyes. He could see her wrapped in a sheet, twisted this way and that, sleeping. She looked helpless and beautiful. Her breasts heaved slowly to the rhythm of her steady breathing, her red hair flowed across her forehead and down her neck. Her shoulders were uncovered, and one breast was barely visible above the top of the sheet she was using for a covering this warm night. She was sleeping in the nude, as Lark always wanted Fran to do. Unlike Fran, who insisted that she could not sleep in the nude and who seemed perturbed every time Lark did it, Jennifer lay dreaming upon her bed only a few miles away with nothing on except the sheet. She rolled upon her tummy, revealing gently curving buttocks. She seemed to be saying something which Lark could not make out.

"Are you alright?"

"Huh?"

"I said, are you alright?"

It was Fran's voice. She had come into the room as Lark sat in his chair staring out the den window, his back toward the doorway. Suddenly, he realized it was Fran who spoke, not Jennifer. He swung the chair toward the doorway and began to rise from his seat when he noticed a familiar tightness to his pajama bottoms. He held his ground and gently reseated himself.

"I didn't hear you get up," Fran said, as she studied her husband in the subdued light of the den. "Is your tooth acting up?"

"Yes," he said, regaining his composure in Fran's presence. How could he have fantasized about a woman he hardly knew?

"Did you take anything for it?"

"Yes," was all he said.

Fran looked at him quizzically. Nothing more was said by either of them. She turned and walked back toward the stairs which led to their bedroom. He got up, relieved to note that his pajama bottoms now fit him as they did the first time he wore them, walked to the doorway, switched off the light, and ascended the stairs behind his wife.

In bed, Lark pondered what was happening to him. His heart pounded as his wife gently settled down into sleep once more. He rolled first to one side and then the other. One thing was abundantly clear to him; this was a new sensation. He thought of Jennifer during most moments his mind was not occupied. The more he pondered it, the less attention he paid to his jaw, until he was suddenly and pleasantly aware that the pain was gone.

Lark's mind, weary of these early morning ruminations, drifted off to sleep. The many questions and few answers available to him would have to wait as his body took time off for rest.

Chapter 11
THE DAY THE LORD HAS MADE

The congregation later on this day of rest was the typical summer Sunday crowd. Pastors don't see many parishioners on summer Sundays. Even bad weather, the likes of which greeted those who arose early on this day, did not keep worshipers at home so their presence could grace sanctuaries around the county.

Lark was not surprised to see the sanctuary half empty when he walked onto the chancel from his study, shortly before Elsie finished the prelude. His only surprise was who sat in the fourteenth pew on the south side of the sanctuary. Jennifer was dressed conservatively in a dark-blue shift and a simple white hat. She smiled, as the sight of her nearly caused Lark to forget the Solemn Declaration at the start of the liturgy.

By the time the choir had processed to the words of the opening hymn, Lark had recovered. By focusing upon Fran and the children, sitting in their usual spot—three pews from the front on the north side of the sanctuary—Lark was not to stumble again throughout the service. His sermon was delivered with the usual professional flair for which he had become well-known in the city. The hundred or so worshipers this Lord's Day sang each hymn with enthusiasm. The eleven members of the choir performed their anthem as the offering was received with a polish not found in many houses of worship in Lancaster city on summer Sundays. Even Chet's special music, a violin solo which set a neighbor dog to howling throughout its performance, did not deter the congregation from praising God with solemnity.

Following the worship service, the members filed passed Lark at the front doors of the church, wishing him a good day. As Jennifer took his hand, she looked directly into his eyes and said, "Very nice sermon, Reverend." She was different today, but, he wasn't quite sure how.

Doc and Millie inquired as to how Lark and his family were spending the day. Doc remarked that if he didn't know better, he would have never guessed Lark was nursing a sore tooth. Millie and Fran stood in the narthex, chatting for some time, while the three Wilson children went their merry ways home.

Lark was the last to leave the building, as usual. After making sure all lights were out, he dashed across the parking lot and into the parsonage. The children were upstairs with Fran, getting into summer play wear for the day. Lark ran upstairs. A sudden impulse had come over him.

Entering the bedroom where various decisions about clothing were being debated, Lark looked at Fran and said, "It's stopped raining. We have time. What do you say we drive to Philly and watch the Phillies play the Cubs?"

"Oh Lark, I don't know," Fran said.

The kids were game, but Fran didn't know what they could eat. She had used most of her picnic provisions the day before, although she did have some peanut butter and jelly. They would take that, and what bread was left.

Within minutes of unpacking things from the day before, and packing what foodstuffs there were available in the house, the family was in the station wagon and driving east out of Lancaster toward The City of Brotherly Love.

Thirty miles into the sixty-five mile trip, it began to rain once more. The children moaned in the back seat as the wipers were engaged. Fran shot Lark a concerned look. Lark simply shrugged, looked at three disappointed souls in the back seat, and implored, "Have faith!"

Soon they were parking their car in the huge lot adjacent to Veterans' Stadium. It was twenty minutes to game time. Lark and Fran took the children, the food, and a thermos in hand, walked to the admission gate, and awaited their turn to purchase tickets up in the outfield grandstand. The Phillies were so bad, they hardly ever sold out a game. Buying general admission seats for the family cost $15, after which you went first to the seats you bought, then moved forward as far as you dared, depending upon the number of people at the game.

At the gate, the friendly attendant checked the bag and thermos to make certain no alcoholic beverages were being brought into the stadium. "Hope you folks enjoy the game," he said. He waved them into the ball park, which from the air looked like a giant sugar cookie but which from this vantage point simply looked huge.

The rain had stopped, but the clouds still looked threatening as they found their seats high atop right field. From this vantage point, Lark doubted that any of the children could make out the players upon the field. They looked so small from where they sat, Lark wondered if the kids would get much from this experience at all.

Soon, the national anthem rolled across the half empty stadium. The kids stood rigidly with their hands across their hearts, oblivious to the fact that a flag could not be seen from where they stood.

The sun finally came from behind the clouds during the fourth inning, and the weather became very warm and humid. By the seventh inning, all of the Kool-Aid was gone, and they had yet to eat a sandwich. Lark walked the boys to the rest room, after which they purchased sodas for all and returned to their seats. Walt and Saul were more interested in the snack bar than anything else they had encountered during the game. Saul, who seemed more interested in the Phillies than anyone else in the family, seemed to come to life in the first, fourth, and sixth innings.

Mike Schmidt was his favorite player. He watched with disappointment, as Mike was having a terrible day at the plate. Ferguson Jenkins, the Cub's crafty pitcher, was shutting the Phillies out, two to nothing, going into the eight inning.

Suddenly, the kids were hungry. The Cubs were batting with the bases loaded, and it probably was wise not to focus much attention upon the field at this time. Fran began to unpack the peanut butter, jelly, and bread. That was when she discovered that, in her haste, one important kitchen utensil was missing— the knife.

The children watched Fran dip her fingers into the jars and spread their sandwiches with her hands. They giggled as she spread the gooey peanut butter, her fingers sticking together as she prepared each sandwich. It was ugly, thought Lark, but, not as ugly as what was happening on the field. Fans were leaving in droves as the Cubs scored six more runs before Fran had finished all of the sandwiches. Left with nothing with which to clean her fingers, she simply licked them clean and drank her Coke, glad that no one was sitting within seventeen rows of their family.

They all laughed and kidded Fran on their way home. It was unanimous, the game was awful, but the sandwiches were great. The Phillies lost eight to one. Mike Schmidt, after striking out three times, did manage a ninth-inning home run with no one aboard. The Wilsons stood on their feet and shouted as Mike trotted around the bases. Saul beamed with pride. Walt jumped up and down and warned the Cubs that their day was coming. Leigh Ann simply glanced around, no doubt noting that hardly anyone was left in the ball park with two outs in the ninth.

By six-thirty, they pulled into the carport. Lark, exhausted, quietly told Fran he was going to bed early this evening. His tooth was starting to ache again, and he felt that rest might do him good before his visit to Doc's office in the morning. She agreed she was bushed, also. The kids, on the other hand, after sitting in the car, were raring to go as they dashed into the backyard and started to play baseball their way.

Fran fixed a quick supper of noodle soup and tuna fish sandwiches. By seven-thirty, all had eaten, and the wear of the day was becoming evident. The kids were grouchy with one another in the backyard. Lark sat half-asleep in the living room. Fran cleaned up the few dishes from supper.

Finally, Lark arose, walked to the yard, and announced it was bath time. The usual protest was merely perfunctory. Within minutes, Lark was giving the boys baths, and Fran was waiting to help Leigh Ann with her bath.

Thirty minutes later, Lark himself was showering as Fran entered the bathroom. She climbed into the shower with him, soaped his back, then stayed there after he climbed out to towel off. As the sun left Lancaster for that Lord's Day, so did the Wilsons. Each journeyed to that solitary place dreamers visit nightly, but seldom remember at all.

Chapter 12
THE FATHER OF MORPHEUS

Lark entered Doc Willard's office at precisely eight. Lark was punctual for appointments, almost to a fault, as he wanted others to recognize him as a professional. He detested being made to wait by another professional, especially one of the medical profession. He always protested to Fran that it was simply a lack of professionalism on the part of physicians to make their patients wait for hours in their offices. Hence, Lark usually wished to be the first patient of the day.

Doc was aware of his patient's habits. He endeavored to oblige this morning by arriving early and welcoming Lark at the door when he arrived.

"Pretty bad, eh?" he inquired.

"Kept me awake all night," Lark responded with a grimace.

"We'll just take an x-ray, and then I'll know for sure what we're dealing with, here," Doc said with confidence.

"Okay," Lark said quietly.

Doc went right to work. The modern x-ray device swung toward Lark's jaw, and ever-so-slightly rested against it.

"Open wide," Doc commanded.

Lark obediently opened his mouth, and Doc placed what appeared to be a piece of folded cardboard inside his mouth.

"Bite down and hold," Doc instructed.

After Lark did as directed, Doc again checked the placement of the x-ray lens and then quickly left the room. In a few seconds, he was back and, after taking the piece of cardboard from Lark's gaping mouth, he was gone again without a word.

Lark sat in the chair, thinking of his first experience with a dentist. He was six years old at the time.

His father and mother were upstairs, getting ready to go dancing while Lark played in the living room with his brother. Suddenly, he remembered something he hadn't told his mom during supper. Running to the stairs, he began to bound up the treads two at a time when he missed the third step and slammed face first into the stairs. In an instant, his front teeth were missing and he was screaming in pain and terror as blood flowed from his mouth.

Lark's mother was the first to the head of the steps. She joined Lark in screaming as his father came into view, cursing loudly at his son. After his dad stopped cursing and blaming Lark for everything from the depression to World War Two, he picked his son up from the stairs, shouting directions to Lark's mom to call "a damned dentist." He carried Lark's little body to the bus stop one block from their row house. He said nothing, but his face said everything: he was angry; he was disappointed; Lark had failed again to meet the expectations of his father.

Soon, Mom was standing alongside, a tissue in her hand. Lark's two front baby teeth were wrapped carefully in the tissue. Lark's mother thought the dentist would want to see them. She assured Lark's dad a neighbor was caring for Lark's brother. Lark's dad said nothing. He was fuming.

The bus trip was brief. The dentist had left an evening meal and was waiting for them when they arrived downtown. Although Lark's mom had clearly shown the dentist the very cleanly extracted baby teeth, the dentist decided to numb Lark's jaw so he could take a closer look and remove any chips still remaining.

Lark spied the long needle as it came from behind the dentist's back and proceeded quickly toward his open mouth. Lark screamed. Dad, who was standing beside him, yelled, "Shut up kid, or I'll give you something to scream about."

The needle pushed into what felt like the bottom of Lark's skull. The dentist was anything but gentle. Thinking back on it years later, Lark surmised that the dentist was probably inebriated. He clumsily pulled the needle from Lark's upper jaw and brushed against his nose so hard that it began to bleed. Lark's little heart raced wildly. His mother was weeping quietly behind her son. His father was cursing once more, and this time, his venom was directed at the dentist.

"What the hell's the matter with you, boy?" his dad screamed.

The dentist didn't respond. He could sense that Lark's father was pretty upset, and he didn't want to get any more involved with this family than he had to at this point. Nothing more was said until the dentist had finished his examination.

"I couldn't have pulled those teeth better myself," he exclaimed. "Clean as a whistle. You say he did this climbing stairs?"

"He was running up the stairs," his mother said quietly. "He's always doing it. We've told him not to many times," she continued matter-of-factly. It was then that she opened the tissue and showed the teeth to the dentist.

He inspected them briefly, then patted Lark on the head. "You ought to study dentistry, son. You're really good at it," he smiled.

Lark began to cry anew as he caught a glance of his teeth.

"Here folk," the dentist went on, "give him these pain packs to chew on tonight." He gave Lark's father a box of what looked like little sponges. "I don't think I'll need to see him again," the dentist said with some relief of tension in his voice, "he'll be fine in a day or two."

"Well, I've got some bad news," Doc said, shaking Lark out of his remembrance.

Lark looked to the nurse who accompanied Doc into the room for reassurance. She was not at all like his mother of many years before. She simply stood there by Doc Willard's side looking very professional.

"What is it, Doc?" Lark managed to say through his growing pain.

"It's a very abscessed tooth. You will definitely need a route canal on it. I'll do the best I can to save it for you," Doc said, in what sounded like the best professional voice he could muster.

"I've never had one. What's involved?" Lark inquired.

"At least four visits, I'm afraid," Doc responded. "We'll need to relieve the pressure today, then give you some antibiotic for a few days. Then, after it has settled down a bit, we'll have you come back in to begin the process."

It was sounding harmless enough. Lark would, at this moment, accede to any process to get rid of the pain. There was only one problem: he hated needles. This process would definitely involve them, many of them.

"Does this process involve lots of Novocaine?" he inquired.

"I'm afraid so." Doc nodded gravely.

"No other way?" Lark asked.

Doc stopped; he seemed to be lost in thought for a moment. Then, he said, "There is another way to handle this, perhaps."

"I'd be interested," Lark said eagerly.

"I believe you'd be a good subject," Doc said. He studied Lark's face. In fact, he had always suspected Lark's intelligence would make him a very good subject for his avocation. But fate had never presented the opportunity.

"You mean hypnotism," Lark said.

"Yes," Doc Willard almost shouted. "I believe you'd be perfect. You won't feel a thing!"

"I'm game," Lark said meekly.

Doc looked at his nurse. "Do we have the time?"

"Sure," she said.

"Okay, let's try it."

Suddenly, the lights which had shone in Lark's face since the chair had reclined lowered in intensity. That effect alone was a welcome relief, thought Lark.

"Now," Doc began, "I want you to think of a very pleasant experience. Perhaps you are by a mountain stream, stretched out in the sunshine, resting upon your back, without a care in the world."

The dentist seemed to talk in a slightly different tone of voice, now. It was a loving presence and a strong command. Every sentence was said with a cadence that suggested a very slowly marching army. Lark could almost envision the ants that would have been undoubtedly crawling around his body were he stretched out by a river bank in the summer sun.

Lark closed his eyes on Doc's command. The scene opened up before him: beautiful, peaceful, timeless.

Somewhere deep in the cosmos Morpheus, the god of dreams, shook his father from his slumber. Hypnos, the god of sleep arose, stretched his arms and legs, and embarked upon his journey through the stream of human consciousness, until he found the tributary for which he searched. Swimming its fast and dangerous current, Hypnos finally reached his destination. Taking a needle from his back pack and testing it to see if its contents were readied by his twin brother Thanatos, Hypnos inserted it into his target and extracted just enough of its contents to induce his client toward a blessed anesthetic rest and peace. Hypnos always pondered, at such moments, what it would be like to administer the final ounce of the solution to one of his clients. Just once, he'd like to finish off a client like his brother Thanatos did constantly. But, true to his calling, Hypnos stopped short of presenting his client for postmortem positioning. Looking upon his client, Hypnos pitied the man; he would not know what Doc suggested during his sleep which aped death, at least, not right away. With one last glance, Hypnos climbed back down to the banks of the tributary and swam away, leaving his client to the fates.

Lark awoke refreshed. The pressure in his jaw had somehow been relieved. Doc had said to him, "At the count of three, you will awake: one, two, three," and he did.

"Doc, you're amazing," he heard himself exclaim. "I didn't feel a thing."

"Well," Doc chuckled, "I thought you'd be a good subject. You were better than I expected."

Lark felt a sense of pride at Doc's compliment. "You're done for today, then?" He asked.

"Yes. Ask Sandy to give you an appointment on Wednesday. Here is the prescription you need to take to get that nasty infection out of your system," Doc instructed.

"Thanks, Doc," Lark said. As he got up to leave the patient room, he was not sure on his feet, at first. His legs felt tingly, and he couldn't quite feel that his feet were beneath him. But, he managed to get to the reception area and lean against the desk while Sandy checked her appointment book.

"How about Wednesday morning, Reverend?" she asked.

"What time?" Lark asked.

"Eight-thirty," she said.

"That will be fine," Lark said. He was feeling more awake now. He began to walk from the plush suburban office when he glanced at the clock on the wall behind the desk. It was ten-thirty. Lark could hardly believe his eyes.

"Is that the right time?" he asked Sandy.

"Sure is," she said with a grin. "Time flies when you're having fun."

She laughed as Lark left the office. He returned via Lancaster Shopping Center, where he picked up the prescription Doc had written for him. Within thirty minutes, he was in his office, ready to tackle the day's challenges.

Chapter 13
MONDAY, MONDAY

Lark used Monday to outline his sermon for the following Sunday, catch up with any reading, and prepare the week's reports, assignments, and tasks. This morning was to be no different, only shorter.

He hadn't bothered to check in with Fran and the children upon his arrival back from the suburbs. Hence, the first call to interrupt his ruminations was Fran's.

"Hi! How are you?"

"Doc says I have an abscessed tooth. I'm going to need root canal."

"Sounds serious, but, I'm not surprised."

"Oh?"

"You haven't been yourself since Saturday morning. I could tell you were in a lot of pain when we went to the lake."

"Actually, it wasn't too bad," Lark replied. He had never liked to complain to Fran about any of his aches, pains, or disappointments. Once, a clinical pastoral education instructor had inquired about this particular reluctance, and Lark was at a loss to explain it. One couldn't exactly attribute it to pride on Lark's part, although there had always been some inner pressure upon him to perform anything and everything to Fran's imagined expectations. Both the instructor and Lark suspected that this trait resulted from Lark's childhood experiences.

Fran knew him well enough not to press. Hence, she changed the subject. "What are your plans for the rest of the day?" she asked.

"I'm going to catch up with things here until lunch time, then I'm going to the YMCA to shoot some hoops," he replied. Unless he were flat on his back with a raging fever, he'd always assumed he could overcome any minor or major physical inconvenience by playing some basketball, golf, tennis, or by jogging. Anything physical seemed to take him to another place where pain, misery, stress, and anxiety could not follow.

"So, we won't see you until supper?" she asked.

"I was thinking we could go out for a burger and maybe some time in the park with the kids," he answered. "Around five or so?"

"Okay," she said. "Take care of yourself, today."

"See you," he said. He put the receiver down and returned to reviewing the New Testament text for the following Sunday. He read an original Greek version, as he loved the language from the first time his eyes embraced it. To Lark, language study represented a mystery to be solved. Such study opened vistas of understanding and interpretation that translations and paraphrases simply lacked. He even believed that one of the reasons the faith became so easily acculturated and distorted, was that much was lost in translation.

It was nearly noon when the phone rang again. "Good morning," he muttered absent mindedly, fully expecting to hear Fran's voice respond to his lack luster greeting.

"Where are you?" a now-familiar voice asked.

"Obviously I'm here, or I wouldn't be talking with you."

She laughed. He could see her throw her head back a little and smile.

"How may I help you?" he asked.

There was a rather unsettling silence. Finally she said; "I was just wondering if you're free for lunch?"

He pondered her inquiry for a few seconds. "I have an appointment," he lied.

"Too bad for me," she said coyly. He could imagine what she looked like when she pouted. This was fun, he thought.

"Well, actually," he hesitated, then continued, "I play basketball with guys from the winter league every weekday at noon, so I skip lunch."

"Hmm," she murmured, "that's how you stay so thin."

Lark warmed to this woman like a barnyard dog on a frosty morning by the cook stove. He was about to relinquish his plans to play basketball when she said, "I'll take a rain check then."

"You're on," he told her.

"I'll see you Thursday night, then?" she asked.

He agreed they'd next see one another Thursday night at the planning meeting. However, he wondered to himself whether there could be a way he'd have a chance to talk with her prior to the session. Just to get to know how she thought, he assured himself. As he sat talking to this beautiful redhead, he pictured her in his mind. Glancing at his desk calendar, he noted that Wednesday evening offered a spot for him to have coffee with her and go over the history of the group, so she'd feel more at home with those she would meet.

She received his invitation for coffee with unusual enthusiasm. He jotted it on his calendar.

For the few moments that they chatted, he forgot his pain, his week before him, his necessary trips to Doc's office, his wife, and his children. He was simply carried along by the sound of this woman's voice. He was especially touched when she ended the conversation, "See you soon, Lark."

The way she said his name seemed to wrap him in sweetness and comfort. It was almost maternal. It hinted at deep care for him as a person of interest and worth. She knew nothing about him. She barely knew his name, yet she said it so quietly and assuredly. There was a lilt to the sound of his name. It wasn't couched in the familiarity of wife and family, all of whom knew how to pronounce his name for effect as well as kin. Lark had always been vulnerable to the sound of his name upon the lips of a woman, especially a woman who wanted to be friendly.

He still recalled the first time he heard his name upon the lips of a person of his age and of the opposite sex. She too had said his name sweetly as she gazed into his eyes.

He had been seriously ill with strep infection when he was a boy of only ten years. Left unattended by his family, the infection had settled deep into his body and was complicating his kidney function. He was one very sick little boy when he left the school yard early that day, telling his buddies that he could not keep on playing baseball.

When he got home, he fell asleep on the living room couch. That is where his mother found him upon arrival home from her job downtown. He was feverish and sluggish. With no little difficulty, she aroused him and got him upstairs into the bathtub, where she sponged his little shaking body, then wrapped him in blankets and gently laid him in his bed. He shivered as he lay there, awaiting his dad's homecoming.

It was his father who brought Betsy into the room. She was one of the neighborhood girls who frequently sat on the school yard hillside, watching the boys play baseball, football, and soccer. She sometimes joined the games, when she felt like it. She had sparkling red hair, freckles everywhere, and a fiery spirit to match. She was Lark's junior by one year. She lived across the street.

Lark peered over the covers as she and his father stood at the foot of the bed.

"Betsy has come to see how you are, Lark," his father said uncharacteristically softly. Lark detected a look of guilt as well as concern upon his father's face. Lark had first complained of an earache. Then, it had progressed to a sore throat. He hadn't been able to swallow his food. When his temperature had spiked to 102 degrees, Lark's father had relented and taken him to the family doctor, only six days earlier. The physician diagnosed it as strep. He gave Lark's dad penicillin samples from the large medicine cabinet that stood behind the doctor's desk. He assured him it should take care of it in a couple of days; it hadn't.

"Betsy has something for you, Lark," his dad continued. She handed his father a rolled up piece of paper. He opened it and chuckled as he read what she had printed upon it, then handed it to Lark. Betsy stood motionless as Lark scanned the piece of paper.

Betsy had taken the lyric of a popular song, changed the words a bit, and composed a poem to cheer him up. "O Lucky (Betsy had started calling Lark Lucky when she was three years old her mother had confided to Lark's mother one day in conversation, and she simply continued referring to him by that name), O Lucky, How you can kiss!" the note read. She watched him closely as he read her composition. When he finished, he looked up at Betsy and his father. Then, he rolled up the piece of paper and placed it under his pillow.

"Thanks Betsy," he said, then began to shiver anew.

It was then that this childhood friend who had never uttered his name smiled and said, "I hope you're better soon, Lark." When she said his name, he almost felt better for an instant. It was so good to hear her say it. She had crossed a threshold with that poem, and she had entered his heart with that single word, Lark. He had never forgotten her. Lark looked for her in others, and from time to time, he almost found her.

Fran was Betsy in the way she said his name. She was Betsy in the way she played games with him. She was Betsy when she kissed him and held him closely and gazed into his eyes. She was Betsy in spirit. But, Fran was many others, also. It was Betsy who said his name first, beyond members of his family and teachers in school. And, it was Jennifer who said his name most recently, who resurrected all of those feelings he first felt for Betsy.

Oh Lucky, Oh Lucky, how you can kiss.
When you're not on the playground,
It's you, it's you I sadly miss!

Oh Lucky, Oh Lucky, how you can kiss!

Love,
Betsy
xxxxxxxxx

He felt the basketball in his hands. And, after playing for nearly an hour, he showered, dressed, and drove back to the church office to finish his self-appointed tasks for the day. The afternoon passed quickly with a flurry of mail to process, letters to dictate, documents to type, and the first paragraphs of a sermon to write.

Lark liked to write the introduction and conclusion on the same day. That gave him, along with the outline, the foundation for the body of a sermon. If time did not permit him to finish the manuscript by the following Sunday, for a pastor had to recognize early in his professional life that ministry really meant being open to interruptions, these would place him in good stead on Sunday morning. "People were captured by the introduction and always remembered little but the conclusion. Hence, these had to be crafted well, in order to preach successfully," he told another parishioner who had asked how he wrote so many sermons in a year's time.

It was four-thirty before he knew it, and he was about to wrap it up for the day when the phone rang for the first time this afternoon. It was John.

"Hey, buddy," John began as soon as Lark picked up the receiver. "What are you doing in the office? Isn't this your day off?"

"Yeah," Lark answered. "But this is how I make it look so easy the rest of the week."

"Fran told me you've been ensconced in your office all day. What's up?"

"Nothing much. I'm just trying to stay afloat."

"Is everything set for Thursday night?"

"As far as I know. I put the finishing touches on the agenda an hour ago. We might have a visitor from New York," Lark informed his friend.

"Who might that be?"

"The new instructor at F&M," he replied.

"I didn't know she was interested in peace," John said as if to no one in particular. It was his familiar way of needling a friend. John had a certain way of saying things which often bordered on double entendre.

"She's very interested," Lark continued as if he didn't hear the inflection. "She might join us on the march."

"You don't say," John feigned interest while barely concealing his concern. "I'm anxious to meet this woman who is getting so cozy with you, all of the sudden."

Lark did not respond. He simply sat back and smiled as John continued to ramble.

"Anyway, I was wondering if you and Fran could get away for a little R and R tonight. We could go over to the Horse and lift a few. What do you say? I haven't seen that beautiful wife of yours in a while, buddy. I need a fix!"

John was helping Lark refocus. He assured John he would get back to him after he'd had a chance to discuss this with Fran. As he said it, he could already anticipate Fran's response. She didn't like bars. She rarely agreed to venture to a bar or tavern for any purpose. He was sure she would grant him permission to go with John later that evening, but she would not be accompanying them. John's flattering comments would do nothing to dislodge her from the resolve to keep free from the entrapments which awaited mortals who frequented pubs. If he wanted to see her, John would have to come to their house. That would be the way Fran would handle the invitation. That is, after she'd inquire if Lark really wanted to go, himself, since he had such a bad abscess.

Hence, nothing about their ensuing conversation surprised him. As though scripted, Fran looked as he thought she would when he brought the subject up—like a school teacher who had just discovered her pet pupil misbehaving while she had been absent from the room for but a moment. That look, a mixture of anger and disdain that emerged whenever the subject of alcohol crossed their threshold, never changed. Fran's answer was precisely as Lark expected. It was prefaced by her concern for him. It was punctuated by her turning her back on him after declining John's invitation.

Within minutes of his arrival home, he dialed John's number and informed him of the plan to meet at the Horse around nine that evening sans Fran. This didn't surprise John; he was used to it. As he explained to Lark with a chuckle, he'd been turned down by women rather frequently, lately. So much so that he guessed he'd have to check out some new aftershave lotions. He managed to share with Lark, before hanging up, that he had read about a new aftershave lotion which women simply had no power to resist whenever a male used it. Both men laughed heartily when John continued to explain that the article said the only factor which had kept the lotion from being marketed widely was the effect it also had upon animals, particularly cats.

The evening passed quickly: supper, family games, a trip to Long's Park; taking turns pushing the kids on the swings; a bag of broken dried bread shared, communion-like, with the ducks that paddled near the shore, then ambled upon dry land to gather up the crumbs offered by the Wilson children; finally, ice cream. They returned home to the ritual of baths, nighttime story, and hugs for each child just before evening prayers as a family. These were the bonds that held the couple firmly in place. The three children brought joy, love, and promise into a home which, without them, would have been monotonously routine for Lark and absolutely lonely for Fran.

At nine-thirty, Lark parked their wagon along the curb adjacent to the entrance to the Horse. John's car was already in place, half a block down the street. Lark climbed the stairs to the second-story entrance to the tavern. He could hear the rock music playing softly inside as he approached the door.

The Horse was named for the fact that it was constructed, as was the practice in colonial America, above a stable. Stagecoaches and their charges were housed in the first floor of the three-story building. The tavern, where weary travelers could refresh their appetites, was located on the second floor. Sleepers could pay an additional fee and climb the ladder, still located along the south wall of the present-day tavern, into the dormitory loft above and take their chance on a few hours sleep upon fresh beds of straw. Eventually, beds replaced the straw and hourly fees for sleeping upon them were instituted by the innkeepers.

Now, two apartments graced the first floor and a storage room occupied the third. The Horse Tavern awaited its well mannered customers with its dark orange and brown interior, soft music, oily chairs, rough wooden plank floor, appearing to the untrained eye, as though it were awaiting the next stagecoach full of 18th century travelers.

At first, Lark didn't see her. John had risen from where he sat the very second Lark entered the room. He came toward Lark with an outstretched hand.

"Hey, buddy, come see who's here," he said with a grin.

Then he saw her; it was Jennifer. They were the only ones in the bar at this hour, which really wasn't that unusual for the Horse on Mondays. As he got to the table, she was on her feet, extending her hand.

"We meet again," she said with a smile.

"Fancy meeting you here," was all Lark could say. John stood silently by, eyeing both of them as they fumbled for ways to accommodate one another in a place neither had expected to meet.

"Jennifer tells me she met you on the train the other night," John said with a wink of his eye, as they all sat.

"What'll it be?" asked the bartender, who had walked into the room from behind the bar to serve the newcomer.

"Rolling Rock," Lark replied.

Jennifer sat, eyeing both of the men silently. She seemed nervous. This was an affectation Lark had not seen in her before. It was something new about her. She bit her lower lip, just a little. It was charming. She was dressed in what appeared in the darkness of the room to be tan slacks and a dark-blue blouse that seemed to hint that she was braless. Her face was only slightly made-up, as far as Lark could tell in the dim light. Her hair fit the scene perfectly. It was swept back to the right side of her face and down the back of her neck, like a woman who'd just climbed down from a horse and removed her riding cap.

"You researching the community?" Lark directed the question to Jennifer.

"Friends told me this was a neat place to visit while I'm here," she said rather nonchalantly. "Not very lively tonight, though."

"You can hardly get in the door on weekends," John informed her. "They make great Chesapeake Bay crab cakes here, and the raw oysters are out of this world."

Jennifer grimaced.

Lark laughed. "I think you got that backwards, John. You have to be out of this world just to eat a raw oyster." Jennifer laughed as the bartender returned with Lark's little green bottle of beer.

"The boy's a big drinker," John quipped. Jennifer laughed again as he lifted his Manhattan, the drink he always ordered. Jennifer lifted a glass of wine. The two touched glasses with Lark's bottle of beer in a mock toast to whatever, then settled into conversation.

None seemed convinced that President Nixon fully intended to end the war in Vietnam. John thought it unfair and unjust that so many black youths were sent to fight. Lacking the cultural underpinnings of the black church and the mentoring which black communities gave their young, John predicted these soldiers would be utterly lost in this great society following the war, and that they would produce offspring more lost than they. Lark spoke to the need for both political parties to make space for those within them who dissented. Jennifer spoke passionately of the need for this nation to take Former President Eisenhower's warning regarding the influence of the military industrial complex seriously.

When it came to sex, all agreed that the so-called free love generation would wash up on the shores of disappointment by the time they reached forty. John spoke of animal longings which

101

were being unleashed in acidic music. Lark talked of several young couples he'd recently counseled regarding marriage. One couple, he said, after having a third Rolling Rock, had slept together for three years prior to deciding to marry. She was sixteen and he was twenty-one, Lark informed his companions. And, in the midst of the counseling, it had become very clear that the girl had never experienced an orgasm and was already disillusioned with life's great mystery. Jennifer spoke of the historic illnesses brought about by such loose living and predicted a new scourge of sexual diseases.

After an hour of comfortable conversation in which it became very clear that these three were going to see a lot of one another in the weeks ahead, Jennifer rose to leave. John and Lark were on their feet to say good evening immediately. Lark watched with interest as she walked from the bar, seemingly unaffected by the two glasses of wine she had consumed while he and John consumed their usual trinity of drinks.

It was John who spoke when they resumed their seats. "She is very intelligent," was all he said. He stared at Lark for some response, but he said nothing.

Funny. Lark had not once thought of her intelligence this night. He was instead captivated by her charm, her ease of being with others, her sense of comfort with herself in the presence of relative strangers. All of this was most disarming.

"A penny for your thoughts, old buddy," John said finally.

"What?" Lark said, called out of his fantasy.

"I said—"

"Oh, I know what you said," Lark mumbled, a little embarrassed.

"Well?" John asked as he peered into Lark's face.

"I don't know, John. This woman is interesting, isn't she?"

"Like the old Chinese proverb says, 'May you live with interesting times.'" John chuckled.

"Isn't that 'in interesting times'?"

"I didn't think that preposition appropriate tonight, old buddy," John said with a knowing grin. "I can see and feel some kind of chemical reaction going on between you two. You'd better watch your step, boy. I'd say that gal's been around."

"It's that obvious?" Lark genuinely asked.

"It has been since the other night on the train," John said seriously. "Don't screw up your life. God knows there shouldn't be two of us."

Both men laughed at John's comment, which eased the tension between them for the moment. Friends rarely dare to cross such boundaries. These two men had shared many of their most intimate failings with one another. John was in dangerous territory now. Lark felt somewhat violated, yet affirmed by John's reflections. He was doing his best to keep from becoming defensive with his closest friend.

"I don't want to talk about it right now," Lark replied.

"Okay, but you know who'll be there when you want to talk about it, don't you?"

"Yes," Lark said. "Thanks." He meant it. After wishing each other a good night, they parted company at the foot of the stairway.

Lark pulled into the carport at eleven. Knowing that Fran would be in bed, he was quiet upon his entrance to their home. Traversing the stairs in the dark, shoes in his hand, he stepped upon some leftover toy. As it crunched beneath his feet, a pain shot from his foot to his head for an instant. He sat down immediately, cursing quietly to himself, using words he'd heard his father use years before, as he rubbed his foot.

Sitting there on the stairs, he remembered he had not taken his medicine. He walked back downstairs and into the kitchen. Once there, he could turn on the light. As he did, he noticed that Fran had put her usual note to him upon the refrigerator.

Lark

A 'Jennifer' called just after you left to go to the Horse. She said it was nothing important. She'd see you Wednesday. Who's Jennifer?

103

See you in bed.
Love,
Fran

Lark stared at the message, then simply wadded it and threw it in the waste basket which stood beneath the kitchen sink. Getting a glass of water, he reached into his pocket and pulled out the little bottle of white pills Doc had prescribed. As he was getting one of the pills from the bottle, he noticed a warning the pharmacist had not mentioned. "Do not use alcohol with this medication." Now is a good time to note this, he thought. No doubt he would pay for this evening's relaxation, he concluded.

Later, as he crawled into bed beside Fran, he thanked God for this day. Even with its surprises and challenges, it had been a good day.

What were those words of the anthem he loved to quote at funerals, he pondered? The anthem told the story of Jesus and his disciples caught in a storm upon the Sea of Galilee. It compared their experience with that of modern life, with all its dangers. Try as he could, the words would not fully come. All he could recall were a few lines, words capable of carrying him to sleep:

And when the storm winds drive us from the shore
Speak, lest we fear no more
'Peace, be still.'

Chapter 14

ANOTHER DAY
AT THE OFFICE

Tuesday rolled along as most second days of the work week. After breakfast with the family, Lark was at his desk, coffee brewing, radio tuned to WGAL, newspaper folded and lying upon one of the office chairs, Bible open upon his desk. Lark indulged in personal devotion before anything else.

"O Giver of all good gifts, Who has enriched my life, I have many needs this day." Lark needed to sort out his feelings about Jennifer.

"Grant me the gift of patience so that I may live in harmony with all."

Lark thought of Doc and others in the congregation with whom he was in conflict over his position on the war. He knew he needed infinite patience for ministering with these people. And he knew he had the support of others, as he dared to stand against the tide of the nation's leaders, many of whom were being bolstered by more conservative clergy to continue pursuing the objectives of victory in Vietnam.

"Grant me the grace of compassion so that I may not bypass anyone in need," he said aloud in his office.

He had been counseling a man stuck in a September/May marriage. Hank had come home from work at Armstrong Cork one recent afternoon to discover all of his worldly possessions lying on the sidewalk in front of his row house. She had a new love, the note said. After four children, one of whom he knew wasn't his, Hank simply could not believe this younger woman would forsake him. He was suicidal. He would be back this afternoon for a session and Lark wanted to refer him, but felt this parishioner would take the gesture as yet another rejection.

"And give me enthusiasm for the tasks of this summer day so that I may invest it with your love and life. Amen," Lark concluded.

Lark scanned the hymnal for a favorite verse or two to sing alone in his office. He loved singing. It was probably the music of the church which first attracted him to ministry. He loved the combination of major and minor keys which prevailed in instrumental church music, especially that which is arranged for organs. Lark sang alone in his office this Tuesday morning, while coffee dripped and the phone lay off its receiver. "Restored to life each morning new, I rise up from the dust to follow God whose presence gives me confidence and trust. I praise the name of God today; in God I put my trust."

To the tune of Brother James' Air, this new wording for the hymn originally composed in 1650 for the Scottish Psalter, moved Lark deeply as he continue to sing, "Goodness and mercy all my days will surely follow me; and where God reigns in heaven and earth, my dwelling place will be. My shepherd blesses, cares, and leads through all eternity." A shepherd lad who became king of Israel is credited with this sentiment, thought Lark. A leader of religious folk who himself had known considerable difficulty with women. David paid dearly for his indiscretion, thought Lark. Yet, God used him mightily. This God of Israel is a mysterious one, mused Lark.

Devotions completed, Lark opened the newspaper. There were the usual headlines regarding the continuing war in Southeast Asia. Body counts seemed to drive this futile effort to suppress the free will of people far away. Estimates of enemy dead numbered in the hundreds daily. Tonnage of bombs dropped on ancient rice paddies and jungles were reported in newspapers and shown exploding on television. It was all rather depressing to Lark. He quickly turned to the sports page and checked last night's baseball scores. The Tigers, his favorite team, had won. They promised to be in the thick of it until the season ended.

Having finished the paper, Lark arranged items for Jane, who would be arriving shortly. They were a good team. Jane never spoke with anyone regarding Lark's personal plans or schedule. Ever the professional, she referred all matters to the pastor or appropriate church leader.

Never having much to say, Jane was the picture of perfection, as far as Lark was concerned. She was a fantastic listener. He poured out his frustrations from time to time and they simply left with her, never to be heard from again. He shared his dreams of justice and peace with her. These left as well. Jane, in a word, rarely interacted in any way so as to reveal what she thought, felt, dreamed, or regretted. She simply came to the office, did her work, and, went home. She was loyal to Lark and Lark alone from the day he had hired her. He never needed to explain a routine to her more than once. When they reviewed policies, manuals, bulletin setups, membership lists, stewardship mailings, and other weekly, monthly, and annual routines, Jane was on top of them all. She was the absolute perfect secretary. Lark thanked God for her almost every day.

He never pressed her to learn anything about her personal life. She seemed to prefer it that way. She had a family, a husband and two children. Their pictures stood upon her desk, faces smiling at her as she typed. She never discussed them. Although they lived within two hundred feet of the building where Jane worked several days each week, Fran and the children had never met her. Lark preferred it this way.

Jane was religious. Her Bible sat upon her desk beside the portrait of her family. From time to time, when things were a bit slow, Lark would happen upon her as she read a passage from Scripture. He never asked her what she was reading, and she never volunteered the information. He simply thought it good that his

107

secretary was religious and attentive to her spiritual growth. He hadn't hired her for her faith, but for her proficiency.

After going over the day's duties and tasks with Jane, Lark left to make pastoral visits in the two local hospitals. He could walk a short two blocks to Lancaster General to see those who were hospitalized. He liked to visit church members in the mornings, so that families were never encountered. He had learned that parishioners were more open in their concerns and needs when he saw them alone. And, although one often was challenged by the early morning routines of tests, baths, and doctor/patient interaction, Lark had learned to visit during the hour before noon for the best stewardship of his time. He also had learned that by visiting in late morning, he could work out any tendencies to identify with patients by playing basketball immediately afterward.

Two patients in Lancaster general were listed as members of St. Andrew Church on the pastoral directory, but neither was a regular attendee. Lark knew both of them, however. Mrs. Rouser was a patient whose pernicious anemia, misdiagnosed by one of the local family physicians, had developed into the more difficult disease of aplastic anemia. Her doctor was making her as comfortable as possible. She was assured she would be home soon, although her color was worse than anyone Lark had ever seen. He wondered, as he talked and prayed with her, just how close to death this seventy-two-year-old woman truly was at the moment.

Mr. Dickbernd had suffered a mild heart attack a week before and was now going through the obligatory deep depression that almost always followed such events in men's lives. He looked good, although he complained about fatigue when he took his walk each day, and he wasn't really certain what his doctor had in mind for him in the next six weeks. Lark recognized the denial which was worming its way into Mr. Dickbernd's psyche and patiently waited while the fifty-year-old man complained of feeling worse since the heart attack than he did before it happened. Lark listened attentively as the man, only twelve years his senior, talked of the sudden pain which overtook him as he lifted a piece of sirloin toward his mouth. Bang! He had wanted to get up and stretch, to get that elephant off his chest that had suddenly sat on him with full force, but knew he couldn't move, for fear the pain would get worse. And, now, this forced rest. He hated it.

After a moment of silence between them, Lark was uncertain how to end this visit. Could they pray to a God, who had allowed this to happen to a father of four teenagers? Was this God's punishment of a man who had not really been serious about his relationship with the Almighty? Does God really count the cigarettes and bottles of beer until weary, then zap every poor sucker who thinks he'll live forever, simply because the bank account is full from working overtime? And, if God does that, how can we pray to such a being, Lark thought as he sat listening patiently to Mr. Dickbernd's woes.

Lark arose to leave Mr. Dickbernd to figure it out, when his parishioner reached out and took his hand. "You've got to promise me something, pastor," he said. His eyes held an intensity Lark had not noticed until now. This man was genuinely afraid of dying. Something was not quite wrapped up in his life, and he wasn't sure he had time to do it.

"What's that?" Lark asked.

"Promise me you'll never tell anyone what I am about to tell you."

"I can do that," Lark assured him. He took the seat beside the bed once more.

Holding onto Lark's hand, Mr. Dickbernd began to cry. Tears flowed as he wailed aloud, his body shaking uncontrollably for what seemed like hours. Regaining composure, his grip on Lark's hand loosened as he went on, "I am not a good man, pastor."

Lark sat quietly waiting for him to continue.

"I have a good wife and four wonderful children, all of them bright and two of them truly gifted. That's quite something, for a man with as little formal education as I have. My wife has been good to me all through our marriage and, as far as I know, she has never been unfaithful."

The man stopped and stared at Lark. He was trying to gain the courage to tell Lark his great secret. The two men sat silently for a moment or two, before the bedridden man continued his confession.

"I don't have much faith, pastor. You know that. You don't see me or my family in church very often."

Lark resisted the temptation to reassure this man that it was perfectly all right for him to be unfaithful to God and the church.

"I have so much to be thankful for," he went on. "A good job in the auto business, a fine family, a great house in Eden Township—who could ask for more?"

Lark nodded.

The man continued to pour out his heart to his pastor after a longer silence between them. "There's another woman," he said almost imperceptibly. "Met her at an auto show five years ago." Shame showed in his face, as his eyes scanned the floor at Lark's feet.

"I tried to break it off after that, but something inside me just wouldn't let go. She lives in Lebanon, and I get up there once or twice a week. Sometimes we go dancing or to a show. Most times we eat in and have a good time in the sack. My wife doesn't suspect a thing."

With each sentence, the man seemed to regain the courage that led him to the threshold of confession in the first place. Lark listened as the man revealed how ashamed he was. Lark felt the man's desperation at the thought that what he had suffered was divine retribution for breaking his marriage vows made twenty-seven years earlier at St. Andrew Church. That was why he had not attended church lately. That was why his life was ruined and his health was endangered. She had even dared to visit him in the hospital and almost met his wife. In a panic that day, Mr. Dickbernd had almost suffered another heart attack.

Lark had witnessed this before. The pain this man was experiencing was most evident. Lark knew it was too early to work toward any resolution. The best he could do was promise

110

to stand with the man, as he sought to work his way through this difficulty once health and strength were regained. That seemed to be enough for today. So, they prayed God would help Mr. Dickbernd regain his health and strength and that God, who awaits the repentance of us all, heard this poor man's confession with compassion.

Shortly after noon, Lark was on his way to the YMCA. Patients in St. Joseph's would have to wait until Lark had spent what physical and psychic energy he had stored since Monday at noon.

The crowd of men who were engaged in games of pick-up basketball when Lark arrived was larger than usual. The day had already grown warm outside, and the air conditioned gym offered some relief, if only for a little while, until he worked up a manly sweat on the courts.

Lark was into the game in minutes and feeling no pain whatsoever, as he pounded up and down the court, trying to help his temporary teammates get to ten baskets before their opponents accomplished the feat. Winning meant one stayed on the court. It was not unusual for Lark's team to stay there for a half hour or more, on most days. Today's team would make that feat nearly impossible.

Lark surmised that there wasn't a man under forty on his team, except himself. The key to their staying on the court depended upon his pushing his game up a notch or two. He set about doing just that. Dashing up court the very second he saw one of his team members snare a rebound, Lark received long passes, thrown nearly half the length of the court, dribbled three or four times with such ferocity that it could be heard in the next gym, and suddenly pulled up, twenty feet from the hoop, and pushed beautiful arches of shots toward the solid steel ring. He was putting on a clinic in jump shots and, to no one's real surprise, carrying this team of old men to their first victory of the noontime wars at the Lancaster YMCA.

After twenty minutes of turning back assault after assault of new teams from the sidelines, the old men on Lark's team

111

began to show their age by no longer jumping for rebounds or holding up their hands on defense. The opposition began to drive through them for layups as though they were merely plaster statues at Caesar's Palace. Within six minutes of their fourth game, Lark's team was walking from the floor toward the showers.

In the locker room, one of the men approached Lark and introduced himself. He was an insurance salesman who had been impressed with Lark's playing, and he wanted to know where he had played in college. Upon learning that Lark had attended Franklin and Marshall, he exclaimed that he himself had graduated from the college in 1955. Lark had missed him by five years. Each man talked about how the campus had changed, now that it was coeducational.

"I can't believe they don't swim in the nude anymore," the man said as they showered.

"It sure would make it more interesting than when we were students," Lark joked.

"And, how about all the female professors they've got?" the man exclaimed.

"All we ever saw were old men. Do you remember Thurman?" Lark asked.

"Who could forget that old galoot?" the man howled with laughter. "He always took roll before every lecture, but never looked up to see who was answering."

"I heard a student attended every class, took the final exam in ancient history, and failed it before the old man learned it was all a hoax," Lark replied.

"That story persists, so it must be true," said the salesman. He dried off in the locker room. "Say, what is it you do?" he asked Lark.

"I'm a pastor," Lark replied. "I serve St. Andrew Church, a couple of blocks from here."

"I'll be damned! I would have never guessed you were a Reverend, the way you play basketball," the man responded. "I think you could have gone pro."

"I was never that good," Lark said with pride, as he buttoned his shirt at the adjacent locker. It felt good to be praised for something he always enjoyed doing. If the truth were known, all of his life, Lark felt cheated when it came to basketball. He was always very good at shooting and running, and he was more than average at defensive coverage. But he constantly was overlooked. His high school coach never played him. Actually, he had been cut from the squad twice. But each year, he went out for the team. He made the team his senior year, only to sit on the bench, watching less skilled players on the courts.

Once in a while, he'd get to play. It was magic, how he always lit up the scoreboard. The *Morning Herald* would report his feats from the night before, and Lark's reward would be to sit out the next three games. His coach was never truly convinced Lark was fast enough to play. Whenever he did play, it was embarrassing to the coach when the crowd, pleased with his shooting, would shout toward the bench, "Where's he been?" Soon, Lark was playing only road games, where nobody knew the kind of treatment he was getting back home in Hagerstown.

It was a road game in Martinsburg, West Virginia, which attracted the attention of an F&M graduate, who called coach Woodrow F. Sponaugle the next morning. "Woody," as the press, players, and opposing coaches knew him, listened attentively to the description of this gangly kid from Hagerstown who seemed to know where the basket was, even when he had his back toward it. But, to his disappointment, every time one of his assistant coaches journeyed the hundred miles from Lancaster to Hagerstown High to see this possible recruit play, he sat on the bench.

As the story goes, one night Woody called coach Hanley and inquired about Lark. He was told that Lark was "not very teachable and, besides, he has slow feet." The first time Woody saw Lark practice on the Lancaster Armory floor, he was heard to mutter, "I don't care if that kid has slow feet. Hell, he's got the best eye on this team!"

Lark played at F&M. Even his hometown paper did a full-page story about him and another ex-Hagerstown High player who had gone to John's Hopkins in Baltimore. That player and Lark were to play against one another that week in an important MAC game, the paper explained. The story hinted that this game would settle, once and for all, the controversy around Lark's lack of play during his high school years. Their pictures, in college uniforms, showed each young man had matured since high school. The game, which was to be played in Baltimore, promised to be a barn burner.

The teams played, and F&M won, yet neither player was important to the outcome. Lark had stepped off the bus after the St. Joseph's College game three nights before and, slipping on a piece of ice, strained his Achilles tendon. Pat, the other Hagerstown player, had contracted influenza. Coach Hanley breathed a sigh of relief when he heard that Lark had not made the trip to Johns Hopkins.

Lark looked at the man as he buttoned his coat and picked up his gym bag. "Hope we can play again, sometime," Lark said to the salesman. He shook his hand.

"Say," the man said to Lark, as he looked at Lark's hands, "you've got some really banged up little fingers there. If I didn't know better, I'd think you'd been a baseball catcher."

"That comes from catching too many basketballs. I don't know how many times my little fingers have been disjointed or broken," Lark explained.

"My grandmother used to say to my sister that if a man had a crooked little finger, he'd become rich. Hell, look at these," he said, as he held up his hands, "not even a cuticle." He laughed.

"Well, you know I'm not rich," Lark said. "Nobody goes into ministry to get rich." They both laughed at that comment.

Then, the man looked at Lark seriously and said, "Oh, I don't know about that. Seems to me Elmer Gantry got some big bangs for his bucks." They both laughed again. "Anyway, I hope to see you around," the older man said. "Take care of yourself, Reverend." He turned and walked away. Lark grabbed his bag and was out the door in seconds. He made a mental note to check out Sinclair Lewis in the city library.

114

After checking on the family at home, Lark crossed town to visit patients in St. Joseph's Hospital. He parked the wagon two blocks east, and as he walked, he thought of how good he felt. The medicine was truly helping. In fact, he felt so good, he wondered if the trip to the dentist the next morning was really necessary.

There was a maternity call to make at St. Joseph's. Harve and Phyllis had been blessed with their first born, a son. This couple, both of whom came from blue-collar families, had traversed a very trying first four years of marriage. Neither was very good at managing a household. In short, neither could keep track of their spending. They were the types who could easily be seduced by salespersons.

When they had finally asked Lark to visit them one evening, their pastor was quick to discern that this couple needed financial counseling badly. It was obvious that they were in big trouble, for they owed $510 monthly and only earned $398. Having no resources to draw upon except their parents, they were quickly wearing out their welcome in both homes.

Now they had a third mouth to feed. Lark determined to simply remain supportive, as best he could, and hope for the best. Grandparents, he had learned, come through for their grandchildren when they no longer really care for their children.

The child, Billy, was born earlier that morning. This made him "Tuesday's child," exclaimed the parents as their pastor sat with them in the visiting room. Wasn't he beautiful, they asked? Any child born on Tuesday would be physically attractive, they explained, based upon an old German tradition. Lark made a mental note to ask Jennifer when she had been born.

"It was a waxy full moon last evening," said Harve the father. "That means we'll have another son." His wife grimaced, remembering all too well the pain of the past several days. Lark listened attentively and wondered how many more German superstitions there were, for there seemed to be no end to them in Pennsylvania Dutch country.

"Were there any clouds last night?" Phyllis, the mother, wanted to know.

"I didn't see any, hon," said the proud father. Lark had learned that German superstition held that during childbirth, one should look up to make note of cloud formations. If the clouds take the form of sheep or lambs, the child being born will enjoy good fortune throughout his life. Lark remembered a cloudless sky the night before when he exited the Horse. He didn't share either fact, however, with his young parishioners.

The scene reminded Lark of Ed and Judy's first child, a daughter, who was born while they attended Lancaster Seminary. They, like this couple, were ecstatic. They had come from Maine where popular sayings were a dime a dozen. It was Judy who happily said, when they brought their daughter home from the hospital; "First a daughter, then a son, the world is well begun!"

"What happens if a couple has a son?" Lark had asked her.

"First a son, then a daughter come, trouble follow after."

"You seem preoccupied, Rev," Harve said.

"Sorry," Lark responded. He paid closer attention to the conversation after that. Baptism would be in two weeks. The grandparents would stand as godparents for the sacrament. Lark was invited to visit the new family's home within a week to discuss the meaning of baptism. They prayed, thanking God for new life and all of its promise. Lark was out the doorway to the visiting center before the next round of coos began to rise from the parents, who looked at their newborn through the glass windows which separated those in the world, with all its dangers and temptations, from the innocents who nestled in the nursery, no doubt dreaming of that fairer place from which they'd recently come to grace their parents' lives.

As he walked toward his car, a voice behind him said, "Hello!"

Turning, he saw her standing there in a lime jump suit, white pumps, and straw hat atop her fiery hair. She just stood, several feet away, looking at him with a pouty kind of smile.

"This is a pleasant surprise," he said, and he meant it.

"We're going to have to stop meeting like this," she said, not changing her smile. She could be absolutely beautiful, he thought.

"I was visiting new parents," he said.

"That must be quite a thrill," she said. She stepped toward him slowly. Two steps and she was almost leaning upon him, gazing into his eyes from behind her sunglasses, her eyelashes blinking as she spoke.

"Yes it is," he responded. "They are very excited."

"How was it for you?" A strange question. He hadn't thought about it until only moments before, and then the thought bothered him a bit.

"Very exciting," he lied. Actually, it was most frightening and anxiety producing. Fran's first pregnancy was horrendous. Childbirth for Fran was also a very scary experience. The baby was breach. The forty hour wait after labor began was agonizing for Lark and exhausting for Fran.

"Got any free time?" she asked. "I could use a cold drink."

"Sure," he said. "I could use some iced tea myself."

To that, she lifted her right hand to her sunglasses, tipped them down upon her nose and gave him a rather incredulous glance.

"Iced tea?" she asked.

"I never drink anything stronger when I'm working," he said curtly.

"I'll remember that," she said. She slid her arm into his and moved against him. The movement took him by surprise. It brought both a sense of pleasure and pure terror. He moved away from her a bit.

"What's the matter," she asked seriously. "Don't you like me?"

"Yes, I do like you; I like you a lot," he heard himself admit almost with disbelief. He was very attracted to her at this moment and wasn't sure how he was going to handle this scene.

"I make you nervous," she said matter of factly.

"No."

"Well, do you have the time?" she asked. She bit her lower lip just a little.

"Yes, I do," he said, more at ease now that they were not touching, but simply standing close enough to catch each other's scents.

"Where to?" she asked.

"How about Lou's Corner?" he suggested.

"Where's that?"

He thought it strange she hadn't discovered this little cafe, which stood half a block from the F&M campus. He gave her directions. They met there five minutes later and each ordered iced tea with lemon. Lou's Corner was a simple little cafe with three tables and twelve chairs against one wall while the kitchen, what there was of it, stood against the opposite wall. Pictures of past F&M athletes graced the walls of the cafe. Lark had always dreamed of his being there one day, but his accident ended all hope of that his senior year. There was no one else in the cafe except for Lou, the owner, head cook, local philosopher, and part-time unofficial tutor to F&M students for over three decades.

"Why'd you call my house last evening?" he asked as they sat sipping their teas.

"I wanted to talk with you," was her only answer, his directness seemingly catching her off guard. Silence crept between them. Once in a while, she would look up into his eyes as she sucked the tea through a striped straw.

Finally, he asked, "What about?"

"Nothing important," she said quietly. She was more interested in hearing him talk about his F&M days. She said she needed some insight into the history of the place so she could feel that she fit in as guest lecturer this summer. It was tough to get in, she claimed. The faculty were stuffed shirts, she said. They both laughed at that one. The air between them softened.

He told her of his days on campus: how he enjoyed studying history; how he fell in love with Greek while a student at F&M; how he had dug a foundation for his favorite professor's backyard patio; how he was propositioned by several homosexual professors; how he was almost too embarrassed to learn to swim in the nude; how he enjoyed the visits by female students from Hood College in Frederick, MD and that other women's college in Chambersburg, PA, which he could never recall the name of because their girls were not as attractive.

They laughed and sat gazing at one another from time to time. She even reached across the table to touch his hand occasionally, indicating how much she was enjoying his company. The air softer still.

By the time he glanced at the clock above the grill, it was nearly three o'clock. Four empty tea glasses stood on the table between them, She said it had been wonderful to run into him. He said how nice it was to meet up with her and how much he looked forward to their date the following evening. That was when she suddenly recalled why she had called his house the night before.

"I wanted to ask you if it would be alright if you came to my apartment for my orientation?" she explained.

It would be no problem, he heard himself say to this gorgeous woman who was suddenly everywhere he turned. "I'll be there by seven-thirty," he promised.

She gave him directions to her apartment as they stood and walked toward the doorway of Lou's Corner, arm in arm. It was Lou who broke the spell.

"Hey," he called, "which one of you two love birds is going to pay me for the teas?"

They stood back and looked at one another. Then, laughing aloud, Lark reached into his hip pocket, pulled out three dollars, and said, "Keep the change."

At curbside, they shook hands and parted. She walked toward her car with the sway Lark had noted in Pennsylvania Station. Getting into his car, he glanced in the rear-view mirror and watched her pull from the parking space and race around his wagon. Driving back across town to St. Andrew he whistled to himself a tune he'd heard several days before. What was it? Something about a free man. That was it—"a free man in Paris."

He thought about his experiences as a war protester as he drove across the city. Lark had marched with Dr. Benjamin Spock and Professor H. Stuart Hughes of Harvard, co-chairmen of SANE, along with 35,000 on the White House just twenty-five days after Norman Morrison, a young Quaker from Baltimore set himself ablaze within forty feet of Robert McNamara's Pentagon window. The crowd chanted toward the residence of Lyndon Baines Johnson as they peacefully walked on Pennsylvania Avenue that crisp, clear, November afternoon. It was the beginning of a movement which would eventually attract even Vietnam veterans to its cause.

Lark had talked with many black veterans over the past five years. For them, the anti-war movement began with the awful evening in April, 1968, when Dr. Martin Luther King was assassinated and America was in flames overnight. In losing Dr. King, blacks found themselves once more without hope in a racist country which had left their young men little to do except go to war. It mattered little to some of them whether the battle was in da Nang or Watts.

It was a common experience by 1970 for anti-war protestors to be accused of cowardice and draft dodging. Lark had all but been forced out of his first parish because of his sympathies with those who opposed the war. When he buried a seventeen-year old who lasted only two days in Vietnam after lying about his age to join the Marines, Lark was fully galvanized against the war. He resented the fact that those coming back were telling of casualties far exceeding those being reported in the press. He was angered by the stories of the expansion of the war in to Laos and Cambodia. He would have voted for anyone who promised an end to the stupidity.

Senator Eugene McCarthy seemed the only choice following Bobby Kennedy's assassination in June, 1968. The nation was reeling, and this seemingly quiet, thoughtful man of peace promised an end to the futility and suffering. Despite Lyndon Johnson's best efforts to promote social renewal and racial equality while fighting a war to contain Communism, the nation was coming apart at the seams. Its only hope, it seemed to Lark, was Eugene McCarthy. He worked in the McCarthy campaign during primaries, and this only angered his parishioners more. Lark found himself at odds with his congregation and began to look for another place to serve that spring of 1968.

Totally disillusioned by the political process observed by many Americans as they watched the Democratic Convention broadcast from Chicago, Lark decided to put all of his energies toward working with those who would take their causes to the streets. From that fateful summer of 1968, Lark's passion was to turn the nation around from what he saw as its total destruction at the hands of those calling the shots in Washington. It mattered little to him any longer who served in the White House or Congress; no one was making sense.

Lark talked with returning servicemen every chance he got from that summer until the present. They came back dazed and lacking any conviction, it seemed. Many were especially concerned that they were being asked to defend a country which didn't want to defend itself. And some of them believed that what was happening in Vietnam was nothing less than a revolution like this country had experience two centuries earlier and that we were on the wrong side.

Lark listened and sensed what was only being rumored in the press: there was growing unrest in our armed forces. Protests were taking place on the very bases where young soldiers were being trained to go fight for this country. For the first time in American history, returning veterans from a foreign war were grouping to protest its continuance.

Lark recalled that day, in the fall of 1970, when over one hundred Vietnam veterans marched the same roads America's revolutionary soldiers trod near Valley Forge. They whistled "Yankee Doodle Dandy" as they marched carrying toy guns and wearing fatigues. They reenacted "search and destroy" missions as people watched in little villages along the way.

Lark and fifteen hundred other supporters of the veterans awaited them at Valley Forge National Monument. When the veterans marched into the park, cheering and applause erupted across the sacred fields. The crowd began to chant "Peace Now!" The veterans, once they reached Lark and the others at the center of the crowd, threw their toy guns upon the ground, and stomped on them, as they joined in chanting "Peace Now!"

Lark had seen the short film made of this event many times. Several times, he even thought he caught glimpses of himself in the crowd that day. They would use a copy of the film to inspire marchers the night before they would go to Washington, he thought to himself. They would also sing the Vietnam Veterans Against the War marching cadence. Lark remembered with fondness the first time he heard the vets sing it in a peace march. As he drove, he began to sing it softly to himself:

> *The moral of the story son,*
> *Death for profit is not fun.*
> *If they want to start a war*
> *Be sure of what they're fighting for.*
> *Sound off - one, two,*
> *Sound off - three, four,*
> *Bring it on down.*
> *One, two, three, four.*
> *Three, four!*
>
> *I do believe the COs lied*
> *When they made us use that herbicide.*
> *They said it only killed the trees*
> *But now I 've got this strange disease.*
> *Sound off - one , two*
> *Sound off - three, four*
> *Bring it on down.*
> *One, two, three, four,*
> *Three, four!*

Lark hardly knew where to begin orienting Jennifer. The "peace train" had been coming across this country for eight years now, and so many more were getting on board who knew little or nothing of the sacrifices America's sons and daughters made prior to Kent State and the two national presidential conventions in 1972.

Lark knew that the Klu Klux Klan harassed black and white soldiers in the South in order to silence their voices of protest. Like the VC in Vietnam, the KKK used force at night to keep coffee houses empty where veterans could chat with college students. Their ardor wasn't cooled when returning veterans shot back at them at times. The press ignored this unrest. The protest movement knew of it, nevertheless.

In the North mainline churches were targeted by pro-war supporters. Pastors were being fired regularly. The press began to portray mainline churches as ultra liberal and seized upon more conservative movements like the "Jesus Folk" as more representative of America's religious traditions. "Jesus Folk" to Lark were little more than young people numbed by the struggles of the times who were seeking escape from anxiety in some kind of unenlightened form of the faith.

Yet the tide, seemed to be turning. Pro-war supporters, backed into a corner by veterans who were returning and joining those in the streets of the nation in protest against the carnage in Vietnam, were getting harder to find by the summer of 1973. It seemed as though everyone carried a certain uneasiness about them, when it came to the war in Southeast Asia. Even those, like the outspoken in St. Andrew who still supported our nation's policies in Vietnam, were growing uneasy, and, less predictable.

Sure, life went on, the day-to-day life of earning a wage, keeping a family healthy, and planning for the future. Yet a kind of schizophrenia had grown in the nation since President Eisenhower had sent "advisors" to that tiny nation far away, so they could protect themselves from the incursion of Communism. Wariness of certainty and weariness of reality set into the recesses of America's consciousness. The peace movement would eventually reawaken the country—Lark believed this passionately. He hoped he could share enough of that passion with Jennifer in the short time he would have with her before the march on Washington.

Chapter 15
THE FIX

"Let's see," Doc muttered to himself as he stared deeply into Lark's open mouth. The drill began to pound away at Lark's jaw, slightly pushing aside enamel, pulp, and decay, while the patient sat dreamily staring into some far-away scene conjured up by Doc as he put Lark under hypnosis only minutes earlier. Doc knew that his patient could sustain any pain this process inflicted, for Lark was really mentally on the beach in Eastern Maryland. While Doc couldn't see the scene Lark was seeing, he knew it was pleasant enough to keep his patient distracted.

Doc talked with Lark as the two men strolled the beach, the waves rolling ever inward, carrying salt water and oceanic debris across the tops of their feet as they went. The sand felt warm beneath Lark's bare feet, and the water across the top kept rolling over and swinging under his toes. The sensation was so pleasant, he really never wanted it to stop. He could have walked here with his friend for the rest of his life.

They talked of issues which would have made other men converse with care, always taking opposing sides. But their trust of one another ran deep enough that they could sustain such disharmony. The war had torn other friends and families apart,

124

but not Doc and Lark. They were brothers in Christ. They knew what it meant to share deeply what such times meant to them, and they knew that God's will would be done, regardless of what each thought.

They talked of family and friends. They spoke of fears and desires. They spoke of things men talk about with other men only when their bonding is such that each knows the other can be trusted with life itself. And so, they talked eventually of Jennifer. She was so beautiful, so bright, and so interesting. Doc agreed with everything Lark shared with him about this woman he had only met recently. And, as they talked, Doc agreed that Jennifer shared Lark's commitment to resisting the war. Doc encouraged Lark to continue the relationship while Jennifer was in town.

Doc was a good friend; he understood these things. Doc was there with Lark, on the beach, walking upon the sand and hearing the ocean roll, wave upon wave, as they strolled under the warm sunlight that wonderful morning...

Doc finished the procedure on Lark's tooth. It was time to bring him back to Lancaster and send him on his way. Doc's pastor had much to accomplish in the next day or so, and Doc felt he had prepared his pastor in the best way he could. Doc leaned over his patient and spoke reassuringly to him.

"Tide is out," he simply said.

Lark's eyes blinked once. He stretched in the dental chair, for since he went under the hypnosis, his body had not moved, except to breathe.

"It's over?" Lark asked.

"Yep," Doc exclaimed with a smile. "You are a great subject."

"Wow, I didn't feel a thing," Lark said enthusiastically. "That was a good idea, to have me picture Ocean City. I could even feel the sand."

"It's all in the wrists," Doc joked. "We'll see you next month, after your trip to Washington, to finish up the work."

"Thanks, Doc," Lark said. "I really appreciate your making space for me. My tooth hasn't hurt me much since we started this process. I know it will be just fine for the demonstration."

"I have all the confidence in the world it'll be fine," Doc said.

Lark got up from the chair and started to leave the dentist's office. Doc watched him as he walked into the outer room and talked with the secretary. To Doc's eye, Lark was going to be just fine. He walked into the lobby to say goodbye to his pastor.

"You be careful with that tooth for the next hour or so," Doc said with a smile.

"Okay," Lark replied. "And, Doc," he continued, "sometime I want to talk with you about the possibility of hypnosis for weight control."

Doc laughed. This had been a joke between them for some time, since Lark had learned of Doc's avocation. Doc, more than a little overweight himself, could have used such a remedy.

"Thanks again, Doc," Lark said, as he turned and walked out the door.

The dentist waved him off and walked back to his office. He had to make a telephone call. There were other patients to prepare. Doc felt fate had handed him the one opportunity he longed for in dealing with this young pastor who was hellbent on protesting against the nation's patriotic duties in Vietnam. Doc needed to share the news that his pastor's tooth was fixed.

Chapter 16
THE TELEPHONE CALL

Fran called shortly after Lark arrived at the church office. She said a reporter from the *Harrisburg Patriot* had called for Lark at home and would be calling the office around eleven-thirty. Lark awaited the call, reading the newspaper, particularly the auto ads. Lark always looked for something in the midst of automobile ads that would stir him to investigate a car lot. This had become a habit with Lark, and he could no longer remember how it had started.

He couldn't help but wonder if his father suffered the same unending search for the perfect car. He really didn't know much about his father, in this regard. All he really knew was that he didn't see much of his father as a child and even less an adult. The two men simply didn't have that much in common. Was parenthood depreciated by every new generation, Lark wondered. Or, was it just the latest of a long list of modern psychological afflictions suffered by millions as they dashed headlong into each new day with the same enthusiasm as children at a beach.

The image of a beach brought back something of Lark's experience in Doc Willard's dentist chair. But, try as he might, the thing his mind wanted to recall just wouldn't surface. A warm feeling came over Lark as he sat at his desk, daydreaming, and,

127

suddenly, a vision. It was Jennifer, dressed only in a bikini swim suit. She was gorgeous in his fantasy. She lay on the beach, tanning, her top drawstring undone.

Lark sat for what seemed like an afternoon, just focusing on this scene. Finally, the phone jostled him from his late morning reverie. Jane buzzed his desk. He pushed the intercom button.

"Yes," he said.

"It's a reporter who says he's doing a story on Vietnam protests," Jane reported.

"Did he say he is with the *Harrisburg Patriot?*"

"I believe he did."

"Okay, I've got it." Lark picked up the receiver.

"Hello, this is Lark Wilson."

"Pastor Wilson, I'm with the *Harrisburg Patriot*, and we're getting a story ready on the forthcoming march on Washington, DC. My sources tell me you are one of the leaders from the Lancaster area, and I thought I might get an interview from you about it," the man said unevenly at the other end. Either the connection was bad or this reporter was a novice, Lark thought.

"When would you like to do it?" Lark wanted to know.

"I have a bit of a time crunch," was the broken response. "I could drive to Lancaster this afternoon, if you have some time. It would only take a half-hour or so."

"Well, Wednesday is the day I usually do the Sunday bulletin and weekly newsletter for the church, so I'm here all day. When do you think you'll be here?"

"About three."

"I'll look for you then," Lark gingerly responded, thinking of the possibility of getting some good publicity for the march and maybe some more recruits from across central Pennsylvania.

"Good," the man responded. "I'll see you at three o'clock. It won't take long; I promise." The reporter seemed to be warming up to Lark as they talked. His voice was becoming less strained and more reassured. Lark could envision a very young man just starting in the business of gathering news. Lark anticipated a good time with this rookie.

"I'll see you soon," Lark said as he hung up the receiver.

Before going to the YMCA, Lark walked across the parking lot to the parsonage, where Fran and the children were just finishing packing a picnic lunch to take with them to the neighborhood park. The day was pretty warm already, and the humidity was low. This was one of those rare summer days in Lancaster county when one could get by without resorting to using the air conditioner. Lark hadn't even turned on the window unit in his office yet today. The open windows sufficed to keep his office comfortable.

"You look tired," was Fran's greeting as Lark sat at the picnic bench.

"Maybe it's the work Doc did on my tooth. I don't feel particularly tired," Lark said. He got up and gave his wife a hug. Her response was to continue packing the lunches while the children came scampering from the living room to say hello to their daddy. Each one excitedly tried to talk over the other to inform him he was really going to miss something if he didn't go to the park with them today.

"Daddy's tired, kids," Fran said. "He's had his tooth worked on this morning."

"He doesn't look tired to me," Saul said, eyeing Lark inquisitively.

The other two children, glancing at their brother, said nothing further to attempt to coerce their father into joining them for the picnic. Perhaps they knew it was futile, for basketball games at noon were known to be a ritual as important to their father as church on Sundays.

As if waiting for a reply, Saul remained focused upon Lark as the other two children ran from the kitchen back to whatever it was that occupied them before their father's sudden appearance.

"Daddy has to go to the Y," Lark said to his younger son.

"To play basketball?" Saul asked.

"Yes," Lark replied.

"You could play basketball with us," said his son hoarsely.

"Your father needs more exercise than that," Fran nervously said to her youngest child. And, with that, Saul turned and walked toward the living room. "He's kind of cranky today," she said to Lark, as he sat once more at the picnic table and watched her finish her preparations for the picnic.

"I guess he's right," Lark said quietly. "I could play with them more often."

Fran sensed the guilt in Lark's tone. She turned to face him, but said nothing. She sat down across the table from her husband and peered deeply at him.

"What's the matter? You just don't seem very energetic today?"

He couldn't answer her. How could he? He just didn't know. All he could think of at the moment was that somehow, some way, his family was becoming less important to him. Was it the march? Was it his tooth? Was it the pressure of ministry? Was it just the sultry days of summer in Lancaster? Or, was it the fact that his mind kept returning to the woman who seemed to be everywhere the past few days?

"I haven't noticed anything," he lied to his wife.

She eyed him somewhat suspiciously, then continued, "Is it the stress of the march?"

"Perhaps," he conceded.

"Well, when that's over, why don't we all take a few days and go down to Stone Harbor? A few days at the beach would do us all good," Fran suggested.

For whatever reason, Lark, suddenly, felt absolutely wonderful. He reached across the table and embraced Fran's hands in his. At this moment, he really wanted to make love to his wife. Maybe it was the light in the kitchen, or the sound of her voice measured by concern for him, or just the moment they were stealing together in the midst of a very busy day. She noticed the change in him and began to withdraw her hands, sweaty as they were from frantically getting the picnic lunch ready for the children.

"Save it, big fellow," she said. She rose to turn back to the counter top where the picnic basket sat. Lark arose, embraced her, and kissed her passionately upon her lips. She seemed to begin to respond, slightly tilting her hips into his and grinding herself against him ever so softly. Then, just as suddenly, she stepped back from him.

"You'd better go play basketball before you spend all your energy on me," she said, smiling cutely at him.

Just as quickly as it had come over him, it left. The feeling, so overwhelming only seconds before, now was lost in the vast memory bank where married couples store such moments so that they can sustain whatever feelings might exist after ten, twenty, thirty years of being intimate with another human being. The disappointment he felt was nearly equal to that of the passion of the moment before, however.

He would never understand how Fran could simply compartmentalize life. He had learned this about her, almost from their very first date. It seemed to become progressively more pronounced with the birth of each child. There was a time for everything in her life. Eleven-fifty on Wednesday morning, just prior to a picnic lunch with her children, was not the time for romance. That would have to wait for her favorite time of the week—Saturday morning.

In a flash, Lark said goodbye to his little ones and was off to the YMCA for the noontime games. This noon, Lark just wasn't himself. As a result, he sat and watched every seven minutes or so and was one of the last noontime regulars off the floor. No team he played for won; he could not seem to find the basket. His buddies joked about it. Various comments were made after he shot one "air ball" after another.

"Tough night last night?" asked one, as Lark ran, dejected back up court.

"You really ought to get another sport, kid," said Bill Rose, as he ran by Lark on the other team.

"They say the catfish are biting today, Lark," Teddy shouted from the sidelines. "Maybe you could hit the Conestoga with a cast!" Everyone laughed to see one of the best noontime players struggle with a game he usually dominated.

"Keep this up, and nobody will pick you for the league," said Gabby, as he meandered past Lark on a slow-motion drive to the corner. Lark stood and watched as the old timer gathered himself in the corner, fired one up, and swished the net. He ran back past Lark to get set for defense, muttering, "Where the hell were you, Lark?" On any other day, Lark would have dashed to the corner and stuffed the ball so far down Gabby's throat, the old man would not have ventured there for another year. But, not today. It seemed everyone noticed Lark's lethargy and took advantage of it.

As he showered alone in the locker room, he thought of the afternoon before him: knock out the Sunday bulletin; get Jane started on the weekly news; be ready for the reporter at three; make a quick visit to see Mr. Dickbernd; have supper with Fran and the kids; and, visit Jennifer at her apartment for the orientation to the march. It was when he got down the list to the visit with Jennifer that he began to feel like a teenager who had just stolen his first glance at a Playboy centerfold. He was glad no one was present in the shower at that moment; and he avoided thinking of her the rest of his shower.

Back at the office, he put the bulletin together quickly. Lark had actually worked on this coming Sunday's sermon for several weeks. It was to be the foundation argument for his involvement with the peace movement. No one, after hearing Lark's sermon, would question why he was so committed to peace in Vietnam. He and the organist, a recent flower child herself who at times had expressed significant interest in Lark sexually, but also had keen interest in a relationship with one of the single women in the church choir, had worked together on the final hymn for Sunday's service. They would use the tune "Melita," whose stirring chords moved people of America so profoundly at JFK's funeral. Elsie, the organist, who dressed like everyone did at Woodstock, had written a paraphrase of First Corinthians 13. The words would be sung to the tune as a recessional. It would send people off with a good feeling, as Lark always truly strove to do in worship services he planned. And, it would send them off thinking about the present war and its devastation of America's values. Beginning with the processional "God Of Our Fathers," moving through the sermon hymn, "God Help Our Country," and including the offertory duet sung by two members of the youth fellowship performing the popular "Universal Soldier," it would be virtually impossible for any parishioner to attend this worship service and not think about their complicity in the evil war in Southeast Asia.

Lark was fully aware that this kind of service didn't endear him to people like Doc and others of Doc's generation who had, like Lark's relatives, fought in World War Two. But, Lark's goal was to move those he served to consider the subtle differences between theologically expounded "just wars" and what was taking place in Vietnam. Dylan was right, Lark thought. The times were changing. And, he was helping them move. Lark's sermons were peppered with references to the loss of self-respect his beloved country was developing with each napalm canister fired and one-ton bomb dropped upon rice paddy workers in that beautiful land he had only seen on television.

A quick check with Jane indicated that no new members had been added to the local hospital patient list. He gave Jane the name of the newborn son of the congregation, as well as instruction to order a rose for the altar which would mark the birth for all the congregation. He also made sure Jane put the announcement in the bulletin regarding the two weddings he had scheduled for the last Saturday of the next month. The first involved a young couple he had only recently met in the neighborhood. They were already living together and decided to wed and join the congregation as members after they returned from their honeymoon. The other couple was from established families in the congregation and community. Their wedding, which would take place on Saturday evening, would be a major social event. Neither family was thrilled with Lark's being the celebrant of the rite which would bring their children together. The young couple, on the other hand, was delighted. It was they who blocked the attempt by the bride's mother to bring back a beloved former pastor to perform the wedding. The bride made it clear to her mother that if Lark couldn't perform the wedding in the church, they'd ask him to marry them privately at Long's Park. Once the reality of that ultimatum settled in, the mother of the bride decided to be cordial to Lark in the months before the wedding.

Lark glanced at the bulletin cover which was set for Sunday. The message on the back, provided by the denomination, was written by his former New Testament professor at seminary. It dealt with the doctrine of the Holy Trinity. A close-up of a tree trunk out of which a new limb was springing and the question upon the lips of Nicodemus to Jesus by night, "How can a man be born when he is old?" simply would not relate to the service Lark had planned.

He planned to read Isaiah 44:6-22 as the basis for his sermon entitled "If I Had A Hammer?" Everyone would recognize the significance of the title and the relationship to the peace movement. Lark liked to select titles based upon popular songs for he had discovered that when they were announced in local newspapers, visitors would simply come to hear what he had to say about the subject. His Christmas Eve candlelight sermon title based upon the Doors song, "Come On Baby, Light My Fire," had been particularly effective in bringing visitors to the church.

The youth of St. Andrew held Lark in high regard for such behavior in ministry. It was they who insulated him from much criticism. The visitors at services also helped keep the wolves at bay, regarding Lark's ministry. Lark felt safe in doing what he did and the way he did it. The numbers showed that the church was growing and changing radically in membership make up at the same time. This worried some of the old timers. But, the sight of newcomers in the pews gave new life to the old church, and people kept relatively quiet about their young pastor's radical views.

Most people, that is. Lark was aware of some grumbling which took place in the Older Ladies' Bible Class and among the military veterans of the church. He sought, at times, to placate these members by planning worship services in which old-time gospel songs were featured and stirring patriotic themes were presented. He even sang solo, himself, on a July Fourth Sunday, utilizing the old standard "The House I Live In." But these groups always saw the political ploys of their pastor for what they were: ploys. They were not fooled; they felt patronized. And they had every right to feel this way.

Lark had absolutely no idea how deep the animosity was toward him in such groups. He felt its strength from time to time, as he met with consistory and the Spiritual Council. He was on the defensive in those meetings. Although, he was glad there were some newcomers to the church among the membership of these leadership groups. He was glad he had made allies of a few old timers who sought, through him, to settle scores with others like themselves over issues relatively few could even remember any longer.

The weekly newsletter was easier to put out than the bulletin, even though it was mailed to every home. It was a single sheet, folded, addressed, and stamped piece with a bulk mail permit on one side. On the other outside fold was an announcement of the service times for Sunday, the Scripture readings, and the sermon title, as well as any other pertinent information regarding the forthcoming services. Lark felt this format enabled him to literally publish his sermon title for every mail carrier in the city and many in the suburbs. He envisioned this as an evangelistic tool of some importance. The consistory disagreed with him. But, as long as newcomers graced St. Andrew Church nearly every Sunday, the leaders didn't press their pastor too hard on this matter.

Inside, the weekly newsletter, the weekly calendar and brief articles of interest to members of the church, were placed. Lark scanned the forthcoming week's calendar: softball game on Monday evening against Highland Presbyterian Church; Junior and Senior Choir on Wednesday evening; another softball game at Conlin Field on Thursday evening against the First Baptist Church. It would be an easy week. Lark saved his trip to Washington and the peace demonstration as a special article of one paragraph, inviting anyone who cared to accompany their pastor to the nation's capitol to call by next Wednesday.

These tasks now securely in the able hands of Jane, Lark simply sat in his study and read over his sermon notes as he awaited the reporter from the *Harrisburg Patriot* to make his appearance.

If I had a hammer, I would swing it with all my might at the phony monuments to death in our world. Man was not made to die—but to live. Man was not made to kill his fellow man—but to live in harmony with mankind and nature, all of God's creation. Down with those monuments and statues that glorify death and destruction—and those who've advocated them as signs of maturity and heroism. Mankind has served this kind of patriotic ego-trip long enough! If I had a hammer, I'd use it to build the bridges, the dams, the houses, the cities, the factories, the mass transit systems, the communities all persons on the earth have a right to enjoy. Why wouldn't such industrial endeavor also be good for world economies? Why can't this nation spend seventy percent of its national budget on constructive world pursuits, instead of military defense and offense? It is true now, as it was true in the day of Jeremiah the prophet, when 'the noise of battle was in the land, and great destruction! Behold, how the hammer of the whole earth is cut down and broken!' A hammer is a tool—perhaps the first tool fashioned by man—and can be used both constructively and destructively, depending on the whim of mankind. It is a neutral tool that we should seek to place in the hands of every able-bodied human being that we might, as both Isaiah and Micah suggested, 'beat this world's swords into Ploughshares' and get on with the business of building the new world 'upon the cornerstone' which builders have rejected constantly. If I had a bell—

The telephone rang, and soon thereafter, his intercom buzzed. "It's someone named Jennifer. She wants to talk to you," Jane said. Lark sat forward in his chair and quickly told Jane he had it.

"Hello," he said. "This is Lark Wilson speaking."

"It is, huh," she said with a giggle from the other end. "I just thought I'd call and see if you are still planning to come by tonight."

"I am," he said.

"Around seven or seven-thirty?" she inquired.

"Sometime like that," he said. Their conversation was taking place so fast and so professionally that Lark thought of it almost as a code. There was little warmth from Jennifer's end, after her initial giggle. For Lark, this call was a bit disturbing. He wasn't sure he wanted Jennifer calling him at his office. It made him feel guilty. Neither Jane nor Fran had any awareness of Jennifer now, except for her name. And after Fran's initial inquiry about who she was, there had been no further pursuit of the subject. Lark preferred it that way. But, now, here was Jennifer calling the church office in the middle of the afternoon. He was so startled, that for a few seconds, he couldn't picture her. Gradually, an image took shape as they talked.

"You sound busy," she purred suddenly, after a few seconds of silence between them.

"Going over my sermon for Sunday and I have an appointment to see a reporter in five minutes," Lark replied.

"Well, I was just here at the library and got to thinking about our date tonight."

"Our meeting—our orientation," he corrected. He suddenly became aware that Jane might have her phone on speaker reception, listening to every word they were saying to one another. Jennifer seemed unperturbed by his interjection and correction.

"Whatever," she said calmly. "I can tell this isn't a good time to talk. I'll see you tonight."

"Thanks," was all he said, as he replaced the receiver. He would have to tell her not to call his office or home. It was too risky. His heart was pounding as he sat and stared toward the doorway, where any second, a young, inexperienced reporter would enter to be educated about the peace movement. Sweat trickled down the inside of his shirt sleeve.

He suddenly became aware of the warmth of the study. He got up and walked to the window air conditioner. The switch had two settings: low and high. Lark had never noticed a significant difference in the effect either choice had on the comfort of the room. Only the difference in noise the unit produced, depending upon which choice one made, had any impression upon Lark during the three years he had used the contraption. There were days when he believed the air conditioner didn't even cool the room; it simply made noise. So, the choice was ultimately between what level of noise he wanted to put up with as he worked. Today, his choice was low.

He returned to his desk and Sunday's sermon notes as he awaited the reporter's appearance.

The other evening at Catholic High School's Summer graduation, right here in Lancaster, State Secretary of Revenue, Robert P. Kane, told graduates that the greatest threat to our society right now is public apathy borne of self-centered living by citizens who increasingly express concern only about their personal problems and rarely show any compassion toward others. 'If we have a threat to our way of life, it is because we have withdrawn from the community and said, 'let George do it' said Mr. Kane. We Americans love freedom; no one can deny that. But, with an almost equal ferocity, we hate discipline. We question any authority which might seek to limit our freedom without discipline, without responsibility. Henry Steele Commanger, seeking to define the average American at mid-20th century wrote: 'Two world wars have not induced in us either a sense of sin or that awareness of evil almost instinctive in most Old World peoples...War has not taught the average American discipline or respect for authority.'

So, if I had a bell, I'd ring it like the Liberty Bell of old—to call all people together—to call us to certain realities about ourselves and our world—to call us to the realization that 'too many persons have died' in the name of a great ideal for which far too few are willing to live. Freedom without discipline and responsibility can only lead to anarchy just as discipline without freedom will only lead to tyranny. For neither a country run by tyrants nor run down by anarchists am I willing to fight and die and become a marble chip in a memorial stone to racism, nationalism, and materialism. But, for a third nation, one promised on the pages of our history, one realized in true moments of glorious advance in this grand experiment of social freedom and civic responsibility called America—for that nation I am willing to work and live until I die!

Lark paused. A glance at the clock revealed the reporter was already fifteen minutes late. He got up from the desk and walked to the rest room downstairs. He glanced in the mirror above the sink. His eyes were a bit red. Maybe that was what Fran saw when she thought he looked tired earlier in the day. He splashed some cold water on his face and did not bother to dry it. The feel of the water upon his skin gave him some relief from the slowly building headache, which had begun to announce its presence about an hour after the noon games.

As he came up the stairs to return to his office, he overheard Jane talking softly to someone on the phone. He could not make out the conversation, for the door to her office was tightly closed and the air conditioner in the church office was humming loudly. The sun hit her office rather mercilessly in the late summer, for it stood along the southwest side of the century-old building. Jane enjoyed that aspect of her office in the winters, and tolerated it without complaining during the summers, as long as the air conditioner worked.

Arriving back at his study, Lark continued to rehearse the Sunday sermon notes:

And, if I had a song, who but Christians can best teach a song of love between brothers and sisters to a nation hellbent upon war and destruction?

We come from an international, inter-racial, transcultural and thirty-five century old historical family of singers. Moses and Miriam sang and danced at the water's edge as their people celebrated freedom from slavery. Deborah and Barak sang of the commitment of their people, the discipline which kept them free in a time of national danger. It was with songs of praise that Israel rebuilt the walls of the city and the morale of their people under Ezra and Nehemiah. It was with loving songs of the servant of God that Isaiah first foretold the coming of our Lord. It was with songs of 'glory to God in the highest and peace on earth' that our Savior's birth was announced. It was with a song on their lips and in their hearts that Jesus and his disciples left the upper room for Gethsemane and Calvary. The song is love; that is all. All you need is love. Learning to love this world as God does is challenge enough for us all. Love—this is the song which the writer of the Book of Revelation envisioned. It is the song of the Lord. And it is the rhythm to which the universe is tuned. For we were not made to hate and die. Both hate and death are enemies of the image in which we are created. We are made to love and live. No more fitting tribute can be paid to those who have gone before us in this nation—to those who have given their lives for our freedoms in the various follies of war after war which have so dotted our historical landscape—than for us to strive to live in love and peace with all humanity. For us as Christians, this is not a choice, but an imperative. We simply cannot claim we love God and harbor hate for any of our fellow human beings.

The phone rang again, interrupting Lark's thoughts. Jane buzzed the intercom and told Lark it was the reporter from the *Patriot*. Lark glanced at the clock and noted it was now four. He buzzed Jane's intercom.

"Yes," she said.

"It's time for you to go, Jane. I'll take this call and finish up here afterward," he told her.

"Thanks," she replied.

Lark reached for the telephone receiver and tried to anticipate what the reporter's excuse would be. "Hello," he began.

"Look, I'm sorry; I'm running a little behind," the reporter nervously responded.

"Well, are you going to make it?"

"Yes. I'm in Mount Joy, and I should be there in twenty minutes or so."

"I'll be here," Lark said. He hung up.

Jane walked past his office on her way to the parking lot. She rarely said anything, but this time she stopped before opening the door and came back to stand in his doorway.

"I'll see you tomorrow, boss," she used this little term of endearment from time to time. It was the only time she shifted from a totally professional relationship with Lark.

"Uh oh," he said with a smile, "it must be time to renegotiate your contract!"

They both laughed heartily. Jane was plainly attractive at moments like this. She developed an almost girlish manner, and Lark caught glimpses of what this woman must have been like when she was a teenager. Not so different from those who graced the church building on Friday nights, he thought.

"Have a nice evening," she said with a smile. She turned and walked out the door, not waiting for any reciprocal comment from Lark. As he sat in his desk chair, he could hear her footsteps descend the concrete stairs to the parking lot. Only a moment later, he heard her sports car fire up and drive out of the lot. He made a mental note to try to learn just a little more about this amazing woman who had worked with him for nearly two years. He also wrote a note to send a memo to the head trustee about raising Jane's salary at the beginning of the next calendar year.

Lark sat and read what he had typed. He made editorial notes at the places he would change in the final draft of the sermon. By the time he had finished the quick read-through, the document looked as though a two or three year old had stolen into his study and scribbled upon the homily.

It was precisely four-thirty when he heard a car hurry into the parking lot, a door slam, and running feet come up the stairs and through the doorway. The reporter hurried right past, and was halfway down the hall when Lark called out to him.

"If you are from the *Harrisburg Patriot,* I'm in here," Lark shouted. The footsteps stopped for just a second, then retreated to his study's doorway. There in the doorway, out of breath, stood a young man in his late twenties, dressed in blue jeans and a tee shirt with what looked like a peace symbol tie-dyed upon it. Atop his head was a Phillies baseball cap which, like the team, looked like it had seen better days. Regaining his composure, the young man stepped into the room and extended his hand to Lark.

"Hi! I'm Rolf Finness, with the *Harrisburg Patriot,*" he said. "And, you must be Pastor Lark Wilson."

"I'm glad to see you have a well-developed power of deductive reasoning, Mr. Finness," Lark said. He shook his visitor's hand rather vigorously. "Have a seat. Can I interest you in a soda or something?"

"No thanks," said the reporter. He sat across the room in one of the study's three chairs. Lark had never succumbed to suggestions that the furniture in his study include a couch or richly upholstered easy chairs. Lark preferred a stark appearance for two reasons: it suggested a frugality which stood for good stewardship; and, it kept people focused upon the reason for which they came to see the pastor in the first place. In short, good stewardship led to less loitering in a busy pastor's study.

"Well, then," Lark went on, "let's get down to the interview. It's getting late, and I have a meeting to go to tonight after supper."

They really didn't talk for very long. The reporter obviously was well-trained in the basic journalistic formula: who, what, where, when, and why? Within ten minutes of scribbling notes feverishly as Lark talked, the reporter indicated he was finished. He closed his stenographer's pad very deliberately and stared at Lark for a moment without saying a word. Lark wasn't sure whether he was witnessing a seizure, or just watching a weary young man recharge his batteries. Finally, the reporter rose from his chair, walked to Lark's desk, bent down, and stared Lark in the face.

"Is anything wrong?" Lark asked him.

"No," said the reporter. "I just wanted to get a closer look at you. You and I are about the same age, I would guess."

"Well, I'm thirty-four years old," Lark said, as he began to relax in the reporter's presence. "How old are you?"

"Twenty-eight," the reporter went on. "I guess you and I like the same things."

"Yes, I bet we do," Lark said.

The reporter stepped back from the desk, took a handkerchief from his pocket and wiped the sweat from his face in a manner most dramatic, almost like a motion used by an umpire to sweep home plate or a gas station attendant when removing dirt from a windshield.

Lark watched with fascination.

"Well, I gotta go," said the reporter as he replaced the hanky. "Thanks for your time, Mr. Wilson."

"Don't mention it," Lark said, rather lazily. The man was gone before Lark could turn off the lights in his study, shut off the air conditioner, and leave the building for supper.

As Lark walked out into the early evening summer sunlight, the brightness of the day assaulted his eyes. Lark walked into the kitchen and glanced up at the clock in amazement. It was nearly five forty-five. He didn't think he had spent that much time with the reporter. He thought it odd that the time had sped by so quickly.

"You're rather late tonight, Lark," Fran said to him as he stood gazing at the clock. "Did you forget you have an appointment this evening?"

"No, that reporter was late," Lark said. He gave each child a hug as they sat at the table waiting for supper. "How was the picnic?"

All three started to tell him all about the picnic and the park as he sat down at the kitchen table. It was Leigh Ann's turn to say grace. She prayed: "God is great and God is good. So we thank God for our food. Amen." The rest of the mealtime was spent listening to each youngster's exploits, some of their grievances against one another, and some talk about the plans for the forthcoming weekend.

By six-thirty, Lark and Fran were alone in the kitchen while the children played wiffle ball in the backyard. They were just about finished the dishes when Fran turned to Lark with a quizzical look.

"Did you say that the reporter was late?" she asked.

"Yes, he didn't say why. He was supposed to be here at three but didn't show up until almost five," Lark said.

"That's funny," Fran said.

"What?"

"Well, around twelve-thirty, just as we were about to go to the park, I got a call from a man who said he was a reporter with the *Patriot*. It sounded like the same man who called earlier. He said he was going to have to cancel his interview with you today."

"What?" Lark said incredulously.

"He said he had tried calling your office, but the line was busy. He didn't want you to waste your time waiting for him."

"Why didn't you call me and tell me?" Lark asked his wife.

"I did call the office. I told Jane," Fran went on. "She said she would tell you when you came back from the Y."

"She must have forgotten."

"I guess," Fran said, a question lingered.

"Anyway, he called the office this afternoon," Lark continued, "and said he was running late. He got here after Jane left for the day. It's not like her to forget things."

They finished the dishes. Lark rushed upstairs to the bathroom, brushed his teeth, and combed his hair. As he glanced into the mirror, he noted the redness had increased in his eyes. He would make it a quick evening, and then get to bed early.

Back downstairs, he bade his children good night, promising he would look in on each when he returned, and if they were awake, he would sing them a song. He loved this nightly ritual with the children, and they almost always waited in the room for the appearance of their father to tuck them in. He kissed Fran on the cheek and turned to leave.

"You still look ragged around the edges, Lark," she said quietly.

"I know," he said. "I'll be home early tonight."

Out the door he dashed. Almost late, he turned out of the parking lot and began the trek across town to Jennifer's apartment.

Chapter 17
It Must Have Been The Tea

Lark drove across the city in the early summer evening light and barely noticed the traffic around him. The twenty-six blocks or so to Jennifer's apartment were behind him within fifteen minutes. And he was bounding up the stairs to the apartment complex doorway with the energy of a teenage paperboy on his last block of deliveries before a hot date.

Jennifer buzzed him through the security door with a cheery, "Get yourself up here!"

Lark ascended the stairs to the second floor, knocked on the door, and was greeted by Jennifer, dressed in a simple cotton polka-dotted design. Without make-up and business suits, she was even more alluring to Lark.

"Hi!" She smiled. He stood at the threshold and stared at her. "Are you game to come in?" she asked, as he hesitated in the doorway. He laughed and walked into her apartment.

It was simply furnished with a temporary feel to it, like most of the furniture had been donated by a well-meaning church group to a distressed immigrant family. Jennifer picked up on his impression and indicated it was indeed donated by Franklin and Marshall. She would only be here for the summer semester, and this was the apartment reserved for all visiting scholars. He sat on the lone sofa and glanced around. It was simple but livable. A TV sat in one corner, and end tables right out of the 1950s adorned each side of the sofa. A rocking chair nestled upon a throw rug in the other corner. Several potted plants stood around at various angles. A hallway led from the living room into which the apartment door emptied. Lark assumed that the first door on the right was the bedroom, the second, the bathroom. He could see just barely into the kitchen area as he sat on the sofa. Small, but cozy; just right for a single woman. Not too much housecleaning needed meant no lost time in domestic duties for one who was here basically to lecture post-pubescent males attending college to avoid the draft and rich young females looking for a future doctor husband.

"I didn't think you'd come," she said. She stood in the center of the room and gazed at him, hands on her hips.

"I see you're dressed rather casually," he said.

"Oh, this old thing," she said. She glanced at her dress and pretended to smooth its non-existent wrinkles with her palms, a motion downward across her body which accentuated her hips for just a second. "I got this in a crazy days sale two years ago. It's nice to wear on summer nights when I'm not doing anything special."

"Oh, I see," Lark said, getting into the banter which seemed so easy with Jennifer. "I'm not special."

She smiled and gave him a maternal look, "You're special, alright!" She turned her back and sauntered to the rocking chair. "Well," she said, as she sat in the rocker, "Would you like some iced tea?" As she sat in the chair, she raised her legs to rest her feet upon the seat of the rocker. It was one of the most seductive moves he had ever seen a woman use. She rocked slightly and smiled as she waited for his response. "You've got time before my orientation, don't you?" she asked girlishly.

"Yes," Lark said nervously. He felt a little warmer. Maybe it was the dash up stairs finally catching up with him, or maybe it was being alone with this beautiful woman, he couldn't be sure. But, iced tea would be fine.

Jennifer arose and walked barefoot into the kitchen. The chair rocked slightly where it sat, and Lark was beginning to doubt his wisdom at making this arrangement. They had always been together in public before this moment, he was feeling nervous.

As he thought about what he would share with Jennifer about the upcoming demonstration, he could hear her humming to herself in the kitchen as she opened the refrigerator and withdrew a pitcher of tea and some iced cubes. He heard the cubes dance into the tall glasses, and then the splash of the liquid as it was poured. The door of the refrigerator opened once more, no doubt to return the pitcher to its cool, dark resting place. Then the phone rang. He listened as Jennifer picked up the receiver somewhere in the kitchen, out of his view.

"Yes," she said. And that was all. The conversation was so swift, had he not heard her say yes, he would have thought it had been a wrong number. He leaned back into the sofa as she walked up the hallway from the kitchen and stepped into the living room with a tray on which two tall glasses of iced tea bearing colorful umbrellas glistened.

"I got these in New Orleans." She purred as she bent forward to hand Lark one of the glasses. A quick glance informed him she was not wearing a bra and her breasts swung easily with the forward motion of her lithe body. If she had caught him steal the glance, she never let on. She resettled upon the rocker and stirred her tea with the umbrella in her glass.

"They serve a drink in New Orleans called 'the hurricane' in glasses like these. I'm not sure, but I think the drink contains rum."

"It does?" Lark said, getting nervous once more. "I wouldn't know. Never been to New Orleans," he said curtly.

"You'd like it, especially the French Quarter," she said. She smiled across the room.

"Why?" he asked.

"They've got lots of pretty women there," she said. She laughed and sipped her tea.

Lark giggled, too. Jennifer seemed to have an understanding with him. It was alright with her that he saw her as beautiful and attractive. It was alright with her that he, at times, felt more comfortable with her than any woman he had ever met. It was alright with her that they got along in conversation like two persons who had known each other for a long time. It was alright with her if he stole a glance down the front of her dress.

As they drank their tea he rehearsed the schedule of the demonstration with her. She let him talk and talk. They would leave at six in the morning, five busses, mostly students from Franklin and Marshall and Millersville State nearby. He was the "patrol leader." There would be a bus captain with each group. She was not to become alarmed if, when they entered the nation's capitol, they were met with armored military vehicles and soldiers on every corner. This was a common practice of the administration. It had been going on since the 1950s, and it was meant to intimidate more than protect.

Jennifer listened, seemingly engaged by his knowledge and insight, his strategy, and his understanding of the politics of Vietnam. She moved from time to time as he explained which church would host their group for brunch before the march was set to begin, and how they would rendezvous at approximately five o'clock, near the Washington Monument, to board the busses back to Lancaster. It would be a long day, he explained, but it would be like a church picnic: lots of people, some fun, heat, and discomfort, all to be followed by a delicious fatigue. Unlike a church picnic, this day would end with a sense of having played a role in history, perhaps saving lives, and bringing our nation back to its senses.

Without a word, Jennifer arose from the rocking chair and walked across the living room to the sofa where Lark sat. She sat down next to him and looked longingly into his eyes.

"Do you mind if we just end the orientation session now?" she asked dreamily.

"No, not at all," Lark heard himself say slowly.

"Do you have time for some more iced tea?" she wanted to know. She was so close to him now that he could feel her breath on his face as she spoke. She was so beautiful at this moment, he could hardly respond to her.

"I don't think so," he said. Panic moved across the back of his neck and down his spine. He was responding to Jennifer in a way he hadn't intended.

"Could we talk about something more personal?" she murmured. She took his hand in hers and held it ever so gently. He felt powerless to pull away from her. She inched closer, until her hip brushed against his and his hand was suddenly resting in her lap.

"What would you like to talk about?" he stammered as her right arm arched over his head and came to rest around his shoulder.

"I think you know," was all she said. She turned toward him, her eyes ablaze with passion, lips slightly parted, and face flushed with just a slight shade of red around her eyes.

A vision flashed across his mind. He and Jennifer were on the beach, the ocean pounding against the shore nearby and soft breezes sweeping across her hair. She is beautiful. He notices their bodies are naked as they embrace upon a blanket. Arm in arm, leg in leg, they rub against each other, a prelude to that act of intimacy for which they were bound from the moment they met. He draws her close to him. She is ready. Her kisses tell him she wants him now.

Things are mixed up a bit. She is kissing him passionately upon the mouth as she places her hand upon him. Then, he sees himself in the apartment. This isn't happening on the beach but in the apartment. He is responding, but he is not sure whether he is a spectator or a participant. His mind is foggy as she moves around his body taking control of his every reaction to the passion of the moment. She bites and tugs at him between the beautiful lips he had kissed only seconds before. He can't quite stand this. He reaches across and places his hand upon her as she undulates. The beach is a wonderful setting for making love, he thinks to himself. Suddenly, he is more conscious. This is not a fantasy.

Startled, he shoves her away from him. She falls to the floor at his feet. He is confused and frightened. This is not what he intended to do no matter how he may have felt about their flirtations. And yet, he wants very much to make love to her. He is so confused, so angry with himself at being where he is, so frightened now of this woman staring up at him. She lifts her dress above her hips as he stands over her. She is surprisingly submissive, lying upon the floor while motioning for him to come down with her upon the floor. Quickly she slips her dress over her head so he can see all of her gorgeous body. Her fingertips move up and down across her body.

It is like a dream. A bad dream. Lark wants to finish what has started. Every ounce of his manhood is pushing him over the edge. But, something deep inside won't let him do it. Disentangled, he turns and walks toward the apartment door, adjusting his clothing.

Jennifer jumped to her feet, buttoned her dress after slipping into it quickly, and giggled as she literally leaped in front of him at the door. "What's the matter? Don't I please you?" she asked petulantly like a teenage schoolgirl.

Lark didn't know what to say. He sensed it wasn't wise to say much at this point. He was so confused. His mind awhirl with contradictory emotions, he struggled to be rational, he felt dizzy, and he decided the truth should be spoken.

"Look," he began, "a few moments ago, I could have gone all the way with you. But then what? I'm a married man with three children. How could I look at them ever again? What would I say to my wife tonight?"

"I knew all of that, Lark," Jennifer said quietly. "I just thought you wanted me." She gazed into his eyes and reached toward him once more. He felt himself stir anew. She held him around the waist and looked directly at him. "We could go to bed in there and no one would ever know. I want you." She had a sad look now as she gazed at him.

"Jennifer," he said quietly, almost to himself. "I may want you with every ounce of my being, but I can't do this. You are

151

beautiful, and we've had some good times together this past week, but I just can't. I hope you understand."

She kissed him again as he finished speaking. This time, the kiss was deeply passionate. He responded immediately as she maneuvered her hands up and down his frame. He could not move. She kissed him again, and this time, slid her tongue into his mouth as she tried to persuade him to return to the living room. Her body moved against his with ease now, as kiss after kiss warmed his face. Her breasts, nipples hardened, bumped against his arm, then his chest. Her hand around his waist gently tugged him against her. It was maddening.

He could not move. He simply stood at the doorway, wanting with every bit of strength he had in his body to disengage. But Jennifer was kissing him, and she was now saying softly that she loved him. He wanted to cry. He felt faint as she took control anew. He could not let this happen. He had never experienced this in his entire life. He wanted to, but he couldn't. It wasn't right but it felt so good. The conflict of emotions overcame him. He began to weep. Great cries erupted from his throat and he started to cry uncontrollably.

Jennifer arose and gazed into his eyes. She reached her hands to his face, "What's wrong?" she asked.

"I must go home," was all he could say between what seemed like orgasmic spasms overtaking his body.

Jennifer stepped back in amazement. She glanced at his contorted face looking deeply into his eyes. "You really are a good person," she said in abject disbelief. "Go on, put yourself back together and get out of here," she said somewhat spitefully, as she moved out of his way and returned to the living room. Lark again put his clothes in order as he watched Jennifer take a seat on the rocking chair in the corner of the room. Her feet were once more resting upon the seat of the rocker. This time, she was sitting like an untrained child upon the chair, rocking it quickly back and forth. She didn't say a word as he turned to leave the apartment.

Once the door was closed behind him, he took several deep breaths. He felt as though he were regaining control of himself, yet he felt sick to his stomach as he slowly walked down the stairs. Reaching the landing, he heard the door open above him. He turned, and there was Jennifer, standing at the top of the stairs.

"I'm sorry," she said, "I truly am sorry. You're a good man. Go home to your wife."

"Good night," Lark said. He turned and walked out into the fast waning daylight. Lightning bugs were making their first appearances in the darkened corners of yards. The heat was lessening. The station wagon stood at curbside, waiting to take its passenger home to his family.

Lark could not believe what had just happened. It was as though it were a dream at points. He was highly agitated as he reviewed the sequence of events which had just taken place. He questioned himself as he drove home. His guilt was only exceeded by the growing sickening feeling in his stomach.

Upon reaching the parsonage, Lark simply sat in the carport and tried to piece together what he might have done to avoid this evening. He shook convulsively as he remembered how good it felt to have Jennifer in his arms. He thought he could smell her body upon his. He didn't know what to do or say once he entered his home. He whimpered as he recalled his breaking down and crying in front of this beautiful woman, who seemingly only sought his pleasure. He took his handkerchief and rubbed his face, so as to remove any trace of her unpainted lips. He wretched as he thought of how he might have sacrificed his integrity had he stayed in Jennifer's apartment one moment longer, if he had gone into her bedroom as she invited him to do, if he had stooped to the floor and lay with her as she begged him to do. Shame overtook him as he got out of the car and walked into the kitchen. His stomach rumbled and a pain shot across his chest as he walked toward the refrigerator to get some iced water before walking into the living room where Fran was watching TV. He couldn't contain it. Bending over the sink, Lark regurgitated, his body shaking with each upward movement of his esophagus. He was still vomiting when the kitchen light suddenly came on and Fran stood quizzically in the doorway.

"What's wrong, Lark?" she asked with concern.

Lark turned to face her, and she gasped at what she saw. He looked like he had been in a fight. His eyes were puffy and red. His face was contorted in pain. Saliva and various stomach fluids dripped from his chin. He did not answer her, but turned to heave into the sink anew.

Fran came to him and wrapped her arms around his stomach, like she did for the children whenever they were sick. Her touch was welcomed, and Lark began to regain his composure as his wife rested her head against the back of his neck and held him tightly. The convulsions lessened and ended. For a moment, Fran was gone as Lark turned from the sink and sat at the picnic table, his head in his hands. Then she was back, wiping his face with a damp cloth and soothing his brow with light strokes of her other hand.

"You look terrible," she said. "What happened to you?"

"I don't know," he lied. "They had some iced tea at the meeting tonight, and there might have been something wrong with it."

"Well, you look like you've got the flu or something," Fran said, comforting him. "Are you going to be alright?"

"I think so," he answered. He took her hand in his. "Thanks." Meaning it, he squeezed her hand.

Fran sat down beside him on the bench. She was freshly scrubbed and powdered. She always used a powder in the summer months, due to the humidity. He put his arm around her and held her tightly against him. He was sweaty and smelled sickly, but Fran didn't seem to mind.

"You going to take a bath now?" she asked coyly, gazing into his eyes. "I hope you have something left for me, after the day you've had."

"I'll be down after I say goodnight to the kids and get cleaned up," he said.

She squeezed his hand, a little movement that communicated she would wait for him to get ready. They both got up and left the kitchen. Lark had made it through the first few moments. He would be alright now. He would not be alone with Jennifer again. Perhaps he would never see Jennifer again. That thought saddened him, as he went up to say goodnight to the children, shower, and then return to Fran's favorite place to make love. Yes, he would be alright now. Maybe it was the tea and nothing more. At home, he felt more like himself. Surrounded by familiar furniture and rooms, Lark began to settle down. It would be fine, he told himself as he bounded out of the bathroom and came downstairs to the living room with nothing on but a clean pair of boxer shorts.

Fran lay on the couch, staring at television. Perry Mason reruns were Fran's favorite for summer viewing. Although she had most likely seen the crime solved before, she was glued to the inevitable finale. She motioned for Lark to come and rest his head upon her lap, as she sat up to greet him.

"This one's really good," she said, as Lark lay across the couch, resting his head upon her generous lap. Within minutes, the court was listening to the great defense lawyer both spare his client the shame of being convicted and lowering the credibility of the prosecuting attorney by solving the case with ease.

It was all rather amusing to Lark. The outcome was as predictable as tomorrow's crack of dawn. Yet millions of Americans like Fran watched each week as Erle Stanley Gardner's pet lawyer got his man or woman, or whomever, to suddenly stand where they were and confess. Americans obviously believed so deeply in human conscience that this is the only outcome that could be written by those who produced the scripts.

As tonight's show ended with the music everyone in the country recognized, Fran stroked Lark's hair. "How are you feeling?"

"Better," he said.

She bent over and kissed him fully upon the mouth. There was never any mistaking when Fran was feeling amorous. Her lips gave her away. Lark was amazed at how full her lips felt on his when she wanted to make love. At any other time they seemed like tiny, tight little bundles of lipstick across her face. But when she was ready to make love, her lips seemed to find some new flesh and blood. They literally covered his mouth as she kissed him. Fran's kisses, when she wanted him, were as sensual as any woman he could imagine. Only, as she kissed him tonight, he found himself comparing her kiss with that of Jennifer's of only an hour before. His wife was moving atop him and kissing him very passionately.

"You want to go to bed?" she asked.

"Do you?" He knew she really didn't want to go upstairs right now. Ever since their daughter had walked into the room to see what was the matter with her one very amorous night three years before, Fran had been somewhat reluctant in the bedroom. When they made love in bed, she seemed to be only going through the motions. Preferring lots of room and relative privacy, Fran liked it best on the large woven rug which lay in front of the fireplace. In the winter, they would rub oil upon one another's bodies while the flames licked the inside brick and danced toward the flue, sparks jumping and logs cracking to cover Fran's little murmurs. In summer, with the windows opened and the breezes blowing, Fran was less amorous. But it was better here than anywhere, and Lark always obliged.

As they lay in one another's arms, he was not as ready as he wanted to be, and she was patiently waiting for him. He kissed her as she rubbed against him, her bare body presenting its various folds of softness and familiar pleasure spots that married couples learn to address at such times. Familiar places to touch, familiar moves, and soon, he was ready. Lark's mind divided as they made love. He was aware that his mind was really two different places. He was in the living room making love with his wife, but, he was also on the beach making love with Jennifer. It was confusing at first, seductive at the end. Fran didn't seem to notice that, at times, his mind was miles, maybe dreams, away.

Afterward, they lay together, as was their custom, and held one another until each was assured it was alright to get up and prepare for bed. As he was slipping on his boxer shorts, Fran turned to him and said, "Are you going to be able to sleep?"

"I think so," he said. "Why do you ask?"

"Well, you were so sick and—" she hesitated.

"What?" he asked her.

"Well, you didn't seem like yourself just now," she said.

He didn't think she had noticed. Panic arose anew.

"I'm alright," he said, nervously. "I guess that tea had something in it I shouldn't drink. I feel better now. Really, I do. Thanks for your concern."

Fran kissed him lightly upon the cheek as she walked by him toward the stairs. Her day-to-day lips were back. He followed her upstairs and into their bedroom. As they crawled onto the bed, she rolled over and gave him a hug.

"Thanks for loving me," she said, and she rolled away from him onto her right side. Sleep came quickly upon Lark, and within minutes, he was lazily drifting toward that land all of God's creatures go to rejuvenate their minds for the day ahead. Just before he fell soundly asleep, he saw Jennifer, lying on her living room floor, beckoning him to make love to her. He rolled onto his left side, and blackness overtook him.

Chapter 18
THE DREAM

Lark stood before his congregation at St. Andrew looking across the vast space of the sanctuary. The sparse service crowd listened raptly as he explained it had all been a mistake. He would make it right, he promised. They would see a different pastor from now on. They smiled at him as he spoke. But from somewhere in the smokey sanctuary a laughter began to arise. It sounded like Doc. Lark scanned the room, the shadows within it playing tricks upon his eyesight. There he was, sitting in the back pew on the right, chuckling to himself as Lark spoke. Then there was more laughter; the sound of it more familiar than Doc's.

Suddenly, Lark was aware that this laughter was coming from the organist. Elsie was rocking on the organ bench, shaking her head as she laughed. Lark looked at her and as he did, she puckered her lips to throw him a kiss. Then she threw her head back and laughed out loud.

Lark was feeling quite agitated now, as he tried to get on with the apology to the congregation for his indiscretion. The congregation was beginning to fidget. The laughter of Doc and Elsie was taking its toll upon the attention of the people in the pews. Then, he heard a new laugh. This one had a quality to it which suggested great pain and derision. He looked in the direction *of the person who could manage to laugh in such a fashion, and there was Fran. Tears running down her face, she shook almost uncontrollably as she laughed knowingly while Lark tried to explain to his parishioners what had happened. The congregation began to look in all directions as he endeavored to continue. He was losing control, and he was being drowned out by the three persons who now laughed aloud in the midst of the service.*

Then, it happened. The doorway to the nave opened and in walked Jennifer. Her smile broadened as she walked down the aisle in a brilliant red evening dress with red pumps and a jaunty little red purse swinging at her side. She came right toward him as he froze in the pulpit. All eyes were glancing from her to him as she moved closer. She stood, right in front of the pulpit, looked up at him, and laughed right in his face.

"Now, what are you going to do?" she wanted to know.

"Quit," he screamed out loud, as he sat up in bed. "Quit," he yelled again, so loudly that Fran jumped up from a deep sleep and turned on the light.

"Quit," he yelled once more, his eyes still clenched tightly shut. Sweat was pouring out from what seemed like every pore of his body. His bedclothes were soaked with perspiration, and he seemed to shake like a person in the grips of a deep fever.

Fran startled by the sight of her husband, barely knew what to do. She sat beside him, took his hand, and stroked his forehead, waiting for him to awaken fully from whatever nightmare had gripped him. She noted that every part of his body was rigid as steel. She waited as he began to cry.

The children, awakened by their father's scream, were calling out to them, wanting to know what was wrong with Daddy. Fran quietly got up and walked to their bedroom, where she explained, "Daddy has had a bad dream." The children understood; this explanation satisfied them, and they settled down once more for the night.

When Fran returned to their bedroom, Lark was fully awake. Yet he sat and stared at the window across from the foot of their bed.

"Are you alright, now?" she asked quietly.

"I think so," he stuttered.

"You'd better change your pajamas. You're soaking wet," she said to him like a mother to a child.

"Yeah," he said, as he got up and walked to the bathroom. She followed him and eyed his every movement.

After relieving himself, he took off the wet pajamas, threw them into the clothes hamper, and walked back to their bedroom. Fran followed him. He was very quiet.

"You're not feeling like throwing up again, are you?" she asked, as he slipped on clean boxer shorts and a tee shirt.

"No," was all he said, as he got back into bed.

She turned out the light and lay down beside him. His breathing was easier now. His body was relaxed. She touched him on the arm. "You were having a nightmare," she said quietly to his back. "Do you want to talk about it?"

Stillness came upon the bedroom and tried to get between them.

"Lark," she whispered, after a few minutes, "are you still awake?"

"Yes," he mumbled.

"Are you feeling better now?" she queried.

"I think so."

"What has you so upset? I've never seen you like this."

"I'll be fine, Fran," he said. His body suddenly shook unexpectedly.

"Are you cold?" she asked.

"No," he replied. "Maybe I am coming down with the flu or something," he lied again. "I hear there is a summer version of it running around Lancaster."

"Good night," she said as she kissed the back of his head. "Call me if you need to."

"Okay," he said as she turned onto her right side and rested her bottom against his spine. He reflected upon the dream which had awakened his entire family. He saw it all. There was a helpless quality to it, a certain inevitability.

He lay there, unable to fall back to sleep. The evening at Jennifer's began to come back into focus. Try as he could, the events stood out of his mind's grasp as he lay there, staring into the darkness of the bedroom. Everything seemed in place, yet the sequence was not quite right. There were jumps now in the memory, like a film which is broken and spliced back together. Lark ran and reran the frames. As he did, the inability to put it together without gaps began to bother and intrigue him.

He was enjoying this challenge when sleep overtook him once more. It was welcomed and embraced, but not before he noticed something in the sequence he hadn't seen before. He was going back to that blip in the evening's events when darkness draped his mind with the soft raiment of sleep.

Chapter 19
THE DREAM
RETURNS

"What's wrong?" he was asked. "You're not gay, are you?"

The confrontation of that question shook him to the core. The voice was familiar, but its body was out of sight. Jennifer stood in front of him, pleading with her eyes to finish what she had started. He was aware that every bit of his manhood had responded to her sexual whiles. But, he was also acutely aware that it was wrong. He was married. He had gone before God, family, and friends, and declared his love for Fran. His grandmother had bid them a wonderful life, as she reached up from her wheelchair to embrace them prior to their departure for the honeymoon. He was a father of three wonderful children. He loved them all. He could not do anything which would make them think less of him. And, what of those he served? And his colleagues? How could he let them down? He wouldn't. And, God? How could he let God down? He just didn't have time for this, not now.

"I know that, but I thought you'd find time for me," she whispered to him as she rubbed his body.

The lie of it all now faced him in his dream. There was yet another reason. It was something no one would accept, standing *in the arms of a beautiful young woman like Jennifer. He couldn't mention it now, not even to himself. But, he knew what it was. It was a threshold he had vowed never to cross. It was a barrier he thought he would never transcend. Many throughout history had done so, but Lark never could. To do so would mean breaking not only marriage vows, but promises that suddenly were even more important to him.*

He stood there, in his church, all eyes upon him. The ministers gathered around him. He knelt at the altar, and they placed their hands upon him, one by one. The Synod President was speaking.

"Beloved brother in Christ; consider well the true nature and significance of the Christian ministry. The first ministers were the Apostles, who were called and sent forth by Jesus Christ himself. Other men were chosen as pastors and teachers in the Church to succeed them; and this from generation to generation the office of Ministry has continued unto the present time..."

That yoke had been laid upon him. The office, the ministry, it was sacred. He could not bring it down to the level at which he now stood in Jennifer's apartment. She wouldn't understand. He hardly did, himself.

"The Ministers of Christ are set in the world to be the representatives of his authority and the ambassadors of his grace...Such is the character of the office to which you are called...Pray earnestly and daily for divine grace...Remember that your sacrifice is not of yourself, but of God. Devote yourself wholly to your office that you may be able to give full proof of your ministry and show yourself an example to others..."

He looked upon himself. Shame descended upon him more heavily than he had ever felt in his life. Unable to tell Jennifer to stop what she was doing, he began to cry. There were more people in her living room now than when he first arrived. He had failed them all: Fran, his children, his family, his congregation, his friends and colleagues, his God. He could not go on. He would bear the incredulity of the questioner. Any conclusion drawn by the inquisitor was acceptable, even if totally inaccurate. He would not continue. He began to cry.

He lay awake, whimpering as Fran awakened to the sound. She rolled toward him and placed her arm around him. "Lark, what's the matter?" she asked. "Were you dreaming again?"

Through his tears, he muttered, "I must quit the ministry."

"Why?"

Lark didn't say a word as he began to regain his composure anew. How could he tell her what had happened? He didn't understand it all himself.

"Do you want to get up and have a cup of tea or something?" she asked him, as they lay in the darkness.

"Okay," he said.

Soon they were in the kitchen, sitting at the picnic bench, sipping an herbal favorite of Fran's. Neither had spoken since they left the bedroom. Lark was trying to piece together what he might say, and Fran was apparently content to wait until he was ready to talk. The tea was good. This moment brought back memories of Fran pregnant, sitting upon the back porch of their first parsonage, sunlight flitting across the lawn in early spring, drinking coffee, and chatting about their first child who was due in less than a month. Lark remembered the joy of that moment. They never seemed to have that kind of time anymore. There was so much to do: three children to raise; a bigger parish to manage and serve; Lark's involvement in the community and wider church.

"What are you thinking?" she asked. She sat across the table from him. "You seem so far away."

"Fran," he hesitated, "I don't know where to begin."

Something in the way he began obviously struck a chord deep within Fran, as a single teardrop rolled from her left eye and down her cheek.

"Go on," she said, "you can tell me." Her face was sincere. Only her eyes reddened with deep concern. Fear, uncertainty, and shame seemed to emanate from him.

"I met a woman in New York," he began. Fran started to weep. He told her everything; he left out no detail. His body contorted with shame when he got to what happened at Jennifer's apartment. He struggled with putting it altogether and didn't know why. He assumed his guilt was getting in the way. When he finished, they simply sat and looked at one another.

What does a woman say to a man who has just confessed attraction to another? How does a wife respond to a husband who has just described a tryst narrowly escaped, but obviously not without damage? This was unchartered territory for both of them. She struggled to stay calm and rational; her face betrayed her. Lark could see the recrimination in it. It was hardening like cement. But nothing was said. They just sat and looked at one another and sipped the hot tea.

"Is there anything more you want to tell me?" she finally asked, putting her cup down. One who didn't know Fran might suspect the question was an attempt to enable the confessor to reflect upon any missing pieces, any unmentioned details. Lark knew better. Her face and tone hinted that the jury was in and the verdict about to be read. Only this time, no Perry Mason was in sight who might save him from the prosecutor's case against him. No one was going to stand up and confess at the last second. He was guilty; Fran had decided it. He heard it in her voice.

"I don't think so," he said weakly as he lowered his eyes.

"You don't think so?" she mocked him. "You traipse around with a young woman you met in New York City, you have drinks with her in a bar and in a diner, you go to her apartment, she makes a pass at you, and does God know what with you—and you don't think so?" Her voice rose with the indignation she felt. She arose and threw her teacup into the sink. The sound of breaking glass reverberated throughout the house.

Lark held his head in his hands and wept aloud. There was nothing he could say or do at this moment. Fran would have to work her way through this, as he was striving to do. She would have to make some sense of it. He knew she would, eventually. After her initial emotional response, the Southern matriarch in her would take over, and she would rise above any kind of suffering or indignation she felt at this moment. Like Scarlet O'Hara, Fran always came back to tomorrow. She was determined they would live together until death parted them. Like her mother and her grandmother before her, she would conquer any threat to her happy home.

"Just look at you," she said disparagingly. "You're a fine excuse for a minister—"

Lark didn't hear much more of what she said, as she stood above him and lectured him regarding weakness in a moment of tension, cowardice in the face of the enemy, and wanting to abandon the profession for which he had been so ably equipped by the Almighty. Lark thought he heard traces of old words of encouragement which had passed between them at times of disappointment and discouragement. Fran would always rise to the occasion and help him remember all the things taught at seminary about hard times and how to deal with them.

This time, it just wasn't working. Tears fell upon the picnic bench. He could barely see across the room. He couldn't focus on her words as she continued to remind him of his hard upbringing and how proud everyone in the family had been when he was ordained. Every word she said now made him feel worse. She was repeating the things he had tortured himself with in the past few hours. Fran was sharing the pride and joy with which they had started this journey together, rehearsing how every member of the family now depended upon him to be a man.

These kind of lectures usually worked, but not tonight. Fran's words did little more than assure Lark that his thoughts were correct. Fran was voicing what he could not say to her. Lark had forsaken his calling, the office to which he was ordained. He must not do that. She insisted he must not think that what had happened meant that he had already forsaken the office. This was a warning, a sign, that some rehabilitation was necessary: perhaps a retreat or two. Maybe, a sabbatical, but, not a resignation.

Her voice finally betrayed the fear within her. She sat down again and looked deeply into her husband eyes. His face was swollen with tears, and his eyes were still watery.

"Lark," she said, "you know I love you. Don't do this to us, please."

He could not respond in any way. His heart ached for bringing this pain upon them. Fran was right: he was a sorry excuse for a minister. He knew that to be true. At this moment, all he wanted to do was get out of it any way he could. His only conclusion was to resign the office he felt he had disgraced. No matter what it meant to his family, he knew he had to quit. There would be integrity in that, as there had not been in his recent behavior. He would resign; that was his only conclusion. There really was nothing more to say to Fran.

He got up and climbed back upstairs. After washing his face in the bathroom, Lark walked to the bedroom and got into bed. Fran was right there with him. Silent as a stone.

Chapter 20
THE MORNING AFTER

"Lark." It was Fran's voice arousing him from deep sleep. "Lark, wake up. Doc's on the phone."

Lark stretched and rolled over as he arose. He hadn't heard the phone ring at all. The sun was vaguely shining through the curtains, which waved in the morning breeze that drifted into their bedroom. Picking up the receiver Lark mumbled, "Hello?"

"Hey, pastor," Doc said cheerfully at the other end, "I've got some free time this morning and was wondering if you had time for some coffee?" This was not unusual. Doc often called or dropped by when he got the chance. He seemed to enjoy the mental sparring which took place between them on such occasions.

"I don't even know what time it is," Lark said quietly into the receiver. "But give me a few minutes, and I'll join you."

"Good," Doc said. "Let's meet at the Glass Kitchen around ten."

Lark glanced at the clock on the phone stand. It was nine-thirty. He could hardly believe his eyes. He couldn't remember when he last slept this late. "Okay," he said. He put the receiver down.

Fran was still in the doorway. "How are you?" she asked. Upset was not the word to describe her countenance.

168

"I'm not sure," was all he could say and still look her in the eye. He was very lethargic and hoped a shower would revive him. He was also immensely guilty about last night, and had no idea how he would live with what had happened.

As he walked toward the bathroom, Fran asked, "What are your plans for today?"

Having none, he shrugged and walked into the bathroom, closing the door behind him. Shaving quickly, Lark was soon standing beneath the steady stream of warm water. As he washed images of the night before danced across his mind. He shuddered as he thought about the way Jennifer had kissed and touched him. The embarrassment of it all was nearly too much for him to endure. He was almost glad Doc had called and wanted to see him. This way, he could avoid Fran for a while longer. She was evidently angry and he could not tell, at this time, exactly what her ultimate response would be. Her words in the middle of the night had both stung and bolstered him, as only Fran could do at times. Like a military drill sergeant, she possessed that ability to both scold and encourage with the same words. She could be tough, but one sensed her toughness was for one's own good. This was the first time Lark had experienced it, however, when he knew himself to be absolutely at fault. The heaviness of his heart at this moment was something he had never experienced; it seemed to outweigh everything else.

Drying himself off, he noticed, for the first time since the events in Jennifer's apartment, that his body bore no marks of the intensity of the passion. He wondered, as he stared at the image in the mirror, how it could be that Jennifer was so aggressive with him, yet he showed no signs of it little more than twelve hours later? Absolutely nothing confronted him in the mirror. Amazingly, for one brief second, he doubted anything had happened. It had all been his imagination playing tricks on him. While he instructed Jennifer about the history of the peace movement, his mind had imagined the love scene—that was it. It never happened!

One look at Fran in the kitchen erased the tendency toward denial that had overtaken him moments before. The waters had not completely washed his sins away. Fran said nothing as he took his vitamins before the kitchen sink, into which he had thrown up only hours earlier. She didn't have to say anything. Her face showed deep disappointment, and her silence was all the condemnation Lark needed to start the day.

Moments later, Lark entered the Glass Kitchen. Glancing around, he spied Doc sitting in a booth across the dining area. The late-morning breakfast crowd was lined up at the cash register to pay their bills as the hostess waved Lark through the entryway. "He's over there," she said, as Lark walked past the counter.

"Hi!" Doc said as Lark sat in the booth across from him. "How's it going?"

"Tough time getting started today," Lark said.

"You've got to watch burning that midnight oil," Doc said with a chuckle.

"Yes," Lark responded pleasantly, "I think you've got that right."

The waitress approached them, dressed in the usual Glass Kitchen uniform of heavily starched red and white checkered skirt, white blouse, and white cap. "What'll it be, men?" she inquired.

Doc glanced at his watch and then at Lark. "You got time for a piece of pie?" he asked.

Lark responded affirmatively, since he had skipped breakfast and could easily run it off at noon at the YMCA. They agreed on the Lancaster County tradition of shoo-fly pie and coffee for their late breakfast.

After the waitress left for their order, Doc said gingerly, "I wish you weren't going to Washington for that peace march." This was openers in what Lark sensed would be a great sparring match. "Can't you back off a little on that stuff, right now?" Doc wanted to know.

"You know I'm committed to see this through until that crazy war ends," Lark said simply.

"It's so hard for a vet like myself to accept what's happening," Doc said. He was sincere when he spoke. Despite his limited experience of warfare, Doc spoke often of his service to his country. And, when he did, people listened appreciatively. "I just can't understand why so many people are not supporting our troops," Doc continued.

The waitress returned with the pie and coffee. Doc grabbed the check; this one was on him. They ate their pie in silence until the last bit was savored and second cups of coffee were poured. Then, Doc looked at his watch and asked, "You got a few more minutes?"

Lark nodded affirmatively. He sat and listened while Doc lectured him about the dangers the nation was facing with the rebellion taking place. It had been five years since Lancaster itself spent a very scary night watching the southern part of the city burn and hearing sirens wail into the night, following the news of Martin Luther King's assassination. Doc assured Lark that revolution was not a pleasant sight, but anarchy was worse. "One moment after the battle every revolutionary is a conservative," Doc quoted some philosopher. Doc droned on. From time to time, he glanced at his watch, and then at Lark, as though he were timing his visit. There was a time when Doc's words would have penetrated Lark's consciousness. But this morning, Lark was also preoccupied with what had happened the night before.

"Lark," Doc asked, "weren't the Kennedys' and Martin Luther King's assassinations warning enough that we need to pull together? You know we can't go on like this—doubting our leaders and undercutting our boys in Vietnam the way you're doing. Besides, Nixon has promised an end to this."

"Doc," Lark said sarcastically at last, "Have you noticed that some of our boys are also marching? Maybe they know something none of the rest of us knows. We've heard promises before."

Doc seemed to ponder the statement for a moment, then leaned forward and said, "Lark, I like you. I don't agree with you at all on this one. But I like you. And I just have to tell you that you are in way over your head with this protest." It was received like a slap in the face from a parent. Lark, the child, didn't care

171

for it very much. From deep within him, anger roiled and he, himself, leaned forward toward Doc to the point that their chins nearly touched.

"Doc, I may be in over my head, as you say, but the protest is right. If we don't stop the military industrial complex now, that same bunch of fun-loving guys President Eisenhower himself warned us about twenty years ago, we're going to lose this country just like Germany lost theirs to the Nazis!"

Doc was stung. He sat back, red-faced and sullen. Pastor and parishioner stared at one another for what seemed like an eternity. Then, Doc forced a smile. "Alright, pastor," he said with an edge of sarcasm, "have it your way. But don't ever say I didn't warn you."

Until that point, Lark hadn't quite realized Doc was warning him about anything. He wondered what Doc meant. Doc looked at his watch again and then asked Lark, "Do you have time for one more piece of advice?"

Lark, more relaxed now, assured him there was time.

"Someone in the congregation is circulating a petition to fire you," Doc informed him. Lark let the words hang between them for a brief time, then responded in a manner which seemed to relieve Doc's tension for some reason.

"Maybe I will resign before they get enough signatures," Lark said quietly. There was a sense of resignation in his voice as he heard himself say it to Doc. Now he had uttered the words to both Fran and Doc. Maybe it would be easier to say it to the entire congregation when the time arrived. It felt easier this time. Doc's silence made the words seem all the more plausible to Lark.

Finally, it was Doc who broke the silence. "That will be a sorry day for St. Andrew Church," he said. It seemed to Lark that the old man meant it. Lark was, for the first time, aware that this man, in his own peculiar manner, had tried to be his friend. The circumstances of the nation seemed to always erect a wall seldom scaled between them. But for a brief second, it was transcended now, as the two men sat quietly in the Glass Kitchen and thought about the future.

By eleven, Lark was in the church office. Jane had placed a note on his desk about a call he had to return to Elsie. She wanted to talk about Sunday's service and the music in it. Seemed she had something special in mind for Sunday and needed Lark's approval before moving ahead. He dialed Elsie's number.

"Hello, this is the day God has given us, so let's rejoice and sing," was the way Elsie always answered her phone.

"This is Lark," was all he said. He waited for her to speak. They got along well if Lark didn't push her very much, and especially if he didn't seem to be as enthusiastic to talk with her as she always seemed with him.

"Hi!" she said with a voice that smiled through the phone lines. "I just remembered what we did last year this coming Sunday, and I thought you'd like to mark it some way in worship."

Lark immediately remembered that Sunday a year ago when Elsie informed him that she was playing back-up guitar for a group which was appearing on campus at F&M that afternoon.

She wondered if he'd like to go along and sing with them? Sure, he had nothing better to do. He thought she was kidding. The group's lead singer was a man named Jerry Garcia. Lark had never heard of the group called Grateful Dead. He was glad for the diversion, however. He went with her.

The afternoon was a once-in-a-lifetime experience for Lark. On stage with this band, he was transported to a whole other dimension. Surrounded by the sound of the musicians, he sensed how easy it might have been for him to simply "turn on, tune in, and drop out" as the saying went. He really didn't do much except just stand, become filled by the sound, note the reaction of the audience, and sing when the spirit moved him, which was quite frequently that afternoon. From time to time, Elsie glanced his way and smiled. She had invited Lark many times to join her and run away to Canada to live happily ever after. There were moments during that afternoon when he was ready to do just that. It was as close to living another life as he had ever been. It was as free and wonderful to him as anything he had ever known.

173

Now, Elsie wanted to celebrate it. He couldn't even talk about it with Fran. She never knew how very close he came to disappearing that afternoon. He could see the headlines. "Local Pastor And Organist Missing." What was she planning to do?

"I'd like you to sing one of their songs," she said. "I'll play my guitar, and you sing. We'll just mellow the congregation with one of Jerry's numbers."

"I don't know," he stammered. "I don't think I can."

"Sure you can," she assured him. "You've got a great voice. And, it'll be our way of pulling one over on the hard asses." She laughed. To think, at one time, he actually liked this brash young woman. Now, he feared her more than liked her; she knew him too well. She knew there wasn't much standing between him and the freedom she sought with him, except his commitment to his family and maybe to God. But he also knew she had seen him step outside that commitment once, when Lark had stood there in the midst of the performing group and lost all his inhibitions at once. She saw it. He knew she saw it, so he feared her.

"I'll give it some thought," he went on. "We don't have to decide this morning."

"Well, we might want to rehearse, you know," she said with a chuckle to her voice. In the early days of their working together, she often maneuvered him into meetings and rehearsals. Once, at her apartment which she shared with her partner, Elsie slipped him something in a lemonade. He was just alert enough to get out of there before something happened they would all regret. He saw the look of fear on Maria's face as she walked into the living room and saw Elsie sitting on Lark's lap, smiling at him like a lost puppy which had been found. That was the last time they met in her apartment for any reason. He was also careful about what food and drink he shared with the organist after that night.

"I'll let you know by Saturday morning," he said with a finality she seemed to accept.

"Okey Dokey," she replied. "Let's do it for old time's sake!" Then, she was gone. The nice thing about Elsie was Lark

174

could count on her forgetting most of their conversations fifteen minutes after they occurred. There was always the chance that by Saturday, she wouldn't even remember what day it was. She was a gifted musician, but she was lost in the generation someplace. A Mary J devotee, Elsie could be anywhere at any time. No one seemed to care. As long as she could play the organ the way she did, the congregation was most forgiving of all her idiosyncrasies. She was there to stay, as far as he could tell. He had learned to live with her by keeping his distance. He would manage this again, especially this week.

He thought of his and Doc's conversation at the Glass Kitchen. Doc really believed Nixon, who was a shoo-in at the Republican Convention, would keep a campaign promise and end the war in Vietnam. How could he? Didn't he know Nixon and those around him, especially the Pentagon leaders and chiefs of staff, had all lied about the realities of the war and our involvement beyond Vietnam's borders. Lark knew all of this. He read as much about the war and the politics behind it as he could get his hands upon. What infuriated him was that intelligent people like Doc couldn't understand why he took the positions he did.

Of course, there were some who did indeed understand and encouraged Lark to move the congregation toward ever-deeper involvement with the anti-war movement. These were the few who often commented on Sunday mornings, as they left the sanctuary and headed home, how very much they appreciated Lark's courage and integrity. Unfortunately, all of these persons seemed to live near the edges of the institutional church. Very few, if any, had sat around the tables of leadership during Lark's tenure. Ministry at St. Andrew Church was a lonely position because of this.

Lark had found support from a few seminary faculty and professors from F&M. And there were the few ecumenical colleagues like John who stood alongside Lark as he built the coalition of community protesters. Most recently, Lark had thought Jennifer would be a great addition to the group. But after last night, he knew that he would have great difficulty working with her, if at all.

175

As he sat at his desk, feeling generally sorry for himself and the mess he knew himself to be in at the moment, Jane walked into his office unexpectedly. She rarely came into it unannounced. She quietly sat in one of the chairs facing his desk. She waited for him to focus his full attention upon her presence.

"What is it?" he asked her. She looked worried, but maybe it was just the unusual heat of the morning, which Lark was gradually becoming aware of himself.

"Reverend Wilson, I received a very disturbing telephone call this morning, before you came in," she began rather shakily. "The man who called did not identify himself at all. He—" she hesitated.

"Go on," Lark said. The hairs on the back of his neck began to stand at attention.

"Well," she seemed unable to verbalize what the stranger had said to her, "he said I should be careful around you." She sat and stared at Lark. This woman, whom he knew to be an absolute professional, was now acting like a frightened sophomore with an experienced senior. Lark needed to know more.

"That was all he said?" Lark asked her.

"No," she hesitated once more. This seemed to be very difficult for her. Lark waited patiently for his secretary to gain the courage to share the message. He wondered, as he participated in this unprecedented conversation, whether this was what Doc had warned him about. Paranoia was beginning to drape its icy arms around the pastor of St. Andrew Church.

"He said they had proof that you are cheating on your wife and that I should not go near you."

There it was. Jane shook convulsively as the last part of the sentence slipped from her lips. She looked at Lark for some reassurance that this was some kind of prank. She waited for him to speak. He didn't. He was stunned by what she had just said. He understood her reaction, as he was having it, as well.

All at once, he thought he saw the outline of a plot. The thought absolutely frightened him. He was frozen now. His body convulsed in the presence of his secretary, but he said nothing.

176

"Well," she asked, "what's happening?" There was an edge to her voice now, which he had never heard before. He couldn't quite locate the tone in his library of human sounds, in order to interpret her question.

"Nothing," he said. "There's nothing to it. Probably just some kind of prank."

Jane smiled. She seemed to be such a trusting individual. She arose, seemingly more relaxed than when she entered the room.

"Do you have anything special for me this morning?" she asked. The nervousness was gone. She was back from the edge of the precipice the caller had placed between them.

"Nothing but the usual for today," Lark said with a forced smile. She turned and left him alone once more.

It was then he heard his children playing in the backyard nearby. They were oblivious to the drama being played out at this moment in his office which might have tremendous implications for them. Caught up as they were in their rivalries, one was calling the other what a child's mind perceives to be a bad name. Lark listened and thought what a wonderful thing it would be to be as free as a child again. Too bad children don't realize what an advantage they have in this world over those who must care for, protect, and nurture them toward adulthood.

Of course, there was the war when he was a boy, too. The fear of air-raid drills. The impatience of his parents which he didn't understand or appreciate. The moments of grief on the part of his mother when she got the letter about her brother. Lark had tried to console her, as she stood on the street corner, weeping uncontrollably, holding a crumpled yellow message in her hand. That damned war made his mother cry. Lark, even as a child, learned to hate what war did to those he loved.

As he listened to his children playing in the yard next door, he wondered just how much they were cognizant of the nation's suffering. This war wasn't like the one Lark had known as a child. There weren't rubber matinees, war stamps in school, aircraft factories nearby, every able-bodied man in the block going off to war and moms wearing pants and working in the factories. Except

177

for what they might be watching on TV, Lark and Fran's children had little awareness that young men and women of this nation were dying in a far off place. Lark longed to explain it to them, but Fran felt it would be too hard for them to grasp and that it might upset them.

Hence, instead of playing war games as he did when he was a child, Lark's children really fought over toys, privileges, and favors from their parents. Instead of dying almost everyday from some imaginary grenade, Lark's children lived on in the relatively secure environment of *Sesame Street* and *Mr. Roger's Neighborhood*. A gulf existed between Lark's childhood experience and that of his children, like that which Jesus metaphorically placed in his parable of Dives and Lazarus. Because of it, Lark knew, his children would not comprehend their father's personal involvement in protesting this war. When they became adults, he decided, he would sit and talk with them about his childhood, so they would understand him better.

The ringing phone brought him back. Jane informed him it was John calling. Lark noted it was almost noon as he picked up the receiver.

"Hey," John began, "how's it going?"

Lark was reassured by his friend's voice. "Not so good," Lark responded softly.

"Want to talk about it with someone who won't charge you a nickel?" John said sincerely.

"Yes," Lark said. "Can we have lunch together?"

"What? No game at the Y today?" John asked, startled. "What happened? Did the roof fall in last night or something?" he added.

"Something like that, only, more personal."

"Uh oh," John paused, "where are we going?"

"Let's just get something quick and go to Long's Park or someplace like that," Lark said quickly.

"Okay," John answered. "I'll be there in ten minutes."

Lark felt relaxed as he put the phone back on the receiver. He walked down the hall to the men's lavatory, waving to Jane as he walked by her office at the head of the stairs. Having relieved himself and washed his hands, he went back upstairs and heard Jane talking with someone on the phone as he walked into her office. She stopped talking and waited for him to speak to her.

"I'm having lunch with John today. I'll be back around two."

"No basketball game?" she asked with a smile.

"Not today," Lark said. "I just don't feel like it."

"See you later." She smiled and waited for him to leave before resuming her conversation.

Switching off the lights in his office, Lark walked outside to await John's arrival. Fran was standing in the backyard, talking with one of the children. He walked across the driveway and spoke with her by the fence.

"John and I are going to have lunch together today."

"Really?" Fran said, absolutely surprised by this change in Lark's usual routine. She smiled. He smiled back. "You look tired," was all she said, then turned to tend to the children and their needs, just as John's convertible pulled into the driveway. The top was down, appropriately for this hot, muggy, Lancaster summer day.

"Your chariot awaits," John said in mock servitude, as Lark climbed into it.

"Yeah, yeah, I've heard all of this before," Lark said. The two men laughed heartily as they drove through the church parking lot, and turned on the street.

"What'll it be?" John asked. "Shall we go to Roy Rogers, or McDonalds, or what?"

"You pick. I'm not that hungry," Lark said with disinterest. Little else was said between them as they drove to the newly opened Roy Rogers. Once their lunches of roast beef, fries, and drinks were served, the two men hopped back into the convertible and made their way to the park. Once lunch was finished, it was John who broke the silence.

"I don't believe I've ever seen you this quiet, Lark. What's going on?"

"I hardly know where to start," Lark said. He began to the share the events of the past sixteen hours. John was a good listener; never once did he interrupt, nor did he show any emotional response to anything Lark shared with him. Finally, Lark concluded with the strange phone call Jane had received prior to his arrival earlier this morning. "Then, you called, and here we are," Lark finished up.

The two men sat in silence a moment or two. John broke the silence anew. "Are you alright?" he asked.

Lark became suddenly conscious that his body was shaking. He felt so naked, sitting there with his best friend. He had risked their friendship by sharing this experience, with all of its feelings, just as John had done with him when his marriage was coming apart not too long ago.

"I just don't know," Lark said nervously. "I feel like I'm on a runaway train!"

"What can I do to help?" John asked sincerely. To this point, Lark had only thought about talking this out with someone he trusted. He hadn't thought anyone could help him. But, the sincerity of John's request opened a door Lark hadn't thought was there.

"I feel like I'm caught in some kind of conspiracy, John," Lark said with an edge to his voice. "I don't know whether I'm becoming paranoid. Maybe this is all just one big conspiracy. But —"

"Look, friend," John stepped in, "you are not paranoid. Something's coming down; that's for sure. But, neither of us sitting here knows exactly what the purpose of it is. You want to know what I think?"

"I thought that was what you were already doing," Lark said, relaxing a bit. The two men looked at one another and laughed. John had such a hearty laugh, folks in the early civil-rights struggle days used to say that his laugh could have gotten Bull Conner to pen his dogs!

"Well, I think that Jennifer's the coincidence in all of this that you need to look at differently."

"What do you mean?" Lark asked.

"Well, think about it," John went on. "She was just at Penn Station. She seemed interested in you more than you were in her, as far as I could see. Maybe she's just a very fast operator from the Big Apple, but that's not who she said she was now, right?"

Lark was thinking. There was little doubt he had found her attractive and responded to her playful flirting in ways he probably would have avoided from others. He had let his guard down with this person he hardly knew at all, simply because she introduced herself as a professional educator, seemed very intelligent, and expressed genuine interest in his pursuits of peace. She seemed to know more about him in less time than anyone he had ever met in his life. And this had flattered him to the point of distraction. She had pursued the relationship after their chance meeting at Pennsylvania Station; John was right about that.

"You're right," Lark said with growing confidence. "I have to confront her and get to know who she really is. Would you help set this up for me?" Lark felt he had an idea that just might work. John could invite Jennifer for a drink at the Horse, and Lark would just show up. The two men could then confront her about her past and present identity. Yes! To Lark, this made sense.

"What do you want me to do?"

"Make a date with her for tonight," Lark said. "I'll handle the rest."

"Oh, you sly one," John winked. "But aren't you forgetting something?"

"What?" Lark asked him.

"I don't like redheads," John said. He started to roll with laughter. "Seriously, Lark," he continued, getting control of himself, "I'll help. Give me an hour alone with her tonight, then you show up. I'll work my way out of the place so you can confront her. I'll use my good ol' southern charm on her, she'll be so soft and cuddly by the time you show up, she'll just be purring like a kitten!" He laughed again as Lark chuckled with him.

"You call me and let me know where and when," Lark said.

The two men stood up, embraced, and walked to the convertible, humming as they went. Lark felt more relaxed that he had in days. He had to know if Jennifer was part of some plot to bring his ministry down. A suspicion was growing. And, anger was beginning to replace the fear which gripped him before. To think that someone or some group wanted to get rid of him so desperately, they would think not only of despoiling his reputation as a minister of the gospel, but destroy his family as well, seemed to galvanize him at the moment. Suddenly, through his conversation with John, he was regaining courage for the struggle. More than that, Lark was awakening. He smelled something in all of this suddenly, and he was getting ready to go on the prowl. Whoever was out to get him was known to Doc, had spoken to Jane, and no doubt, felt safe at the moment. This wouldn't protect whoever it was from the vindication Lark would win in the end. There was almost a spring in his step as he exited John's car in the church parking lot moments later, bounded up the steps, and entered the hallway which led to his office.

Chapter 21
THE DELIVERY

Only minutes after Lark entered his study, Clyde arrived, red-faced and agitated. This was the last man Lark wanted to see, but, here he was. Clyde, the retired FBI investigator assigned to Lancaster nearly twenty years before his retirement because of some blown case nobody could remember, finished his years of service by tracking down rustlers in the Lancaster stockyards. Forever angry about his sudden and irreversible decline in the ranks of government, Clyde was known to be short with everyone in his family, anyone with whom he dealt socially, and impossibly acerbic with those who crossed him.

For St. Andrew Church, Clyde was not a welcome addition to the membership. He joined after Lark became its pastor and after rejection from seven other churches of various denominations during his residence in the city. Pastors were known to have got down on their knees to thank God each time Clyde came into their studies and demanded a letter of transfer of membership.

In short, Clyde could be a royal pain in the ass, even to God. And Clyde had somehow managed to get himself elected to the leadership of St. Andrew two years ago. This meant, for Lark, that there was one, always in the midst of important meetings of the consistory and of the congregation, of whom he was especially wary. Having Clyde walk into his study today, looking as he did when he arrived, was nothing but bad news, and the pastor knew it.

Clyde didn't even wait for the usual niceties to occur. He walked straight to the pastor's desk, threw an envelope upon it, and demanded in a voice which might have been heard three blocks in all directions, "All I want to know is what the Hell is going on."

He stood and waited as Lark hesitantly picked up the envelope and opened it. Eight black and white photographs fell in a random mix upon his desk. One glance at them, and Lark knew he was in big trouble. There, before his eyes were scenes from the night before in Jennifer's apartment. Lark at the door in an embrace of Jennifer. Lark and Jennifer in various stages of undress. Lark and Jennifer making love on her apartment floor. What could Lark say? The pictures seemed to put the events of the night before together in a way his mind could not. And, yet, there was something not quite right about them.

As Lark looked at each one a second time, studying each with more scrutiny than his first perusal of them, little details stood out. The only one which showed his face was the parting embrace at Jennifer's door. The other seven photographs did not reveal his face, but Jennifer's was ecstatic. Jennifer, hair thrown back over her shoulder, atop Lark, seemingly enjoying every movement of her pelvis. Jennifer kneeling before Lark, whose back was to the camera, his hands resting ever so lightly upon her shoulders. Jennifer, upon her back, legs around Lark's waist in a lover's embrace. It was all there. Lark could not deny it. The photos seemed to reveal to him, the participant, the truth of the night before.

Lark was suddenly very ill. His stomach turned and he knew he must exit, or he would throw up all over Clyde. Clyde must have sensed Lark's dilemma, for he stepped back from the desk and began to sit in one of the office chairs. Lark arose, dashed outside the building and leaned upon the railing atop the stairway landing. His gut wrenched. He knew he was losing it.

Grabbing the railing, Lark did the only thing a person can do in such circumstance. It was totally involuntary and absolutely embarrassing. Lark heaved his entire dinner over the railing and into the parking lot.

Until the vomit hit the paved lot, Fran and the children had been oblivious to Lark's presence only a few yards from them as they played in the postage-stamp backyard of the parsonage. It was Leigh Ann who spied her father just as he heaved anew across the railing. This time, it was breakfast.

"Daddy's sick," she said. She pointed toward the church building. Turning, Fran could see in an instant that her husband was violently ill. She instructed Walt to take the two younger children inside, while she attended to Daddy. Then, she dashed across the parking lot and up the stairs. She gently took Lark into her arms and held his body as he convulsed across the railing again. Lark groaned as his body lurched forward again and nothing came up. Sweat broke out upon his forehead, and a cold sweat began to trickle down his back.

Fran wiped his brow with her hand and stared at him. "There, there," she said, just as she had done with the children many times. "What's the matter, Lark?"

"Oh, Fran," was all he could muster before he jerked forward involuntarily once more. She held him and tried to calm him, as she gently sat him down upon the concrete landing.

"I'll go in and get you some water and a cold towel," she said. "You just sit here. I'll be back in seconds." With that, Fran entered the church building before Lark could stop her. As he sat outside, he could hear Clyde's agitated voice inside. Then he heard Fran scream. The sound of her scream was like a trapped wild animal. Pity gripped Lark's soul, as he pictured the scene now taking place in his office. He had to pull himself together and minister to his wife. Clyde, the old blusterer, must have shown the photos to her.

When Lark entered his study, Clyde still sat in the chair he had taken as Lark dashed from the room. "I tried to stop her," Clyde said to Lark's back. Lark's attention now was riveted upon his wife. She stood in the center of the room, stooped across the desk, peering at each photo and sobbing.

Lark stepped forward to console her as she had done for him only moments before. Fran recoiled at his touch and twisted away from him, throwing the pictures upon the floor as she walked from the study.

"Fran," Lark called to her in vain. The door slammed behind her and her feet moved swiftly down the steps. Lark walked around the room, picked up the photos, and returned to his desk.

"I know this looks horrible," he said to Clyde quietly, his mind hardly focused upon what he was saying. "There is nothing I can say to you about this at this time."

"What the Hell's that supposed to mean?" Clyde yelled just as Jane appeared at the study doorway with a look upon her face which Lark had never seen before.

"I don't know what I mean right now," Lark continued in a tone which suggested he was in control. But inwardly, his life was coming apart. He shot Jane a glance as if to say 'it's alright, I can handle this.'

"All I know is that you have every right to be upset about this, Clyde," Lark continued. "And you have a right to an explanation. I promise you, there will be one."

Jane turned from the doorway and walked back to her office. Clyde sat, eying his pastor in silence.

"May I ask you a question?" Lark said. "How did you get these?"

"They were in my mailbox this afternoon," Clyde retorted. "How the Hell do I know how they got there?"

"Well, did they come in this envelope?" Lark inquired.

"Obviously," the older man responded, now no longer shouting, but no less red-faced. "Someone put these in my mail box. I don't usually get mail until three in the afternoon."

"I see," said Lark, wondering just how many other people had such special deliveries to their homes since last night.

"I tell you this, pastor," shouted Clyde once more. "I don't give a tinker's damn how they got there or who delivered them.

I want to know what the Hell's going on, and, I'm going to pursue this! You hear me?"

With the last shout, he seemed nearly exhausted. Lark had a new concern, he wondered how well Clyde was, and whether Clyde could handle his lifestyle of anger and paranoia much longer before he suffered a stroke or heart attack.

"May I keep the photos for a day or two?" Lark asked in as calm a fashion as he could at the moment.

"Not on your life," Clyde said, determinedly. "Besides, how am I going to get to the bottom of this without them?"

Lark could never persuade this man to give up a minute of precious time. Clyde was going to solve this, and it mattered little to him who got hurt, or even destroyed, in the process. Lark gave no response to Clyde's question. He simply gathered up the photos once more, looked at them carefully as the two men sat in silence for a few minutes, put them back into the envelope, and handed them to Clyde. It was then that Lark noticed, for the first time, that the envelope had no address, name, or identification of any kind upon it. No doubt it would have no fingerprints, either.

"I promise you, Clyde," Lark said, as he handed the photos to this bombastic leader of the church, "I'll have an explanation for this soon."

"You damned well better," was all Clyde said. He stormed out of the office in much the same manner as he had entered it moments before. Lark breathed deeply as the man exited the building. He wondered to himself how many copies of the photos had been delivered to other church members? He also couldn't help but wonder how it was that a photographer could have been so close in Jennifer's apartment the night before and not be seen nor heard. This was a mystery, but the photos raised other questions, as well. He didn't remember the events of the night before in the way the photos depicted them. Something about one of the photos bothered him, but he just couldn't focus on it.

Walking down the hallway to go to the pop machine downstairs, Lark heard Jane sobbing in her office. As he entered the office, one glance revealed that yet another person had received photos. There on Jane's desk lay copies of the same photographs Clyde had received. Jane looked up, wiped a tear from her eye, and tried to compose herself in his presence.

"These were on my desk when I came back from lunch," she said. "There was no name on the envelope, so I opened it to see what was inside."

"I'm sorry, Jane," Lark said, trying to be as reassuring as he could with her. "I can't talk about them right now."

"I guess not," she said. "May I have the rest of the day off?"

"Of course," Lark replied gently.

"I'm not sure—" she hesitated.

"Yes, go on," Lark encouraged her.

"Well," she hesitated. "I'm not sure I'll be here tomorrow."

Lark now sought to assure Jane that she had nothing to worry about by being in the building alone with him. He told her that there were lots of questions about the photos, and that he and Clyde were working on it. He sought to assure her that she would be safe. He could tell, as he spoke, that she was in grief. This simple product of a genuinely uncomplicated Christian upbringing would need some time to cope with what she had just seen. He backed off. "Sure," he said. "Take all the time you need."

"Thank you," Jane said quietly. She put the photos in the envelope in which they had been delivered. "Here, you may have these," she said. She reached out toward Lark, he took them in hand, and went downstairs.

Moments later he looked at the pictures once more. Lark was overcome with a horrible sadness. He could not think of anything but resigning. He knew he had broken two very important vows. His marriage was in jeopardy. He wanted to walk across to the house and talk with Fran. Yet, he just could not face her; she looked so horrible when she left the office. Now that he knew two sets of photos were out there among church members, he could not help but assume there were many more. Hence, he surmised his career in ministry was crumbling around his feet.

He called the regional office of the church and asked the secretary to put him in touch with the minister who oversaw the region. Explaining very little except that he was going to resign immediately following Sunday's service, and saying only that he wanted to meet the ministry committee to seek a leave of absence, Lark informed the man who oversaw the region for the denomination in a most professional manner. Never too fond of this leader, Lark knew that he would find little if any support from Harry, who had led the region for only three years and who showed very little respect for Lark's involvement with anti-war activities. No doubt, as most church leaders were experiencing, Harry was not very enthusiastic about fielding all of the questions, charges, and complaints he was receiving about clergy like Lark, whose congregations sought relief for their discomfort from the top echelons of mainline Protestant denominations. Harry had publicly stated at a conference that he felt some clergy were acting immaturely and needed to take a more expansive view of history. As Lark looked at US history, he found only two other times when church life in America was so disrupted: there was the revolution which split churches on loyalist and colonialist lines; and, a century ago, it was the civil war that divided the churches into camps from which few had broken until the Vietnam conflict was engaged. So, when Lark took the long view, as Harry suggested, he felt consoled in standing for the positions he did with the people he served.

Hanging up, Lark set about writing a formal letter to the committee on ministry, requesting an indefinite leave of absence immediately following Sunday's service. Knowing that he would have to appear before the committee to formally seek action on the request, Lark avoided the temptation to write details leading up to his decision into the letter. It simply contained two short sentences:

Dear Committee on Ministry:
I request a leave of absence from active ministry following the Sunday morning service at

St. Andrew Church. I will await your invitation to
appear before you in order to act upon this request.

> *Sincerely,*
> *Lark Wilson*

Glancing over the letter, Lark noted that he had not dated it. After adding the date to the top, he sealed and stamped it. Then, he set about the task of writing a formal resignation to the congregation. This would need to be mailed immediately, if the members were to get it before Sunday. After obtaining a mimeograph master from the work room, Lark reluctantly sat down at the typewriter and wrote:

Dear Friends In Christ:

I have decided to resign my position as pastor and teacher of St. Andrew Church, effective immediately following this coming Sunday's service of worship. I do so with a heavy heart, but with the firm conviction that doing so is within the will of God for me and you.

I will ask the committee on ministry of our region to grant me an indefinite leave of absence from ministry, believing that such action will give me the necessary time to discern any future possibilities for service in Christ's name.

Please know how very much I have appreciated your faithful support of St. Andrew Church during my tenure. And know also that I will hold each and every one of you in my prayers, as I trust you will do for me when we part. "May Christ's peace be with you all."

> *Sincerely,*
> *Lark*

Quickly, Lark took the master to the work room and placed it upon the cylinder of that hand-turned machine affectionately referred to in his seminary days as "the prayer wheel." His classmates no doubt would be amused to learn that Lark often did some of his best praying as he stood before this ancient reproduction machine and turned it over and over, as sheet after sheet of whatever he was doing at the time was ejected onto the holding tray. Mimeographing was always a messy job, especially in summer months when one never knew exactly how warm and runny the ink might be.

This afternoon was no exception. From time to time, as copies of his letter jumped from the bowels of the slowly turning machine, giant globs of ink were emitted with them. One always wasted paper with such machines, for invariably, some copies were ruined by giant Rorschach-like blots of ink when they landed upon the paper.

Once the task was done, Lark removed the master from the cylinder as carefully as he could, getting runny ink beneath his fingernails as he meticulously lifted it and threw it in the waste can. Then, he put the brown paper cover back upon the cylinder, stretching it so the end would fit beneath the spring loaded clasp. Lifting the copies carefully so as to not mar the still-wet ink upon each sheet, Lark walked into the church office to look for a set of labels, which he knew Jane stashed in one of her desk drawers. After finding them, he took a box of envelopes and the letters back to his study to prepare the mailing for the congregation.

One hour later, he had affixed the last label and folded the last letter. A glance at the clock on the wall revealed to Lark that all he had to do was walk the letters to the corner mailbox. The mail was not picked up until five. Grabbing the letters, he walked by Jane's office and out the south office door, so as to avoid seeing Fran. He quickly walked to the corner and dropped the letters into it. Breathing a sigh a relief, and with no taste of buyer's remorse, the pastor and teacher of St. Andrew Church walked back with a sense of relief he hadn't expected.

As he entered the building, the phone was ringing. It would be Fran, he thought. He dashed into his study and picked up the phone, slightly out of breath as he answered.

"I can't find her," John's voice reported, with more than a slight edge to it.

"What?" Lark said incredulously.

"She's vanished, man," John said nervously. "She checked out early this morning and nobody has seen her since. The apartment manager said she had only had a one-week lease."

"That's impossible," Lark said, annoyed. "What about her teaching assignment?"

"I don't know whether you are ready to hear this or not, buddy," John continued, "but when I called F&M, nobody knew anything about her."

Lark was stunned. His heart skipped a beat. His head pounded as Doc's words from earlier in the day echoed through his memory. Lark really was into something which was bigger than he had ever experienced. His rumination was broken by John's anxious voice.

"What do you want me to do?" John asked sincerely.

"I don't know," was all Lark could muster. Without even bidding his good friend farewell, Lark hung up the receiver. For what seemed like a century, Lark sat in his office alone, head buried in his hands, weeping quietly. God seemed so far away from him. More than light years away and absolutely immutable. The calm that was his only moments before was gone now. Only torment filled his soul, as he contemplated his personal landscape from a watery point of view. He lay his head upon his desk and wept.

Just before five, Lark lifted his head, straightened his tie, and rubbed his burning eyes. Then, he arose and walked out of the building. He would go home and have supper with the children and Fran. Then, following the evening reverie with the children, he and Fran would talk this out somehow.

But, as he walked toward the parsonage, he could tell at a glance that Fran and the children were not home. The station

192

wagon was not in its usual place. The kitchen looked as though it had been left in a hurry. Luncheon plates and dirty glasses still rested upon the table. Even the Kool-Aid pitcher stood on the table.

Walking through the house, Lark noted that quick changes of clothes had preceded their departure. Children's clothing, which Fran usually was most meticulous about putting into the hamper or back upon closet hooks, was now strewn about on the dining room and living room floors. Lark wondered if there had been another mishap. Perhaps a child had fallen and Fran rushed all to the hospital, but she would have left a note. There was none.

Lark walked about aimlessly, picking up clothes and putting them in the hamper in the washroom. He put the Kool-Aid pitcher back into the refrigerator and washed the dishes, dried them, and put them away. In barely an hour he had the house looking normal, but there was still no sign of his family.

He walked into the living room, now feeling desperately alone. Lark found himself sitting at the ancient piano he had bought two years before from a Lancaster County farmer who had kept it in his barn for twenty-five years. "I'll take a dollar for each year it sat in that barn gathering dust," he had said to Lark.

They drove it home with great excitement that day in a pick-up Lark had borrowed from Ed down the street. Lark spent every hour of free time he had for the next four months refinishing the huge upright. The living room was a mixture of paint brushes, sandpaper, paint remover, new paint, and dust from May until September. Finally, it was complete. All stood back to admire it. The children loved playing it. They didn't seem to mind that, from time to time, important keys refused to respond to their touch; they just chose another key.

As Lark sat before the piano, he remembered how, in fourth grade, he had wanted to learn to play. The teacher asked the class members who had pianos in their homes. Only four hands rose. The teacher worked with those four at the classroom piano. All others were given a handcrafted wooden keyboard upon which they were instructed to play in their minds, as those who already had pianos played upon the real thing. Lark asked his teacher, Mrs. Ryan, many times if he could play on the real piano. Her only response was, "Lark, do you have a piano in your home?" He would hang his head and answer, "No ma'am." That was it. He never played for her or anyone else. He never told his parents how disappointed he was that they could not afford a piano. It was then, in the fourth grade, that Lark determined to get a piano for the children he would parent some day.

His fingers moved across the keys. Without much thought, Lark was playing some pieces he had learned as a seminary student. Hymns were easy to play, he learned, for one already knew how they were supposed to sound. Without any formal training in the art, Lark, as an adult, fulfilled a childhood dream and taught himself to play. "Beautiful Savior" came forth, as his fingers slowly caressed each note and his feet upon the pedal pulled forth each sound for as long as the old strings could vibrate. Then, "Be Thou My Vision," with its haunting Irish melody, was heard through the open windows on the street. And, finally, the song Lark always came back to when his soul was troubled and his heart nearly broken. He could not remember ever working on it. He just sat one day and played it, as he was doing this evening. Suddenly, there its notes were, as his fingers moved gently, playing ever so quietly, "Dixieland."

As he played, one could envision lonely Rebel soldiers lying mortally wounded upon the fields of Antietam or Gettysburg. Lying there upon their backs, gazing into an unfamiliar sky, struggling for breath and life, yet knowing they were going to die, they prayed to go back home. It was not right to die in a strange land, to be buried with hundreds, maybe thousands of others, in a common, unnamed grave, in dirt not one's own, beneath trees which others had planted. One could hear their prayers being lifted, as Lark quietly played the soulful tune which, when played by a band, had become a rallying march, but when played in the manner in which Lark styled it, could only be identified as a mournful dirge.

194

Once it was played, fatigue swept across Lark's body. A tiredness he had never known before embraced his very being. Barely able to move, Lark got up from the piano, walked the few steps to the couch, and lay down upon it. Within seconds, the world was gone.

Chapter 22
THE DESERT

For some time, Lark wandered aimlessly across a land as foreign as any he had known before. Treeless, except for an occasional scrub pine leaning awkwardly one way or another, and absolutely lifeless, as far as he could discern, this land seemed Godforsaken as any he had ever seen. Voices inhabited it somehow, but, they were unidentifiable. He could hear them from time to time, as he seemed to walk toward an endless horizon.

A voice as soft as raindrops in a desert was reading a very familiar text to Lark. He couldn't see who was reading, but he knew what the unseen presence with him on this journey was saying, "The Spirit helps us in our weakness; for we do not know how to pray as we ought...."

The landscape subtly changed as Lark stood to listen to the voice. As he stood, he noted a breeze moving across the land. A sturdy breeze which bent the tall grasses and unusual flowers of this region. Looking up, Lark noted that the sky was a brilliant azure, with sunlight streaming from every direction. He had never seen such a land. It held a mystery and beauty unknown to him.

As he reflected upon the words spoken only moments before, he thought to himself how inadequate his prayers were for those to whom he ministered from time to time. But inadequate as they were, in his opinion, they were far more beneficial than any he had said in his own behalf. God never seemed to have time for this busy minister, thought Lark.

He began to walk once more. And as he did, the landscape around him changed dramatically. Banks of fog slowly rolled across the dreamscape and the air around him chilled precipitously. The crisp, still air produced a deafening silence, as hoarfrost seemed to entomb everything in its reach, freezing it and him.

The voice was heard anew, this time more loudly than before, "The Spirit helps us in our weakness; for we do not know how to pray as we ought, but the Spirit intercedes for us with sighs too deep for words." Lark stood motionless, frozen in time, as these ancient words pricked a level of consciousness in him that had never quite responded before. He felt compelled to ask a question of his unseen host.

He heard himself shout aloud words which were very familiar to him: "Lord, teach us to pray." Lark was now highly agitated and fitful, in this place so strange to him. His body began to shiver in the cold that surrounded him. He noted the plants around him were actually going into their winter hibernation as he watched. Frost-covered plants began to get smaller, then bend toward the ground as snow started to fall—first, great big flakes, and then like rain which might never stop. The wind picked up and began tossing the snow around in all directions, until Lark could no longer see his hands in front of his face. His body stiffened, and he imagined he would die here.

Death, when it comes, is so unexpected, thought Lark. How often we humans project onto animals an inability to comprehend the future and the certainty of their demise. We like to think that this is what separates us from them, what makes us more intelligent. And, yet, Lark often had stood beside a dying patient whose eyes revealed the absolute disbelief in what they were experiencing or prayed with a loved one who, likewise, could not accept the fact of death. Now, Lark mused, here I am dying in this wilderness I have never visited before, and it too, is an absolute surprise to me. Lark needed to make peace before he *breathed his last breath. He could barely feel his skin upon his body. Everything was becoming numb in the cold.*

Lark tried to speak, but the blizzard prevented him from opening his mouth. His body shook convulsively now as he stood, the snow getting higher than he imagined possible. He wanted to cry out to anyone who might be nearby, so that he might be saved from this fate, yet he could not move a muscle. His spirit sank as he resigned himself to dying here, far from anyone he knew, in a strange land, utterly alone. "God have mercy upon me," he breathed.

Above the howling wind and blinding snow, there came the voice once more. Lark strained to hear it. There it was. He heard it again. What was that it was saying? "We know that in everything God works for good with those who love him."

Lark began to cry, the tears freezing upon his face as they fell from his eyes. Those words which he had read at hundreds of funerals were so real to him now that he could almost taste them. The emotions he felt, as he stood freezing in this desert dream, were overwhelming. He cried for what seemed like hours. And, as he cried, out of the snowstorm persons Lark had buried came to him, one by one, and held him close. Their bodies kept him warm and protected him from the fierceness of the storm around him. Soon, they were coming two by two. Each spoke not a word, but simply reached out and hugged their pastor, the one who had helped to carry them across the river to the promised land. Then, as the storm howled against them, all of the people Lark had buried came and surrounded him. Faces turned from Lark into the teeth of the storm. And, as they stood, they began to sing. Lark could hear their voices above the winds which seemed to grow with each stanza that they sang:

"Of the Father's love begotten Ere the worlds began to be, He is Alpha and Omega, He the source, the ending He Of the things that are, that have been, And that future years shall see, Evermore and evermore."

He wondered how long he had been here? They continued to chant Lark's favorite plain song verse:

    "O ye heights of heaven adore Him, Angel hosts,
        His praises sing;
    Powers, dominions bow before Him, and extol our
        God and King;
    Let no tongue on earth be silent,
    Every voice in concert ring,
    Evermore and evermore!"

Suddenly, Lark was in a completely different environment. Almost as cold and sterile as before, except its antiseptic appearance and smell made him aware at once that this was an operating room in a hospital. From his vantage point, he could see the table on which someone was to be operated upon. Surgeons and nurses, along with an anesthetist, were milling about, chatting with one another as they prepared the room. Within seconds, a nurse wheeled the patient into the softly lit room on a gurney. "Here's the patient," she said as the doctors, nurses, and anesthetist hovered around. With one orchestrated lift and heave, the patient was upon its back on the operating table. It was a pig.

The surgical wrap was quickly placed around the squealing critter; its face glowing red with terror at the sight of those around it. Squirming to get free of the straps which had been placed around its legs, the pig pushed this way and that until a mask was placed over its snout and the anesthetist began the countdown into the subconscious journey.

The chief surgeon bent over the now relaxed animal and asked the nurse for a scalpel. Lark watched as the surgeon deftly cut into the pig's abdomen, pushed aside layers of muscle, fat, and gristle, until the ribs were exposed. They heaved up and down to an ancient rhythm as the pig breathed in and out. All leaned forward as the surgeon tied off bleeders as he went deeper into the abdominal cavity. Reaching up under the ribs he announced, "There it is!"

More cutting ensued, as nurses now finished tying off arteries and wiping the surgeon's brow. Suddenly, his hand came forth from the inner part of the pig's body. He was holding something large and yellow in his hand. He had removed it, whatever it was.

Holding it aloft, the surgeon announced, "This is the winter of our discontent!" There was a hush in the room for but a few seconds, until one of the nurses said, "It sure is big, doctor." All agreed as each took a closer look at the organ which had been taken from the innards of the pig.

Then, to Lark's amazement, they broke into song as they repaired the body of the pig, now that whatever it was they wanted to remove had been taken from it. The song was another familiar hymn to Lark:

"In the bleak mid-Winter, frosty wind made moan,
Earth stood hard as iron, water like a stone;
Snow had fallen, snow on snow, snow on snow,
In the bleak mid-Winter, long time ago..."

Lark listened intently, as the group sang better than any choir Lark had ever heard. And, as they sang, they began to move slowly around the operating table in a gentle, snake-like walk:

"Our God transcends all heaven, earth, and its domain;
Heaven and earth shall flee away when Christ comes to reign;
In the bleak mid-Winter a stable place sufficed
The sovereign God almighty, Jesus Christ!"

The mask removed from the pig's snout now, the animal joined in song with those around it, singing solo as they hummed in accompaniment:

"What can I offer, poor as I am?
If I were a shepherd, I would bring a lamb.
If I were a wise man, I would do my part;
But what can I offer: all my heart."

200

Lark found himself upon the plain once more. It was springtime. Birds sang as they flew from high grass to weed. Water puddles stood now, where snow had been before. The sun shone brightly upon the windswept area in which he stood. It was a warm wind, with just a hint of violets in it. Nothing else had changed about this place, however. It was as desolate as when he last came this way nocturnally.

He began to walk across the hills and grasses. They bent easily beneath his feet. From time to time, he stepped into soft earth and mud, which seemed to claim him right then and there.

As he walked, he thought he heard the cry of an animal. At first, it was distant, but as he walked toward the top of a gentle slope, the sound clearly came from the other side of it. The cries became louder. The animal sounded as though it were a young one, lost from its mother, in need of comforting.

Upon reaching the top of the rise, Lark looked down onto a vast, flat plain stretching endlessly before him. At first, he didn't see the animal, for the area before him was so big, it almost took his breath away. Not a tree upon it, the plain before him stood empty save one scraggly little beast. It looked like a miniature imitation of what it would surely grow up to be some day. And, Lark wondered, as he studied the creature crying out, not more than thirty yards below him, whether all young ones were this color? Was this their first coat, the albino fur? The eyes of the creature looked almost blue in the sunlight.

Lark walked down the hill toward where the little calf stood. As he approached, the critter did a most unusual thing. Lifting its rear legs and its right front hoof, the little white buffalo stood upon its left front leg alone. It stopped its crying, and simply stood motionless as Lark walked right up to it. As Lark reached toward the head of the buffalo calf, it spoke to him.

"Come and help us," was all it said. Lark touched its furry head.

"Come and help us," the beast said again more loudly than before.

Lark was startled now, for when it spoke the second time, its voice was like that of Fran's. Again, there it was, the sound of the voice as the image began to fade, "Lark, come and help us!"

Lark awoke to calls for help from his wife. She stood in the kitchen doorway, calling to him. It was dark outside, so Lark knew it was probably the children's bedtime. He staggered from the couch and walked toward the kitchen where Fran stood.

"All of the children are asleep in the car, Lark. Come on, help me get them into the house."

"Okay," was his only answer. He began to come back to reality and awareness of consciousness. Once outside, Lark saw Doc and Millie's car in the driveway. Millie simply said, "Hello," as Lark assisted Fran with the three little ones who rested against one another in the back seat. Carrying each one as gently as they could up the stairs to their bedroom, Lark and Fran said nothing to each other. Having done this many times before, they simply lay each child in his and her bed and walked silently from the room. When Lark returned to the kitchen, he heard Fran saying good night to Millie, and then their car drove slowly away.

For the first time since the morning, Lark and Fran were face to face alone. They stood, eyeing one another carefully. Lark must have looked a mess. Fran didn't appear to be in such good shape, either. Lark glanced at the clock above the kitchen sink for the first time since he was awakened and realized it was nearly midnight.

"I must have dozed off," he said quietly.

"Yeah," was her only response. But, the tone carried a disgust he had rarely felt from her.

"Look, Fran," he continued, "I know how this must look to you. But, you've got to believe me when I say that I am as confused by this as you are."

She sat down at the picnic table, head in her hands, and sobbed. Her body simply quivered, as she tried to keep from crying to no avail. Lark sat opposite her and reached for her hand. When he touched her, she lifted her head and looked at him with such anguish that his heart nearly broke at the sight of it.

"Why? Haven't I been a good wife?"

"Sure you—" he couldn't continue. The lump in his throat was so large. He was on the verge of crying again. The two sat, looking at one another for a long time, saying nothing.

"I never thought you'd do this to me, " she finally said. The hardness in her tone caught him off guard. Her eyes were now fixed upon his face, and a certain resolve grew in them as she spoke.

"I've supported you throughout our life together. I've gone to the limit for you when you were in tough places. I've even taken risks for you. For what?" she asked.

He could not answer. It was her turn to talk. He simply waited for the avalanche to proceed.

"You have a wife and three darling children," she went on, as if rehearsed. "You have a good ministry. Most of the people of this parish really respect you and follow your leadership. You are well-known in our church. You are admired in the city. You have been able to do whatever you like, go whenever you want, and be with whomever you wish. Why this?" she demanded.

Lark did not answer. Fran was determined to speak to him, not listen. This was obvious to him, so he sat and waited for her to continue. With each sentence, her face drew tighter and muscles contorted like a person enraged. But her voice was soft, almost hypnotic, as she spoke.

"My parents will be devastated by this, you know. After all they've done for us, you go and screw around with some whore you don't even know, instead of being faithful to me, your wife, their daughter." She paused.

Lark could no longer look at her as she spoke; it was too hard. She was speaking truth in ways perhaps even she didn't yet comprehend. He had been unfaithful to her. Even though he couldn't accept what the photographs revealed about his visit to Jennifer's apartment, he knew that Fran was absolutely right.

For Lark, this lack of fidelity was based upon his emotional reactions with Jennifer, however, and not upon any physical manifestations of it. Something in him had died when he first talked with Jennifer, he believed. He had obsessed with her in ways he had with Fran when they first met. He saw it all, now.

"And I thought you'd never break your ordination vows," she said in a whisper. "How could you?" Her voice was so low, it was not unlike the way in which Lark had always imagined Eve whispered to Adam in the Garden of Eden, whenever she didn't want God to hear what she said. "Do you have anything to say for yourself, Lark?" she demanded.

Lark knew that he had just been tried, found guilty, and sentenced. What could he say? Fran was sure she had it all down. She was married to a man with no personal conscience, no professional or ethical standards, no Christian morality, and no fidelity. He was very tired. He wanted to lie down right there and sleep. He didn't have the energy to speak or to flee this judgement. His head was pounding.

This time, she waited for him to speak. And when he didn't, she proceeded, "Yes. That's so like you—speechless when found out, helpless when it comes to this marriage, this family. So helpful to others, and so useless here."

Her speech now hit home. As he listened to his wife, he sensed she had talked this all through with her good friend Millie, and the two had devised some conclusion. He didn't know what Fran expected him to do, or how they had rehearsed various reactions to whatever he would say. But he knew that there was definitely some plan of attack which had been talked through, woman to woman. Perhaps Millie, being somewhat older and wiser, had faced a similar crisis in her marriage to Doc and this approach had worked. Lark knew that Fran was the kind of person who would not be facing him down now, if she had not worked this out pretty clearly in her mind and had already not only come to a conclusion, but a definite plan to implement afterward. He decided to wait in silence to see what that plan might be.

"Well," she began anew, "it's just as I thought. You'd sit there and not say a damned thing!"

Fran rarely cursed. Lark took this as a signal of the pending implementation of the plan. "I can't sleep with you tonight. I'll make a bed in the living room. Then, tomorrow morning, the kids and I are going to take a vacation. We'll go to West Virginia. You do whatever you need to do here, but I won't be here to help you with it; not this time. This is your mess; you clean it up! Good night."

She got up and walked out of the kitchen. Lark listened as she went upstairs to the bathroom. He waited while she got some bed clothes from their bedroom, a sheet from the hallway linen closet, came back down the front stairs, and entered the living room. When all was quiet, Lark walked to the doorway. He couldn't see her lying on the couch, but he knew she could hear him.

"Fran," he said, "I have resigned and have sent a request for a leave of absence from parish ministry to the committee on ministry. I'll preach Sunday morning, and then I am leaving."

She did not respond. He turned and walked upstairs, brushed his teeth, and crawled into their bed, alone.

Chapter 23
HELP!

Fran and the children were already gone when Lark arose Friday morning. The quietness of the house notified Lark of this before he observed that the downstairs closet where they stored suitcases was left hanging ajar. Some of the children's toys were not in their usual corner of the dining room. Glancing outside, Lark noted that the station wagon was gone from its stall in the carport. Only his old VW Beetle stood in the parking lot. Amazing, he thought, how much he liked that car when he first bought it, and how he hardly ever drove it after they bought the station wagon. It wasn't only that he didn't think it a fit car for the children to ride in. He, himself was leery of the thin sheet metal in the doors of the car. He often remarked that in a sideways collision, the only thing that stood between him and eternity was about one and half inches of German steel.

After a breakfast of toast and tea, Lark worked in his study until noon. He basically tidied up the room, knowing that, after Sunday, he would never be here again. Lark had no plan for moving but he knew he would need to come up with that soon. The phone didn't ring the whole morning.

Jane barely spoke to him when she arrived and then stayed in her office. Neither of them saw one another the rest of the morning. From time to time, Lark slid the center drawer of his desk toward him and, taking the photographs from their envelope, glanced at them. He still could not accept that the things these photos represented had actually happened. He could not deny the fact that it was his face which stared at Jennifer upon the threshold of her apartment. But this being the only picture in which he could see his face began to gnaw at his mind. There were lots of questions emerging each time he studied the photographs. If a photographer could take his picture as he stood on the threshold, where was he? How could anyone be in the apartment that night and not be noticed? The pictures were so damnably condemning. Each time he studied them he came to the same conclusion: he had done the right thing by resigning. If this actually happened, he was not fit to be a pastor, not at this moment.

After a terrible noon basketball set at the YMCA, Lark quickly showered and returned to the church office.

Jane met him in the hallway. "There are a number of calls for you, Lark," she announced, as he walked into the building. Lark surmised that the mail had been delivered and these were the first of many calls he would have to field for the next couple of days. He glanced at the phone list Jane handed him: "Call Doc, Bev, Clyde, and John." Lark decided to call his good friend first.

John jovially answered the phone with that thick southern drawl of his. "Good Afternoon."

"This is Lark."

"Hey, what's this I hear about you resigning?"

"It's true," Lark said.

"I'm mighty disappointed to hear that, Lark," John said seriously. "You aren't gonna let that little fracas with the trollop scare you into leaving now, are you?"

"I'm afraid it's more serious than that," Lark explained. He told John about the photos, Fran's reaction, and his decision. John listened quietly at the other end, never interrupting.

"What about Washington?"

"I'll be there," Lark said. He had decided that no matter what happened to him personally, he was still committed to bringing an end to the war in any way he could. Suspecting that those who opposed him were now winning this battle at the church, Lark was resolved to continue leading protest marches so that the war would eventually end at the will of the people.

"I'm glad to hear that, Lark," John said. "I thought you might be planning a disappearing act on me." John worked with suicide prevention and perhaps suspected Lark might do something foolish.

"Don't worry about that," Lark replied. "I don't have much of a plan, beyond getting some rest at this point. But I'm not going to disappear."

"Okay," John said. "Glad to hear it." There was relief in his voice. "I'll talk with you later."

They said goodbye, and he proceeded to dial the other numbers in the order Jane had written them down.

Doc's secretary answered for him when he was with a patient. She said she'd have Doc call him as soon as possible. Bev wept as she expressed to Lark her absolute surprise at his resignation. She said her husband would be over to see Lark at the end of the day to try to talk some sense into him. They chuckled at the thought, and wished one another well when the call was interrupted by a hungry baby crying in the background.

Lark dialed Clyde's number. "This is Lark Wilson, Clyde. Jane said you had called."

"Yeah," he answered gruffly. "I've been studying those photographs. There's something weird about them. I can't say for sure what it is, but a couple of them have my interest."

"Oh," Lark said, somewhat taken with Clyde's sincerity at following through with his parting sentiment the day before. "I've been looking at them from time to time today also, and can't quite tell you what I'm feeling when I look at them. But I know something isn't right."

"Uh huh," Clyde said perfunctorily. "Any of them bother you in particular?"

A strange question, thought Lark. "Yes," Lark lied, "there is one." Actually there were three which Lark always seemed to stop and peer at disbelievingly. And all but the first one seemed to Lark to have happened in another life. He couldn't remember any of the scenes the photos represented, except Jennifer's initial greeting at the apartment doorway.

"I wonder if it's the one I have in mind," Clyde went on.

"Which one would that be?" Lark inquired. There was no response. "Hello, Clyde?"

"Just a minute," the old man said. Lark could picture him fumbling with the photographs as he looked for the one which bothered him. "There it is," he finally said. "It's the one with you two on the floor and the shoes and socks lying around."

"What about it?" Lark asked. He found it in the middle of the pile of pictures on his desk.

"I don't know," the old investigator said. "Just a hunch."

"Well," Lark lied again, "that's the one that has bothered me for some reason."

"I thought it would," Clyde said quietly, almost distracted. "Do you mind if I call some of the boys down in DC and see if one of them will take a look at this picture. Maybe they'll see what it is that bothers you and me about it?"

"How could I mind?" Lark responded. "They're not my pictures now, are they? And, besides, it doesn't make much difference to me, anyway."

"What do you mean?" Clyde asked. He obviously had not gotten his mail yet today.

"I've resigned," Lark said.

"The Hell you say," was Clyde's response. "You've resigned!" Clyde was now in orbit. "What the Hell did you go and do that for, boy? I told you I'd look into this. I just want to know what the Hell is going on." He continued, his voice rising with each sentence. "Now, look, you didn't think that I—no, I didn't intend for you to resign over this. I wanted to know what this was all about, that's all. I came in to help you yesterday, not fire you."

"Clyde," Lark replied, "it really doesn't matter what your intent was yesterday. What matters is that I have made some horrible mistakes in judgement, and the only honorable thing for me to do is resign."

"Bullshit! I never figured you for a coward, not with all that marching and stuff you do, what the Hell's the matter with you? You aren't the first attempt at crucifixion, you know!" he screamed over the phone.

Lark feared he might have a stroke. Up to this point, he never realized how much the truth mattered to this former FBI employee. Nor had he realized how much this man respected him. Lark almost felt ashamed.

"Clyde," Lark continued, "I have to do this. Please understand."

"That's the whole damned trouble," Clyde swiftly retorted, "I don't understand any of this that's going on." He stopped talking.

"Clyde," Lark inquired, "do you want to have some coffee or something?"

"Hell no," the old man said. "I got work to do." He hung up.

Lark sat with the receiver to his ear for several seconds, unable to move.

An hour later, the phone rang and Lark was buzzed by Jane on the intercom. "It's Doc," she said. Lark picked up the receiver to hear the familiar voice at the other end.

"Pastor, Millie and I are truly concerned about you. Fran called Millie this morning from Harrisburg. She told Millie she's considering leaving you and—"

"What?" Lark quickly said. Fran hadn't mentioned leaving him, but she certainly would have reasons to do so. But it wouldn't be like Fran to tell someone else before she would express it to him. Maybe spouses act this way when betrayed. Lark didn't know; he had never betrayed his spouse before this.

"Didn't you know?" Doc asked incredulously.

"Well, yes, I knew she was going to West Virginia to see her parents but—" Lark searched for words to say.

Doc didn't hesitate. "Millie and I think you might be having a nervous breakdown," Doc said in his most concerned voice. "Is there anything we can do? We're just heartsick about this. We read your letter at lunch and couldn't believe it!"

"I guess everyone will have to get used to it," Lark said, regaining his composure. His mind was still reeling from the thought that Fran might leave him. What the members of the congregation thought or felt now mattered little to their pastor. He was more concerned about what Fran might have decided, and how her parents would react when she told them. This thing had gotten so complex. Yesterday, resigning seemed to settle it. Now, there was so much more to consider.

"Would you like to have supper with us tonight?" Doc asked.

"That's very nice of you, Doc," Lark replied. "Please tell Millie I thank her for her kindness, also." Lark was deep in thought now about what the future held for him and Fran. He knew he had much to do to make amends. But, what if she wouldn't wait for him to do it?

"Then, you'll be there?" Doc wanted to know.

"What?"

"You are going to come to dinner?"

"Well, yes," Lark said. He felt the need to talk with someone. Doc and Millie were as near to him, at this point, as anyone in the congregation. Furthermore, Lark had learned that once a pastor resigns, the conversations can, at times, be much more forthright.

"Good," Doc replied. "We'll see you at six."

He was gone. The conversation over. It was three in the afternoon. Lark sat and stared at the pictures on his desk once more. Each time he did so, he felt like screaming. He couldn't remember any of this. Jennifer hugging him from behind and kissing his neck. Jennifer atop him on the sofa. Jennifer kneeling before him with only her shoulders appearing on either side of his torso from the rear. Shoes and socks and pants akimbo, as the two embraced upon the floor, her atop. She sat astride him, totally nude, with her head flung back in ecstasy, her red hair flowing over her sweaty neck. She atop him, resting after that sweet surrender, clothes pushed aside and the coffee table just visible at the edge of the photograph. He sat and stared at what the pictures clearly presented as fact. His only trouble was having no memory of this!

His memory of the scene was entirely different. Jennifer, the seductress, begging him to join her upon the floor. Jennifer, half naked, inviting him to be her partner. Jennifer whispering in his ear how much she loved and wanted him. Jennifer's perfume and hair and sounds mixing together in a whirlwind of feeling: his revulsion, his fear, his confusion, and seeking escape. And, her question of him as he stood frozen before her, "What's the matter? Are you gay?"

He felt terror at the suggestion. He remembered feeling inadequacy with this beautiful woman. He recalled his attempt to leave the apartment, and, her final words to him that night, "I'm sorry. You really are a good person."

This was all he could put together. Try as he did, nothing more came to him. Everything seemed very hazy and jumbled. Up until he drank the iced tea, he could recall, almost word for word, everything the two of them had discussed and done. But, after the iced tea, everything seemed to get jumbled, moods changed, scenes rotated quickly. And, each time he sought to put it together to make some sense, he was overcome with fear and trembling of such a nature as he had never known.

Maybe he was losing his mind. Maybe a nervous breakdown feels this way, he thought. Perhaps all those people he had met in psych wards of hospitals were this confused about their lives, and that's why they ended up where they did until drugs and psychoanalysis helped them reconstruct a life of order. Lark feared that this was precisely what was happening to him. Especially whenever he looked at the pictures. They were so different from what he remembered. And yet, they did portray certain fantasies he had entertained. And they did reflect the basis of a rationale for resigning, as he had already done. Maybe his mind was really denying what truly took place and the pictures were a Godsend to him, revealing the beast he had become? Lark could not be sure any longer.

At five o'clock, he walked across the parking lot to his home. Bev's husband had not shown up, and Lark was just as glad. He decided to shower and rest a bit before driving out to Doc and Millie's place in Eden Township.

As he showered, a vision crept across his mind's eye. It was the picture of Jennifer kneeling before him as portrayed in one of the pictures. Only now, the picture was moving. Jennifer begging Lark, fumbling with his clothing, pain and power, regret and longing, converged. He stiffened in the shower. In his mind's eye he heard Jennifer begging him to let her have her way with him right there and then. He quickly turned the shower water to the cold position and screamed at the top of his lungs, "No!"

The icy cold water streamed down upon his forehead and across his body. The vision gone, Lark pondered its appearance and wondered if it represented a truth he had not considered to this point. Stepping out of the shower and toweling off, he thought of Fran and the children. They must be in Berkeley Springs by now. Probably sitting down for supper or sitting in his in-laws' backyard sipping iced tea.

Lark could hear their hushed voices as they discussed Lark's dilemma out of earshot of the children. He could see the concern on his father and mother-in-law's faces as Fran explained to them the events of this week and Lark's decision to resign. Sam's brow would deepen as he listened, while Mary would wring her hands and repeat; "Oh dear," and "Did you ever?"

Lark stretched across the bed, determined to take a fifteen minute nap before going to Doc and Millie's for supper, when the front doorbell rang. Damn, he thought, as he hurried to throw on some shorts and a tee shirt. He dashed downstairs, half-hoping it was his children returning with their repentant mother. Spying through the curtains Fran had placed upon the vestibule door for privacy, Lark saw what looked like just another vagrant male standing upon the parsonage porch. This was normal; they usually showed up at meal time or on a holiday when the family was just about to leave. The man seemed about to step off of the porch and head to a neighboring church parsonage several blocks away,

213

when suddenly, he walked up to the doorbell and rang it once more. A determined cuss, thought Lark. He decided to open the door and see what the man wanted.

Opening the door, Lark stepped onto the porch in his bare feet. "May I help you?"

"Naw," said the man. "I was just wondering if you knew how to get to St. Joseph's hospital from here. I've been driving around this damned city for thirty minutes and can't quite make sense of the directions I was given."

"Where are you from, then?" Lark asked.

"Reading," the man answered. "I came down Highway 222."

"Well," Lark replied, "it's not so difficult to get there from here." Lark outlined the trip for the beleaguered gentleman and saw him off. When the car was out of sight, Lark turned to go back into the house. That's when he saw that someone had painted what looked like a hammer and sickle upon the brick wall of the parsonage. Lark stood and stared at it for what seemed like a very long time. He could barely believe his eyes. Lark and his family were used to neighborhood thugs stealing things from their yard and picking on their children. This neighborhood around the church was in transition, and it hadn't quite decided what kind of face it was going to present to the city. Uneasy truces abounded between what was left of the old guard and the newcomers who now rented parts of what were once family dwellings. Hateful slogans had been chalked upon the sidewalks and upon the telephone poles around the church and parsonage. But never had such a sight graced the parsonage walls themselves, until now.

Lark walked up to the symbol which had obviously been done in a great hurry. He touched it with his right index finger, noting that the paint was still wet to touch. It must have been done just before the man rang the doorbell, while Lark was showering. Rushing into the house, Lark looked for some old rags which would serve as blotters and erasers of the unsightly art work on the front porch.

When he returned, he quickly rubbed the paint as hard as he could, getting most of it to come off onto some old boxer shorts he had given up wearing. When he was finished, all that remained were some oddly shaped splotches of white paint. He would paint the brick on Saturday, mixing water with the barn red paint in the basement of the church which the janitor used for just such occasions.

It was nearly twenty to six when Lark was finished dressing for supper. Dashing down the back stairs of the parsonage, Lark grabbed the Volkswagen keys from the key holder near the kitchen doorway, slammed the door behind him, and trotted out the gate toward the Beetle. Once inside the car, he depressed the throttle pedal several times before turning the key. The car responded by rumbling and belching. The air-cooled engine in the rear was so noisy on the few highway trips Lark dared to take with this little blue car, he often wondered what it was that made this model so damned popular in the first place. The floor pedals were so very close together, that whenever Lark drove it, he depressed both the clutch and the brake as he sought to change gears. Roaring and belching some smoke out both its chrome-plated tailpipes, the pancake-driven piece of tired steel rattled out of the parking lot behind the parsonage.

After rather perfunctory greetings, the three sat for a light supper of spinach salad with warm bacon dressing and some delicious powder biscuits, one of Millie's specialities. Little was said between them as they ate, beyond some chatter about the sticky weather and the Phillies' poor performance lately. Lark noted that Millie was most hesitant to speak of anything. She let Doc do all of the leading.

After Millie cleared the table and took the dishes to the kitchen to clean, Doc and Lark sat alone in the spacious dining room with a large double door leading to an even larger patio which overlooked the gently rolling Conestoga Creek nearby. It was Doc who finally opened the conversation to the matters at hand.

"I received a copy of the pictures in the mail today," he said. "They must have been quite a shock to you," he continued.

"Of course, Millie shared with me some details Fran had told her. Poor girl, Fran. She's quite upset." Doc seemed genuinely concerned about her.

"She went to West Virginia," Lark struggled to add. "I don't know when she'll be back."

"So, what do you do after Sunday, Lark?" Doc wanted to know.

"I hope to use the next month to get my things together, leave the parsonage, and take some time for myself," Lark confided. "Beyond that, I haven't a clue."

"Of course, the consistory will permit you to stay in the parsonage for a month, if you like," Doc said in a conciliatory tone. "I guess I was hoping that you'd not act so impetuously."

Lark, annoyed by the condemnation of his decision, responded, "What else could I do?"

"You might have considered coming to the consistory with this, asking for time off for some counseling, get your life with Fran and your family back on an even keel, and then come back to us at St. Andrew for a while, as you looked for another position," Doc reflected.

Lark had never thought of any of this. He realized that in his panic, he might have acted precipitously. But he was certain his decision was correct. A peace had come over him he had not known for some time, and this he took as a sign.

Often, Fran had remarked how tranquil Lark appeared in the midst of crises. She often remarked that she envied this quality about him. He knew that it was just a perception others had of him; inside, he was angry or frightened at best. But, this time, it was different. Once he had mailed the letters of resignation, Lark was ready for whatever God had in mind for him. Be it punishment of the worse kind, he knew he deserved it for what he had done.

"Lark, we could still have an emergency session of the consistory on Sunday if you like," Doc was saying to him. "I'm sure folks will be understanding. You don't have to just walk away from us so fast." Doc seemed nervous as he spoke.

"Doc, you saw those pictures," Lark said matter-of-factly. "You know pictures don't lie. How many other people have copies of them lying on their kitchen tables or on their desks right this minute? This—whatever it is—is beyond my control."

"Yes, it does look bad," Doc said now, as he listened to Lark. "I suppose to you, it seems hopeless."

"Pretty near it," Lark said. "Look, Doc, I probably deserve this for being so foolish. I admit I was infatuated with this young woman. She is beautiful, and she showered me with attention these past few days. I just succumbed to her and walked right into somebody's trap."

Doc sat up straight as Lark spoke. He seemed to seriously consider every word his pastor used, as Lark continued to explain his rationale for resigning.

"The way I see it, somebody wants me out of here. Why? I'm not sure. But whoever it is, I can't beat them. Not only is my professional life in ruin, I am about to lose my family, too. I don't think anyone would try to hang on in such circumstances; do you?"

Doc stroked his chin and leaned forward to speak directly across the table to his pastor. "Lark, I believe you're right about somebody wanting you out of here. But I don't believe that the goal was to ruin your family life."

"Well, you'd have a hard time proving that, in light of the photographs and the fact that more than one person in the church has received copies of them these past few days," Lark said with some irritation.

"I believe that was unfortunate. Clyde called me and told me all about Fran's reaction to them in your office. I am sorry that happened the way it did," Doc said sincerely. Why would Doc be apologizing for it, Lark wondered.

"What would you do, Doc, if it were you in my place?" Lark asked. He waited as Doc fidgeted in his chair, no doubt striving for time to put some kind of answer together.

"One thing, for sure," Doc responded. "I wouldn't try to overcome this alone. I'd draw people into my confidence and face it with others."

217

"I tried it that way," Lark said. He went on to share how he told Fran, how he and John searched for Jennifer the day after, and how he and Clyde had discussed the photographs, along with Clyde's promise to look into the photos a little more. This last bit of information seemed to catch Doc by surprise, as Lark told him of Clyde's plan to have the FBI lab look at the photos. Quickly glancing at his watch, Doc cleared his throat and informed Lark that he had an appointment at eight o'clock at Lancaster General. A man who was to undergo surgery that evening needed to be hypnotized, and Doc had to leave soon so as to not keep the surgeon waiting.

Things moved quickly after that. Millie came into the room briefly to say good night, as Lark thanked her and Doc for supper and their concern for him and Fran. They shook hands and parted.

Lark drove slowly, the Beetle coughing and sputtering as it pushed him homeward. The doors barely closed and never seemed to stop rattling from the time the engine started until it stopped. The seats were sticky light-colored plastic, which in winter and summer were most uncomfortable in Lancaster County. The kids liked this old car. They often climbed into it and pretended they were driving it, as it stood silently in the parking lot behind the parsonage.

Pulling into the parking lot this evening seemed odd to Lark: no lights on in the parsonage, no children in the yard, no Fran there to greet him. He walked lazily into the kitchen just as the phone was ringing.

"Hello," he answered.

"I thought you'd want to know that we are safely here," Fran said.

"Thanks," Lark said.

"Where have you been? I called six times this evening," she inquired.

"Doc and Millie had me for supper," he answered. "Oh," was all she said. "Well, I guess I'd best hang up. I just wanted you to know we are alright."

"Fran" Lark whispered.

"Yes." She waited.

"I am so sorry. I never wanted any of this to happen," he stammered.

"Yes, I know," she said, but not kindly. "Mother and Daddy were horrified when I told them. It was all I could do to keep Daddy from driving up there like a maniac. He wanted to break your neck, he said."

Lark was glad they lived so far from the in-laws.

"Fran," Lark had to ask her.

"Yes." She waited again.

"How long will you be gone?"

"Forever," she said with finality. Lark knew she had worked all of this out over the past twenty-four hours. She hadn't gone home to cry on her parents' shoulders, but to simply inform them that she was separating from Lark. Lark's chest felt heavier than he had ever noticed, as the meaning of her response blossomed into his consciousness. There was no point in trying to dissuade this woman. Lark knew her too well. She meant every syllable: for-ev-er. That was it. She and Lark were through. He would lose the possibility of living with his children as they grew. It was too much for Lark to bear at this moment, when all else was lost. He didn't respond to Fran, but hung up the receiver and ran from the kitchen into the backyard.

It was there, in that postage stamp of a yard, where his children played as though it were the entire world, where the scene shifted many times to accommodate their imaginary environment, where rocking horse stood alongside electric car and inner tube hung crookedly from the lone tree limb. There, the family had gathered for picnics on warm summer nights, birthday parties for each child were attended by neighborhood children, where Fran and Lark sat on quiet spring Saturdays and drank coffee as they awaited the appearance of the first towhead to come through the kitchen door. Right there, as he dropped to his knees in the middle of that yard, Lark cried out to whatever god might be listening.

"Help me," he screamed into the twilight sky, tears streaming down his face, body swaying from side to side in a rocking motion.

Doc was right. This couldn't be faced alone. He needed someone to lift him up, hold him, and keep him safe. Childlike, he whimpered as he knelt there in the grass, looking heavenward.

"Are you out there somewhere?" he demanded of the Almighty. "Help me," he screamed again, and quietly added, "please." Falling to the ground face first, he lay in the darkening yard for several minutes. Then, getting up, he walked into the kitchen once more. After drinking some ice water, Lark walked up the back stairs to the master bedroom and flung himself across the bed, quickly falling into a very deep sleep for the rest of the night.

Chapter 24

ANOTHER SATURDAY MORNING

Lark arose at five. He showered, shaved, dressed, and then drove downtown to a diner for breakfast. The diner was half full at six. One cook worked where everyone could see him prepare their food. The waitress who commanded the night shift was putting in time, waiting for her replacement at seven.

She came to Lark's booth and asked what he would have. No menus here; it was pasted upon the wall for all to see. Lark liked the simplicity of this place: no pretense, no style, just food. That's what people came here for whenever the pangs struck them, for this place served food twenty-four hours of each day of the year, no exceptions. Lark ordered two eggs and toast with some coffee to help awaken him.

Within minutes, his meal was before him and he devoured it as though he hadn't eaten in weeks. The others in the diner paid him no mind, as they chatted with one another about the game the night before, in which the Phillies blew a ten-run lead after seven innings.

The cook was into it with two guys at the counter, who insisted the Phillies would do better if they fired Gene Mauch, the manager. The cook saw it differently; players play the game.

"If the food in here is bad, don't blame the manager, blame the cook," he explained with a hearty laugh.

The point was made in such a sensible way, the two men at the counter changed the subject to this weekend's weather forecast. Did the cook think it would rain, as predicted? Lark listened to their friendly banter about the uncertainties of most anything, especially Lancaster County weather forecasts.

Suddenly, a new subject arose between the three. The waitress joined in as they all jabbered about 'Nam and the marches across the country which were to take place soon. Each of them had an opinion. None of them supported those who marched. The sum and substance of their comments was that those who couldn't support our nation should leave. What an idea, thought Lark. Some of the best young minds of the nation, as well as some of the most patriotic of congressmen, not to mention returning servicemen themselves, had raised a defiant arm in protest of this war. Where had these people in the diner been?

After finishing his breakfast he walked to the counter to pay his bill, having left the tip on the table behind him. The waitress eyed him as she rang the amount, and placed the money in the till, and handed him a quarter. "What do you think?" she asked.

"About what?" he asked in return.

"About the war," she said, and smiled. Something about her smile unnerved Lark.

"What do I think?" he said. "I think it is just about the biggest mistake this nation ever got itself into in its history. That's what I think."

"I thought so," she said with a grin. The others were listening to their exchange, but they said nothing. Lark turned and walked out into the fresh morning air. There was but a hint of how warm it might become. And there were some clouds milling about in the heavens, he noted.

Lark walked toward the city square. He liked to walk the children uptown on Saturdays, get a newspaper, and treat them to something. Entering the newspaper shop was always a treat, for the proprietor also sold exceptional aromatic tobacco for pipes. Lark often wished he were a pipe smoker, the place smelled so good each time he entered it. The New Era, Saturday edition, was proudly displayed on the counter of the small shop.

"Good morning," shouted the proprietor, as he walked up to the front of the store. "What'll it be this morning? And, where are those darling children of yours today? Snoozing, I bet."

Lark quietly handed the owner a quarter and replied, "They are away with their mother for the weekend." God, how he wished that were the truth. Choking back the lump in his throat, Lark walked from the little store quickly, the New Era tucked beneath one arm.

The walk back to the car took very little time. Soon, he was driving North on Lime Street and turning into the parking lot. He had decided to just talk with the people on Sunday. He would scrub his sermon and simply speak from the heart. Lark had no idea what he would say. Whatever came would be fine, Lark thought, for it would be the last time he would talk with the people of St. Andrew Church.

The rest of the morning hours dragged by, as Lark began to pack those things he would need to take with him wherever it was he could go. How would he tell his parents that his marriage was over? They had grown so supportive in their later years, especially his father. The love they showered upon their grandchildren was sometimes a bit much, Lark felt, but, he never had a sense that his parents would ever interfere with the domestic patterns Lark and Fran had established.

What would his parents think? They had found a way to stay together even though there were times, Lark knew, when it could have been over for them, too. Lark recalled one stormy night when his parents argued into the wee hours of the morning in the adjacent bedroom. Whatever it was that had made them cross, never a word was spoken to Lark or his brother. The next day was the same as that which preceded it. Lark's mother and father went off to work, while Lark and his brother walked to school.

From time to time, in Lark's home, an unnerving silence overtook his parents, usually following upon the heels of one of his father's explosive outbursts. Barely speaking to one another, they went through their tasks around the house almost as total strangers. Yet neither of them ever complained about the other to their children, as far as Lark ever knew. And, all of this seemed to fade into the past as they grew older.

His parents would be stunned by this news, even more so by the awareness that it was Lark's foolishness which brought all of this upon him. Lark's dad always said, in his own crass manner, "Son, never lose your head over a piece of ass." Lark was losing more than his head, in this case. They would be absolutely devastated, especially if Fran chose to isolate the children from them.

By lunchtime, Lark had scarcely packed two suitcases and several boxes. This was going to take more time than he thought. By mid-afternoon, it dawned on him that the phone had not rung all day. Most unusual, even for a lame-duck pastor, he thought. The sun was bright, and if it were going to rain, it wasn't going to do so in the next hour. Lark decided to take a walk around the neighborhood, if for no other reason than he needed to be out of the parsonage for a while.

Eventually, he found himself walking on College Avenue, Franklin and Marshall College to his right and Lancaster Seminary to his left. Lark knew both institutions intimately. As they had shared a large portion of Mercersburg the century before, the two institutions now stood opposite one another on College Avenue in Lancaster.

Lark recalled the history of the two institutions from which he had graduated with honors over a decade ago. He remembered that the first president of Marshall College was a world renowned psychologist, Dr. Frederick A. Rauch. How he would liked to have met Dr. Rauch walking this avenue this afternoon. Perhaps they would spend some time in Lou's Deli, and Lark could share with the great doctor what was resting now very heavily upon his heart. Certainly, one so famous would be of some help, offer some word of support, lend some insight to this poor lost soul.

Lark stood at the base of Old Main Hill on the campus of Franklin and Marshall. Standing here, gazing at the buildings, Lark felt as though a whole lifetime had passed since he had attended classes at his alma mater.

Dr. Rauch, when he wrote, taught, and administered what insights there were into the human psyche in the mid 1800s, had no awareness of Freud when he became president of the college. Freud would not be born until twenty years later. With no id, ego, or libido to rest upon, no Oedipus, or Electra complex, no understandings of the relationship of narcissism and neurosis with which to tackle the pastor standing before him, what would Rauch say? How would he counsel this man who presented such despair? Freud would have envisioned a pleasure principle at work in cases like Lark's. What would Rauch begin with as he tackled the problem, Lark wondered?

No doubt, Lark mused, Dr. Rauch would rest more heavily upon that interesting interface of soul and mind which the ancient Greeks called the "psyche." Dr. Rauch, unlike Dr. Freud, would insist his client be alert and awake as they spoke. Dr. Rauch's counsel would undoubtedly rest upon Christian understandings of human beings as sinners, capable of falling from God's grace at any moment. In such cases, a healthy repentance was necessary for healing. A turning away from that course upon which one had journeyed to arrive at this juncture. Yes, that would be it, thought Lark.

And, what if young Dr. Freud came into Lou's Corner while the pastor and the elderly Dr. Rauch engaged in psychological confession and absolution? Lark thought of this as he walked through the seminary parking lot and grounds toward the deli. Dr. Freud would, no doubt, find this tale amusing and simple. Lark was basically a narcissist who had projected his love of himself onto Jennifer, just as he had when Fran could turn his head every time she walked into a room. Jennifer now became the obsession of a man who genuinely loved himself. And, the behavior in her apartment? Most natural, in such cases, Freud would say. Anxiety has an unmistakable affinity with expectation.

Freud would point out to Lark that he went to Jennifer's with very high unconscious expectations for the evening. She confronted all of his instincts with a demand that triggered an internal conflict. If he had sought gratification with her, the internal danger would have manifested itself externally. His helplessness in the situation, both in Jennifer's apartment and in his own kitchen with Fran, was simply a continuation of the conflicting dangers Lark faced when he stood in the arms of Jennifer. Basically, Lark was fearful of losing the one thing in the world he truly loved above all else —that sense of self which he had cultured and bred over the years. When faced with a choice between what he wanted for a moment and what he sought and loved for a lifetime, Lark made the right choice, at least in his mind's eye.

"Hello," said Lou as Lark entered the deli. "What will it be on this muggy afternoon?"

"I think I'll have some of your lemonade," Lark said. Thankfully, Lou did not engage him in any further conversation but let him alone after serving the cool drink. Lark continued to fantasize Drs. Rauch and Freud discussing his malady here in Lou's Corner.

"The transition from physical pain to mental pain corresponds to a change from narcissistic cathexis to object cathexis. The object whose presentation is highly cathected by instinctual need plays the same role as the part of the body which is cathected by an increase of stimulus," Freud explained to Dr. Rauch who listened with rapt attention.

"I do not know what you are talking about Dr. Freud," Rauch eventually admitted. "But, I do know the torment of a man who has escaped the grasp of Satan but must live to tell how he almost enjoyed such an embrace."

Lark pictured them so deep in discussion, that eventually, they discussed him as though he were no longer present. Growing tired of the fantasy, Lark arose and left the two giants to fight it out, right there in a booth in Lou's Corner. With one last glance at that corner booth, Lark emerged into the real world of a late summer Saturday afternoon and walked slowly back across town to the parsonage.

When he reached the parsonage, he instinctively checked the mailbox. Along with the usual fourth-class junk that postal workers deliver on their routes everyday was one postal note with multi-colored mice scampering across the envelope. It was addressed only to Lark, and there was no return address upon it.

Lark broke the colonial-style seal and unfolded the note to read its contents.

> *Dear Lark,*
>
> *Sorry, because of Gil's family, we won't be with you at service on Sunday morning. We will be with you in thought at least. I have mixed emotions about it all and a deep, deep sadness within me. I hate to see you leave, and I'm so unhappy with the many things precipitating it. I hope and pray your new life will be a healing experience that gives you joy and satisfaction.*
>
> *Sincerely,*
> *Betty Smythe*
>
> *P.S. I'm hoping to see you, Fran, and the children sometime before you leave here. B.*

Betty and Gil Smythe had been among Lark's most ardent supporters when he first came to serve St. Andrew. Lark recalled how both of them had shown up the evening the moving van arrived, each carrying a hot container of food. They greeted one another warmly. Fran was obviously nervous about the appearance of her new home, but Betty assured her that clutter was their middle name. Gil, a prominent banker in Lancaster, laughed at that one. The tension eased and the meal was thoroughly enjoyed by the entire Wilson family. Lark could picture Leigh Ann sitting upon Betty's lap, leaning back upon her and gazing up at her face as the seven of them talked of this new beginning.

Lately, the Smythes had not been seen as often in church services. Gil had gotten elected to some national banking association position, and Betty often traveled with him whenever he left town on business. Betty, a former church secretary, had a sense of the tensions pastors live with, as they juggle the roles of servanthood and parenthood. She often offered to sit with the children so Fran and Lark could have some time on their own, away from all of the pressures of clergy life. Betty was around the house so often, especially in the early years of Lark's ministry, that she was like one of the family.

But, as Lark thought about it, in the past year, he had seen less and less of the Smythes. The deeper Lark became involved with the anti-war movement, the less he saw of them. Only four or five months before, Lark was so concerned about their sudden disappearance that he called upon them late one evening. Gil and Betty graciously welcomed their pastor into their modest home near Willow Street. After some small talk, Lark asked the couple if something had happened which had led to their falling away from church.

Without warning, Gil launched into a verbal assault upon Lark for what he termed the "leftist lacings" of his sermons. Never in all of his years of belonging to church, Gil shouted, had he been subjected to such one-sided points of view. Furthermore, Gil seethed, he was embarrassed by news stories in which his pastor was quoted as saying he felt President Nixon should be impeached for not keeping his promises to end the war. Betty sat silently through the entire tirade, as did Lark. This was a side of Gil Lark never imagined existed; he had always seemed so jovial and easy-going. Red-faced, Gil, when finished delivering his lecture to the pastor, did not wait for any response, but loudly stomped from the living room.

Lark and Betty looked at one another. Betty shrugged her shoulders as if to say there was nothing she could do about Gil's anger. Lark apologized for having been the catalyst of this

228

unfortunate break from the church. Betty assured him that everyone had to do what was right in their own minds, and each of us has to answer to God for our response to God's call. She spoke in such comforting tones that Lark left their home that night, assured that Betty was, like he, longing for their relationship to be what it once was, but could never be again. They shook hands. Lark saw Betty in church at least a half a dozen times since that visit, but only spied Gil on Christmas Eve when their children came home for a visit and the entire family came to the candlelight service at eleven.

The letter from Betty meant a great deal to Lark this day. The Smythes had been good friends. Although differences in political philosophies and expectations had led them to a parting of the ways, Lark knew that, when all of the struggle was over and people finally knew the truth about the war, he would be vindicated in that respect.

It was later, after supper, that Lark thought again about Betty's letter and realized that it implied nothing about his incident with Jennifer. The Smythes had not been sent copies of the photographs. The "many things" precipitating Lark's resignation must have meant nights like that experienced in their home, thought Lark. The letter implied that Betty, although rarely in church most of the past six months and absent as a visitor in the Wilson home since last Christmas, when she came with a basket of oranges for the family, had kept up with the mounting tension Lark was undergoing in the church and in the city. She had, no doubt, read the series of letters to the editor of the New Era last winter, in which Lark was named several times as "pastoral rebel not without flaws." At first amusing, then nearly libelous, the letters to the editor hinted that Lark was not really a pastor, but a community organizer using the church as a base for political purposes. One letter suggested to parishioners of St. Andrew that they "regain their senses and dismiss this pastoral rebel not without flaws immediately."

The letters, always signed *Bill Smith,* provoked considerable response from readers each time they appeared. Some joined the fictitious Mr. Smith, whom Lark suspected was nothing more than a *New Era* reporter having some fun, while others took him on. For weeks, after each one appeared, the *New Era* would print pro and con responses to Mr. Smith's diatribes. Lark never responded. Having checked with the paper as to who this person truly was and being informed that it was the policy of the newspaper never to give the addresses of persons who wrote in, Lark gave up trying to speak with the author personally.

Betty, no doubt, was probably also aware of the petitions which had floated through the church earlier in the spring. Rumored to have many signatures, though never shown directly to the pastor, the petitions reportedly asked for people to indicate whether they would vote to dismiss the pastor. A few of Lark's supporters in the church would report to him each time one of these mysterious documents made its way through the congregation.

One morning, Chet came into Lark's office and excitedly told him that he had just been approached by a member of the Ladies' Bible Class and asked if he would sign a petition. Chet hadn't seen the petition yet, but he thought Lark would want to know right away. Having delivered his message, Chet quickly left the pastor's office and never mentioned the subject again.

There were days when Lark truly wondered whether there actually were petitions to fire him, or whether there were just the rumors that such petitions existed. Either way, the news of them always demoralized him. Lark couldn't think straight for hours, each time he heard of the elusive documents against him. Hence, just the news of the operation was having an effect upon the pastor. Little by little, Lark drew further from the congregation as a whole and grew more distrustful of the people for whom he had been called to serve in Christ's name.

He had talked this over with John many times. Both men agreed that whoever was behind this was getting the job done without even producing a name. John always encouraged Lark to simply ignore the rumors, but both men knew Lark couldn't accomplish that. He simply was too much of a people person.

His sensibilities were such that word of disappointment with him gnawed at him at times, until he was almost totally distracted by it.

The evening passed in silence. His supper of tuna sandwiches and a bottle of cola consumed as though he were operating on auto pilot, Lark watched television for nearly an hour. Blankly staring at the multi-colored screen, until fatigue embraced him, he got up from the sofa, turned the TV off, and walked upstairs to prepare for bed. It was eight o'clock. Fran had not called, no one had visited, and only one letter of regret regarding his resignation had been delivered. Lark anticipated, as he brushed his teeth, that his final sermon at St. Andrew the next morning would be difficult, to say the least.

He looked at himself in the mirror. His eyes were reddened by the numerous times he had wept throughout the day. His face was puffy, his color a bit pale. Taking a washcloth from the rack and running it under some cool water, he lifted the cloth and covered his face entirely. It felt refreshing and gave some relief to the tension in his face. He repeated this several more times, before wringing the cloth out and replacing it on the rack.

He walked to the bedroom after tossing all of his clothes in the hamper in the hallway, and stretched across the bed on top of the sheets. It was going to be a warm night. The moisture which had not come during the day as rainfall now inflicted the good citizens of Lancaster with one-hundred percent humidity. No breeze crossed the threshold of the window sill; only the sounds of the occasional car racing up the street punctuated the damp stillness of the evening.

Lark turned away from the dusk light which illuminated the floor near the window and stretched as far as it could into the bedroom, before being conquered by the darkness. Curling upon his side until he was comfortable, Lark drifted toward that other world in which human consciousness dares to venture in search of meaning.

Chapter 25

FAREWELL

The parking lot was nearly empty. He ate breakfast, brushed his teeth, made sure his hair was presentable, adjusted the clerical collar about his neck, and grabbed his Bible from the dining room buffet. Walking into the church on this bright Sunday morning was difficult for Lark. Various church sounds greeted him as he entered the building not through the office doorway, but through the main entryway off Lime Street. This had become a habit with Lark, and he found it often enabled him to speak to worshippers as they also were arriving.

Like any other Sunday, Lark mingled with folks as they opened the large red doors of the church. People were cordial as they came into the building and saw their pastor in his usual Sunday morning spot, talking with one or more who had gathered. No one said a word about his resignation. Lark found this strange behavior for a congregation about to say farewell to its pastor. When the organ prelude began, Lark walked quickly downstairs to greet the choir members, who had come to sing the morning anthem and assist the congregation in the liturgy.

Very few choir members were in the practice room when Lark ducked in to say good morning and share a prayer with them prior to worship. Only five persons, two men and three women, were present. Elsie was already upstairs, playing her usual five-minute prelude.

"Good morning," Lark said rather matter-of-factly.

"Is it?" Chet piped up.

"Let us pray," Lark directed.

Dutifully, the five singers lowered their heads and listened as Lark asked God to help them bring meaning and substance to worship this morning. With the amen, Lark noted one of the women wiped a tear from her eye as the five choir members sauntered down the hall toward the front stairs of the church, from which they would emerge at the introductory chord of the first hymn, march down the aisle, and take their place by the organ at the front of the sanctuary.

Lark hurried to his study, put on his robe and green stole for Trinity Season, and stepped into the chancel via the office door, just as Elsie was finishing her prelude with a haltingly beautiful quiet refrain on the higher pitched pipes. It was then that Lark recognized Elsie was playing contemporary composer Frank Ferko's musical setting for a text of Hildegard of Bingen, a Benedictine mystic known as a visionary and spiritual guide. Glancing at the congregation, Lark noted that there were barely fifty persons in the room. Their faces revealed that they had no understanding of the music they had just heard Elsie play. To them, it must have seemed like little more than an organist practicing chords or tuning the pipes. "O verbum Patris" was not known for stirring audiences, even if musicologists found both the text and the setting to be moving.

Lark preferred the text to the music; Elsie knew this about him. They had actually discussed the piece of music one night when the two had gone to hear the Gettysburg College Choir perform at Trinity Lutheran Church a few years back.

"I find the mystical quality of the music to fit perfectly with the text, don't you?" she asked, as they drove to her apartment.

"Not exactly," Lark replied. "Why didn't they just have a woman sing the solo parts? The man couldn't quite hit the notes."

"Oh, Lark, you don't know your musical history, let alone church history," Elsie chided him, as only she could.

"What do you mean?" he had asked.

"Well, good pastor, you men have held such power in the church for so long that you don't even confess your sins any more, do you? Don't you know that women weren't aloud in church choirs until the 19th century? The composer simply wrote this in the manner of the 16th century, when it was common to ask a bass to sing falsetto voice in parts that ordinarily would be sung by tenors," she explained with a laugh.

"Oh yes," Lark replied good-naturedly. "I had forgotten about the castrated boys' choirs!"

Elsie shook her finger at him as they drove.

"Seriously though," he continued, "I must confess that I find the text itself to be intriguing. I'll have to read some of Hildegard of Bingen's work some day."

"Hmm," was all Elsie said at first. Then, she confessed that the text interested her. She found its metaphoric reference to creation as a spinning wheel to be very feminine. She dared entertain the thought that God might indeed be female. They laughed about that as they neared her apartment.

Lark confessed that the part of the text which he found most interesting was the suggestion of the foreknowledge of God. To him, it almost sounded Calvinistic. And, he especially appreciated the last several phrases which, as he recalled, went something like "hidden in the center of your potency...you knew all things from the beginning and you created...all, having no beginning nor brought down by any end."

This morning, that last sentiment especially comforted him, as he stood to pronounce the Solemn Declaration to the sparse crowd of the faithful who had come to hear his farewell words. "In the Name of the Father, and of the Son, and of the Holy Spirit," he intoned.

"Holy, holy, holy, Lord God Almighty," he continued, standing before them at the center of the chancel, "which was, and is, and is to come." He thought of Hildegard's words. How appropriate that Elsie played that piece. No doubt she did so just for him this morning. How thoughtful of her, he mused.

Then he led them in the call to confession of sin. All eyes were glued upon him as he bade them to draw near to God with true hearts and ask God, through Christ, to grant forgiveness. Facing the alter, he led the congregation in the unison prayer, and then intoned the Kyrie.

"Lord, have mercy upon us," he sang, much like a 16th-century bass trying to sing a tenor part.

"Lord, have mercy upon us," the congregation sang, with Elsie's accompaniment.

"Christ, have mercy upon us," Lark sang with more fervor, for he always imagined Jesus to be merciful and understanding.

"Christ, have mercy upon us," responded the congregation with assistance from the choir, which was standing in place, at the rear of the nave, ready to process with the first hymn.

"Lord, have mercy upon us." Lark sang the final verse of the ancient trio of verses so softly, it was barely above a whisper. Elsie, caught by surprise, was still waiting for him to sing the third verse when the handful of worshippers broke into singing their response without aide of organ or choir.

Lark turned toward the people to give them the Assurance of Pardon and noted that some were weeping openly as they awaited those very familiar words from their pastor.

"Hearken now unto the comforting assurance of the grace of God," Lark began to recite. He always changed the words of this beautiful passage in their hymnal to make it first-person plural, rather than second-person plural. At first, folks reacted to this subtle change, but eventually they grew to appreciate it and expect it from him. As he finished the assurance, he felt the words were meant for him this day, more than for anyone else in the church.

"Unto as many of us, therefore, as truly repent of our sins," Lark concluded, "and believe in the Lord Jesus Christ, with full purpose of new obedience, it is announced and declared, that our sins are forgiven, according to His promise in the Gospel; through Jesus Christ our Lord. Amen."

Turning once more to face the altar, Elsie and the choir led the congregation in singing the "Gloria Patri." Usually, the choir was so large that their voices issuing forth through the congregation from the narthex was quite a moving way to get ready to sing the opening hymn. But, with only five voices and maybe fifty persons scattered about the large sanctuary, the praise to God was weak this day.

Elsie did her best, as she played the introduction to the first hymn, to rouse the congregation to sing with more fervor. The trumpets blasted before each stanza of "God Of Our Fathers." But, their hearts, as well as those of the few choir members, just weren't in it today. People wiped tears from eyes as the choir marched toward Lark, standing at the center of the chancel. The hymn was played very well by Elsie, but the congregation just couldn't lift up their hearts to sing. By the fourth verse, hardly a person was singing. All of the women in the choir were crying. Tears trickled down their faces. The two men struggled to maintain their composure. Lark, too, was fighting back emotions he did not think he'd feel this morning. He looked at the congregation from time to time and imagined Fran and the children in their usual places. But that pew was as empty as his heart this day.

"Refresh Thy people on their toilsome way," was the final line of the hymn hardly anybody was able to sing. Elsie finished it with her usual flair, stretching the "Amen" chord to the limit, as all took their seats and endeavored to regain some sense of worship.

Lark turned and faced the altar as he led the members in the Collect for the day. Then, he walked to the lectern from which he was prepared to read the Lectionary texts for the day. Lark struggled to get through the Jeremiah reading, in which God is pictured as simply wearying of the false prophets who had scattered His people and not cared for them. The words stuck in his throat as he read them, finding relief only when finished. Lark then turned to the Epistle to the Ephesians, the second chapter, where the writer taught his gentile converts that it was Christ who had built them into the living temple. Lark had often preached this comforting passage during his ministry. But this morning, Lark had decided to base what words of farewell he could muster upon the Gospel from Mark, chapter six, beginning at verse 30, in which Jesus bids the disciples to take a "leave of absence." He read the lengthy passage as the congregation listened intently for some clue as to what might be forthcoming from their pastor. They knew him to be an excellent Biblical preacher, and they were certain these words he was reading would be further enhanced by the sermon to come. Two miracles later (the feeding of the multitude and walking upon water), the text closed with Jesus and the disciples entering new territory and discovering that wherever he went God had already placed persons who were in need of his ministry awaiting him.

"Blessed are they who hear the Word of God and keep it," Lark said as he closed the large Bible. Elsie immediately introduced the hymn "What A Friend We Have In Jesus." The congregation, now reasonably recovered from the opening minutes of the service, sang as best they could the words many of them had committed to memory over the years.

"Have we trials and temptations? Is there trouble anywhere?" they plaintively sang. "We should never be discouraged, take it to the Lord in prayer! Can we find a friend so faithful, who will all our sorrows share? Jesus knows our every weakness, take it to the Lord in prayer!" They seemed to be advising Lark as they sang.

During the final verse, Lark descended the chancel stairs and sang as he walked toward where most of the congregation was sitting, about halfway back in the sanctuary. He had never done this before, but felt moved to be closer to those who came to say farewell to him.

> "Do thy friends despise, forsake thee? Take it to the Lord
> in prayer.
> In His arms He'll take and shield thee, Thou wilt find a
> solace there."

There being no "Amen" chord composed for this hymn, written in the same year Marshall College left Mercersburg and united with Franklin College in this very city, Elsie simply stopped playing. The congregation looked up from their hymnals and were startled to see their pastor standing so close to them.

"My friends." He began to say farewell to them, moved to speak of the necessity to withdraw from active ministry from time to time, in order to be of service in the next place, to which Christ would lead us all. More than that, he would never be able to remember, as it was such a moving time with the people he had grown to love and respect. He talked of the necessity to be absent from ministry for a time, and one or two of them were heard to protest. "No," they murmured and then lowered their heads in embarrassment. Assuring them that he believed his leaving to be within the will of a gracious and loving God, and encouraging each of them to "fight the good fight," Lark closed the farewell message with a blessing nearly as ancient as humanity: "May the Lord watch between you and me, while we are absent, one from another."

Lark often wondered aloud with parishioners why this passage was used the way it was in churches of their tradition. Did not folk know the story? One time an elder claimed that Reformed people did indeed know their Bibles. It was their pastors, he said, who didn't catch the meaning of this passage: its reconciliation and joy at the end, its hope, and its dependence upon God watching over sinful humanity that no harm may come to any. After that lecture, Lark felt more comfortable leading congregations in saying it. This Lord's Day, it seemed somehow to fit most perfectly.

Lark walked toward the chancel as the congregation arose to repeat the words of the ancient Creed of the Apostles, after which he led them in the morning prayers, closing with the words of the Saint Chrysostom. Then, he invited those gathered to offer their morning sacrifices, as the five choir members stood to present their offering. Elsie introduced their anthem for the day, no doubt hurriedly rehearsed only forty minutes earlier. Lark knew within seconds what they were going to sing, and for the first time a tear welled in his left eye.

> *"God of the prophets! Bless the prophets' sons;*
> *Elijah's mantle o'er Elisha cast;*
> *Each age it solemn task may claim but once;*
> *Make each one nobler, stronger than the last."*

They sang with such dignity. The congregation listened attentively as the ushers passed the offering plates among them.

> *"Anoint them prophets! On Thy service bent,*
> *To human need do Thou their hearts awake,*
> *With heavenly speech their lips make eloquent*
> *To preach the right, and every evil break."*

The ushers now stood at the rear of the nave, awaiting the end of the anthem, which this small band of singers was presenting as though God himself were in the building.

> *"Make them apostles! Heralds of thy cross,*
> *Forth may they go to tell all realms Thy grace;*
> *Inspired of Thee, may they count all but loss,*
> *And stand at last with joy before Thy face!"*

The choir closed the anthem with a sturdy "Amen" and remained standing for the "Doxology," as the ushers brought forth the morning offering and handed the plates to Lark. He turned toward the altar, and prayed, "May the work of our hands be established, oh Lord. Yes, may your Church prosper forevermore. Amen."

Elsie played the introduction to the closing hymn, a lyrical arrangement of John Newton's 18th-century benediction, usually reserved for evening services. Pastor and people sang to one another this parting hymn.

"May the grace of Christ our Saviour and the Father's
  boundless love,
With the Holy Spirit's favor rest upon us from above.
Thus may we abide in union with each other and the Lord
And possess, in sweet communion, joys which earth cannot
  afford.
Amen."

For what might have been the first time in Lark's professional career as a minister of the Gospel, he did not use the second person plural in pronouncing the Benediction, but took the role of priest, dispensing God's favor upon these people he would never see again. "The Lord bless you and keep you; the Lord make his face to shine upon you, and be gracious unto you. The Lord lift up his countenance upon you, and give you peace. Amen."

He lazily proceeded to walk down the center aisle of the church toward the narthex, not glancing at either side to meet the faces of those who worshipped with him, as was his custom, as the choir sang the first verse of "Bless Be The Tie," after which Elsie launched into Karg Ellert's "Nun Danket Alles Gott."

It was finished. He awaited the people's departure, the final handshakes, as one by one, they left the sanctuary, some milling around like persons after a bowl game, not quite wanting to leave yet. When the last one had said goodbye to him, he noted that throughout the entire experience, no one had asked about Fran or the children. Very few asked him what he might be doing after this, and no one asked him why he had resigned.

As he walked back to his study to gather up what few personal items he wanted to take with him, he saw Elsie sitting at the organ, staring into space. He walked past her on his way to the study.

"Where was everybody?" she shouted. The sound startled him, but he kept walking. He did not want to engage her in any conversation, at this moment. In fact, he wasn't sure he'd ever speak with her again. Grabbing a few items, he started to leave the study. Suddenly, she was there.

"Hey," she said. "Aren't you going to say farewell to me?"

"What's to say?" He shrugged. "We both knew this day would come. As you can see, I'm not that great at saying goodbye."

"Is that why Fran isn't here this morning?" she inquired.

"I don't want to discuss this with you," he snarled.

Elsie walked toward him and looked up at his contorted face. "My God, Lark," she said. "What's going on?" She reached out and held him tightly, as his body shook in her arms. Gently, she guided him to a chair, made sure he was seated upon it, and then began to stroke his hair like a mother with a fevered child. It was comforting, this human contact after so many days of struggling alone and the poor attendance at this morning's service. Many people were notably absent. Doc and Millie were not in their usual pew. Clyde was missing from the back row, where once in a while, he would growl at one of the ushers as they talked among themselves during the service. Bev and Bill were not there up front giving their support to Lark as he led worship. Lark knew Betty wasn't coming. But, where were all of those whom he had ministered over the years? At this moment, he felt so desperately alone that Elsie's touch was comforting.

Regaining his control, he shared with her everything that had happened during the week. Elsie continued to stroke his hair and murmur softly as he, occasionally, shook convulsively, as he told her of each event. When he got to Fran's leaving, and her message from West Virginia, Elsie tensed somewhat, but said nothing.

When he was finished, Elsie pulled a chair next to where he sat and stroked his right arm. Lark felt like he had run a marathon: all of the energy with which he had come to church that morning had dissipated. He turned and looked at Elsie for the first time. Her face revealed the pain she was feeling.

"I'm sorry," was all he could mutter.

"You're freezing," she said, her facial expression changing to one of almost delight. "Let's go get some dinner and warm you up a bit." Ever the seductress, Lark thought. She had seen

241

the opportunity to live out her fantasy with him that now was hers. Still, she did represent some human contact which worship did not provide. He agreed to go with her, but only for lunch.

The two, soon-to-be-ex-colleagues, rode in Elsie's sports car to a tourist restaurant famous for Pennsylvania Dutch cooking and frequented every day by bus loads of folk from New York and New Jersey. Since most locals knew it was virtually impossible to avoid a crowd at Plain and Fancy, it was a great place to be fairly anonymous.

Elsie chatted all the way to the restaurant and through their meal about the fun times the two had working together. It was interesting to Lark how he could have one view of their labors together, and hers were completely the opposite. After an hour of this reminiscing on Elsie's part, Lark simply gave in to it without offering more caveats to the contrary.

But halfway through their meal, Elsie's mood shifted. She was known to make sudden turns like this. It would be evident in her body language, as well as the content of the subject with which she happened to be dealing. Lark was not prepared for it when it came, this time. He had just begun to slip into denial once more about what was really taking place this day.

"Did Fran leave you?" Elsie asked bluntly.

"Why, yes," Lark stammered without thinking. There it was. He had said it to another for the first time. It felt terrible. He was immediately angry, and slammed his fork on the table so loudly that guests nearby looked up.

Elsie stared at him in silence, waiting for more to be said. Her face betrayed a slight smile, and her eyes twinkled just a bit as she waited. Lark knew he had to be more careful with the rest of this conversation.

"She took the kids to West Virginia to visit her parents," he cautiously said, lowering his tone.

"And." She waited.

"She doesn't know how long she'll be gone," Lark said, half-hoping it was true.

"That leaves you with the packing and arrangements," she coyly stated with a knowing smile.

"Yes, I guess it does," he said, regaining his control.

"And then what?" Elsie was going to pursue this. She wanted to know her chances, he assumed. She had made it very clear to him before that her plan would be to go to Canada and take him with her, if he ever truly wanted to just simply bolt this scene. He remembered how he had laughed when she suggested it. But he also never forgot how serious she was about the proposal, and how hurt she was that he took her so lightly.

"I'm not really sure, Elsie." He continued to give her only what he felt would not entangle them again. "I'm going to take a leave of absence for a while."

"And what does that mean?"

"I just won't work for the church for a while. I need some rest and some time to think through what I'll do next," he said, gaining more confidence as he spoke.

"And what will your family eat? Where will they live?"

"We haven't worked that out," Lark said, losing his composure a bit. Her question made him think of his children and reminded him of Fran's anger. He felt warm across his neck and face.

Elsie seemed to take note of the blush and pressed him more with her questions. "I don't know how ministry works, Lark," she said. "Is there a fund of money you can draw on to support you during this leave you're planning?"

"No, nothing like that," he said flatly. "I'll have to find some employment somewhere to tide us over."

"And a place to live," she said ruefully.

"Yes," was all he could muster.

The two finished their meal in silence. After paying for it, going back to the table, and leaving a tip, Lark rejoined Elsie in the parking lot. They walked to where she had parked.

"You know," she said, reaching out and taking his hand, "God always opens a window whenever a door closes." She said it with confidence as she squeezed his hand.

Lark had seen a miniature tapestry with that phrase on it in the lobby of Plain and Fancy. No doubt Elsie had seen it too, for she was always drawn to such sentiments. He did not respond.

Riding back to the parsonage and its emptiness, loneliness, and the solitary aspects of decisions yet to be made, Lark began to feel an anger grow within him. He could barely contain himself as he made small talk with Elsie, as she drove fairly slowly back to the church lot.

As they pulled beside the house and she stopped the car, Elsie turned directly toward Lark as he began to exit the vehicle. "It is not proper for me to say this, I know," the organist said now, more earnestly than he had ever heard her speak. Never taking her eyes from his, she continued, "The fact that Fran is not here today, the last day of your ministry with St. Andrew, says volumes about your relationship. I just want you to know that my offer still stands, Lark." Her eyes teared as she spoke directly to him in tones he had never heard from her before. "We could be very happy in Canada. I know it!" She smiled and leaned forward to kiss him on the cheek.

Lark turned away from her instinctively and grasped the door handle to leave the car. Then, he turned back toward her and said, "Thanks, Elsie. I really have appreciated our friendship. And I especially appreciate your taking the time to have lunch with me today."

Her face fell, and a darkness gathered behind her eyes. "Yeah," was all she said, as she put the car in gear and turned her face away from him. Lark got out of the car and hopped the fence which stood around the parsonage yard, walking quickly into the house without looking back.

The clock read two as he entered the kitchen. The phone was ringing. Picking it up, he heard Fran's familiar voice on the other end.

"How was it?" she asked.

"Not as tough as I thought it would be, " he said, trying to hide his disappointment about the size of the congregation and the virtual silence from those who attended regarding his leaving.

"Were there a lot of people?" she asked.

"A normal summer Sunday," he answered, this time not as careful about hiding his disappointment.

"Well, how are you doing?"

"About as well as a man who has just resigned, said farewell, and doesn't know what he's going to do, can be," he said, an edge to his voice. He felt like saying that despite the events of this week, he felt she ought to be here instead of where she was at the moment.

"Well, I guess that's alright then," Fran said flatly. "The kids miss you," she continued in a tone which seemed to suggest that things were not as cozy in West Virginia as they had been twenty-four hours before.

"Yeah," he said, "I miss them, too!"

"And," she said with what sounded like a gigantic question mark attached to her forehead, "I guess I miss you, too. I've felt miserable all day long knowing how difficult this day is for you."

Lark could not contain his anger. He screamed at Fran, "You made your choice, Fran."

"Lark," she said very quietly, "I'm very sorry. I just don't know what to do."

"You leave me, and now you want me to feel sorry for you?" Lark shouted, tears of anger flowing down his face. He wanted to shout more at her over the phone, but he could not get the words out.

"Lark, please don't," Fran pleaded with him. "We need help now; we'll get through this, I know."

Lark wasn't sure he was included in Fran's "we," or whether she meant only herself and the children.

"So, what's your plan today?" he asked sarcastically. As angry as he was with Fran at this moment, he hoped she would return and they would find a way to work out their differences, forge a new life together, and get on with rearing their children. There was no response, at first. Fran needed either time to think of an answer or rephrase her answer, so as to lower the tension which prevailed.

"Daddy says we can spend the rest of the summer here, if we like," she finally answered.

"Well, then," Lark said, feeling the anger rise anew, "you just do that, Fran!" He hung up with such force, the phone base nearly was dislodged from the kitchen wall. Within minutes, it rang again. Assuming it was Fran, Lark ignored it. It rang several times more during the rest of the afternoon as he packed clothes and a few books for a trip. He fought the urge each time it rang to run and ask for Fran's forgiveness. He simply let it ring.

After eating a sandwich of bologna, lettuce, and tomato, Lark carried the suitcase and box of books to the car. He started the car, not really knowing where he was headed, but only knowing he had to leave. The old car shook to a start, and Lark drove away from the church parking lot, glancing once in the rear-view mirror as he turned into the alley, just to make sure he had not left any lights on in the house.

Driving west, Lark passed the seminary and college, then continued toward Columbia, across the Susquehanna to Wrightsville and on to York. The Beetle purred as it passed the hills and farmhouses which faced the roadway. Lark thought of how often he and Fran had come along this route, at first as newlyweds, later with friends from college, and more lately, as a family with three growing children. A mixture of remorse and anger propelled the car toward York, the White Rose City.

Traffic was heavy through York's inner city as the sun began to sink behind the hills and houses. Lark continued driving until he came to Gettysburg, where he had to make a decision as to which way he would travel on to Hagerstown.

Driving through the circle in the center of this historic little village, Lark decided to take the quicker route across the Sunshine Trail through Waynesboro, rather than the route Confederate troops took after they burned Chambersburg a little more than a century prior.

Lark rehearsed his story, which he decided needed to be told to his parents, as he shifted gears up and down the mountain trail that led through the Micheaux forest area and past beautifully moonlit lakes. This could be a very challenging drive in winter, but on summer evenings with the car windows down, it was quite refreshing.

Passing through Waynesboro, Lark turned south toward the Maryland border. Hagerstown lay only twelve miles away now, and he hurried along toward the city of his birth. Suddenly, it dawned on him, as he was only five miles from Hagerstown, that he had not phoned his parents. They had no idea he was coming for a visit. It was nearly ten o'clock on a Sunday evening, so he hoped they'd still be awake, for he had much to share.

He parked the car and walked onto his parents' porch. His dad's laughter came from within the screened windows of the living room. Lark was home. He opened the door and simply walked in. Like a child, he had come home to share a tale of woe and to ask for understanding and love. Here, he knew he would find it. It embraced him as he crossed the threshold.

Chapter 26
KNOWING IT FOR THE FIRST TIME

Lark's parents were accustomed to catastrophic news coming late at night. Having lost their other son in an auto accident three years before, the news of the dissolution of Lark and Fran's marriage, the shameful collapse of his ministry, and the uncertainty of their son's future was not as devastating. They sat in rapt attention as their unexpected visitation brought them news which would have destroyed many a parent. But not these hearty two souls who had weathered the Great Depression and World War Two with all of the human suffering in their wake. They sat, bodies erect, eyes focused, and hearts open to whatever it was which had brought their son to their doorstep this late Sunday evening. And, though they both were expected to rise early the next day, as they had throughout most of their lives, to go to work for minimum wages, they gave their son the most gracious hospitality their aging bodies could muster.

After attending to Lark's need for nourishment, Lark's mom joined her son and husband in the living room while the TV blared in one corner and the four thirty watt bulbs screwed into the aged overhead ceiling light illuminated the trio. Lark, from time to time, cried, as he related the horrible guilt and shame he bore for having broken both his marriage and ordination vows.

248

Despite the softness of his voice, at times, the elder Wilsons never asked him to repeat once any of the sordid details. And when Lark told how the sight of the photos had sickened him and eventually led to Fran's departure, both his parents looked at one another with abject sorrow and pity.

One could only guess what they thought or felt about this distressing revelation. They said not a word. They simply sat and listened as Lark poured his heart out to them, not pausing until he told them how he left the house this very day. For a few minutes after he finished, his parents simply sat and looked at one another, as if to determine who would speak first.

"So, what is it you wish, son?" his dad asked simply.

Lark didn't answer at first. That gave his mom a chance to introduce her agenda.

"The kids and Fran will stay in West Virginia the rest of the summer?" she asked quietly.

"I guess so," Lark said to his mom, as he turned his head toward his father, ready to answer the first question. "I had hoped I could stay here with you all, until I figure out what's going to happen."

His dad smiled. Lark, until this very instant, had forgotten that his dad was opposed to the wedding with Fran from the start. He perceived her to be from a family with pretentious airs and felt from the start that Lark would be happier marrying one of the neighborhood girls. Somehow, Lark's dad saw, from the very beginning, that the union was not going to be an easy one. His slight smile reminded Lark that his dad, under any other circumstances, would have been quick to say 'I told you so.'

"Of course, you can stay with us," his mother responded. She shot her husband a look only the Irish can give to loved ones. Lark's dad's smile quickly evaporated. "Yes, we'll make up the bed in the guest room, and you can stay as long as you like."

"Your mother and I will be happy to have you with us, son," his dad added. "You can come and go as you need to, and when you are certain what you want to do next, just let us know when you'll be leaving."

"Thanks," Lark said lamely as his mother got up, stretched, and left the room to prepare the bedroom which would become Lark's. His dad cleared his throat after his wife was out of earshot.

"I believe you want to say something further to me, Dad," Lark said.

"Not really. You know that your mother and I love those grandchildren of ours. When parents of grandchildren call it quits, someone has to be sure the grandchildren don't become the scapegoats."

This last comment hurt Lark deeply. Not until this very moment had he even thought that his children would somehow be harmed by what was about to happen between him and Fran. His face must have revealed the wound.

"I'm sorry, Lark," his dad said genuinely. "I don't mean to upset you any more than you obviously are. But you know I have always been realistic, lad. So what I'm about to say to you is meant for you to ponder, not respond to right away."

"I'm not sure I want to hear it, Dad," Lark said meekly. He glanced at his father's face, trying to read what it might be that he wanted to say.

"I hear that," his dad went on. "But you must know, somewhere deep inside of you, that no man strays from a wife and children unless the wife simply isn't there for him any longer."

Lark looked at his dad; this man, who had never gone beyond seventh grade, had more wisdom than some of the wisest sages who ever taught at universities. The words rang as true as any Lark had heard in months. He knew that he was correct— something wasn't right between Fran and him, and it wasn't new. With the birth of each child, Lark not only felt, but realized that he was less important to Fran. She had shut him out of most of the nurturing of the children, except to be a comic relief person on family outings or the threatened heavy who would come home to straighten them out, if they didn't listen. Lately, Fran was not as amorous as she once had been. Her life was so compartmentalized, Lark only found himself received during several time slots each month. He was always cast as one or two character parts in the family drama Fran directed with such heavy handedness, Lark felt utterly constricted.

Yes, his father had named it. There was no confrontation. Lark simply arose, said good night to his dad, and walked upstairs to assist his mother with the preparation of the bedroom. When he arrived, she was just throwing the top sheet onto the bed. She was crying, and hence, she was startled and embarrassed when Lark walked in the room.

"Mom, I'm sorry to bring this home to you and Dad," Lark said. He stretched out his handkerchief to wipe the tears from her face. "You know I didn't want any of this to happen."

"Lark, I don't think like your father, you know," she said. "I always felt you and Fran were perfect together. Each of you brought something special to your marriage. I just can't believe that you are parting," she said, as she started to cry anew.

"Mom, don't cry, please," Lark begged. "Nothing is final yet. Maybe Fran will reconsider. We'll have to get together to discuss moving out of the parsonage. That should give us a chance to talk, I hope," he said, almost believing it himself. He hoped his mother would latch onto it with hope, for now, even if he didn't.

She wiped the tears from her eyes and face, finished making the bed, and excused herself for the evening after informing Lark there would be clean towels and a wash cloth in the bathroom for him to use. They wished one another a good night. It was midnight, and his parents quietly went to sleep as Lark lay restless for nearly an hour before falling asleep himself.

In the two weeks that followed, none of the Wilsons heard from Fran or the children, presumably staying with her parents just forty miles from Hagerstown. Lark journeyed to Harrisburg on Tuesday for his first meeting with the committee on ministry and to formally request a leave of absence. It was granted by the committee without any inquiry, following Lark's explanation that his marriage was disintegrating and he needed time to put his life back together. Harry said little to him before, during, or following the meeting. On both Wednesdays, Lark went back to the parsonage in Lancaster to pick up the mail and begin boxing those things he knew he wanted to move with him. A week later, Lark went to the peace demonstration with the Lancaster contingent. People were cordial but distant with him throughout the trip. Only John was his old self around Lark, joking from time to time about past experiences not only in peace marches, but in other battles the two men had faced. Only once did he inquire about things between Lark and Fran. John did not ask Lark what it was he might be doing down in Maryland.

That weekend, a calm Sunday evening, the phone rang and Mom called Lark to the kitchen. "It's Fran," she said as she handed him the receiver.

"Hello," Lark said.

"Lark, the children, Daddy, and I are going to Lancaster this week to get things out of the parsonage that we want to take with us," Fran said matter-of-factly.

"You're leaving me, then," Lark said to her.

"I thought I had established that some time ago," she said bravely, but with a slight quiver in her voice. "I don't see any other way to handle this. Do you?"

"I guess not," was all he could think of saying.

"That's what I thought you would say," she said a little more sharply. "So, Daddy and I were wondering which day you might be there, so you and I can discuss what you may need and what we want to take?"

"Fran, you don't have to do this," Lark said. "You can have anything you want, need, or would like. You can have it all, if you want. I'll just take my clothes and books."

She was not expecting him to be so compliant. There was a silence over the phone lines, during which he wondered to himself how it was that she knew to call his parents' home.

Finally, Fran calmly said to her estranged husband, "Thanks, but I think it would be best if we had some kind of meeting of the minds on this. Besides, the children want to see you."

There it was. The first hint that someone in his family might be missing him. No sight or sound from any of them in nearly a month. He guessed his mother and father-in-law must have run out of ways to divert the children's attention from their father's absence.

"Of course," Lark said, "I miss them something awful."

"Well then," Fran said, with what could have been interpreted as a slight lilt to her voice, "what day will you be there?"

"Wednesday," he said. "I'll be there all day Wednesday."

"See you then," Fran said, then hung up.

It was only then that Lark became aware that both his mother and father were standing in the doorway of the kitchen with rather expectant looks upon their faces.

"Well?" his mother asked.

"We're meeting Wednesday to divvy up the furniture," Lark said angrily. "Her dad is coming up to help."

"That's not good, son," his dad said. "That old drunk will only be a jerk about everything."

"Hush," Lark's mom commanded.

"No, Dad's right," Lark said. "Fran's father is hard to get along with, and he'll be gunning for me this time."

"How did she seem?" Lark's mom asked.

"No different, Mom," Lark said quietly. "She still wants a divorce, I think."

They spoke no more of it. When Wednesday came, Lark drove early in the morning, leaving Hagerstown at five, for Fran had not made it clear when she would arrive. He wanted to be there when she did, so he could have as much time with her and the children as he needed.

They arrived around nine, about two hours after Lark. Fran's father was driving the wagon. The children leapt out of the car when it stopped just short of being beneath the carport canopy. Walt jumped into his father's arms, hugged him, and said, "I love you Daddy!" Leigh Ann and Saul approached more cautiously, but each took a turn at giving Lark a hug and kiss. The old man said nothing, and Fran simply said, "Hello," as the six of them walked into the disheveled house.

Within minutes of their arrival, the doorbell rang to reveal that Betty Smythe had come to care for the children for several hours while Lark, Fran, and her father made preparations for the move. Betty was friendly, as always. She would be back with the children by two, she informed them.

"As I told you over the phone, Fran," Lark said for openers, "I only plan to take my books and clothes. You are welcome to take everything else."

Fran's father grumbled something as he walked out of the kitchen, in order to leave his daughter and her husband alone for a few moments. No doubt the old man had a stash of booze somewhere in the wagon, thought Lark, but he said nothing.

"Lark," Fran said, "I really was hoping we could work something out here today."

"Really," said Lark. "Why'd you bring Ebenezer Scrooge with you then?"

"I couldn't make this trip to Lancaster and back all by myself in one day," was her excuse. Lark knew better. She had brought him along, just in case she needed someone to out muscle her husband for whatever he would be reluctant to give her. "Besides, Daddy pays his way, plus ours."

"Fran, it was your idea to leave me. Don't blame me for your lack of resources when it was you who left, okay?" Lark said. He was giving in to a rising anger.

"You would have left had the situation been reversed," she said with such self-assurance, Lark thought he might jump across the room and slap her where she stood.

"Look," he said instead, "this isn't getting us anywhere. Take whatever you like. How could I possibly care about any of this stuff? You've already taken the ones who mean more to me than anything in this house. Take it all; I don't give a damn!"

Fran's face flushed as he spoke, but she kept whatever she might have been thinking to say to herself. She simply walked past him into the dining room. She gathered up some of the kids' favorite toys and began to carry them to the carport. Lark stood motionless in the kitchen, watching his wife begin the process of dismantling their household.

Fran eventually went upstairs to pack several of the suitcases she had brought from West Virginia. Lark walked outside to the carport where her father stood, smoking a cigarette and gawking at the neighborhood. The old man turned toward his son-in-law and grumbled something so guttural, Lark could not make it out.

"What?" Lark asked.

The old man swore and turned away from him. This gesture was the absolute last straw for Lark. He had watched his children leave only moments after they arrived, a plan obviously choreographed by Fran. Now the old man was actually shunning him.

Lark walked toward his father-in-law, shouting as he approached, "Look, this wasn't my idea."

The old man turned and faced him, toe to toe, shouting in return, "I suppose it was all my daughter's doing, then, you son of a bitch."

"Don't give me any of your lip, damn it," shouted Lark. Both men stood close enough to whisper, but were yelling nevertheless. "This is really none of your business!"

"Oh sure, you goddamned asshole, I told her not to marry you!"

For the first time in all the years Fran and Lark had been married, the words were spoken which Lark always felt were just beneath the surface everytime they were together as families. He was crushed to hear it, even if he did suspect it. The older man continued to shout at him, telling him he was nothing but white trash, that Fran tried her best to rescue him from the gutter, that Fran had given him three wonderful children, and it was she who had provided such a wonderful home. All so her husband could go whoring around.

That said, the older man took one step back and swung his fist directly at Lark's face. Only the younger man's quick reaction saved a broken nose. The blow glanced off Lark's shoulder but was delivered with enough force to knock him off balance.

As he was falling, the older man swung with his left fist, catching Lark, this time, face first, right above his right eye. The force of the upper cut was just about the hardest hit Lark had ever taken in his life. For a second, or two, he saw stars, as he reached out to catch himself. His father-in-law had recovered his balance and next used his right foot to deliver a rib crushing kick to Lark's chest. The air seemed to rush from Lark's lungs, and he gasped for breath at the feet of his father-in-law. Lark's head was spinning, when he heard Fran's hysterical screaming from somewhere in the carport. She ran to where Lark lay in a heap upon the parking lot.

"Are you alright?" she asked, as she cradled his head upon her lap.

Blood now spurted from Lark's right eyebrow, as Fran sought to comfort him. The old man continued to swear, as he turned and walked away from both of them. Lark, in the arms of his estranged wife, began to come back to some sense of reality. His father-in-law had just royally kicked his ass. Some part of his manhood quickly developed a bit of respect for the old man. His head, shoulder, and ribs hurt like hell. He wasn't sure what was worst. Finally, his dizziness past and the air returning to his lungs, Lark sat up.

"I am sorry, Lark," Fran said sincerely. "I shouldn't have brought him along."

Lark nodded agreement, but he knew that he was somewhat responsible for provoking the old man. Had he just let his father-in-law alone, this would not have happened. His anger now beat out of him, Lark simply wanted to get this over with as quickly as possible.

"Fran, I'm going back home," he said meekly. "You and your father just do whatever you want, then lock up when you're done."

"But Lark, I thought—" she started to say, as Lark got up on his feet and staggered toward the house, "I thought you, and I, and the kids would have some supper before we left." She called after him, as he entered the parsonage, "Don't you want to see the kids again?"

Fran now turned her attention to her father. Lark could not hear what she said to him, but he watched her gestures through the open dining room window. The old man said nothing to her. He took his verbal reproach defenselessly. When she was finished talking with him, he turned and walked up the street by himself. Fran walked toward the house as Lark stepped away from the window.

"Lark," she called as she entered the kitchen.

"I'm in here," he said. He sat down at the dining room table.

"Are you alright?" she asked. She sat opposite him at the table. "Do you need to go to the hospital?"

"No," he said, "I will heal."

"I am so sorry," she said. "I never thought he'd act like that toward you."

"Well," he answered, "you did say he wanted to knock my head off. He sure tried out there, just now." There was something very clarifying about a licking. When Lark was a kid, he always was able to look back on a fight and understand that he deserved the whipping. He glanced at Fran and chuckled at the thought of being knocked over by her father.

She smiled slightly, then informed him that her father was going to take the train home to Martinsburg, call her mother to pick him up, and wouldn't be a problem the rest of the day.

Lark listened as Fran, genuinely embarrassed by her father's behavior, was doing the best she could to make this day more positive. They agreed to go get some lunch together after getting the house in some semblance of order. They agreed that they would simply store the furniture neither needed at this time. Each would have a key and the freedom to come to the storage garage to take anything he or she needed in the future, no questions asked.

Those decisions made, Lark called several storage businesses before he arranged for one, while Fran continued to gather clothing for the children and herself. As she moved about the house, she informed Lark that she and the children would probably not stay at her home in Berkeley Springs any longer than necessary. They might even come back to Lancaster, rent an apartment, and return to school in the fall. She told Lark she felt it would be better if the children did not experience too many changes. He agreed with her. She obviously had given this transition far more thought than he. Lark always respected Fran's ability to implement plans in this manner, even if it was boring to him, because such organization rarely left much space for spontaneity.

By noon, Fran had the wagon packed for the trip to West Virginia and Lark, feeling much better than he had two hours before, also had all of his clothes packed into the back of the Beetle. Two boxes of books were stacked in the passenger side front seat. Only Lark's gym bag fit into the little car's front trunk. Lark watched Fran load the final box into the back of the station wagon. Her red and white cotton blouse was out of her cut-off blue jeans, and her hair was mussed and damp from both the work and humidity. As she closed the back door, she turned just in time to note that Lark had been admiring her backside. She brushed her hair from in front of her face and simply smiled at him.

Lark walked toward her and took her into his arms. She didn't resist, as he held her tightly. But when he tried to kiss her, she squirmed away from him.

"No," she said, "I can't."

Rejected, Lark stepped back. "Okay," he said, "where will it be for lunch?"

"You pick," she said. "I'll go in and freshen up a bit."

Five minutes later Fran emerged, hair in place, shirt tucked in, and face and hands washed for lunch. She got into the wagon, and Lark climbed into the passenger side. "Have you decided?" she wanted to know.

"Yes," he said, "let's go to McDonalds."

They drove out the Lancaster Pike to the nearest McDonald's. It was crowded with business people and students from McCaskey High, all grabbing a quick lunch. Two hamburgers, orders of french fries, and chocolate shakes later, the Wilsons drove back to the parsonage. They had barely spoken.

"Fran," Lark said as they drove into the parking lot, "I don't want our relationship to end." There, he had said it. The one thing he feared saying for weeks was finally out in the open.

"Why?" she asked.

Lark knew what he should have said. He knew his parents were correct when they said that, as far as they were concerned, no matter what had happened between these two, Lark still loved Fran. They suspected that Fran still loved Lark, too. He loved his children. He didn't want to lose them this or any other way. Fran waited for him to say it. He couldn't.

"I just think we can work this thing out," he said. "I'll do better; you'll see."

Fran turned to him and took his hands into hers. "Lark, I believed promises once. I need more than promises now," she said. There was nothing more to say. He had risked, and he had lost once more. As he got out of the car, he noted that his head now hurt where Fran's father had punched him hours before. His ribs were aching where her father had kicked him. His shoulder was touchy where the first blow had errantly struck. But, his heart ached most of all, because he couldn't find a way to stop what was very obviously going to happen. Fran was leaving him for good. There was nothing he could do to change her mind.

"I think I'll go now, " he said, as she walked toward the house. She stopped and turned to face him. A tear ran beneath her left eye. "Don't worry about the things," he continued. "I'll call a mover and make arrangements for everything next Wednesday. I'll send you a key to the storage garage. Call me if you need anything else."

She stood her ground as he spoke, squinting just a bit in the early afternoon sun, which now was beginning to bake the city anew. She said nothing as he spoke.

"Tell the kids I had to leave. I don't want them to see this black eye," Lark concluded.

He turned, and walked toward his car. Fran never left the yard as he drove out of sight of the parking lot. He imagined her driving the children south. As he drove, Lark reproached himself for not offering to buy gasoline, not checking the wagon to make sure it was ready to travel, not seeing the children off, and not telling Fran he still loved her very much. Why was it, he mused, that the sins of omission are paid so little attention, when it is those that afflict the soul of the perpetrator the most?

The remainder of the summer, Lark made the necessary transitions one makes when families break apart. The household furniture was stored in Lancaster. The parsonage was completely vacated. The post office was notified to forward all mail addressed to him to his parents' home, while all mail addressed to Fran went to her parents' home, in Berkeley Springs. The keys were turned into Jane in the church office and all bills were paid. Lark left Lancaster on Labor Day, assured that he would not have to return to the city ever again. He dropped a birthday note to his daughter in a city mailbox as he left. Leigh Ann's birthday was September 7. He imagined her opening it and reading:

Dear Leigh Ann:

Ten years ago today a beautiful blue-eyed daughter came to live with me! She was fat, cute, cuddly, and bright eyed! I held her and fed her and sang to her and played with her. I watched her grow up into a beautiful, fine young lady. And, I've enjoyed her laughter, her jokes, her cute ways of eating and even getting mad. All the things my daughter is have made me extremely glad to be her Daddy.

And, if I were there today, Leigh, I'd invite all our special friends together and we would have a great big surprise birthday party for you, sweetheart! 'Tickle Bug,' 'Kiss Bug,' 'Pinch Bug,' would all be there with me, Debbie, Connie, Carla —and all the new friends I am sure you are going

*to make in Berkeley Springs. Have a happy
birthday, honey. I hope to see you soon.*
Love,
Dad

With that last detail accomplished, he drove toward a
future he had not planned with a sense of relief.

It was later that September that Lark's dad came home
with the news that the warehouse was looking for someone to
replace old Charlie, who had retired in August. Hence began
Lark's new career. He would unload boxcars at the siding next
to the food warehouse and load trucks for delivery to various
grocery stores in the Western Maryland region.

Lark's dad had worked for this outfit for nearly thirty
years, having landed the job right after World War Two. When
Lark was a teenager, he had worked several very warm nights at
the warehouse, unloading grain cars. It was the most difficult job
Lark had performed as a teen. Hence, Lark had no errant
preconceptions about this job. It was hard work. It meant minimum
wage. But when his dad suggested it, Lark agreed to fill out an
application. Within two days, he was hired.

Thus began some of the happier days of this unplanned
interlude of Lark's life. Lark and his dad went off to work together
each morning, lunch pails in hand, worked throughout the day,
then drove home at five each night. They took turns driving: Lark
drove one week, his dad the next. The two men gradually grew
to enjoy one another's company. Lark found he could converse
with these hard-working men in much the same manner as he did
his parishioners. People were people; some just worked harder
than others, got dirtier at it, and received lower wages. Lark grew
to like every one of the men at Merchants. Especially after they
stopped calling him "Preacher" every chance they got and began
to refer to him only as "Lucky." Lark knew his dad had negotiated
that change and he could only guess how.

Lark did little else but work all day and watch television
every night. Lark drifted into the lifestyle of his parents easily that

first fall. The rhythm of this lifestyle left him lots of time to think about himself, his family, and his future. His parents kindly left him lots of space. Although he helped buy groceries, assisted in yard and house work, did his own laundry, and kept mostly to home, his parents never suggested that he do anything other than what he wanted to do.

With each passing month, Lark was beginning to feel at home again with the two people who probably knew him best. His mom and dad listened as he talked about past experiences in each church he served, about special times with the children and Fran, and about dreams he once possessed regarding teaching graduate school theology. As was their custom, they listened without much comment. They simply were there any time he needed to talk. As the months passed into November and December, they noted that Lark talked less and spent more time in his room alone. The pain of separation was most keen as the holiday season approached.

Mail had come. Lark opened all but the letters obviously addressed in Fran's handwriting. These he simply stored in the shoe box, promising himself that he would open them when he felt strong enough to do so. In another shoe box, he placed letters from members of St. Andrew Church. There were not as many: three from Clyde; one each from Doc and Millie, Chet, and the Smythes. These were, like the letters from Fran, simply filed for some future time, when Lark believed he would have the strength to deal with whatever their contents might be.

From time to time those first months of his new life, the phone would ring, and Lark noted that his mother brightened as she chatted with those at the other end. A few times, he thought it might be Fran and the children, but, he didn't ask, his mother didn't say. Her mood was definitely upbeat after each of the mysterious calls. She smiled more. She laughed at TV more heartily. And, she seemed to walk with more of a spring in her step. She even joked with Lark's dad after these calls. Lark thought he heard them discussing the contents of the calls from time to time, as they prepared for bed in the adjacent bedroom.

On Christmas, the phone rang just as the three of them had sat at table for some of Mom's turkey, filling, mashed potatoes, and cranberry sauce. Mom always gave a reprise of Thanksgiving on Christmas day. This time, she came back to the dining room, looked at Lark, and said, "It's for you."

"Hello," Lark said.

"Merry Christmas, Daddy," three very excited voices said from the other end. Father and children talked joyfully with one another. The children thanked Lark for sending them games, clothes, and new books for Christmas.

"We miss you, Daddy," Walt said.

"When are you coming to see us?" Leigh Ann wanted to know.

"Are you warm, Daddy?" Saul inquired.

Lark assured them he missed them terribly, he hoped to see them soon, and he was keeping warm. It wasn't until hours afterward that Lark surmised his younger son's question was a query about his father's new job. Somehow, the children were aware of what he was doing. He guessed that his mom was giving Fran this information, and it was being passed on to the children. He had not written to tell them what he was doing. His letters to them always talked about past days and dealt with present questions about their happiness.

When Lark returned to the table, his parents had eaten their fill. "You want me to warm this up for you?" Lark's mom asked.

"No, I'll be alright," he said. Yet his appetite for food had all but disappeared. Later that day, as he and his dad watched the Blue/Gray Football Classic, Lark ate two cold turkey sandwiches and drank a beer. His dad snacked all day long, until he could keep his eyes open no longer. Saying goodnight to both Lark and his mom, his dad trudged off to bed, one weary and overstuffed Christmas reveler of the original Wilson household. He never awoke.

Three days later, Lark helped his mother out of the car and toward the gravesite where the pastor would intone the final

263

benediction for the dearly departed. A massive coronary, the doctor said; he never felt a thing. Lark's mom had screamed, just as Lark was climbing out of bed to get ready to go to work. The next two days were spent arranging the funeral, comforting his mother, and making sure all were notified.

Fran and the children came to the funeral. So did her parents. They were all sincerely supportive of Lark's mom. The children, glad to see their daddy so soon after Christmas, had some difficulty understanding the sobriety of the event. Fran, stoic, and self-assured, spoke to Lark only once and spent the rest of their time together paying particular attention to Lark's mom. Fran's parents simply expressed their sorrow, seemingly meaning every word of it, and left the mourners alone for the rest of the day.

Lark's cousin Ike invited everyone back to his home for a light luncheon following the funeral. Fran, the children, and her parents, ate quickly and left so soon folks scarcely noticed they had gone. Only Lark's mom spoke of them after they left. She remarked how Fran and the children looked so good and how good it was to see the younger Wilsons together again as a family. A neighbor remarked, not quietly enough that Lark could not hear her, that it was a shame it took Lark's dad's death to bring them together.

When it was over, Lark and his mom drove back to their home in Dad's old sedan. She guessed she'd sell it, she had said, as they drove to the funeral earlier in the day. She couldn't drive, and Lark didn't need two cars. It was the only decision his mother seemed to have made since she cooked Christmas dinner. The rest of the week had been a blur for her, and for Lark.

Chapter 27
LIFE WITHOUT FATHER

In the months that followed, Lark lost interest in world events. He barely noticed that President Nixon was now having troubles of his own. A two-bit break in of the Democratic Headquarters in a Washington hotel threatened to undo the Republican President. Lark simply worked at the warehouse, and then spent every evening with his mom, helping her adjust to the rest of her life. She needed so much help. Lark taught her how to keep a checkbook, make the most of her money, and even how to drive, once the weather improved. Mom handled the old sedan's push button drive automobile better than Lark expected her to, and she had earned her license by May of the first year without Dad.

Having the freedom to move about at will, seemed to make a new woman of Lark's mother. She took to delivering meals on wheels to shut-ins three days a week. She joined a women's bowling league and volunteered to drive her team to nearby towns for tournaments. Lark watched her seemingly enjoy life more than he would ever have dreamed. It wasn't unusual for him to come home from work around five and see a note attached to the refrigerator door, informing him that she would be absent and he was to care for himself that evening.

Following Lark's father's death, the men at the warehouse grew more sensitive around Lark, often inquiring about his mother's welfare and what new adventure she might have had that week. They stopped referring to him as Preacher, and eventually dropped calling him Lucky. They referred to him simply as Lark and seemed to have developed a respect for him which he couldn't explain. From time to time, he would be invited to one of their homes for supper, get a chance to meet the "better half" and sometimes, the kids. These excursions into normal family life reminded Lark of his family, now removed from Berkeley Springs and relocated in Lancaster. He often left such visits in a melancholy mood. This was especially true for him as he and his mom spent their first Christmas alone.

Miller was one of the men in the warehouse with whom Lark felt most comfortable. A generally confrontational person, Miller could also be kind. Lark learned, as the two men worked side by side loading and unloading grocery cases, that Miller had an intense interest in people. He listened deeply as others shared their lives with him. And he had almost a sixth sense about which questions he could ask and which ones to avoid.

Hence, it was no surprise to Lark when Miller asked him, out of the blue as they sat at Municipal Stadium for a minor league game one very warm evening, just days after Richard Nixon left the White House lawn and flew into history, leaving the mess in 'Nam for Gerald Ford to clean up, "When are you and Fran going to get back together?"

"What?"

"You heard me, buddy," Miller said with a grin, as he sipped a beer.

"What makes you think that's possible?" Lark asked his friend, as the big first baseman of the London, Ontario, Tigers, hit one nearly four- hundred feet over the right field wall with two men aboard.

"Well, you two aren't divorced yet, for one," said Miller. "I've watched you at work lately, especially after you've been with your kids or had a chat with Fran over the phone. You're different, man."

266

"What's that supposed to mean?"

"Oh, you're more—what's that you religious folks say? Contemplative," Miller said with a grin a mile wide.

It was true. Lark had thought about calling Fran and seeing if a visit from him on days other than holidays would be welcome. More than that, he had fantasized going back to Lancaster and visiting, unannounced, on Leigh Ann's next birthday. He, too, had wondered why Fran had never served papers seeking a divorce. It would be uncontested by him, if she did. With each passing month, Lark had hoped this was a good sign. The two had been apart for two years now. He had not opened any of her letters. They came once a week after Dad's death for a while. Then, this spring and summer, letters came less frequently. He suspected Fran still called his mom from time to time. And, for all Lark knew, maybe Mom had visited Fran on one of her bowling trips. Tonight, he felt he could give that process a start. Miller had struck a nerve.

"I didn't know it was that obvious," Lark said to his friend, as the new reliever finished his warm-up tosses.

"Oh, one can tell you are not meant to work at Merchants forever," Miller said. "Besides, your brain will get soft if your muscles get too big, you know!" Miller laughed at his own little joke, lightly slapped his knee, and nearly dropped his beer cup on the patron sitting in front of them in the bleachers.

"My mom needs me, " Lark suddenly remembered.

"Your mom is sending you all kinds of signals that she is capable of taking care of herself," Miller said seriously. "No mother wants her son around forever. It was a godsend you were here last winter when your dad died. But, hey, that was months ago. Your mom is doing fine."

Lark had to agree. With each passing week, his mother grew more independent. Come to think of it, Lark had seen very little of her since June, except evenings when her favorite television shows were on or the weather was threatening. Mom didn't like the thought of being out on the road somewhere and getting caught in a bad storm. Lark left earlier for work in the morning than his mother did for her job at Kresge's, where she had worked her way up to being head of the housewares department. In fact, Lark had seen so little of his mom this summer following his dad's death, he was beginning to wonder if she had another man stashed away someplace.

The reality was, Lark's mother had discovered a whole new side of herself. Widowhood seemed to liberate her spirit to explore new worlds hitherto unknown. Lark was proud of his mother's adjustment. He had seen this in other women his mom's age. The death of their husbands either made or broke them for the rest of their lives. Mom, having little of what this world terms luxury, was able to make the adjustment to a lesser income more easily than most. The only thing that worried Lark was whether she could have made this adjustment as easily without his moral support, ability to teach her, and patience to teach her to drive. Hence, he agreed with Miller's analysis that his presence had been a godsend.

The two men watched the rest of the game, joking with those fans who remained seated near them at the ineptitude of the Suns, the local farm team of the Baltimore Orioles. When the game mercifully ended in the bottom of the ninth, the two men walked to their cars, bid each other good night, and took their individual routes home.

It was eleven when Lark walked through the front door and heard his mother weeping in the living room. He flipped on the light and she sat up, startled by his presence.

"What's wrong, Mom?" he asked. He sat on the sofa opposite her.

"I had an accident," she said.

"Are you alright?" Lark asked most solicitously.

"Just shook up," his mother said, "and utterly embarrassed."

"What happened?" Lark asked, sensing his mother was regaining her confidence as she shared the incident with him.

"I parked the car up on the corner of Prospect and Washington and went into the church to pray. When I came out, the car wasn't there. I looked up and down the street and there, one block away, down at Jonathan, were all kinds of police cars and ambulances," his mom said.

"I naturally walked down to see what the excitement was and to tell the police that my car was stolen and—"

"What, Mom?"

"There was the car."

"Where?"

"Halfway into the plate glass window of Kay Jewelers, it was!"

"What?" Lark asked incredulously.

"They said the car came through the intersection at thirty miles an hour, never braked, and just smashed into the jewelry store."

"And the ambulance?" Lark asked cautiously, ascertaining that she had forgotten to engage the parking brake at the top of the hill, and the car simply had rolled down until the building stopped it at one of Hagerstown's busiest corners.

"They came for the driver of the car," his mom said. "The policeman I spoke with said that when a driver could not be found, he had called for backup because they then believed the car had been stolen and the teen who had taken it might be armed, or that it was part of a robbery."

"What did you say then, Mom?" Lark asked with a twinkle in his eye and a smile in his voice. He was now assured that nothing was hurt, but his mother's pride and the old sedan, which had seen better days anyway.

"Well, I told the young man that the car was mine and that, as far as I knew, no one had been driving it at the time of the accident," she explained.

"And did they cite you for the damage?" Lark asked.

"No," she answered. "When I explained that I was in the church praying, the officer seemed to change his mind about ticketing me."

"What did he say?"

"He looked at me and said, 'Lady, your prayers have been answered.' He told me nothing was hurt much but he doubted the old car would run very well ever again—something about a frame, I think."

"The frame is bent," Lark said quietly.

"That's it, totally," his mom said, as she searched Lark's face for some hint of recrimination to come.

Lark got up, walked to his mother and gave her a hug. "I'm glad you're okay, Evel."

"Hey," she shot back. "Who's Evil?"

"Oh, Mom, haven't you heard of Evel Knievel? He's a daredevil driver who does all kinds of stunts with motorcycles and cars."

"Never heard of him," the old woman said with a smirk.

"Well, just like you, he always crashes them and walks away unscathed."

"Oh," she said.

"Mom," Lark said now seriously, "I'm glad you're alright. I can't think of a better way to have your first auto accident than to simply not be in the car at the time."

They both laughed. Lark learned from his mom that the tow truck driver had taken the car to the collision shop. He explained that Lark could see it the next day and make any decisions about it. His mom had simply caught the next bus home, after standing in Hagerstown square for nearly thirty minutes, waiting for it.

She seemed more relaxed when Lark explained to her that if her car were totaled, as the policeman had suggested, her insurance would pay her the wholesale value of it, and they could then go purchase a used car for her to drive. She seemed satisfied. In fact, she was relieved. It was then that Lark realized his mother was grieving not simply the loss of the automobile, but the loss of her freedom of mobility. Both slept better that night, knowing all would be well in the morning.

The next day, Lark did look at the old sedan. It wouldn't have been impossible to fix it up so it would look better. But he worried that it might be unstable as its frame was bent badly. He decided to claim it a total loss. That night, he picked his mother up after her work ended at six o'clock. The two of them went car shopping, Lark promising to make the down payment for his mother and assuring her that the insurance would cover the rest when it arrived.

Two hours later, his mom drove a used car off of Sharret Motors' lot. They paid $1200 for it. This car, much smaller than the sedan, but of the same blue color, seemed to please his mom immensely. Lark followed her in his old Beetle. The two sat in the kitchen, eating sandwiches as Lark's mom explained to her son how much easier this new car was to drive. As Lark went upstairs to prepare for bed, he heard his mom dial a long distance telephone number and, after a few minutes of quiet conversation with whoever she had dialed, he heard her laugh heartily and say good night.

Several weeks later, Lark sat on his bed and stared at the two shoe boxes on his desk. He decided to open the letters from church members and leave the ones from Fran unopened for a while longer. There were sixteen letters, dating back to the first week he was absent from St. Andrew Church. Seven of them, in fact, were dated that first month after he resigned. Four were from Clyde, and the rest were from individuals who only wished to say how much they had appreciated Lark's ministry during some crisis or other. The first two from Clyde were somewhat disconcerting. The first, dated two weeks after he had left, informed him that as far as Clyde was concerned, at least two or three of the photographs were questionable. He hadn't heard from Washington yet, but expected a reply from the lab in two more weeks. He asked Lark where he could reach him, if need be, to inform him of the results. The second letter, also mailed to the parsonage address and dated thirteen days after the first, revealed the startling news that FBI film lab specialists were convinced that the pictures Clyde had questioned were actually taken at different times than the rest, and that there was the distinct possibility that some of the rest of the pictures had been touched or brushed, so as to alter them in significant ways. Clyde again asked where he might reach Lark, so they could discuss the next steps they might take to get to the bottom of this mystery.

271

Lark sat and reread the second letter. He reproached himself for not opening this letter and seeking some resolution to the pain, still deep within him, caused by the photos and his inability to reconcile them with his memory of the night at Jennifer's apartment. Clyde had also added a "PS" to his letter, in which he asked if Lark had drunk anything that night at Jennifer's apartment. He hinted that this fact could be significant, but said nothing more. He would await Lark's response.

There were two more letters from Clyde in the church letter box. Both of them were mailed before the forwarding ran out in the Lancaster post office. One was dated in September a year ago, and the final one came one week before Halloween. Both of them begged Lark to respond and hinted that there had been more developments in Clyde's investigation that just might prove Lark had indeed been set up by some group in the church. Reading these letters brought all of the pain rushing into the foreground of Lark's consciousness. He threw himself upon his bed and tried to calm down. But he could both feel and hear the blood pulsing through his head. He was angry at everyone again. He pounded his fist into the mattress over and over again and shouted, "God, why?"

There was no one in the home to come to his aid. Lark's mom had gone bowling. He was alone. He considered going into the bathroom, filling the tub with water, slashing his wrists, and sitting down in the warm water to die. That would end this once and for all, he thought. All of the feelings of confusion and doubt surfaced once more as he lay upon the bed, face down, pushing toward some resolution of the feelings which now twisted and turned his every thought to those of hatred and revenge.

After several minutes, Lark sat up, rubbed his eyes, looked about the room which had been his home for over a year, and got on his knees just as he had done growing up in this house as a boy. He wasn't sure what he might say to God, and so he just knelt there, at the bed, waiting for something to come.

Finally, he prayed. Aloud, he asked God to help him forgive even those who did him wrong, for he confessed once more his

272

complicity in any plot that was used to oust him from ministry. He asked God to continue to give him the strength to live through this leave of absence without self-pity or thoughts of destruction. He thanked God for giving him this time with his mom and dad. He ended by thanking God that Fran had not closed the door altogether on the possibility of their ever living together once more as family.

As he prayed, great pauses interfaced with words he said aloud. During those pauses, an unexpected peace began to embrace him, as a mother takes her newly cleansed babe in arms and walks him to the crib for the night's rest. Lark felt the touch of God during this prayer, like he had not felt for a long time. Surely, the Lord is in this place, he thought to himself with awe and amazement, as he knelt silently by the bed. He understood why the apostles wanted to build booths and never leave mountain tops. Lark half hoped he'd never have to get up on his feet again. Perfect peace, began to fill his being.

Finally, he lifted his weary body onto the bed and slept in a way that night that made him absolutely refreshed when the morning came. Miller shot him a knowing glance several times at the warehouse the next day. Lark smiled to himself as Miller smiled, knowing that it was something far greater than a call from Fran or a letter from one of the children that had lifted Lark's heart this day. It was none other than the Spirit of the Lord.

Chapter 28
MARKING TIME

Lark continued to work at Merchants, seeing the children twice every month, on their birthdays, visiting at Christmas and Easter, and living with his mother as she approached retirement. Nothing much changed between Lark and Fran. She gave him no hint of wanting to reunite with him, and he lacked the courage to take the initiative in seeking reconciliation. The truth was, as a couple, they had drifted into a comfortable arrangement. Lark was sending a portion of his income each month to support the growing children. He was writing about a half a dozen times a month. All had adjusted to being a family that lived this way, including Lark.

Each time he drove to Harrisburg to earn another year of leave, the committee on ministry seemed more interested in what he was doing to keep up his reading or any other aspect of ministry. Following Nixon's resignation as president, Lark had lost interest in demonstrating against the war; he had found a new cause.

It began one Saturday, the summer after Nixon resigned, as Lark walked out of the Hagerstown Gas Company, after paying one of his mom's bills. He noted a terribly disheveled man sitting on the sidewalk, singing an army cadence to himself. The man was filthy. As Lark approached him, the stench of urine and excrement wafted from the pavement to assault his nostrils.

"How you doing today?" Lark asked the man out of courtesy.

No response. The man just rocked himself and sang "one, two, three, four, three, four."

Lark sat down beside him, having decided to take another tack. "Hey soldier," Lark said above the man's off-key singing, "tough duty, huh?"

"Toughest there is, Captain," the man said in response, as he kept on rocking back and forth on his backside, banging against the wall of the building with each back swing.

"How's that?" Lark asked.

"Shore patrol," the man shouted. He turned and stared right through Lark. "Damned sailors be all over this here town, and I jest about give up trying to corral 'em," he said through teeth so ground down and brown, it looked as though the only thing this man had ever eaten was beef jerky.

"Well," Lark continued for some reason, "you round them up, and I'll pray for them."

The vet smiled, reached out his hand toward Lark, and said "Fuckin' A!"

Thus began Lark's ministry with Vietnam vets, who were beginning to show up on streets in America as veterans hospitals turned them out. Post-traumatic stress syndrome, the newspapers called it. Lark had seen it before. When he was a child, he learned that some men, following war, never make it back to reality. They are simply left to wander the streets of this jungle we call America.

Lark returned each day to that same corner, but didn't see the sailor until a month later. There, sitting beside him as he rocked, sat a man with only one arm, dressed no better than the one who brought him to meet the preacher. Within a month, there were a dozen or more men who gathered with Lark on Saturday evenings, just off the square in Hagerstown, right there on the sidewalk, for prayer and some Scripture reading and study.

Some of the men knew their Bible better than they knew their names. Most were from fundamentalist or Pentecostal backgrounds. Hence, they would punctuate Lark's prayers and commentary upon the Scriptures with "Amen" and "Praise the Lord," and "Right on, brother." From time to time, Lark could hear the apostle of the group, the one he had met first and who he judged responsible for gathering the men together, mutter softly to no one in particular, "Fuckin' A."

The *Herald Mail* took note of the motley congregation one Saturday evening, and when the flash bulbs went off in the middle of the prayers, the vets screamed, ran, cursed, and threw bottles against walls. It took Lark more than a month to reorganize the group. Some never returned, but some new ones showed up.

Old Zion Church, the first in Hagerstown and the place where its founder's body was buried, on the corner of North Potomac Street across from the YMCA, offered one of its halls to Lark for these gatherings, as winter approached. Having arranged, through his mom, to have some soup and bologna sandwiches served with lots of hot coffee and milk, Lark talked it over with the men. They agreed that if supper were going to be served, they'd stay for prayer afterward. So, that fall and early winter, Lark was serving as strange a congregation as any pastor ever faced. Each Saturday evening, about half-past six, the men would start to straggle into the basement of Zion Church's fellowship building. By seven, most were chattering and slurping their soup through mouths which would have made good patterns for jack-o-lanterns' faces, come Halloween. Then, a young pianist who Lark had coaxed into the coming each Saturday evening would tickle the ivories for twenty minutes or so. Steve was a down-and-out junior college student who worked at Merchants during the day, and then played gigs in local bars and clubs at night to make enough money to go back to college. After Steve's playing, which bordered upon religious but never quite made it, the prayer service would begin. The men always wanted to sing "Jesus Loves Me," and "What A Friend We Have In Jesus," and it was difficult for Steve to ruin these. It was also useless to try to teach them any particular liturgy. Their attention spans had been all but shattered by land mines, booby traps, shattered hopes, and various hallucinogenic drugs in Vietnam.

Lark carefully selected texts, read short passages of them, commented about them, and, asked the men what they thought about them. Some of their responses were quite unusual. Lark never contradicted them or endeavored to teach them differently. He did at first, but not since the night they discussed the passage about Moses and the children of Israel crossing the Red Sea, when Miriam had danced at the victory of the Lord over Pharaoh's army.

"Why do you suppose Miriam danced when it became apparent to the children of Israel that Pharaoh's army had been destroyed?" Lark asked.

"Because the dumb bitch didn't know any better, man," said one of the scruffiest of the vets. He sat at the table beside the apostle, the founder of the group.

"Yeah," shouted another. "She was probably just one of those dumb ass USO broads sent over here to 'Nam to make us guys feel good!"

With that, all of the men were into it, shouting obscenities and gesturing with their middle fingers to imaginary stages. Then, it was the apostle's turn to speak directly to Lark. He stood as he addressed the preacher.

"Look, the guys here are trying to tell you something, preacher, that you need to pay attention to. Every fuckin' army and navy in the history of this old world has got to use sex from time to time to get soldiers minds off killing. We saw so damned many shows over in 'Nam that were just like this Miriam dame, that it made you want to throw up! Women jiggling up there on stage where you couldn't reach them, getting you all hot and bothered, celebrating the fact that you just blew some poor goddamned Vietcong daddy's brains out. Shit, man, after we reflected upon it, we'd like to shoot Bob Hope!"

All of the men laughed, shouted and applauded as the apostle sat down. Lark tried one more time to get their attention back to the meaning of the text. He tried to explain to them that Miriam led the children of Israel in a dance of liberation. It was a scene of joy. They were free after four-hundred years of captivity and slavery.

That was when Lark was interrupted by one of the black soldiers. He jumped out of his seat and came right up and stood in Lark's face.

"Listen, man," the black man shouted. "No white man knows nothin' 'bout slavery. You honkies just won't ever get it!"

Lark truly didn't know what he had said to so roil the men this evening. They got angrier by the minute, as they shouted back and forth to one another. It was the apostle who stood once more and calmed them with his philosophy.

"Men," he said quietly, "the preacher's in over his head on this one. He doesn't know that if anybody had the right to dance and sing in 'Nam, it wasn't us. We were there as the taskmasters, not the children of Israel. We were Pharaoh's army, and, we got our ass kicked, just like Pharaoh did."

The men roared with approval. Lark turned to the pianist to seek help, and he started to play "Beautiful Savior," another of the men's favorites. The congregation regained some degree of decorum as they sang, and Lark gave them a final prayer and blessing as the service ended.

As Lark told of this group, the committee on ministry listened most intently. They sensed that Lark was onto a need that few of them ever had a chance to meet in their stained glass sanctuaries and their well-ordered church services. They were eager to learn as much as they could about his experience. Even Harry Sawyer was more than cordial toward Lark. He seemed genuinely supportive in his enthusiasm for this new form of ministry. Harry summarized the session with the committee on ministry by saying that he wasn't sure, given the report Lark gave of this ministry with ex-servicemen, that Lark should be granted another leave. It appeared to Harry that Lark had accepted a call to ministry once more. All of the committee nodded approval, but granted the leave, as was their right to do, and in accordance with Lark's request.

Lark could have shared so much more. What about the time Mom forgot to tell the women who helped on Saturdays what time they were to come serve supper? Lark and his mom scrambled and recruited the early arrivers to assist them in slapping slices of bologna between hastily mayonnaised slices of white and wheat breads. Or of the time, two months into the program, when Wayne, the pastor of Zion Church, informed Lark that the consistory wanted to speak to him about some damage done to a sofa in the basement? They were convinced one of the men had smoked a joint and burned the sofa? Or what of the time, shortly before Halloween, when the *Herald Mail* called and asked if they could interview some of the men following the Saturday night prayer service? Lark had a terrible time convincing the apostle that he should be the chief spokesman. Three quarters of his conversation with the reporter could not be printed. The picture which graced the Sunday edition, the next day, showed Pastor Wayne, two members of the consistory, and Mom, all smiling into the camera, while the apostle fittingly leaned a little to the left away from the more normally dressed folk with a slight sneer upon his face which should have been captioned, "Fuckin' A."

It was after that particular night's service that attendance began to dwindle. In fact, the apostle did not return. Lark assumed that it was because the men did not like the publicity. By Thanksgiving, there were only two or three men showing up on Saturday evenings. Lark and his mom could handle the crowd with no assistance from others. Steve also begged off, since his studies were taking more time and the weather wasn't always right for the trip. Lark paid him $100 and wished him well.

The third Saturday in December, only one man came to the service. He had said little or nothing all of the months he was attending. He simply ate, sometimes sang, but always seemed to be listening intently. Until that night, Lark dared not ask why the men were no longer coming. But, when it was just he and this very emaciated young man chomping upon their sandwiches and drinking coffee, Lark asked him, "Why aren't the men coming any longer?"

"They're not here," the young man said, as he took the last bite of his sandwich.

"What?"

"Gone South where it's warm, man," the young vet said.

"I hadn't thought of that," Lark muttered, mostly to himself. "Where do they go?"

"Mostly Texas, Sir," the soldier replied quietly. "They hop freight cars and ride the rails to warmer climes. The damned railroads know we do it all the time. They pretend to be policing the freight yards, but, hell, one of those guys sees you, and he simply hauls ass away from you."

"Why haven't you gone?" Lark asked the young man.

"Can't this time," he replied. "I've got to go to the VA over in Martinsburg 'cause I've been feeling poorly lately."

Lark looked at him. He indeed was not well: his eyes had receded into his face, his skin had a gray tone to it, and he seemed to be made of simply skin and bone.

"What does your doctor think is wrong?" Lark asked sincerely.

"I don't have a doctor," the young man said. "I just know I've got to go to the hospital. I've not been sleeping well, and I hurt real bad."

Lark offered to drive him to Martinsburg, twenty-three miles from Hagerstown. The young soldier thanked Lark for his offer but declined, saying that he had a sister who was going to take him the next day. When Lark got back to his mom's house that night, he informed her that Saturday services were ended until the men came back the next spring and he could recruit the apostle to rebuild the group. He also told his mom about the young soldier with whom he had spoken that night and of how sick the man appeared. The two of them sat and talked of the little congregation Lark had served that year. They laughed as they remembered each man. They recalled how one very hot Saturday night, the apostle became incensed because there was no iced tea. He lectured the women in the kitchen for not being genuine Southern ladies, or they would have certainly brewed some tea, spiced it with mint, and loaded it with lemon and sugar in the true Southern way.

That winter was particularly harsh, and Lark's mom, one year from retirement, missed several days of work due to influenza which had struck the households of the city in epidemic proportions. Mom coughed all through the winter and seemed to be irritable more than once with little things she would have handled with aplomb otherwise.

With the coming of spring, however, she seemed fine. She went to her work with enthusiasm, heading, as she liked to say, into the "home stretch" of working for a living. Lark noted that the men were returning from the South where they had wintered. Hence, his congregation began to grow, old Zion Church was used once more on Saturday evenings, and Lark's favorite sport returned to Hagerstown in the form of the Class-A Suns.

As the spring thawed the waterways and brought fresh aromas of gardens and green grass to the city, so things began to go better between Lark, Fran, and the children. This year marked the first time since the separation that Lark invited the children, one each weekend, to come Hagerstown and visit with him. Beginning in May, he saw each child this way every month and spent time with them, except on Saturday nights, when each of them helped him with the veteran's service. In August, Fran took the children with her to West Virginia to be with her parents.

These outings meant Fran and Lark had to talk more over the phone. Often, the conversation turned to Lark's ministry with the veterans. The children had come back to Fran with such tales, she wondered if they were telling the truth. They were. The men now numbered nearly fifty each Saturday evening. The Bible studies were livelier than any Lark had ever experienced in a local church as pastor. They asked little or nothing of Lark, except that he be ready to guide them on Saturday evenings and lead them in prayer. Though he would often see one or two wandering the streets of downtown Hagerstown throughout the week, none ever approached him or asked him for any kind of assistance. They seemed genuinely satisfied with Saturday nights; that was all they wanted of him.

"You mean," Fran said one night, as they chatted amiably under the pretense of getting their timing straight for Lark's arrival to pick up one of the children on Friday evening, "not one of these men has asked you for a nickel?"

"Yep," Lark said. "I guess they're getting all the money they need from pastors in the area."

They both laughed at that one, for their experience in the parish had been one of constant panhandling at the doors of the parsonages they lived in, from both vagrants and parishioners.

"Sounds to me like you've got yourself a genuine New Testament church, Lark," Fran concluded. Lark hadn't thought of it that way, but he guessed it was pretty close. The pastor of this flock was unpaid and unharried by the day-to-day operations of the faith community. He simply taught the Gospel to those who gathered each Sabbath. That probably was the way the church had started.

Miller pressed Lark one Tuesday evening that summer, as they sat in the bleachers at Municipal Stadium, watching the rejuvenated Suns win easily. "Why don't you ask Fran to visit you some weekend?"

"I've been thinking about it," was all Lark said. He had been on the verge of it many times. But he knew there was unsettled business between them, and he wasn't sure he was ready to deal with it. She didn't suggest their getting together, either. Perhaps she was as comfortable with things the way they were as he. He'd just think about asking her, nothing wrong with that, he thought.

Chapter 29
MOM'S
RETIREMENT

December 31, 1975 was the date. Everyone who worked at Kresge's knew it. Mrs. Wilson's last day of work for the company would be marked by a brief party, some punch and cake, and a short speech by the manager. Then, some kind of gift, usually a wall clock with the company logo on its face, would be presented to the retiree. Then, all would go home and promptly forget the person who so faithfully had shown up for work, year in and year out. Mom had seen several of these gatherings. Now, as her date approached, she talked excitedly about having only twelve more weeks to work.

One evening, however, just before Halloween, she was depressed. Lark took this to mean that the fact of her retirement was finally realized. But that wasn't what had Mom down. No, she had been inexplicably reassigned to a new department. After nearly twenty years in housewares, the manager told her that day she was being demoted to assist the person in charge of toys. Mom was so depressed, she could hardly eat as the two of them sat in the kitchen together.

"You'd think they would wait until I was retired to make changes," she said sullenly to her son. "Makes me feel like I did something wrong," she said. She just sat and stared at her tomato soup, which Lark had prepared, along with toasted cheese sandwiches.

Lark listened as the old woman poured out her grief at losing the one job she ever held which gave her a sense of importance. All she was now was a glorified clerk; that was how she saw it.

"Why don't you talk with the manager tomorrow, Mom?" Lark suggested. "Tell him how you're feeling about this."

"Won't do no good," she said sourly. "Sam's God at Kresge's."

"Well, try not to let it get you down," Lark tried to cheer her up. "The pay is the same, and the work is less taxing. Relax. Enjoy your last days at Kresge's."

Lark's mom just looked at her son as though she couldn't believe he had said what he had. She got up and left the table. The two of them didn't talk the rest of the evening. Lark's mom was deeply hurt by what had happened, and being the tough woman she was, she determined to deal with this problem in her own way.

The next evening, she announced that she was thinking of quitting before her retirement came. She couldn't or wouldn't adjust to assisting in the toy department. She knew nothing about toys. She didn't like the department head. She just didn't see why she had to make all these changes so close to her retirement. Lark listened as she rambled on about how she had talked with other employees and they supported her in this decision. As he listened, he sensed that his mother's pride had been hurt, and this was the only way she saw that she could save face.

When she was done, Lark asked if this decision would affect her pension. She hadn't discussed that with anyone. She would the next morning, she promised. That seemed to be the only impediment to her strategy for dealing with a manager, who seemed determined to make her final days at Kresge's miserable.

When Lark discussed this predicament with Miller the next day at Merchants, the older man was quick to point out that this maneuver was one he had seen at other places. In fact, Miller thought it just might be a strategy on the part of the company to rook Lark's mom out of her pension. He warned Lark to tell his mom to proceed carefully, for it could affect her future.

That evening, as Lark and his mom sat at the table, he asked her if she had discussed what would happen to her pension should she quit before her retirement date. She seemed reluctant to talk about it at all.

"Well, did you ask your manager the question I suggested?" Lark asked her point blank.

She sat starring into space. "Yeah," she responded, finally. "And?"

"He said I'd lose half my pension if I quit," she responded angrily.

Lark looked at his mother to try to determine if that answer were one which would dissuade her from her plan. He couldn't tell. He knew she was giving it considerable thought, for she didn't talk much that night or the rest of the week. Lark knew enough about her not to press her while she was mulling something over. She could be very stubborn. He thought he heard her talking on the phone about it with someone later in the week but he couldn't make out what she said, or to whom she spoke.

Over the next weekend, Lark's mom seemed preoccupied. She wasn't herself at all. She decided to sleep in, instead of going to church on Sunday. This was most unusual for her. Lark became concerned that she might be slipping into some kind of depression. She didn't seem interested in anything. She didn't watch TV, talk on the phone, or even go out over the weekend. Something was brewing, but Lark kept his distance.

Finally, on Monday evening as the two sat down to supper, Lark's mom announced that she had decided. She was going to move into a senior citizen's apartment downtown, and she was going to quit. Lark was stunned. He didn't know what to say to her. For all he knew, she might have given her notice that very day. And the apartment came as a complete surprise to him. His face must have shown how surprised he was, for his mother reached across the table and took his hand in hers as she spoke to him.

"Don't worry, son," she said. "You can still bed down in my apartment. I got it all figured out. With the money you make, I thought you might just want a place of your own someday soon, anyway."

"But, Mom," he started to say. Over half of his money was being sent to Lancaster to support the children.

"Now, now," she went on, "I've decided, and that's that. We'll get along just fine. I put my name in for one of those Walnut Towers Apartments today. The man said there is a six-month waiting list, at least. I just can't take that manager anymore. I know when I'm being screwed, and I'm not going to put up with it!"

Her jaw stuck out as she spat the last sentence across the table. Lark had rarely seen his mother this angry. Whatever had been said between her and the manager at Kresge's, he was sure it wasn't pleasant. His mother was the kind of person people either respected, or they simply were dropped from her acquaintance.

"Okay," he said, "I'm sure you and I will make it. We're survivors."

"I knew you'd see it that way, Lark," she continued, "I feel really good about this decision. I'm not getting any younger, and this place is just too much for me now, with your father gone and all."

Lark looked at his mother. Her hands were older, her face creased, her eyes dulled, her body a little smaller than he remembered. He was seeing her as she actually was—a senior citizen. He realized that he hadn't looked at either of his parents as approaching this age, when he came to live with them. To him, they had not changed, but the reality was that both of them had aged. His dad was gone and his mother was nearly sixty-five years old. He was seeing her this age for the very first time, as they sat at table discussing their future. As they talked, she explained that she had given her manager the necessary one-week notice. He assured her that one half of her pension payments would be honored, and they would commence immediately after she filed for them. Lark promised his mom that she would not have to file for them until she filed for social security. He would cover their expenses for the next three months. Fran and the children would understand, he said.

The two of them drove out for some ice cream later that evening. They chatted about old times and how much they missed Lark's dad. They even talked about the children and Fran and how some day, perhaps, Lark's family might be reunited. Mom never gave up on that hope, she said.

When Lark called Fran later that evening to tell her of the developments, she didn't seem surprised. She matter-of-factly informed Lark that she and the children would make out alright for three months. She said little more. But she seemed supportive of the plan.

Three months later, Lark helped move some of his mother's possessions into the third-floor apartment on South Walnut Street. It was a neat one-bedroom unit with a sizable kitchen and a lavatory set up for handicapped persons. It really was nice, but hardly sufficient for two generations to live in together for very long. Mom's bedroom suite fit into the bedroom very well. The new sofa bed for the living room seemed awkward at first, but after a few weeks, they got used to Lark making his bed each night and getting up early each morning to straighten the living room for any guests who might arrive during the day. There was only one parking space per resident, so Lark simply left his car parked at the Merchants' parking lot three blocks away. He walked to work each morning. When he wanted to drive his Beetle, it was ready and waiting at Merchants. Mom's car was rarely standing in its appointed place, except overnight. The old woman was always going someplace and seemed to genuinely enjoy her newfound freedom.

Between Social Security and her half-pension payments, Lark's mom was able to more than handily cover the expenses of the apartment and groceries for the two of them. They did more than survive. The two of them seemed to enjoy the liberation from caring for the house the Wilson family had rented for forty years. Retirement living for Lark's mother was better than either expected.

Chapter 30

BICENTENNIAL

Lark wasn't sure whether it was his mom's idea or not, but he liked to say it was, as he explained to Fran one wintry evening in February, that he was planning on taking the children to New York City for the big nation's bicentennial in July. Fran liked the idea and was sure the children would enjoy seeing more of the nation, now that they, could grasp a bit of history as they journeyed. The plan was to pick them up in Lancaster on July 1, drive to Philadelphia and see the Liberty Bell and Independence Hall, then go on to Valley Forge and spend a night camping where General Washington and his troops nearly froze to death before the battle of Trenton. Next, they'd rush up to Boston and see where the Battle of Bunker Hill took place, and then get back to New York City in time to see the tall ships enter the harbor on July 4. It was to be quite a dash. Lark wondered if he could borrow the wagon. Fran obliged. He also wondered if she would want to go along. She begged off on the trip, saying it would be special for the children to spend the time with their father. After all, Walt was getting older and soon would be old enough to drive. Next year, he'd be in seventh grade, Leigh Ann in sixth, and Saul in fourth. His children were getting to that age where they needed him more than their mother, she explained.

Lark didn't complain or try to persuade Fran to change her mind. He spent the next five months going over and over the routes, making reservations at camping sites, and getting tickets for the gigantic celebration in New York Harbor. As the date for the trip drew nearer, the children called more frequently. Each time, one or more of them had suggestions as to what additional sights they might see. Saul suggested, no doubt at one of the older children's urging, that they visit Mystic Seaport in Connecticut. When Lark asked him how he had learned of the place, Saul giggled and gave the phone to his sister, who deftly made another suggestion.

All seemed to be having fun discussing the proposed trip and making suggestions to Lark. Even Lark's mom had a thought or two, but surmised that she'd stay far away from the East Coast that particular week. She pictured all kinds of reveling and danger on the highways. She promised to pray for Lark and the children.

Miller also made a suggestion. What about Yankee Stadium? The kids ought to be introduced to the greatest stadium in all of baseball, he said. It would be sad if they were to spend a day or so in New York City and not take in a game. When he and Lark checked the schedule, however, they discovered that the Yankees were set to play in Kansas City that weekend, only the Mets were in town. They were to play the Giants, hence, any possible ardor Lark might have had to give in to the national pastime on this trip was squashed. Besides, this was to be a camping along-the-roads-of-history vacation.

Lark opened the ministry to the veterans at Zion Church on the last Saturday evening in May. They talked of their adventures during the winter, but one notable member of the group was missing that first evening, the apostle. Lark inquired about his whereabouts and was informed that he had taken ill during the winter. He was in Martinsburg, at the VA hospital. Lark made a note to visit him first chance he had. The men were in good spirits as they left that evening. Lark had talked several pastors of the community into joining him for this ministry. They would work together as a team the first month or so, then take turns on

Saturday evenings the rest of the time the veterans wandered the streets of Hagerstown.

Lark was concerned that these men get some help beyond simple Saturday evening meals and prayers this year. He talked with several local psychiatrists about joining the ministry team. He also talked with some business owners about joining them on Saturday evenings, to see if they could spot one or more of the men as possible part-time or full-time employees in their businesses. Nearly all of the fast food restaurant managers agreed to stop by, along with several warehouse managers. Even Merchants would be represented on a Saturday and seek to recruit one of the men to work for them over the summer, to help unload boxcars.

By the end of June, five of the men had been hired, and two of them had been fired from their jobs for insubordination. Lark knew this wasn't going to be easy, but he felt it was worth the try. Somehow, these men who risked so much and gave so much to their country had to be brought back into the mainstream of American society. Lark knew few of them would ever make it back. He felt there must be some who, with encouragement and patience, just might end up spending the winter working here, instead of riding the rails south to live in the woods, and cardboard boxes, panhandling.

The last Saturday of June, Lark heard one of the men tell another that the apostle had passed away that day. The men said a special prayer for the one who had been so instrumental in getting this ministry started three years before, and who now was with Jesus in heaven. Lark was particularly glad that Captain Paul of the Salvation Army was helping that night. The Army personnel could speak many of these vet's languages in ways Lark never could.

Lark had seen the apostle just the week before. That was when he learned the man's name for the very first time: Corporal David Hoskins. He looked so pale lying in the large ward bed at the VA hospital in Martinsburg.

"How are you doing?" Lark asked the man, as he approached the bed.

"How the hell do you think I'm doin'?" the apostle shot back. "I'm dyin', man."

"Oh, come on," Lark started to argue a bit.

"Get off it, Chaplain," the apostle went on. "A fightin' man knows when his number's up. Just say a prayer for me, and get the hell out of here."

"You're feeling that bad, huh?" Lark asked.

"Chaplain, if I felt any worse, you wouldn't be talkin' to me now," he replied seriously.

"I'm sorry," Lark said. He meant it. This man had come to mean a great deal to Lark, and now death was going to part them.

"I am, too," said the apostle, almost in a whisper. "Fuckin' A."

Those were the final words Lark ever heard pass the apostle's lips. After a few moments of silence, Lark offered a prayer for him as he held his very cold emaciated hand, then quietly left the ward. A nurse glanced up at him as he walked by, as if to say thank you.

After the Bible study the men all wanted to know if Lark was going to do the funeral for the apostle. He informed them that he had not been contacted. Inwardly, he was glad he hadn't been, since it more than likely would take place early the following week, and he had plans to go on the history vacation with his children. The men were sure that Lark would be contacted. The apostle had already decided it, some time ago, they said. He would be buried in Arlington National Cemetery. He came from a really important family; they continued to inform Lark, as though preparing him for what he might say about the dead man. In every generation of his family, going back to the American Revolution, men had served the United States with honor.

The call from Martinsburg never came, however. Lark didn't know where the funeral was held. And, when he next led Bible study that summer, there was no talk about the apostle. With a group of believers like this, Lark knew that people came into and out of their lives all the time. There were few long-term relationships and even fewer regrets when one no longer related with them. It was sad, in a way, but liberating also. The group made no demands, even upon one's memory. Perhaps they had given up on ever finding a place in this world which would give them a sense of community or of belonging. They were like children who would simply go from experience to experience, person to person, without engagement, enlightenment, or entanglement.

Yes, there had been three men who made it through the summer in their jobs, sweeping floors, unloading box cars, and lugging large cartons of paper through a local paper warehouse. But, these three were the minority. The rest were simply going to live the rest of their lives upon the edges of the culture. Unseen, unheeded, and unwanted, is how one of them described the group, one night at Bible study. All the men yelled in approval and clapped at the self-description. That was enough for them.

Hence, what first looked to Lark as though it were a group which might be rehabilitated and restored in much the same manner as one might think of resurrection, took on the appearance of the Biblical Valley of Dry Bones in Lark's mind. Only the breath of God could restore these men to their once proud manhood. It never occurred to Lark that perhaps many of these men had nothing to start with, in life. It was simply the turns of the political wheel which caught them in the Far Eastern conflict know as Vietnam, then spewed them back upon these shores to fend for themselves not any more improved than when they left. Many in their generation had gone on to college, marriage, parenthood, and moved up the social, political, and corporate ladders. These men, most of them, were right where they were when they first departed to that beautiful land far away. What was even worse, many of them came back with nightmares. These were the slag of America's misadventure in Vietnam. Lark didn't hate them, he just felt hopeless in the face of them. He determined that he would step aside next year and let local clergy try their hands at winning these souls. Never being good at maintenance kinds of ministry,

Lark had the good sense to back away from projects when they moved toward being simply pedestrian. He decided he would announce this to the men in the fall, after the numbers had dropped a bit, and then the word would get around.

The trip that first week of July was everything Lark and the children imagined it would be. For the children, it would have been enough to simply spend a week with their father anywhere. For Lark, it was the opportunity to really spend what he had learned to call "quality time" with them.

They were fascinated with the Liberty Bell. Saul wanted to run his finger down the crack, but the fencing around it prohibited him from doing so. He was truly growing too large to carry, and Lark, tempted as he was to grab the boy and lift him toward his goal, decided to let Saul experience the pain of a goal just out of reach this time. Leigh Ann suggested that the desks in the meeting room of the first Continental Congress weren't any larger than hers at George C. Ross Elementary in Lancaster. The children seemed fascinated by the quill pens with their feather plumes at all angles around the room. Walt wanted to know if the buckets which seemed to be standing at the end of each row of desks were truly spittoons, which he had read about in a *Weekly Reader.*

The night at Valley Forge was magnificent. The park ranger led a large group of intergenerational campers in a lecture about the colonial army and its hardships. The children listened with great attention to detail and later asked Lark how many men didn't have shoes that winter at Valley Forge.

"Why didn't General Washington just go to a store in Philadelphia and buy some," Saul asked innocently.

His brother and sister reminded him that there was a war going on and a price on Washington's head. He seemed to grasp it.

The next day, as they hiked around the battle field, Lark could sense the children were losing some interest. It was hot and muggy, and there truly wasn't much to look at, except rises in the ground and fences. So, Lark cut this part of the trip short and asked them if they would like to make a detour on their way to

Boston and go via Mystic Seaport? All three of them beamed with approval.

At Mystic Seaport, later that evening, they stood in front of the Mall, by an old two-seat wagon. Another tourist took a picture at Lark's request. Saul stood in front of Lark, almost armpit high, and smiled into the camera, as his sister, standing to his left with her arms folded behind her back, peered nonchalantly at the lens. Walt stood stiffly, much like a guard at Valley Forge with his hands in a framed position, the backdrop a white framed wooden Congregational Church building. The children loved Mystic Seaport, particularly the seafood they ate that evening. As they bedded down in their tent, they all swore they could hear the waves beating against the shore several miles away.

The next day, the four rode to Boston and visited the site of the Battle of Bunker Hill. The children's eyes were wide, as the tour guide talked of Crispus Attucks, the first black man to die in the Revolutionary War. Walt reminded his sister and brother that there was an elementary school in Lancaster named for him. They knew, they said. Lark thought to himself how ironic life is, really. One dies almost accidentally in a gun fight which now is remembered as the first battle of the American Revolution and is remembered forever. How unlike the men with whom he had ministered these past three years, Not one of them would be remembered, perhaps not even by their families, let alone have schools, cultural centers, or streets named for them in the future.

The following day, the four of them broke camp at five and after a breakfast of donuts, raced toward New York City for the big celebration that evening in the harbor. The plan was to drive to Newark, then take the train under the harbor and the subways back to the point where they could stake out a claim to the bleachers which looked out upon the harbor toward the Statue of Liberty and New Jersey. Despite the crowds, the four of them were down by the pier by six, having eaten nothing but junk food all day long. Aside from Saul being cranky at times throughout the day, everything worked to perfection.

Gazing at Lady of Liberty, Lark thought of his mother's ancestors, who had come to this country in the 19th century during the Irish Potato Famine. What must they have thought when they landed in Boston Harbor? There was no statue welcoming them, as there were so many in 20th-century New York City. Many were robbed or tricked out of what few possessions they were able to bring with them. But, they, like their Italian, Eastern European, and Jewish counterparts, were all survivors. That was what America was celebrating this week, Lark thought to himself, as the children craned their necks to see the ships spouting water and blowing their fog horns as they moved about the harbor. Bands played and people milled about as happy as those who first stepped off the boats at Ellis Island to begin their lives of freedom. It was quite a sight and quite a celebration. From time to time, Lark looked upon his children and smiled as they gazed about at a throng of people they'd likely not see again for a long time.

Downing more hot dogs, soft pretzels, and sodas from push cart vendors just before the fireworks began, the Wilsons huddled together and gazed into the night sky, as the cacophony of explosions accompanied the multicolored displays of Chinese pyrotechnics to celebrate America's birthday. And, when it was over, they walked to the dockside and looked into the murky waters, still reflecting the gaily lighted ships and adrift with paper from the fireworks' return to earth following their one brief shining moment of glory.

It was as they stood there, arms around one another, that Saul jerked forward and threw up right over the edge. Lark held onto his son as his body lurched forward, bringing with each resounding gurgle, everything he had eaten that day. Tears ran down Saul's face as he apologized over and over for getting sick. When Lark felt his son's forehead, he could tell there was something more happening than just an upset stomach. His head felt very warm to the touch. His face, even in the darkening harbor's edge, was reddening. Panic, for one brief moment, spread across Lark's being, for he did not know much of New York hospitals, and he had promised to have the children home early in the morning.

After ascertaining if Saul felt well enough to walk to the subway, the four of them started toward the stairway. The plan was to catch the next northbound subway into Penn Station, then catch the train to Newark, get their car, drive to the Holiday Inn, and bed down for the night. But, Saul threw up again as they rode the subway. His body shook, as his father sought to comfort him, while his siblings, embarrassed by the scene, were seeking to disassociate from him altogether.

An elderly gentleman, who had sat across from them, stepped forward as the car came to a halt in Penn Station, and asked, "Is he okay?"

"I think so," Lark replied. "We've had a big week, and, today, all we've eaten has been junk food."

Instinctively, the old man reached out to touch Saul's head with his palm. "He looks flush with fever," the old man said, "and, he's very warm. Do you mind if I take a look at him in the station? I'm a doctor."

Lark relaxed immediately. He could not believe their good fortune to be riding in the one car with a doctor in it on a night like this, when hundreds of thousands of people had just one thing in mind following the celebration, getting home.

Once inside the station, the old man asked Saul to lie down on one of the station benches. He again placed his palm on the lad's forehead while Walt and Leigh Ann watched with caution. Then, the old man took Saul's pulse and timed it by the second hand on his watch. He felt Saul's neck and then turned to Lark.

"This lad is very sick," he said.

"What do you think is wrong?" Lark asked him. Saul began to cry.

"Do you think he'd let me probe his abdomen?" the doctor asked.

"Saul, can the doctor feel your tummy?" Lark asked his son gently.

"Yes," the boy bravely replied through his tears.

The minute the doctor touched his right side, Saul squealed in pain and rolled away from him. "Just as I thought," the doctor

296

said to Lark, "this lad has acute appendicitis. Has he complained of any pain during the day?"

"No," Lark said, beginning to panic once more.

"Why don't you check him into a hospital here in the city, just to make sure," he suggested.

"We're on our way to Newark tonight, doctor," Lark said. "Is there a hospital there you'd recommend?"

The doctor shot Lark a look he'd seldom seen in his life, except from his mom. With a glance, the old man had told Lark he'd better forget going to Newark or any other place until this crisis was attended to. He simply said, "I don't recommend it."

Here it was eleven o'clock in New York City, with three tired children, and one of them was very ill. Lark had to face it; the doctor was right. He sensed the panic Lark was dealing with. So he made a new suggestion.

"Why don't you stay here with your children, and I'll call for an ambulance and make arrangements for a doctor to look at him in a nearby uptown hospital. Then, if I'm wrong, I'll drive you all to Newark tonight."

"That's very kind of you," Lark said to him. "Thank you."

The doctor turned and was gone quite a while. Saul seemed to settle down a bit and was resting comfortably on the bench when the doctor returned with two persons who wore emergency technician uniforms. The doctor introduced them to Lark, and they began immediately to care for Saul. One inserted a thermometer into his mouth while the other took his blood pressure.

"High and low," they said to the doctor, "we better hurry." Lark panicked anew. Within seconds, all of them were walking swiftly toward the exit, Saul being carried upon a stretcher by the two EMTs. There would be room in the ambulance for all of them. As soon as they climbed in and the doors were shut, the driver sped along the city streets, traffic parting to let them pass. Within thirty minutes, Saul was prepped for the necessary surgery. Their entrance into the hospital emergency room that evening was so choreographed, Lark almost thought he was dreaming, at times. Both Walt and Leigh Ann teared up as their brother was taken from them by a rotund nurse who assured them all that Saul would be fine as soon they got that sick appendix out of him. Lark explained to the children, as they sat in the surgical waiting room of the hospital, that an appendix is no bigger than a little finger, and it really has no purpose. Yet it could become inflamed and make a person very ill. They seemed to understand and, of course, wanted to know if Saul could travel that night to Newark. Lark explained to them that they'd probably have to stay in New York a few more days, a message which delighted both of them.

"Are you going to tell Mommy?" Leigh Ann asked.

"I'll call her tomorrow when we know Saul's alright," Lark said. "There's no use worrying her tonight. Besides, she's probably asleep by now."

Lark marvelled that these two youngsters weren't sleepy also. He was worn out. They seemed to gain some new life in the ambulance ride, and they were chatting to one another about it when the surgeon who had been designated to remove Saul's appendix walked into the waiting room.

"He's a brave little boy, Mr. Wilson," the surgeon said to Lark. "The appendix was very inflamed, and so we took a little longer getting it out than we usually do. We wanted to make sure we protected him from infection."

"Had his appendix ruptured?" Lark asked.

"No, not quite," the doctor continued, "it's been infected for some time, and it's a miracle no gangrene has set in around it. That lad must have been having awful pain, and I can't understand how you didn't know."

"He never complained, even after he threw up tonight," Lark explained. "Until then, I had no clue he was ill."

"You're very lucky," the surgeon said, never taking his eyes off of Lark's pupils, seeming to try to read something in Lark's eyes. "He might have died tonight, had you not gotten him here."

"Thanks to that doctor who insisted we bring him here," Lark said.

"Doctor," the surgeon almost laughed. "You mean old dough boy? That guy was a medic in World War Two, a conscientious objector, I heard once. He came back from the Battle of the Bulge so damned shell shocked, he has spent the rest of his life in and out of this hospital. Sometimes he's a patient, and sometimes, he brings in patients like your son."

"But," Lark interrupted him, "he said he'd drive us to New Jersey tonight if he had misdiagnosed my son."

"Hah." The surgeon did laugh at that one. "That old man can't drive! And, even if he could, I don't know what he'd use for a car. Last I heard, he lives under the George Washington Bridge."

"I can't believe this," Lark said, shaking his head in disbelief.

"Well, all I can say is the good Lord was looking out for your boy tonight, if that old geezer convinced you to bring him here. You a praying man, Mr. Wilson?"

"Yes, I am," Lark said quietly.

"You'd best light a dozen candles next time you're at church, because that old man saved your son's life tonight," the surgeon concluded. "And that old man hasn't officially been involved in medicine for over thirty years!" With that, the surgeon turned and walked away.

Lark sat down, very weary suddenly, and took each child in his arms and held them against him. "We'll stay here tonight, kids," he said to them. "Then, as soon as we can see Saul, we'll go into his room and stay with him. And, kids, let's say a prayer of thanks for Saul, okay?"

"And for the doctor," Walt added.

"Yes, and for the doctor," Lark said.

An hour later, as all three were gently sleeping in one another's arms, a nurse walked in and shook Lark's shoulder.

"Mr. Wilson," she gently said to him as he awakened to her touch. "Your son is out of recovery and is resting comfortably in room 1207. You may go up to be with him any time you want."

Walt and Leigh Ann awoke, stretched, yawned, and quizzically looked at this nurse, an older woman with gray hair and big sneakers.

"You children need anything?" she asked calmly.

"No," they replied in unison.

"Thanks," Lark said to her as he rose from the sofa. Each of them used the lavatory, and the children washed their hands thoroughly in preparation for visiting their brother.

Walt and Leigh Ann, as well as their father, were dismayed at the tubes which extended from Saul's mouth and abdomen, each emptying body fluids into separate containers. The one from Saul's abdomen looked especially bloody.

"That's a surgical drain," explained the attending nurse, a young woman with golden hair and a prepubescent figure. "Nothing to worry about. I've seen worse," she informed them.

The room was equipped with a sofa, and soon as the children looked at Saul, they both curled and quickly returned to dreamland. They were truly exhausted.

Lark sat beside his son's bed and from time to time stroked his hair, felt his palm, or touched his forehead. With each touch, Lark thanked God for the lad's safe recovery from surgery. Eventually, sometime during the middle of the night, Lark lay his head upon Saul's bed and went soundly to sleep.

Lark was awakened three hours afterward when Saul pulled his hair.

"Wake up, Daddy," the boy said. "Come on, get up, you sleepy head!"

Lark lifted his head and looked into his son's deep brown eyes, which showed little wear from the ordeal he had experienced.

"How are you, Saul?" Lark asked groggily.

"Hungry," Saul said.

The attending nurse walked into the room. "Welcome back," she said gaily to Saul, as she took his vitals. "Hard to keep a good man down." She turned to Lark and said, "He's going to be fine. Why don't you go freshen up?"

Lark, assured that Saul was alright, walked out to the hallway, noting that it was nearly six in the morning. Once in the public lavatory, Lark washed as best he could, swirled hot water in his mouth to remove the awful aftertaste from the day before, and did his best to straighten his aging hair. Then, he walked through the hallway looking for a telephone to call Fran about the events which had taken place.

Fran was groggy, and Lark wasn't sure she understood everything he was trying to tell her. He hoped she grasped the situation and would not expect to see them that afternoon. Lark promised to call her as soon as he knew how long they'd be in the city with Saul. He asked her what her insurance number was, for he knew he'd have to use hers to cover this hospitalization. Lark finally said goodbye and walked back to Saul's room, ready for the day ahead.

Three days later, Lark drove the children back to Lancaster. Saul was sore, but otherwise fine. Walt and Leigh Ann quickly grew tired of attending to their little brother's every wish and occupied themselves by reading magazines which Lark bought for them in the hospital gift shop.

Fran embraced the children eagerly as they ran into her arms in their living room. She glanced at Lark. "Thanks, Lark," she said earnestly. "When you have time, you'll have to tell me all about it."

They hugged, and he left for Hagerstown. The big vacation, extended by three unplanned days in a New York City hospital, ended at last. Two hours later, Lark parked his old Beetle in the Merchants' lot and walked toward his mother's apartment, took the elevator up to the third floor, opened the door, walked in quietly, and simply collapsed upon the couch.

Chapter 31
THE LETTERS

Three days later, a letter arrived from Fran. It was laying on the kitchen table when Lark got home from work at five o'clock. His mother had prepared a light tuna salad for supper, because Lark had told her at lunch he and Miller planned to go see the Suns game.

As he sat down to eat, Lark's mom asked him if he had seen the letter.

"Yes," he said. He reached out and, without thinking, opened it and began to read.

Dear Lark,

> *Thank you so much for taking the children on vacation this past week. I know they had quite an adventure for it is all they have been able to talk about since coming home last evening.*
> *Saul is doing very well and, if one didn't know better, there would be no way you'd guess he had surgery only five days ago. He is quite a trooper, and told me this morning that you were a great help to him when he got sick. He said the*

*"old doctor" was very nice too, even if he did hurt
him when he pushed on his tummy!*

*You really are a good father to our children,
and I have that for which I thank God, as I think
of the fact that you were with Saul when he became
ill.*

*Well, I must close this letter for now. Maybe
next big vacation I'll take you up on your offer to
go along.*

Affectionately,
Fran

Lark breathed deeply as he finished the letter. It was the
first from Fran in quite a while. And, it was the first letter from
her he had read since they parted. The others still waited to be
opened in the old shoe box behind the living room sofa.

Lark's mom sat across from her son, eying him closely.
"Well," she said, expectantly, "what did the girl have to say?"

"Oh," he said casually, "nothing much. She's just thanking
me for taking the kids on vacation."

"Oh?"

"And," Lark said very quietly, "she said she thinks I'm a
good father."

Lark's mom got up and walked around the table, put her
arms around her son, and said, "We all know that, son—the kids,
especially. Now, why don't you and Fran have a serious talk about
putting your family back together again, for good, the way it ought
to be. You know the good Lord never intended for man and wife
to live apart. You, of all people, know what he said about that."

"Yes," Lark said, a bit disturbed by his mother's sudden
display of concern for his lengthy estrangement from his family.

"You're darn right," she went on. "That's why I've prayed
every night that you two foolish children would never go see a
lawyer about ending this family. I'm sure Fran doesn't want a
divorce any more than you do."

"Well," he interjected, "she never told me she wanted to get back together, either."

"You've got to be more understanding of women, Lark," his mother explained. "She had every right to be hurt by what you did. But that was a long time ago. You know what my dear mother always said about the hurts of life."

Lark knew one more Irish saying was about to come from his mother, and he wasn't sure he hadn't heard this one many times before. He looked up at his mother, as she stood behind him, hands upon his shoulders. Her face was beaming as her mind retraced the quote.

"Lovely inlets of water," she began, "sweet free running streams," she continued. She placed her hands more firmly upon her son's shoulders and seemed to stare beyond him, straight into the fourteenth century. "Though tonight a spent veteran," she finished with a hushed voice barely audible to Lark's ears, a voice subdued by a sudden remembrance of her own, "I lived in pleasant times."

Though Lark little grasped what possible relevance this ancient verse might have to their conversation, he could not help but smile with pride at his mother as she finished the quote, no doubt learned many years ago at the feet of her mother or grandmother in Massachusetts. She walked away from him as though to leave the kitchen, but suddenly turned to face her son. Her message was about to be delivered.

"You, too, lived in pleasant times, my lad," she said. "And I don't mean your growing up here with your father and me. You know in your heart that whatever it is you've got to face about yourself, it's time. It's way over time."

With that, she turned and walked out of the door, leaving the supper dishes for Lark. He slipped Fran's letter into his pocket and quickly did the dishes, leaving them standing in the drainer basket by the sink after he had washed and rinsed them.

Within minutes, he and Miller were in their usual spot at Municipal Stadium. The game was with Winston Salem's entry in the Carolina League. The weather had been threatening to turn wild and rainy all day. But by game time, there were clouds scattered across the Western Maryland sky and the usual summer mugginess engulfed fans, players, and stadium lights in a soft, wet haze by the seventh inning of a well played game.

Miller had just returned from the refreshment stand with two cold beers. The Suns were coming to bat in the bottom of the seventh, when to the west, there were sudden streaks of lightning and loud thunder. Several fans moved immediately toward the exits, deciding to read about the rest of the game in the morning newspaper. Some fans clapped at the building noise to the west, the storm now surely roaring over the hills near Clear Spring. It was just a matter of time before it would bring its ferocity to this southeast part of the city.

The fans yelled and rooted for a rally. If the Suns could score in this inning, they would win, no matter what the storm might do. The first batter singled up the middle. The next walked. The manager for Winston Salem signalled to his bullpen, down the left field line, where Lark often sat as a knothole youngster when the Hagerstown team was known as the Owls, a farm team of the Detroit Tigers.

The next batter struck out, and some fans booed as lightning and thunder drew nearer to the stadium. Lark and Miller decided to stay with it, no matter what nature had in mind. The stadium lights flickered just as the Suns' big first baseman hit a scorching low line drive in the direction of the Pilot's shortstop. Maybe it was the thunder, the lightning, or the stadium lights flickering at just the right time, no matter. Within a millisecond, the shortstop lay in pain just off the infield grass in short left field, holding his right ankle and screaming. No one was sure whether the loud crack which they had just heard was the bat hitting the ball or the ball hitting the opposing shortstop's shin.

Whatever it was, suddenly, everyone was moving. The base runners were streaking from first and second, around the base paths. The second umpire was running toward the shortstop. The left fielder was racing toward the infield in order to pick up the ball and make a play at the plate. And, the Suns' trainer was running onto the field with what looked like a child's first-aid kit in hand. The home plate umpire threw both hands into the air and called time out, but, to no avail. Everyone kept moving. And, as if to punctuate the madness which suddenly appeared in the midst of this sedate baseball game until now, there was a brilliant flash of lightning which, by the time the thunder stopped rumbling around in everyone's ears, extinguished every light in the stadium and the rest of the city at the same time.

People screamed. Some fell right out of the bleachers as though blinded, the paper said the next day. Many had to be treated for bruises, bumps, and lacerations after the melee that took place. Lark and Miller sat, calmly sipping the last of their beers as the rain poured down upon them. Lightning flashed from time to time, and players and fans were caught in its sudden brilliance in various stages of frantic movement like dancers in a disco parlor outfitted with random strobe lighting.

After a couple of minutes of very heavy rain and some wind, the rain slacked off to a soft drizzle and the storm rushed suddenly toward South Mountain.

"Do you suppose we ought to go home?" Miller asked from somewhere in the darkness next to Lark.

"Hell," Lark replied, "why don't we just sit here until our clothes dry! Besides, maybe they'll resume play if they can get the lights back on!"

Both men laughed. Auto lights were now beginning to blink on in the parking lot adjacent to the stadium. This enabled many people to see where they needed to walk, in order to exit the stadium. Some of the players were back onto the field with flashlights in hand, obviously looking for items they had left behind when they dashed for the clubhouse. Lark was sure he heard two of them, from one team or the other, run into the wire fence in front of where he and Miller were sitting when the lights went out. They cursed and stumbled toward the clubhouse, obviously in some pain by what they said to one another.

As Lark sat there in the dark, he thought of the days when he was convinced he wanted to be a professional baseball player. Throughout his childhood, he had wanted nothing other than to be a ball player. But his teen years revealed to him that there wasn't much glamour in riding buses all day and all night to get somewhere to play a game. Little by little, the desire left him. Tonight, Lark thought, confirmed his earlier career decision. Being reduced to playing in a small city like Hagerstown, before a sparse crowd of persons who basically were just out to have some fun for the evening, underneath less than adequate lighting, while some other guy throws ninety mile an hour fast balls at your head, then having to get on a bus in wet clothing, body aching and sore, for $100 a week, just didn't appeal to him any longer. He enjoyed being a fan. There were less risks and less miles to travel. Beside, one could sit in the bleachers, drink beer, have fun, and make more money than the guys in the funny- looking uniforms. Maybe it was his age, but he was pretty sure his decision not to pursue a baseball career had some wisdom in it.

He thought of Fran, and suddenly remembered her letter. It was still in his shirt pocket. Only now, it was considerably damp, if not soggy, like the rest of what was wrapped around his body. Reaching into his pocket, he could feel that the letter was nearly fragmented by the water which had just poured on him, Miller, and everyone else. When they got to their cars, he said goodnight to Miller, stepped into the old bug and drove it to Merchants' lot. It wasn't raining at all in the west end of the city. In fact, some stars were blinking through the clouds, he noted as he walked to the apartment, his feet still squishy inside his sneakers.

Once in the apartment, Lark slipped off his shirt carefully, so as to not disturb Fran's letter and draped it around one of the kitchen chairs. He lay his sneakers upside down in the kitchen sink, so water could drain from them overnight. He hung his pants over the towel rack in the bathroom, then quickly made up his bed and climbed into it, pulling the sheet around him. As he sat there in the dark, he could hear his mother snoring in the bedroom. She was well into her nightly chorus. Whenever it got real bad, Lark would quietly slip to her door and close it, so as to lessen the impact of her sonorous ups and downs upon his sleep.

Sometimes, his mother would say whole phrases in her sleep. Quite comical at times, Lark thought. From time to time, she even swore. "Oh shit," she'd suddenly say. He remembered his dad would sometimes say, "What did you say, honey?" She never answered, of course. The problem was settled the minute she said it. Once in a while, his mom would wail in her sleep. "Oh, no, no," she would cry out. Whatever she saw, anyone who heard her do this would be convinced it was most traumatic. Sometimes she would even sing. One could never quite make out what the words were. Lark would have sworn they were Gaelic. But, there was no mistaking that beneath them, whatever they meant, was a melody much older than she. This night, his mother simply snored away the hours.

Lark switched on the floor lamp next to the sofa. He didn't want to turn the TV on, for fear of awakening his mother. He wasn't quite ready to sleep, and the newspaper quickly bored him. It was then that two thoughts emerged in his mind. His mother's comments earlier that evening about getting back together with Fran someday, and Fran's letters which as yet had not been read. He decided that tonight was the right time to start reading Fran's letters, beginning with the first which came after they parted, to the one that had arrived this very day.

Fran had written weekly, at first, then more sporadically, when Lark answered none of the early ones. In the last two years, she had written sporadically.

Funny, Lark thought to himself, how easy it was to avoid opening them, letter after letter, until it was a simple matter to ignore the entire box. It contained about forty letters. He had no idea what to expect.

When he opened the first one, it was dated just after the unfortunate incident between Lark and his father-in-law. Reading it brought all of the intense feelings of that sad day back to him.

Lark,

 I was very embarrassed and am so sorry
you and Daddy had the brawl in the church parking
lot. In talking about it with Daddy, he admits he
started the fight, just as you said, and he is also
sorry for the whole thing.

 I hope you are feeling better and that the
swelling has gone down. Please believe me when I
say that had I known he was going to act that way,
I would not have brought him along. But, I am so
confused with everything that is happening. I think
it is wise we are apart for a while. But, there are
times when I am simply not up to doing everything
alone.

                    With a heavy heart,
                    F

Lark stared at the letter, Fran's usual signature, simply her
initial, seemed so delicately placed at the end of the note. Perhaps
it simply was the fact that the ink on this note was beginning to
fade.

Lark opened the next dated letter.

Lark,

 How are you doing? The children and I are
still here at Mother and Daddy's but I am planning
to take them back to Lancaster with me in
September. I have applied for a teacher's aide position
at McCasky High. I think this will help me get back
into the profession. Daddy has promised to help
us move Labor Day weekend. Is it alright for me
to take whatever I need from the garage you rented?
Please let me know.

 I must confess, it is stressful, at times, without
you. I find myself thinking of you every day and

309

wondering how you are doing. How are your
mother and father?

I know you will find this difficult to do, but
I hope you write me sometime soon and let me
know what you are doing and planning?

Lonesome,
F

With each letter from Fran it became apparent to Lark
that she did indeed have mixed emotions about her decision, right
from the beginning. As Lark read the next several letters, he could
sense that Fran was attempting to reach out to him once more
and rebuild some of the bridges they had burned between them.
It was also obvious that she was cognizant of the events in Lark's
life in those days in ways Lark never would have imagined. There
was this note which came two weeks after Lark's father had gotten
him the job at Merchants:

Lark,

I think it is wonderful that you and your
father are working together. It must be fun for you
two to trudge off to work and have lunch together
in the same place. Write and tell me all about it,
please!

On this front, I am enjoying my work at
McCasky. There is the possibility that I'll land a
long-term substitute position after Christmas. If
that happens, I'll get a raise. That will be nice.
We've just eked out our living here, and I am glad
we have such a nice place on Lemon Street for as
low a rent as we pay.

The children are all back at George Ross
Elementary School and seem to be getting along
fine. Walt is king of the hill. Leigh Ann is doing
fine. Saul is enjoying his teacher. They all miss you

310

and wanted me to be sure to tell you. Just last night, Walt asked me directly at the table when you were coming back. I told them you were helping their grandfather at work, and that seemed to please them.

Missing you,
F

The next few letters were similar, filled with news about school life. But the letter dated November 2 was most intriguing to Lark, for it contained surprising information which brought up feelings he knew were only banked in a furnace of regret and ire.

Lark,

Though you have not had the time to respond to any of my letters to date, I felt you would want to know this right away and do whatever you see fit with it.

Harry Sawyer called me last night and talked with me for an hour. He asked me all kinds of questions about your incident with Jennifer. I told him everything I knew. He said he needed this information for your file. He told me that the committee granted you indefinite leave based upon what you had told them. I worried, after he called, that I might have said something to further damage your reputation. I hope I didn't. He didn't say much at first; he simply listened and asked me to repeat some things so as to be sure he understood what I was saying.

When we were just about finished, I asked him about St. Andrew Church. He surprised me with his candid response. He said there was an investigation taking place at the request of one of the elders. Harry said that a group of members went to Harrisburg recently and presented a strong case for investigating the incident which led to your resignation. He promised he would be available to me if I had any further insights to share with him. Am I doing the right thing, Lark? Please let me know.

> *Concerned,*
> *F*

Lark was amazed. Harry and the committee, in three years of appearances with them, had never let on that they were investigating the reasons for his resignation. Lark wondered if more information about this were contained in any of Fran's other letters. The letter dated December 18 nearly broke his heart as he read it.

Dear Lark:

The children and I invite you to spend Christmas holiday with us here in Lancaster. We miss you horribly, and we want to be a family again. Please come.

I know that I was wrong to act so hastily and harshly with you. You were not at fault in what took place at St. Andrew Church. Many of us know that now. But, there is nothing they or you can do about that. But we can do a lot about our family. It is not right that families be divided at Christmas. Please say that you'll be here with us.

And, please, find it in your heart to forgive me for being so blind as to what was happening to you.

> *F*

312

He felt ashamed that he had never opened or answered the letter. How could he have been so stubborn? The fact that he questioned it now, as he sat in his mother's apartment on a rainy night in August, three years after he and Fran had separated, was testimony to the growth which had taken place in his life. Like a person miraculously healed of macular degeneration, Lark Wilson began to see some things which might have been right in front of him, but which went unnoticed. He saw that there was a hand in all of these events far greater than his or Fran's, far more mysterious than Jennifer's or Doc's, far more beneficial than Harry's or John's, and far more loving than his mom and dad's.

Religious people always strive to understand the Holy One and are never truly prepared to meet with this mysterious presence which deigns to move and live among its creation and creatures. Encountered by the Holy One, we mortals go about our daily lives as though they rest entirely in our own hands, when in reality, one is there with us all the time who knows our every weakness and strength. Lark reflected, for the first time in quite a while, upon the grace of that one so glibly called God. Once more, he felt embraced by that good presence as he sat, no longer shivering, upon his mother's couch.

He no longer dreaded opening the letter dated January, 1974.

> *My Dearest Lark,*
> *My heart is heavy knowing how very much you must be grieving your father's passing. Please know that I pray for you each night and trust that your mother and you will both find rest for your souls in the fact that your dad is in heaven with our good God.*
>
> *In loving sympathy,*
> *Fran*

313

He eagerly opened more of Fran's letters which, shortly after January, became less frequent and the tone less hopeful. These letters took on the form of newsletters, with lots of information, but little substance. He marvelled at how her letters revealed her awareness of his life. He could only assume that she and his mother must have talked a great deal on the phone.

Her letter from March of that year contained startling news about the church in Lancaster.

Lark,

Harry Sawyer called me last night to tell me that the investigation at St. Andrew Church is over. He told me that your file would be sealed until such time as you wished to deal with the matters. As far as he was concerned, you could take as long or short of leave of absence, as your conscience led you. He informed me that one of the leaders of St. Andrew Church had proven that the photos, all except for one, were phoney. How much damage those photos did to both of us—to think that they were fake makes me sick and disgusted. I can only imagine how difficult it was for you to deal with this, knowing in your heart that the photos were not telling the truth. By the way, Harry said there were copies of the photos in your file as well.

Although you have not answered any of my letters, I thought you'd want to know this. Please accept my apology for not standing by you, Lark. It was childish of me to leave you when you needed me most. Please forgive me.

With love,
F

Lark had not heard his mother walk into the room, as he sat reading this letter from Fran. She startled him when she began to speak. "So, you've decided to read them at last." She said with an early morning growl to her voice, "It's about time!"

He turned and looked at her. "Mom, I'm sorry if the light awakened you," he said.

"No, it wasn't the light," she said. She rubbed her stomach. "I just have an upset stomach every now and then. I thought I'd get up and take something."

"Must have been something you ate tonight, Mom," Lark said.

"Yeah," was all she said, as she went into the bathroom in search of what she called 'that pink liquid.' He heard her rummaging around, then heard her wash the spoon which he had noticed lately in the bathroom but had never mentioned, knowing that if it were there, that was exactly where she wanted it.

"Good night," she yelled, as she headed back to her bedroom for the rest of the night. Lark noted he was over half-through with the letters, and it was nearly two in the morning.

The last letter stirred him deeply. He had long since given up trying to figure what was wrong with the photos. Try as he might, the best he could ever think was there was something about them all except the one of his embracing Jennifer at the top of the stairs which made him feel they weren't exactly real. He became so frustrated with the photos a few months ago, that he walked down to the hallway incinerator on the bottom floor of the Walnut Towers and tossed them into it. He felt better immediately after having done so, and never once regretted burning them. Until reading this letter, he had forgotten about the photos altogether. Funny, he thought, even now he didn't wish he still had them, so he could glance at them once more in reference to Fran's letter. Her letter simply confirmed what he felt almost from the first sight of them.

He lifted his eyes and said, "Thanks!" Then, he thought of Clyde. There was another letter from Clyde which he had never opened. He'd read it later. Lark was sure it contained information assuring him that the photos were touched up and made to look like something they weren't.

The rest of Fran's letters were quite interesting. All were filled with little bits of news about the children and her job, summer vacations, preparing for his visits, and assuring him that he need not write in return. Ultimately, he read the last one written prior to one he opened today. It had been sent nearly six months before.

Lark,

It has become painfully obvious to me that we have each settled into this lifestyle which has developed. The children are getting older. You and I are moving along very separate paths, now. I appreciate all of the help you have given me with the children's costs and the support since you started working. It is especially commendable that you have done this without our having to face one another in court or anything like that.

For a while, I had hoped that you and I could reconcile and be a couple once more. But the silence from you is absolutely deafening. I am sorry that I have hurt you so deeply that you can no longer relate to me. I must move on and look toward the rest of my life without you by my side.

I will always love you, Lark. You have to know that somewhere in your being. But, I cannot go on hoping for something that is never going to take place. Hence, I promise I will make your visits with the children as pleasant as possible, and I will do my best to rear them as we might have done together, were the circumstances different. But from now on I will probably not write you. Let's simply communicate by phone whenever we need to, and I'll depend upon you to initiate those conversations. Please continue to send the kids cards and notes whenever you wish. And, please call them anytime. As for me, I think it best that

316

I begin to face the reality that you are never coming back.

> *Yours,*
> *F*

Lark boxed the letters, shoved the shoe box behind the sofa once more, and curled onto the sofa for a few hours sleep. Tomorrow, he resolved, he would finally answer Fran's letters. Sleep came quickly and peacefully.

Chapter 32

HERE COMES THAT RAINBOW

On Saturday morning, Lark arose, showered, dressed, and walked downtown to run errands for his mom. Paying bills and picking up odds and ends was not his idea of an exciting start to a day of rest and relaxation. Nevertheless, he reminded himself, as he trudged back out West Washington Street, this was the very way his ministry with the Vietnam veterans had started. Now that he had all but relinquished that ministry to local clergy, he rarely made an appearance at the Bible studies, even though his mother stayed quite active in serving the men on Saturday evenings at old Zion Church.

It had been nearly two months since Lark had carefully answered all of Fran's letters. No response had come from her. Lark listened for hints of changes in tone as they chatted by phone, regarding his weekend excursions to Lancaster to visit the children. But he could detect nothing. Perhaps Fran wasn't going to answer his letter any sooner than he had answered hers. At this rate, they would be a quarter century getting back together, he thought.

Each day, his mother asked him if he had heard anything new from Fran. He could give her no more encouragement than he could muster for himself. Of course, news of the children was encouraging. Walt had shown little interest in any sports, except baseball, and that only casually. He, no doubt, would end up being one of those adult males one often sees playing softball on some ball field well into his forties, thought Lark. Leigh Ann, on the other hand, had shown the same prowess on the basketball court as her father had when he was in junior high school. She was playing first string. And, Saul? A football player, no less. He seemed to relish just going out and tackling anything that moved on the field. His coach loved his spirit. His mother feared he might hurt himself, the way he played with such reckless abandon. Lark saw him play one game, and the tackle Saul made on defense was something to behold.

Baseball season was over for another year, except for the World Series, which didn't hold much interest to Lark. It was a time in the sport world during which Lark languished. He was therefore glad he had the excuse to journey to Lancaster each weekend to see the children.

Strangely, now that the war was over, Lark paid little attention to politics. The Democrats had selected a man from Georgia to run for president. He seemed a decent and intelligent person. His Southern Baptist underpinnings concerned Lark, but he thought he'd vote for him anyway, when the first Tuesday of November rolled around.

The last Saturday in September, he decided to take the kids to see Franklin and Marshall College's football team play Widener College. The kids were hoping that Widener would have another runner like one they had seen when they were younger. His name was Billy Johnson. That day, Billy scored three touchdowns within the first eight minutes of play, simply by running to the outside and then outrunning any F&M defender. The fans were stunned by his speed. He wore white shoes, unlike any other player on the Widener team. Some thought he had to, in order to give the opposition a chance to spot him as he streaked down the field.

But, no such luck. On this Saturday, F&M's quarterback dazzled fans with his variety of passes, option tosses to the tailback, and draws, in which he called his own number. F&M beat Widener 28-7, and the Blue and White Diplomat Band marched up College

Avenue, past the Seminary, and turned up Old Main Hill as the bell tolled another glorious victory. The children wanted to walk with the crowd during this traditional victory march, and Lark was only too happy to oblige. He hadn't done it in over five years.

They decided to walk back to Lou's Corner for a drink, before heading for the car which Fran had let Lark take this afternoon. When they walked into Lou's, it was deserted. All around the streets, college youth celebrated, yelling from balconies of fraternity houses, driving by blowing horns, and generally celebrating F&M's victory. But in Lou's, it was relatively quiet.

The old man looked up when the four of them walked in and shouted to Lark, "Hey, long time no see."

"It's been a while," Lark said. "These are my kids: Walt, Leigh Ann, and Saul."

"Hey, fine-looking family," said Lou. The four of them sat down at the corner table, the children glancing around at the old pictures of F&M events long past, "What'll it be?"

"You still serving your lemonade this time of year?" Lark asked.

"Yes, we serve it almost year around." Lou's eyes sparkled. "Seems college kids always ask for it, except when it snows."

"We'll have four," Lark said. Leigh Ann suddenly scowled. Turning to her, Lark asked, "Don't you like lemonade, honey?"

"No," she quickly said. "It's bad for my face, Daddy."

"Wait a minute," Lark shouted to Lou who was beginning to squeeze lemons upon what looked like the first juicer ever invented. "My daughter would like something other than lemonade."

"No problem, for such a pretty young lady," Lou said. "She looks just like her mother."

Lark was startled at the comment, for he had never imagined Lou would remember his wife from the few times he had brought her to Lou's Corner. It had been years since they last sat here.

"What would you like?" Lark asked.

"Coke." She smiled.

320

"You got it," Lark said, and yelled again to Lou to make one of the drinks a cola.

Within minutes, Lou was delivering the drinks to their table. He also had a little basket of popcorn. "Something to munch on after the game," he said with a smile. "I don't get many customers in here on game day afternoons. It's good to see you again. And such a fine family!"

The kids thought the old man was little daft, but they kept it to themselves by simply looking at one another and smiling. Lark thanked him and gave him five dollars, telling him to keep the change.

By four o'clock, they were all back at the house Fran had rented on Lemon Street, a row house utterly indistinguishable from the many on all the blocks around it, save for its not-so-colonial purple trim on the window sills. Fran greeted them all as they arrived and asked how the game went. By the time the kids had finished, each trying to out talk the other, she shrugged at Lark and asked, "Do you want to add anything to that?"

He didn't, but, he did ask if they might all go to supper together. Fran begged off, saying that she had to grade papers and do some research reading for next week's classes. Once again, she deftly avoided being with them during Lark's time with the children. Lark had hoped they could go to one of their favorite spots in Ephrata for supper, and then take in a movie afterward. They would have to do that without Fran.

The old theater in Ephrata was showing the re-release of *Song of the South*. Leigh Ann got her brothers to agree to see it, and the four of them waded through a virtual sea of pre-schoolers who, along with their parents, had come to the early evening performance. As the film ensued, the children in the audience squealed in delight as Brer Rabbit and Brer Fox tried to outwit one another. Even Saul laughed at the Tar Baby scene. Walt, on the other hand, was more amused by the children in the audience than he was by the movie.

They were out of the theater before nine o'clock and back to the house on Lemon Street by a quarter past. Fran was surrounded by papers and had that harried teacher look about her when they walked into the house.

"You children should get ready for bed, now," she said. All three of them debated as to whose turn it was to go first. Apparently, it was Saul's, for he said thanks and goodbye to his dad and ran up the staircase to prepare for bed. As Lark was saying goodbye to Walt and Leigh Ann, he heard the shower start and knew one of these two in front of him would be next to go. Fran got up from the table and walked Lark to the door of the house.

"Thanks," she said, as they walked onto the porch. "It obviously was another great day for the kids."

"I love doing it, " he said, "and, besides, it gives you a break."

"Lark." She hesitated. "Drive carefully."

He looked at her. There was something else she had wanted to say, but couldn't. The whole way back to Hagerstown, he struggled against all kinds of negative possibilities which could have lay beneath her hesitancy, but concluded that if there were someone else, one of the children would have said so. Hence, he concluded, she must have finally wanted to say something about his last sentence in his letter to her. "I know this is awkward, but if you still want to try to get back together I am more than ready to meet you anytime, anywhere."

She wanted to set the date, time and place for their reunion. His heart skipped a beat at the thought. But, now, it was the end of September and still no word from her. Each visit seemed to be a game of cat and mouse, where he endeavored to set up some way for her to participate with him and the children. And each time, she had some other pressing need to attend to while he spent time with them.

Lark felt badly that the next weekend would not afford him the opportunity to visit the children. Harry Sawyer had called to say that the Committee on Ministry was meeting and asked if Lark could be present for his annual leave session with them by three. As he dressed, in preparation for the two-hour drive to

Harrisburg, he wondered what he might say to the committee. His life lately had lacked any sense of movement toward ministry, and what he thought was an open door to reuniting the family was only slightly ajar.

The drive to Harrisburg was not without its first touches of fall beauty. The hills weren't the bright red they would be in a few weeks or so, but a slight hint of yellows, greens, and browns met his eyes. The light traffic allowed plenty of time for observing as the countryside passed by the little windows of the Beetle.

When he turned into the parking lot, Lark noted there were more cars than usual gathered for a Saturday. He assumed that there was more taking place at the ecumenical center this particular Saturday afternoon than just the conference committee on ministry meeting. And, when he got to the meeting room, he was met with only the usual members of the committee: seven people who also were giving up their Saturday to meet with various clergy at diverse stages of their careers.

Harry opened the meeting by making sure that Lark knew everyone around the table. Then, Lark was asked to summarize his past year of leave and make any requests he had considered. When Lark concluded, he asked the committee to extend his leave for yet another year. They nodded approval.

"Is there anything else?" Harry asked him as he sat at table with the committee.

"Not at this time," Lark replied.

"We were hoping that, by this time, you would have given some thought to returning to full-time service, Lark," said one member of the committee.

"Yes, we've sensed progress in your faith journey," said another, "You know the church needs good pastors."

"I think what the committee is trying to say, Lark," Harry chimed in, "is that if they grant you a leave, this will be the last year such leave is normally granted. We are hopeful that any minister who seeks leave will come to some sense of the credibility of her or his call after a year or two. In your case, you are now asking us to grant you leave for a fourth year. That is our limit."

Lark didn't know what to say. He hadn't expected to deal with this question. Silence prevailed around the table, as members shot one another quick glances without engaging Lark's attention.

"I hope to have this question settled soon," Lark said finally.

"Good," said the oldest member of the committee, "because we don't want to lose you." They all smiled as they waited for Lark to respond.

"Thank you," was all he said.

"Lark, will you please step outside, while we debate your request," the chairperson said.

As Lark got up to leave the room, so did Harry Sawyer. "I'll accompany you," he said. The two of them went into his office, which was adjacent to their meeting room.

"Lark," Harry began to say, "it's none of my business, but I guess I want to ask you how you and Fran are doing these days?" Harry had never asked about them as a couple. Lark didn't know what to say.

"We, " he started to respond slowly, "are trying to have a meeting of the minds on our future. I sense positive things are developing between us."

"Good," was all his Bishop said. The two men stood face to face. It was uncomfortable being here, suddenly. Harry sensed Lark's discomfort.

"Look, Lark," he said, "none of us is out to get you. I, for one, don't believe any of the things you were accused of ever happened. And there are many within St. Andrew Church who don't either. Any day you want to return, I am ready to support you."

Lark was encouraged by the tone of Harry's voice, the sincerity of his facial expression as he spoke, and the door which was suddenly opened between these two men who had normally kept such professional distance between them, that their relationship could only be described as cordial.

"Harry," Lark said, "I appreciate that very much. I think I'd like to talk with you about those events sometime very soon."

"Good," Harry said again. The chairperson entered the office once more and asked the two men to come back into the room. When they got there, the committee members smiled at Lark.

"Lark," the chairperson said, "we have decided to grant you a leave of absence for yet one more year."

"Thanks," Lark said in return.

"But, there is a provision," the chairperson continued. "We want you to come back to meet with us every three months. We have set goals for each meeting. Would you like to hear them?"

"Yes," Lark said hesitantly.

"In three months, we want to spend two hours with you, dealing with the events which led to your departure from St. Andrew Church. In six months, we want to invite members of the church to meet with us to reflect together upon those events. And, nine months from now, we want you and your wife to be present to talk with us about your remembrance of those events and how you have dealt with them since." She hesitated, to let Lark absorb the gist of their plan.

"And, a year from now?" Lark asked.

"Our goal one year from now is to determine your fitness for full-time ministry," she paused. "And, hopefully, to celebrate a new call to serve with you."

Lark looked at Harry, who was beaming with pride. Obviously, they had not decided all of this in the little time Lark and Harry had spent in his office. There had been considerable discussion prior to this meeting.

"Are you agreed?" the chairperson wanted to know.

"Yes," Lark replied. What choice did he have? The committee had shown tremendous patience with him. To them, now was the time to deal with this minister before them and bring him back to service in the church or drop his credentials. To allow him to drift any longer would be fair neither to him nor the church.

They shook hands as Lark got up to leave the meeting. Harry excused himself once more from the group, and accompanied

Lark out of the building, into the parking lot. This was most unusual behavior on Harry's part, and Lark took note of it. More was to be communicated.

"Lark," Harry said, as they stood in the parking lot, "you must know that I am aware of all of the events which led to your resignation. The committee, however, is not. And, you know that over the years, I have communicated with Fran and members of St. Andrew Church. All of this is now in your file. I am hopeful that in the coming year, we can add one more page to that file, Lark."

"And, what would that be?" Lark asked.

"That you have been reconciled to those events and that you have rejoined the church as an active minister."

"Harry," Lark said, feeling very awkward about this conversation, "you know that there are aspects of those events that only I experienced."

"Yes," Harry said, "and I am ready to hear any of that you care to share with me."

"Do you think I'm ready to talk about all of that before a committee?" Lark asked.

"I said, I am ready to hear you, Lark," Harry concluded. "I never mentioned the committee. They will hear only what you and I decide to tell them."

Lark looked at Harry quizzically as the two men stood, each waiting for the other to make the next move.

"I'll give it some thought," Lark finally said. He opened the door to the Beetle and stepped into it. Harry said nothing, but simply waved him off as Lark drove away. Think about it is what Lark did the entire drive back to Hagerstown. Though his thoughts were muddled, he did decide to contact Clyde and follow up with that part of the story.

Once back in the apartment where he and his mother lived, Lark looked up Clyde's telephone number and dialed. Clyde's wife answered the phone.

"Hello," she said.

"This is Lark Wilson calling," Lark said.

"Well, I'll be," she exclaimed.

"Is Clyde available?" Lark asked.

There was a considerable pause at the other end, and Lark thought he heard weeping, before Clyde's wife regained enough composure to speak again.

"Lark," she said hesitantly, "Clyde is in a nursing home. He had a very serious stroke a year ago. He just got to be too much for me to handle here at home. He flies into rages when he can't communicate."

"Oh," Lark said softly, "I'm so sorry to hear that."

"Yes," she continued, "wish you were here, Lark. He couldn't get you out of his mind when you left us. He believed you were set up, you know."

"Yes," Lark said quietly. "I hope that didn't upset him too much."

"Oh, please don't misunderstand me," she went on. "You didn't cause his stroke. Clyde's been in poor health for years, and he's always had too much temperament for his own good."

"I was wondering if I could visit Clyde sometime, if that would be alright?" Lark asked.

"It might really cheer him up to see you again," she said sincerely, "as long as he's having a good day."

"I'm coming to Lancaster tomorrow," Lark told her. "Maybe I'll just stop by for a few minutes."

Clyde's wife told Lark that her husband was a resident at the Brethren Home on the old Lancaster Pike. Lark assured her he knew where that was, and that he would not overtax her husband.

As Lark returned the telephone receiver to its cradle his mother walked into the kitchen. "You going to Zion tonight?" she asked.

"I don't think so, Mom," was his response. "I want to do some reading before I go to bed." Lark intended to review the letters he had received from Clyde for any clues as to what the old man might have discovered.

"How did it go today?" his mother asked. She walked to the sink and drew herself a glass of cool water.

"Fine," he said. "They've outlined a course of reflection for my final year of leave."

"This is your final year?" she asked with a tinge of hope to her tone.

"It's the protocol, Mom," Lark said. He explained to her that he would need to go to at least four meetings in the coming year. She listened carefully to his every word, as she stood sipping the water by the sink.

"And," she asked, "at the end of the year, then what?"

"They want me to serve a new call," Lark said unenthusiastically.

"And, what do you want?"

"I wish to God I knew," he answered.

After his mother left, Lark dug out the old shoe box containing letters from parishioners at St. Andrew. It had been quite a while since he first read them, and he looked for the letters from Clyde. As he read Clyde's third and fourth letters, he was surprised by their contents. He had remembered the first two very clearly, as they related how Clyde was continuing to investigate the incidents which led to Lark's resignation, and about the photos. He guessed, as he read the third and fourth letters anew, that he must have been so upset that first night he had read them, that he hadn't fully grasped their content. This time, Lark calmly read them as he prepared himself to see Clyde the next day.

In the third letter, dated the last day of September, 1973, Clyde informed Lark that he had become aware of a substance which was being used by some KKK groups in the South to confuse and accuse political opponents of the Vietnam war of doing things they never did. Clyde recalled Lark telling him, or maybe it was Fran, that Jennifer had given him something to drink before things got hectic in her apartment.

"What you might have been given in that drink is really a controlled substance known as

flunitrazepam. The stuff is odorless and tasteless, and just two milligrams can turn you into putty in another person's hands within twenty minutes.

And, here's the rub, Lark. It causes memory loss and extreme nausea. I'll never forget how you threw up that day I came to see you at your office. You said you couldn't remember everything. Now, it's important that you get back to me and go over everything again. So far, I know the photos are phony. I also suspect you were drugged. And, I truly believe you were set up by somebody in our church. Let's fight this together. What do you have to lose?"

The last letter, dated October 31, 1973, revealed Clyde's frustration with Lark's lack of interest.

"I have called Harry Sawyer and informed him of my findings. I have decided to go ahead without you on this. Whether you are willing to participate or not is irrelevant to me. There has been a serious miscarriage of justice here, and I intend to reveal it to your superiors, not just for your sake, but for our church's sake as well."

Reading the letters this time, Lark was startled by Clyde's absolute certainty that his pastor had been wronged. The photos, a possible drug, and the distinct impression of a set up had gotten this old FBI investigator into full gear. Clyde was not going to stop until he, as he had said from the beginning, got to the bottom of it. Lark had to admire the old man's determination, and his integrity.

The next day, after visiting the children for several hours, Lark waited in the sun room of the Brethren Home for an attendant to wheel Clyde in to see his surprise visitor. Lark was taken back by the figure who was wheeled into the room by the young attendant. Clyde had aged considerably. His frame, now much lighter than Lark had remembered, was curled slightly to his left, with his head seemingly almost resting upon his left shoulder. A dribble ran down the left side of his chin, and his hair was a mess. But his eyes, when he spied Lark, had that same old fire in them that told Lark there resided in this aging human shell the same man who once strode into rooms and struck fear in the hearts of those who sought to avoid the law.

"Larggch," Clyde mumbled, as more dribble moved down his chin toward his neck, "Larggch!"

"Hi, Clyde," Lark said with a smile. "It's good to see you."

"Don't yu kid me," the old man struggled to say, his eyes tearing as he looked at his former pastor.

"I read your letters again last night," Lark continued. "I want to thank you for all you tried to do for me."

The old man seemed to want to say something, but the words would not form this time. Instead, he began to cry.

"There, there," said the young attendant, as she took a tissue from her pocket and wiped his eyes and chin.

Lark sat down next to the old warrior and simply waited for some sign of Clyde's regaining his composure. The young lady never left Clyde's side, but stood at attention, waiting to be of service.

"I nu... ued... come," Clyde managed to say, looking intently at Lark.

"Yes," Lark lied, "I'd have been here sooner, if I had known you were not well."

"Come... to my... room," Clyde said. He seemed to become a bit agitated. The young attendant bent over him to ascertain if he needed more attention from her. Clyde swung his right arm into the air, as if to push her away, but his aim was poor.

"I don't believe I have time today, Clyde," Lark said to the old man who was seemingly very anxious.

With every ounce of energy he had, Clyde yelled, "NOW!" With that, nearly every person in the sun room looked in their direction, as the attendant swung into action by backing Clyde's wheelchair away from Lark, and saying in her most professional manner, "I think he's had enough today."

Clyde nearly jumped out of the chair. "LARGGCH!"

"Perhaps if I go back to his room, he'll settle down, " Lark said directly to the attendant.

"Maybe," she said. "Follow me."

Clyde could not see Lark walking behind them. He struggled and yelled incomprehensibly as the attendant wheeled him quickly toward his room. As they went by the nurses' station, the attendant nodded to one of the nurses to follow them. Lark assumed they might have to sedate Clyde, for he was becoming wilder with each turn of the chair's wheels.

Finally, they entered his room, and when Clyde realized Lark was with them, he settled down almost immediately. With his right arm, he pointed to a dresser drawer and said, "Therrre..."

The nurse quietly spoke to him. "Do you want something from your dresser?" she asked him. He relaxed, and the nurse walked to the dresser which contained but two drawers. She opened the top and turned toward Clyde. His face contorted. She quickly closed the top one and opened the bottom. She rummaged in it a few seconds, and then extracted a large manilla envelope. Turning to Clyde, she asked, "Is this what you want?" He almost smiled.

"I believe this is for you, if you are Lark Wilson," the nurse said. She handed the envelope to Lark. "He's been saving this for you ever since he came here. It took me quite a while to understand this old guy, but after you get to know him, you learn that his bark is worse than his bite."

Again, Lark noted that Clyde almost smiled. His eyes had softened. The fire was gone. "This is for me?" Lark asked him.

"Yas...," the old man said with what seemed like tremendous satisfaction.

"I'll look at it when I get home," Lark said. "You need your rest, now. You've had an exciting day."

331

Clyde tried to reach out to Lark, but his arm fell at his side before he could grasp anything but air. Lark sensed what he wanted.

"Would you like to have a word of prayer before I leave?" Lark asked him.

The face of the old man communicated the affirmative. Both the nurse and the attendant bowed their heads, as Lark took Clyde's right hand in his and prayed with him.

"God, be with your servant, Clyde, and give him rest this day. And if it be your will, give him strength of body anew. We thank you for the nurses and young people who hear your call to serve those in need, oh God. And, we thank you for family and loved ones, who give us encouragement."

Lark paused, knowing what he was also praying for, but not sure he could say it aloud. After a few seconds, he proceeded. "God, forgive me for not trusting this friend and brother in Christ when he came to help me. And may Clyde forgive me also, for not answering his letters before this. Amen."

The two women looked quizzically at one another before they turned to the leave the room. When Lark looked into Clyde's eyes, Clyde seemed to give Lark's hand a little squeeze. His eyes told the tale. They were soft, and at peace. As Lark left the room, promising to return again someday soon, he felt guilty for not having communicated with Clyde all these years.

After another quick visit to Fran and the children, by nine that Sunday evening, Lark was once more at his mother's apartment and anxious to look at the contents of the large envelope. On the outside, it was simply addressed to Pastor Lark Wilson. Lark opened it after his mother had bade him good night and was already snoring, somewhat loudly in the next room.

Chapter 33

THE LAB REPORT

The contents of the envelope Clyde had been saving for
Lark contained several items: a personal letter from Clyde to Lark;
a detailed analysis from the FBI Photo Lab in Washington DC;
a computer background check on Jennifer; a copy of a personal
letter to Clyde from one of his colleagues regarding possible
solutions to Clyde's presented mystery; and a letter from Harry
Sawyer to Clyde regarding a visit made by Clyde to his office in
Harrisburg in early 1974. Lark noted that the date of Clyde's
personal letter to him was March 1, 1974.

> *Dear Lark,*
>
> *I have completed my investigation and am
> utterly convinced you have been victimized by some
> group in our church. The enclosed items clearly
> reveal that a tremendous hoax was played on you
> and others of our congregation by whoever
> manufactured the photos.*
>
> *And as you can read, your Jennifer is quite
> an operator. You were in the hands of pros, my
> friend. If I am unable to locate your present
> whereabouts, I will simply turn over copies of this*

333

information to Rev. Harry Sawyer in Harrisburg, so that he can continue his investigation of this sorry incident with solid facts at his disposal.

One final thought—I know you believe you have done the church justice by resigning. God only knows whether you are correct in that assumption. But, as one and only one member of the church which you at one time believed God called you to serve, I firmly believe you have made a terrible mistake in not staying with us and seeing this thing through. Your precipitous act enabled those who did this horrible thing to you to scurry back to their rat-infested Hell holes from which they crawled.

There, I've said it, and I feel better, even if you don't. I remain your friend in Christ,

Clyde

Lark scanned the photos and the lab criminologist's report on each one. The summary statement regarding all but one of the photos indicated that the photos were taken at different times of the day, due to various concentrations of sunlight that shone through windows and upon furniture. Furthermore, the pictures revealed that the flooring depicted beneath the cavorting lovers was actually two different grains of hardwood. Hence, they couldn't have been taken in the same living room. Two of the photos showed legs of furniture which differed in brand and make. Hence, the couple would have had to move furniture between orgasms, noted the lab person who reviewed them. These facts were not as evident to the naked eye or the untrained analyst, admittedly, but one of the photos clearly was in error, in that a coffee table is partially pictured and is depicted nowhere else in the shots. There also was a hint, when the photos were all studied together as one, that the pictures were not even taken in Lancaster. A lot of technical language followed this thought; the sum and substance seemed to be based upon highly technical studies of gradient light which would suggest they had been taken in a latitude farther south. The conclusion of the analyst was simply that the photos were taken at different times and possibly in different places.

There was one photo which may have actually been taken in Lancaster during a summer evening, depending upon the weather, concluded the analyst. However, that photo, curiously, was the only one which was retouched in such a way as to suggest that the photographer who developed the film replaced the head of the male subject in the picture with that of another person. It was very professionally done, reported the analyst. No one would have noted this, except perhaps the person who was portrayed in the picture.

Lark stared at the picture in which he was embracing Jennifer in her apartment doorway. He never understood quite why that picture made him feel so uneasy. Now, as he looked at it, he could tell that his unease must have been related to the awkwardness of it and how unacceptable that was to him. The other pictures were still hard to discern as phonies, even with the analyst's report, although he remembered that the presence of the coffee table bothered him also when he first looked at the pictures, mainly because he didn't remember one being there at all.

Lark read the analyst's suggestions to Clyde regarding inquiring of his pastor where he bought his clothes, and even whether he could remember whether the clothes he wore that night to Jennifer's apartment were clean or soiled. Lark assumed that the lab analyst had spotted other things and wanted to make sure in the only way one could: asking the victim. Finally, the analyst asked Clyde to check to see which side his pastor parted his hair, for there was a hunch in the lab that the male in the photos had combed his hair unnaturally, so as to seem to be someone he wasn't. The analyst hinted that one technician who had studied the photos wasn't even convinced that the male pictured in the photos was a male. The analyst promised to check one more thing for Clyde. They were going to have a file clerk

335

go through their photo library, to see if there were others like these on file. That might enable Clyde or someone else to actually track down the folks who produced the photos in the first place.

Next, Lark read the letter which had been written by one of Clyde's colleagues. This letter seemed to be the concluding correspondence between Clyde and the FBI. Lark read every word carefully, for attached to it was a computer background report on a possible Jennifer:

Dear Clyde:

By now you have received Ben's photo analysis. Our search of the library of photos has harvested over one-thousand such pieces, which all could have been done in the same darkroom or by the same person. It may interest you to know that our analysis of this data convinces us that this work was not done in our country but in a neighboring nation. There are twelve cases of suicide by clergy and university professors connected with photos from this lab in the past two years. My conclusion: your pastor was targeted by this group, and there will undoubtedly be more like him in the future.

Seems folk in the administration don't take kindly to those they see as aiding the failure of our efforts in Vietnam. Don't forget that they don't call our President "tricky Dick" for nothing.

We have also done a background check on the woman depicted in the photos. It may interest you to know that she is a well-known hooker from the French Quarter in New Orleans. Her real name, as far as anyone knows, is Jacqueline Frantione. If you would like, we could check to see if she was actually missing from the New Orleans scene during the time this alleged incident took place. We are aware that Jacqueline has done some work for the

336

*Mafia in New York City recently, but we haven't
closed in on her or her benefactors, since we're
waiting to see exactly what is up. You know how
that goes, I'm sure.*

   *Do take care, Clyde. There isn't much you
or your pastor could have done about this, for it
is obviously the work of pros.*

Sarge

Next, Lark turned to the letter from Harrisburg, which
was very brief—basically, a thank you from Harry Sawyer for
Clyde's visit and sharing the file he had gathered on the incident.
Harry assured Clyde that the Committee on Ministry would
continue to monitor Lark's progress during his leave of absence.
The final sentence of Harry's letter was the most intriguing to
Lark. "I personally will see that your former pastor is brought
back into service in our Church," Harry had promised the old
man. Two years later, such a sentence suggested more than Lark
had experienced of Harry's administration. Yet, this assurance to
Clyde must have been the factor which led the old man to cease
looking for Lark.

   Questions remained, however. Why hadn't Harry shared
any of this with Lark over the years they had met to review the
leave of absence? Did Fran know any of this? At this point, Lark
felt flushed as he sat with the contents of the envelope spread
before him. Had he chosen to ignore avenues of resolving this
crisis himself for some reason? He knew he had done so, for the
guilt he felt around the incident was so heavy. It was heavy still.
He knew that he was, in effect, hiding out. Hence, he still saw
himself as playing a significant role in his own demise.

   As he sat there, staring at pictures and old letters, he
resolved to find an answer to this last question, for he sensed it
held the key to understanding his very soul.

Chapter 34
BAD NEWS

Lark was stunned by the doctor's tone of voice. Old Dr. Dietz had been a family friend, and Lark knew he could count on him to say, promptly and courteously, what it was that had been bothering Mom these past few weeks. The news daily around Hagerstown noted that an aggressive form of influenza was getting to many senior citizens. Mom was certain, two weeks before, that it was a bad case of the flu which had her feeling under the weather.

But, as the ailment didn't respond to rest or medication, Dr. Dietz had asked her to go the Washington County Hospital and take some blood tests. "Just to be sure," he had said to her. She grumbled all the way to the hospital and back.

Lark thought this was out of character for her, but then, she had gotten more testy since retiring from work. He had to admit that he was concerned that all she had done for the past several weeks, it seemed, was sleep. He would come home from work to find her asleep on the couch, dishes in the sink from breakfast and lunch, when she ate any, and little else that indicated there had been much activity during the day. Her color had grown paler in the past week.

Hence, Lark was somewhat prepared for whatever bad news Dr. Dietz had to share with him. The phone rang shortly after seven o'clock in the evening. Lark's mom did not respond to it, so Lark lifted the receiver in the kitchen.

"Hello," he said.

"Lark, this is Doctor Dietz," said the familiar voice on the other end of the line. "I'm afraid I've got some bad news about your mother."

"Yes," Lark heard himself respond. His heart began to pound. The doctor's voice itself revealed the gravity of the message to follow.

"Your mother has a very aggressive form of cancer," the doctor said quietly. "She needs to be in the hospital, where we can make her comfortable."

"What are you trying to tell me?" Lark asked bluntly.

"Your mother is dying, Lark," the doctor said in a tone to suggest he was speaking of a member of his very own family. "She has non-Hodgkins lymphoma and it is quite advanced. She'll need blood transfusions right away, and she will need to be monitored closely."

"Are you sure?"

"I'm positive," the doctor confirmed. "She has about a week or so to live, Lark. I am very sorry."

Lark struggled with the burden of this news. This couldn't be happening. The children had recently come and stayed with them for several days. Mom was full of life. Now, she couldn't be dying. There had to be some mistake. Asleep in the other room, his mother had absolutely no idea how sick she was. At supper, she had complained that nothing tasted good anymore, and she hoped this flu bug would soon be gone so she would get her appetite back.

"Lark," the doctor's voice sounded. "Are you still there?"

"Yes," Lark said, now functioning as though on automatic pilot. "What do you want me to do?"

"I want you to take your mother to hospital tonight, if you can," Dr. Dietz said. "She needs blood desperately."

"And then what?" Lark asked.

"We'll just have to deal with this day to day, for some patients, there is a point at which we simply cannot supply them with enough blood. They slip into a coma and die peacefully."

"Just exactly what is this disease?" Lark asked.

"It's a very virulent form of cancer, Lark," Dr Dietz said, now adopting a professorial tone. "My guess is your mother is in no pain at all, however, for often, this kind of cancer moves silently throughout the blood stream and attacks everything at once, including the brain. We rarely see patients with this disease in any kind of discomfort. What we do see is increasing lethargy, inability to stay awake for long periods of time, extreme listlessness, and ultimately, total collapse. Their blood simply isn't carrying any nutrients or oxygen to cells, like it's supposed to. Rather, the body's mechanisms are busy trying to fight off what it interprets as an infection. It is not unusual to see tremendous white blood cell counts and a rapidly deteriorating red blood cell count. Literally, people this sick are gradually moving toward an irreversible death. All we do is keep them as comfortable as we can by supplying new blood as long as we can."

"I see," said Lark. Frankly, he didn't understand how one could become so sick so fast. He thanked the family doctor for calling him, and put the phone receiver back on its cradle.

Quietly, he walked into his mother's bedroom. The little woman was lying peacefully upon her bed, breathing steadily, unaware that she was bound for the hospital, then the grave. Lark held the tears in check as he looked upon his mother, the woman who helped him grow up, protected him from harm, stood by him no matter what, and who enjoyed living so much. How could she be dying?

As he stood quietly in her darkened bedroom, listening to the rhythm of her breathing, he reflected how often he had been with others at times like this, knowing what prognosis determined their fates as he witnessed their denial of the certainties before them. There is really so little this culture does to prepare its people for dealing with death. A nation which has consistently looked at death as defeat has little to say to any of us about the finality

340

of life. The Church had long since lost its ability even to speak meaningfully to persons at such times. Ministers, Lark knew only too well, struggled more with this issue than any other, for they were often expected to say things at the time of death that they nor anyone around them had any confidence in, anymore.

These thoughts raced through his mind as she stirred, turned toward him, and opened her eyes.

"Lark," she groggily asked, "is that you?"

A lump welled into his throat as he tried to respond without revealing his heavy heart. "Yes, Mom."

"Oh," she said, "for a minute there I wasn't sure. I thought you were your father."

"I'm sorry, Mom, " he said. "I didn't mean to scare you."

"You didn't," she said. She swung her legs over the edge of the bed and endeavored to lift her rapidly aging body from its resting place. "Did Dr. Dietz call you?" she asked, as she stood up. It was then that Lark recognized she was fully dressed.

"Yes," he said.

"And," she looked at her son carefully, squinting her eyes so as to see him more clearly against the background of the hallway light, "what did he tell you?"

"He says you are very sick, Mom," Lark said, holding back tears. "He thinks you ought to go to the hospital tonight and have a transfusion."

"Does he now?" she said. She pressed her hands down her wrinkled dress. The two stood looking at one another for what seemed like a long time. "Well, then," she sighed heavily, "I guess we'd better get going."

Lark was stunned. His mother seemed prepared; she wasn't going to fight him or Dr. Dietz about this. She walked past Lark and went straight for the closet, where her coat awaited her. Within minutes, they were driving to the hospital.

Upon arrival, Lark and his mother were quickly attended to, and there was little hesitancy on the part of admitting staff. Dr. Dietz had prepared them for this late arrival. Not more than twenty minutes after they had walked from the apartment, Lark's

341

mom was in her hospital room, lying upon her bed, hooked up to a blood pack, which was dripping new life into her veins. Lark watched as drop by drop, the dark substance left its container and began its journey through a series of tubes toward his mother's right arm, into which it would silently merge and bring her body some much-needed nourishment.

Lark watched his mother quickly fall asleep. He sat for about an hour, then walked out into the hospital corridor. It was fairly quiet, for visiting hours were over, and the only sound to come from patient rooms was the din of TV sets at the foot of numerous beds, or nurses talking with patients.

When Lark reached the nurses' station, the head nurse was checking some charts. She glanced up at him and inquired; "How is your mother resting?"

"She's doing fine," he said. He paused before her.

"And you?" She cocked her head to one side as she gave him a serious glance. "How are you doing?"

For the first time, a tear slipped from his eye and slowly rolled toward his chin. "It's all so unbelievable to me," he heard himself respond.

"She'll be comfortable here, and you'll have time to talk with her," the nurse said reassuringly.

"But, she'll never leave here alive," Lark said, almost as a question.

"No," the nurse said, "not as sick as your mother is right now. She won't suffer, but she won't survive. I'm sorry."

Lark wanted to scream at her. This was his mother they were talking about. This was a woman who had overcome innumerable odds against her many times before. How could they be so damned sure? He held his anger in check, thanked the nurse for her concern, and continued walking through the hallway, until he made a full circuit of the fifth floor and returned to his mother's room.

She was still sleeping, but Lark felt she looked somewhat better. There was even some color beginning to develop on her cheeks, where only hours before, she had looked so pale. This was a good sign, he felt. His mother would show them. She would pull through this. A few more pints of blood, and this feisty little woman would rise up and smite the angel of death. It was his only hope. He prayed silently that God would lift her from the valley of deep darkness and spare her life. With his silent prayer, he turned and walked from the room, feeling better than he had since supper. He bounded down the stairs of the hospital, as was his practice, gingerly walked to the car, and drove slowly back to the apartment.

Lark knew his mother better than any doctor or nurse. He knew she would conquer this. They would all see it and marvel at just another one of God's mighty miracles.

Chapter 35
HARRY'S CALL

The phone ringing early on Saturday morning, two days after Lark had placed his mom in the hospital, was most disconcerting. She responded so well to the numerous blood transfusions that she even sat in a chair the night before, chatting about her girlhood and eating deep-fried fish which Lark had purchased at her request. Yet, Lark knew it was only a matter of time, for he witnessed how quickly she sank into lethargy between transfusions. His heart raced as he anticipated bad news at the other end of this early morning call.

"Lark," the voice at the other end said. It was Harry Sawyer! What could he want so early in the morning? It was only seven.

"Yes," Lark said, "how are you Harry?"

"I'm fine," the elder minister said earnestly. "I'm calling you this morning, for our Committee on Ministry is in an emergency session this weekend, and we have some time to process your request today."

"I can't come to Harrisburg this morning," Lark said, "My mom is in the hospital, and I have got to stay here."

"That won't be necessary," Harry assured him. "What happens from here on in is pretty much a formality, since you

344

indicated to us in your last letter that you would be open to a new call. What's wrong with your mother, Lark?"

"She's dying," was all Lark said. A long silence followed, as Harry obviously was unprepared for such news.

"I am so sorry, Lark," he finally said. "I didn't know."

"Neither did I, until three nights ago," Lark said. "She is very ill—some form of cancer."

"How are you handling this?" Harry asked. "Is there family support there for you?"

"Yes, my cousin still lives here," Lark said, although he hadn't seen or talked with his cousin in quite some time. Harry Sawyer didn't need to know that, and he certainly didn't need to hear that Lark was once more trying to deal with something traumatic by himself.

In the months which had followed his visit with Clyde, Lark had pursued every part of the plan laid out for him by the Commission on Ministry. He had also sought to learn more of Jennifer's whereabouts, only to discover that she had been placed in some kind of witness protection program. He would never learn anything else about her. As far as the world was concerned, she never existed. The finality with which the message was delivered by an old friend of Clyde's who still worked for the FBI seemed to help Lark place a lid on the whole episode. Coupled with what seemed to be Fran's inability to bring herself to attempt reconciliation with Lark, the blocking of his pursuit of any other information regarding the incidents seemed to give Lark opportunity to focus upon himself for the first time in years. From that moment on, he did everything the Committee on Ministry wanted him to do to rehabilitate himself. Eventually, he had written, just after Christmas, that he would allow Harry to place his name before search committees once more.

"Good," Harry said. "All I want to be sure of is that you want to give me the green light to place your name before search committees."

"Yes," Lark said, "there really won't be anything here for me, after Mom is gone."

"Lark, I am sorry to hear of your mother's condition," Harry reassured him. "I am sure the committee will uphold you and her in prayer at this time."

"Thanks," Lark said quietly. He began to awaken fully.

"Lark," Harry continued, "there is one more thing."

"I didn't think you would call me this early on Saturday if there weren't," Lark said with a slight chuckle.

"Yes." Harry laughed a bit. "There is a ministry which I thought might interest you, and I need to get your okay on it before I call a friend of mine and recommend you."

"Oh," Lark said, "where and what is it?"

"Well," Harry hesitated, "don't think I'm crazy or anything, but I was wondering if you would be interested in serving a Native American church out in South Dakota?"

This conversation was now beginning to take on the quality of a dream, as far as Lark was concerned. Harry Sawyer wanted to recommend him to a search committee halfway across the nation.

"Well, I don't know."

"Before you say no, let me tell you some things about this," Harry insisted. "As you know, there was a lot of trouble on the Pine Ridge Reservation in South Dakota four years ago. We've had a mission on that reservation in a little town called Kyle since the 1860s, and we want to rebuild it, if we can. That shooting of FBI agents on the reservation has just about torn the community apart. Your stories about how you developed that ministry with Vietnam veterans in Hagerstown got me to thinking that this just might be something that would appeal to you for a while."

There was something deep inside Lark that called as he listened to Harry's words. His mind raced as Harry continued talking.

"There are many veterans of Vietnam and Korea on that reservation, Lark," Harry was saying, "They have been recruited by some radical leftists who call themselves AIM or something like that. You seem to be the kind of minister who is able to enter into other cultures and have a positive impact upon people's lives. It's just a hunch with me, but I had to ask you about it."

"I'm awake now, Harry," Lark said with a laugh. "I don't know a thing about Indians. And I've only ever driven through South Dakota once in my life. I don't even know where the reservation is, for God's sake. I only visited the Black Hills and walked up to Mount Rushmore when I visited there with Fran and the children back in 1969, on our way back from Colorado."

"Lark," Harry went on, "I don't expect you to say yes right now. I just want to know if I can give your name to my friend out in South Dakota?"

"Well," Lark hesitated, "I know I said I would be open to whatever call God placed upon my heart. I suppose, to be true to my own conviction, I should give your inquiry some prayerful consideration. How about I call you Monday morning? Would that be soon enough?"

"Sure," Harry said, "and, Lark, do take care of yourself. I am confident the committee will affirm your request to come back to active ministry. And, if it is alright with you, should any questions arise regarding St. Andrew Church, I'll share the contents of your file that I judge to be relevant. Is that square with you?"

"You have my permission, Harry," Lark said, more relaxed now that the conversation was clearly coming to a conclusion. "Thanks."

"You're welcome," Harry concluded. "I'll talk with you Monday."

Lark gulped down a quick breakfast of cereal and some instant coffee, shaved and showered as quickly as he could, and drove immediately to the hospital. His steps seemed more assured than they had been in years, as he walked up the five flights to the floor where his mother awaited a new day.

Upon entering her room, he was surprised to see her sitting up, eating her breakfast, hair combed and face freshly made up for his arrival. If one didn't know better, his mother would never appear to be near death.

"Hi!" she gaily waved her right hand. "Top of the morning to you!"

He bent and kissed her upon the cheek. "How's my favorite girl today?" he asked.

"I feel fine," she said. She meant it.

"You sure look good," he lied. Her face and hands were now so wrinkled, it was as though she had lived in a desert all of her life. There was a slight yellowish tinge in her eyes. A bag of plasma dripped into her left arm as she continued to eat a breakfast of two once-over-lightly eggs, toast, jam, and coffee. Lark sat down opposite her and watched her eat. Lifting the utensils seemed to present some degree of difficulty, and he noted she was having trouble getting the food to her mouth. It was as though she couldn't quite focus. Various bits of food rested upon the large napkin a nurse had placed around her shoulders.

"Do you want me to help you with that breakfast this morning, Mom?" Lark asked, as he pulled a chair to her bedside.

"No, thank you," she said lightly. She lifted another shaky fork full of egg toward her mouth. "I can do it myself," she said with a grin.

Shortly after breakfast, Mom said she was going to take a bit of a nap. He could go home for a while if he liked, she said. As he tucked her into bed, pulling the sheet snugly around her tiny frame, he bent to kiss her upon the forehead.

"I'm not getting out of here," she said matter-of-factly as she smiled into his eyes.

"Mom," he said, taken by surprise.

"It's alright, Lark," she said. "I'm ready to meet my maker. I'm so tired, and the doctor told me this morning that they are getting to the limit on this blood thing they're doing for me."

Lark didn't know what to say. He had seen this many times before. Dying people were better at dealing with their end than those around them. Lark knew this, but he never dreamed he would live it himself with his own mother.

Taking her hands in his, he asked, "Is there anything I can do for you, Mom?"

"Pray for me, son," she said. "That's all."

"Oh, Mom," he said, with a quiver in his voice. He couldn't speak. He wanted to cry. Tears glanced down his face and dropped onto her bed sheet. He squeezed her little hands, and kissed her on the forehead as she slipped into sleep. She never heard his prayer.

Once back at the apartment, Lark found himself growing restless. He ruminated about possibly living and serving in a strange culture. He wondered if he should call Fran and discuss the possibility with her. The last time they had talked by phone, he had asked her if she had given any further thought to their reconciliation, now that he was getting his life back together and preparing to renew his professional life.

"I just don't know, Lark," she had said, as best as he could remember the conversation, "I feel good about where I am right now: school is going well; the children seem well-adjusted; I just don't know whether it would be right to uproot everything right now and begin to follow you wherever the Church calls you."

The words stung. Lark had never heard Fran put the choice quite so clearly. She seemed to be saying that the only way reconciliation could take place would be if he were to come to them, regardless of his professional dreams and aspirations. The choice between having a family again and having a ministry once more seemed to create a chasm between them.

"Is there someone else?" he remembered asking her. He would never forget the silence which followed his question. It was as if Fran were searching for a way to let him know, so he would not forsake the children as a result.

"Nothing serious," was her response, finally. "There is this widowed teacher who has taken me to a few movies, and we've gone out to eat a couple of times. His wife died two years ago and he is trying to raise two kids by himself."

Something about the way she said "by himself" let Lark know that Fran held this man, whoever he was, in very high esteem. He knew better than to press her for more information, but now that he had asked, she seemed willing to talk a bit about this other man.

"There is really nothing romantic between us," she confided. "He is ten years older, and his two children are in college right now. It's not easy to put young people through school on a teacher's salary, but he's doing it."

There it was once more. The intonation of the voice, almost like a teenager in awe of the star basketball player.

"It's just that we enjoy one another's company, from time to time. It's nothing serious, though," she had confided.

Lark remembered how awkward he felt when Fran stopped talking. He didn't know what to say to her. He knew he couldn't press her for more information, and he felt funny trying to deal with any other subjects. Their call ended shortly thereafter.

That had been shortly after Thanksgiving, and Lark had not spoken to Fran about it since. He could not call her now. Even though he had not told her about Mom, he would not call her until it was over.

After taking a short nap on the couch, Lark drove to get a roast beef sandwich for lunch before going back to the hospital. He gulped down the sandwich with some french fries and a cola. Then, he quickly drove to the Washington County Hospital, bounded up the stairs, and walked gingerly toward his mother's room. Just as he got to the doorway, Dr. Dietz was exiting the room.

"Lark," he said, "I tried to call you, but obviously you were having lunch somewhere."

"What is it?" Lark asked anxiously.

"Your mother slipped into a coma an hour ago. There is nothing more we can do for her, except keep her comfortable."

"But, I thought you were giving her blood," Lark protested.

"Yes, but as I told you, there's a limit to that treatment," the doctor said quietly. "We gave her six pints since last midnight. There is no point going any farther with it. She is feeling no pain, and I doubt that she has had any at all, throughout this ordeal."

The doctor searched Lark's eyes for some hint as to how this message was being received. He truly had been a dear friend of the family, and Lark knew this man was doing everything medical science could do to make his mother's final hours as peaceful as possible.

"Thank you," Lark said. He reached for the doctor's hand and shook it. "I know you are doing all you can. I just can't believe this is happening so quickly."

"This is a damnable disease," the doctor said. "One rarely sees it coming until it is too late. And, with this form of it, well, it's just impossible to predict. Sometimes, massive blood transfusions will halt the progress and actually reverse it for a while. Most times, though, it doesn't. By the time we diagnosed your mother, it was so widespread that she wouldn't have benefitted from chemotherapy, either."

Lark listened to the doctor as the medical man tried to give him some comfort. As he listened, he thought there were innumerable things in life that he rarely saw coming: his entrapment at St. Andrew; his father's sudden death; Fran's new friend; and now, his mother's final hours. His mother used to say to him as a boy, "I'd rather never know what tomorrow will bring. I might not be able to get through the day if I did." Lark thought those rather strange words at the time, but no more. The universe seemed more random to him at this moment than at any time in his life. And, if anyone had dared to bring up the subject of Divine guidance, Lark might have laughed in his face.

"How long does she have?" Lark asked the doctor.

"Hard to say," was his response. "Usually patients just sleep away in hours. On rare occasions, they awaken and actually say something to their families. Sometimes, they report seeing long deceased members of the family standing in the room with them. But my best estimate is that your mother's body is so full of the disease that now, it has ravaged her brain. That usually means a patient has but hours to live. Most automatic nervous functions cease shortly after this kind of coma."

"So, I guess I should plan to stay with her," Lark said.

"If it were me, I would," Dr. Dietz said quietly. "If you need me, call me anytime."

351

"Thanks, Doc," Lark said. The two men parted, and Lark walked into his mother's room ill-prepared for what he would see. His mother now lay on her left side in a fetal position. Several tubes of clear liquid were dripping into both arms. Some kind of ooze was dribbling from her mouth and nose as she labored to breathe. Lark was astonished at the sight, for only hours before, they had talked and she had eaten breakfast, albeit rather poorly. Her skin now felt very cold to his touch, an icy-wet feeling seemed to envelop her total being as she lay curled upon her side. Lark cried openly as he stood by her bed. There were so many more things he wanted to say to his mother that would remain unsaid.

Scenes of his mom from when he was but a boy raced through his mind. She was so full of life, and her laugh was so hearty. He could see her sitting at the kitchen table, puffing on a cigarette, drinking soda, and laughing with one of Lark's dates prior to a high school dance. It was Nancy. He had all but forgotten that cheerleader he dated during his junior year in high school. She was very smart and somewhat intimidating to be around. All Lark wanted to talk about with her was sports, how he was going to be a major league baseball player and make lots of money. Nancy wanted to talk about molecular physics and chemistry. It was eerie, the way she could come across so sophisticated and brilliant one minute, then go out on the football field and jump around like an ancient tribal leader, exhorting her tribe to kill the opposition. Perhaps it was the incongruence of the girl that struck his mother, for there she was sitting and laughing, her head thrown back. Nancy was staring at mom, wondering what she had said that was so funny.

He saw his mother going off to work, lunch pail in hand, to build aircraft in support of his dad and uncles during World War Two. He saw her getting on the bus to ride downtown to work at McCrory's. He saw her behind the lunch counter, throwing hash and hamburgers at hungry Saturday shoppers, as he and his brother waited for the Academy Theater to open for its Saturday double feature and serial. The tears ran freely down his face as he replayed scene after scene. He could tell her almost everything as a boy. Only after he married Fran did he find it difficult to confide in his mother. Maybe it was his mom who barred the way to any conversation they might have had about his family and his feelings. He wasn't sure.

She had been the strong one when Lark's brother died. She held the family together, kept her husband from drowning himself anew in booze, made sure that Lark was comforted throughout the funeral, and never cried until the casket was being lowered into the ground. Lark remembered holding his mother's shaking body as she sobbed.

Then, there were these final years. She and his father had been so gracious toward him and allowed him to stay. His mom handled the death of her husband with grace. She truly was a magnificent woman, his mother. Lark found himself praying a prayer of thanks to God for his mother and all she meant to him and to their family.

From time to time, a nurse would step into the room and check his mother's pulse and temperature, adjust the dripping saline solution, and walk quietly out of the room only after ascertaining if there were anything Lark needed. Each time, he declined any assistance.

Shortly before nine the nurse who was attending his mother stood up at her bedside. "It won't be long now. If there is anything you want to say to your mother, she might still be able to hear it." With that said, the nurse walked from the room.

Lark sat staring at his mother's bed.

Getting up from his chair, he walked to her bedside and looked down upon her lying there like a baby in its crib. This must have been the way he looked to her at one time, he thought. The love he felt for his mother welled within him as he took her cold, wet hand in his.

"Mom," he began to say to her softly. "You were the greatest mother a boy ever had, and I just want you to know that Wes and I really were lucky to be your boys." He choked on the thoughts, but continued. "I just wanted you to know, Mom, that all my life, I have never known a more loving person than you. I love you, Mom," Lark concluded, as tears ran down his face.

Just then his mother's hand twitched in his. It had a familiar feel to its movement for her thumb and forefinger came together, ever so softly, as though she had pinched his hand as she had so many times when he was a little boy. Lark was astounded for an instant. Nothing else about her appearance had changed; perhaps it was just some nervous tic. A nurse earlier in the day had warned him that her body might jump or twitch. It was normal, she had said.

Lark thought he might share one more thing with his mom. Holding her hand, he spoke to her anew. "Mom, don't you worry about me any. I'm going to go back into ministry. Harry Sawyer, you remember him, don't you? He called this morning. There's a chance I might be going to South Dakota to serve in an Indian church. Imagine that, Mom. Your son who grew up fighting Indians from imaginary staircase stagecoaches might be going to a reservation to serve an Indian church. God sure has a sense of humor, doesn't he?"

There it was again. Her hand moved ever so slightly. But, the little pinch by her thumb and first finger was unmistakable. She was listening. Lark just knew she was listening, even though every other thing about her appearance indicated she was struggling mightily now for every breath.

"I guess I just wanted you to know that I'll be fine. You don't have to worry about me at all," Lark concluded. He waited for some response. The room was silent, except for her labored breathing. As he was about to replace her hand at her side, her thumb and forefinger twitched once more. The pinch was there more lovingly than he had ever felt it. She was saying goodbye to her son the best way she could.

Lark sat in the chair and thanked God for this moment of farewell with his mother. As he sat there, he felt a warmth embrace him, not unlike that of covers being drawn up around one's chin at bedtime. He rested within it and waited for the inevitable last breath his mother would draw in this world.

Chapter 36
MOM'S DEATH

Lark's mother passed away at 1:35 a.m. He held her hand as she quietly slipped toward that promised rest. Nothing in her body, except for the cessation of breathing, indicated her change of state. With a slight squeeze of his hand, she passed over the final boundary which awaits every soul.

Lark stood up on his feet and looked upon the woman who bore him. She lay in a fetal coma only minutes before. Now, she seemed as though she were completely relaxed. No more struggles, no more loads to bear. Her time on earth complete, her soul presumably rushed to meet its maker and left this aged body for others to tend.

Lark bent and kissed his mother's damp forehead. "Goodbye, Mom;" he managed to say before tears overwhelmed him. He needed to walk. He'd always done something very physical after funerals, when he was a pastor. Somehow, playing a rough game of basketball, hitting a bucket of balls, or simply running a three-mile course gave him the assurance he was alive and the energy to go forward and assist those with grief to bear. Now, he had the unmistakable urge to run a marathon.

Lark's mom had stood with him when no one else understood. She had professed a blind faith in his integrity. She knew her son, and she knew his character. Now, she was gone, and he could not contain his feelings.

He dashed down the hall of the Washington County Hospital to the stairway. Literally running down the five flights of stairs, he was outside and deep into the dark winter's night before he realized he'd left his coat behind. No matter—he'd pick it up later. His feet began to move faster beneath him, and soon, he was running. Dashing across totally deserted city streets unmolested in the middle of a sleepless night, he ran until he was totally exhausted.

He found himself on Bellevue Avenue. All was dark and still. It was a typical Maryland winter. There was no snow on the ground, at the moment. Lark sat down in the field to his right and rested his head on his knees, breathing like a runner after a dash.

Silently, the realization of where he was came to him. He was sitting on the old schoolyard. A short distance across the field, where many a childhood day was spent playing baseball or football, stood Woodland Way School. Lark had gone to his first nine grades in that building. His mom had seen every one of his school plays. She even had the pictures proudly displayed in her home, until Lark's teenage pride demanded they be put away.

His tears came anew as he sat alone on the old ball field. His body contorted with grief, and he rolled on the cold, dark ground like a deeply tormented soul of Biblical proportions. The one person in this world who never gave up on him was gone.

Words of an old song he'd heard in church as a young lad crept across the back of his memory, only to bring more sobs from his body, "Sometimes I feel like a motherless child." He lost all track of time and circumstance. After crying for what seemed to him an eternity, he simply lay still on the ground—the ground in which he would lay his beloved mother—and fell asleep.

His cousin, Ronnie, found him on the schoolyard at five. When the hospital staff called to ascertain his whereabouts, Ronnie instinctively knew where to find Lark.

"Lark," he called to the man in a fetal position before him. Lark stirred and straightened out on the ground. Then, he rolled on his back and stared into the still, starlit sky.

"What time is it?" he inquired. His senses began to inform him of his situation.

"Five." Ronnie said matter-of-factly.

"My God, I must have fallen asleep!"

"Yes."

"Where's my coat? I'm cold."

"It's at the hospital, where you left it."

Lark began to struggle to his feet as tears began to form anew. Ronnie grabbed an arm and helped lift him from the ground.

"How'd you know I'd be here?" Lark asked him.

"Where else?" was all Ronnie said.

Nothing more needed to be said. This was the place where they'd always come as boys. This was where they'd competed with one another for the attention of every neighborhood girl since they'd been able to walk. This was where they drank beer together as teenagers on warm summer nights. This was where they talked of what they'd be when they grew up. This was where they talked seriously of girls turned to women. This was where they shared their darkest secrets.

Ronnie draped an arm around his cousin and helped him toward the still-running car at the curb. Lark was stiff, cold, and suddenly hungry.

"Let's have some breakfast," he said weakly, through chattering teeth.

"Now you're talking," Ronnie replied.

They drove downtown. Ronnie asked Lark if he were warm enough. He was. Ronnie turned the heater fan to low. They rode in silence until they came to Richardson's All Night Restaurant. When they were teenagers, this had been a favorite haunt. Neither had been here in years. It was one place where they knew they could get a decent breakfast. It had come in handy many times as they were growing to manhood.

They sat in a booth by a window overlooking the Dual Highway. Traffic to Washington and Baltimore was just beginning to move. Both men sat silently, sipping coffee and waiting for their orders.

"Looks like the herd is beginning to move," Ronnie said quietly.

They chuckled.

"What do they see in it?" Lark asked no one in particular.

"Beats the crap out of me," Ronnie responded. "Ask my brother."

"Do you think he'll come to Mom's funeral?"

"He will, if he's in the country," Ronnie said.

Suddenly, the bouncy middle-aged waitress came to their table with their orders. Ronnie got a short stack of pancakes with bacon. Lark had scrambled eggs, hash browns, and toast.

"Will there be anything more, boys?" she wanted to know.

"You can just bring that coffee pot over here, darlin', and we'll drain it for you," Ronnie said in his best imitation of Jimmy Dean in years. She turned and walked away with a well-practiced frumpiness toward the counter.

"Must've been something I said," Ronnie muttered.

They chuckled and then began to eat the first meal of the day in earnest. After they had downed four cups of coffee and scraped their plates clean of any crumbs, Ronnie took out a pack of cigarettes and lit one up.

"You still doing that?" Lark asked him.

"Yep. I know I should quit. But, what the hell, I'm pushing fifty. What do I have to preserve?"

They chuckled.

Then, with a more serious glance, Ronnie inquired, "How you doing, Lark?"

Silence.

It was a good question. It was just that an answer didn't present itself, readily.

Lark had much to do in the next few days. He had to clean out mom's apartment within forty-eight hours of her death. He had to sign all the papers required by the state. He'd need to stop by the funeral parlor at which he'd pre-arranged everything when he knew his mom would never recover. And he'd need to call relatives who didn't live in Hagerstown and tell them when the funeral would take place. He guessed he'd sleep at his mother's place for the next two nights.

"Let's get out of here," Lark said suddenly. They got up. Ronnie paid for the breakfast, and they left. Ronnie inquired as to whether Lark would like a morning paper. The answer was no. They turned and drove past the jail, then headed toward Ronnie's house.

Once there, Lark informed Ronnie he'd need some rest before tackling the day. Ronnie understood; the bed was ready. Lark slipped into it at six thirty and slept soundly until almost noon.

The sound of the telephone ringing downstairs awakened Lark. Ronnie's muffled voice could be heard in the quiet house. Lark arose and wandered into the bathroom. He stared into the mirror. He looked older today, pale and wan, with jaws hollowed somehow by time and gravity. His stubble needed immediate attention. He searched through the medicine cabinet for some shaving cream and a razor.

After shaving, he quickly disrobed and stepped into the shower. The warm water trickling across his body felt particularly refreshing. As he washed his hair, he simply stood for a long time and let the baptismal-like waters run from head to toe. It felt wonderful just to be in this place at this time.

Leaving the shower, he rapidly dried himself and got back into the clothes he had worn since the morning before. They smelled of sweat and dirt, but they also felt like home.

When he came downstairs, Ronnie had already poured him a cup of coffee and made him a turkey sandwich. "I thought you might need a little pick me up," he said.

Lark sat at the table. "Thanks," he said.

"Will you be needing any help today?"

"No."

"I didn't think so. But, I want you to know that I'm here, if you need me."

"Okay," Lark said appreciatively.

"Ike called a few moments ago."

"He knew?"

"Said he'd read it in the morning paper."

"Is he coming to the funeral?"

"Yes. He said he doesn't have to leave the country for a week or so."

Lark finished the sandwich in silence. His other cousin was one less out-of-town phone call he'd need to make. Lark had forgotten that Ike always got the *Daily Mail,* so he could keep up with hometown news as he slowly drove to Virginia side of the Potomac River each day. Seldom did anyone know what Ike did or where he was. But, he rarely missed anything important in his home town. Lark's mom's death was something very important. Ike would be there.

"Could you give me a ride to the hospital?" Lark asked.

"Sure. I was counting on it," Ronnie replied.

The ride was relatively quick. Lark's car was still parked where he'd left it. It now had an overdue parking ticket attached to its windshield.

"Looks like Patrol Patty has been around," Ronnie chided as they drove alongside it.

"The city's got to get its due," Lark quipped.

"You take care today, and let me know if you need me," Ronnie said. Lark opened the door.

"Thanks," Lark said.

At the funeral home, Lark thanked the director for going ahead with the obituary they had planned a week before. Then, the two of them walked into the room where his mother's body already lay, awaiting viewing by friends and relatives, set for the next evening. Lark glanced at his mom's body and was internally grateful for the skill of embalming. Mom wore a silk dress in pale blue which would have matched her Irish eyes, were she awake. Her hair was beautiful. And, her face now looked full, following the battle which had shrunken her to a weak mass of skin and bones.

"Thank you," Lark said to the undertaker. "She looks wonderful."

"You're welcome, Lark."

Back in the efficiency apartment by two, Lark set about the task of calling everyone he knew was still alive and who would not have had the opportunity to read the Hagerstown paper. There were some uncles and aunts in New England who'd want to know, even if they couldn't make the trip for the funeral. And, there were still friends in Pennsylvania who'd kept up with him after all the years, who knew his mom and knew how much Lark loved her. They would need to know. Some said they might be at the funeral. And, each in her or his own way sought to offer Lark comfort in his grief.

By five he had called everyone but Fran and the children.

"Hello?" The voice was so familiar and lovely. For an instant, Lark lost his composure and wept.

"Hello? Lark, is that you?"

He cried.

"I'll be there in two hours," she said. And she was.

Chapter 37
THE REUNION

Lark opened the door, and there she stood. Their eyes met for the first time since Christmas. She waited as they simply stood and looked at one another.

Finally, Lark mumbled, "Come in." As she did, he began to weep.

He looked terrible, he knew. His face revealed the stress of the past weeks. Lines were deeply entrenched at nearly every corner of his countenance. Somehow, he appeared shorter, or slightly bent forward. He turned from her, walked to Mom's lone couch in what passed as a living room and sat. She followed him quickly and sat on one of the faded blue chairs his mother and father had purchased for their fortieth wedding anniversary.

"Are you doing alright?" she asked.

He simply stared at her and nodded affirmatively. To Lark, it was evident Fran had cried most of the trip from Lancaster to Hagerstown. He knew she dearly loved Mom.

"I'm so sorry," she said. He knew she meant it.

He shook in grief, but said nothing. They hadn't been alone in a room for a long time, and this forced reunion was beginning to feel a bit awkward. He wondered if it felt the same to Fran.

"Have you eaten anything?" she inquired.

"A little," he replied quietly.

"Would you like to get a bite? I skipped supper in order to get here early."

"That would be nice," he said.

"Let me freshen up a bit, and I'll be ready," she said. She casually got up and walked toward the small bathroom between the kitchen and bedroom. Boxes of things to be moved or discarded were everywhere, it seemed. But, Fran negotiated the route to and from the bathroom without mishap.

Coming back into the living room, she picked up her coat, as Lark retrieved his from the back of one of the kitchen chairs. He helped her with hers and paused ever so slightly as he wrapped it toward her left arm. His body brushed her back, and a distant urge came over him.

Lark decided they'd eat at the Park Circle Tavern. He hadn't been there in years, but knew they served great steamed crabs. He knew Fran loved steamed crabs. In their early dating days, he'd call the tavern and order some crabs for her. He'd pick them up, along with some beer and cola, and take the feast fit only for Maryland kings to their apartment, where they'd pig out on the succulent crab meat and gulp the drinks to ease their palates of the scorching seasoning used in the preparation. They'd laugh and tease one another about who had made the biggest mess on the kitchen table, spread with old newspapers and various pieces of shell and empty bottles.

They parked in front of the tavern Fran had never entered in her life and walked in. It was practically deserted, except for two men who sat near the television which hung above the bar. They were arguing about an NBA game which was being aired. The Bullets were losing again. It didn't seem to matter who they played; they lost.

Once they were seated, Fran initiated their conversation while they waited for a waitress. "I've never been here, have I?"

"No. You've eaten many a steamed crab from here, though," he replied.

She smiled at the remembrance. "So, this is where they came from," she said. "Those were the days."

"Yep!" He smiled for the first time.

"Do you think they have any tonight?"

"I sure hope so—if we're not too late."

The waitress approached their table. "May I help you?" she asked.

"Do you have steamed crabs tonight?" Lark asked her.

"Yes, I think so. This is my first night," she said in a West Virginia drawl.

"We'll take a basket and a pitcher of Coke," Lark said.

Fran smiled, "Thanks."

The waitress left them and hurried to the kitchen.

"She seems nervous," Fran noted.

Lark did not respond. Soon, the waitress reappeared with brown paper for their table, two wooden hammers, and metal devices resembling small nutcrackers and two picks. Then, she quickly brought the pitcher of icy cola and two glasses.

"They'll be ready in about ten minutes," she said.

Lark poured the cola into their glasses and set Fran's before her. He sipped his and gazed in no particular direction at all. Then he asked, "How are you doing?"

"Fine," was her response. Yet there was a slight edge to her voice. "I have twenty-two fourth graders this year, and they're really a challenge. Fourteen of them are children at risk. They keep me hopping."

In no time, their awkwardness with one another was relieved by the arrival of the steamed crabs. The relative silence of the small tavern was soon challenged by the sound of breaking shells as Fran and Lark settled into the task of rescuing the succulent crab meat from their crustacean confines. There was a pleasure to be gained from the task of feeding oneself in such a manner. It didn't matter that the juices splashed across the brown wrapping paper table cloth, or that it once in a while spit onto a shirt or blouse. Once the feeding began, the taste made one most ambitious for the next morsel of snowy white crab leg or slightly veined innards.

Neither Fran nor Lark were rookies at this best of all Maryland customs. Between crabs, they gulped their drinks, finding relief for their burning throats. The spice recipes used in steaming crabs, Maryland style, are often kept secret. But, one thing every patron knows before the first crab is eaten is that the spices will burn. Such burning can only be soothed by the passing of waters down the throat; preferably mountain waters mixed with the finest barley and hops. But, Lark was deferring to Fran's sensitivities tonight. Either way one quenches the thirst produced, that's living.

When there were but a few crabs left upon the table which resembled their living form, Fran was the first to speak. "Thanks for thinking of this," she softly said to him, as she sucked upon a crab leg.

"Glad you enjoyed them," he said, and he meant it. He was beginning to be glad she was there. Somehow, her presence would help him get through this difficult period, for Fran was usually able to organize time and tasks in even the most dreadful moments.

"They were just as I remembered them."

"It's been a while," Lark muttered, almost to himself.

They sat and looked across the table at one another.

"Do you want to go see Mom?" he asked.

"Of course," she replied.

They left the new waitress a very generous tip, along with the money for the tab they'd received. They quietly drove to the funeral home, viewed the body without a word to one another, then got back into the car.

"Where are you staying tonight?" he wanted to know.

"I hadn't given it a thought, Lark. I guess I just jumped in the car and drove."

"You want to stay at Mom's place? I could sleep on the couch."

"Oh, that would be a lot of trouble. You need your rest."

"I don't mind," he responded, as he started the engine.

"You sure," she inquired.

"It would be good to talk to you again, Fran," he said. The tears began to roll down his face once more.

She didn't answer. There was no need. He'd expressed his need for her. She would stay at Mom's. That was settled.

When they got back to the apartment, Lark looked for some spare bedclothes and found them in the old metal linen closet he had known as part of his mom and dad's household furniture since he was a boy. It had rusted in the corners and around the door handles. More than a few chips of enamel had been knocked from its surfaces, no doubt by children and grandchildren alike. There were few items in it now. Mom had not bothered to get anything new for years. There was no need. Seldom did anyone visit in her later years. Until Lark came home unexpectedly, no one had slept over in ten years. Mom was anything but extravagant, especially with herself and her needs. Lark often thought that his ministry didn't become grounded in his formative seminary years, but in his very early childhood, as he watched how his mother held things together in a highly dysfunctional home.

Lark laid the bedclothes on the end of the sofa and sat down beside them. Fran was resting in the only chair in the living room that had nothing stacked on it. She had kicked off her shoes and was scratching the bottoms of her feet upon the carpet.

"Still have that little problem, I see," Lark said with a slight twinkle in his eye.

"Dry skin never goes away, I'm afraid," she said with a little laugh. She seemed so relaxed. Regaining her composure, she asked, "Have you talked with the pastor?"

"Yes," Lark said. "He'd like to do a simple service. He says Mom had talked with him about three years ago and had insisted that her funeral be as simple as possible."

"That's good for all of us, I guess," Fran said.

"Yes," he said matter-of-factly. "In many ways, Mom was like most of my parishioners in Lancaster. I guess that's why I liked that church so much," he said with a slightly broken voice.

He simply stared into space somewhere just beyond her. "Do you ever go to church there?" he asked her.

"Yes."

"How is it?"

"It's not the same, Lark," she said with all seriousness. "You had that certain thing. What did they call it, Charisma?"

"Stupidity, you mean."

"No, you know you were the best thing that ever happened to that church."

"Don't start that, Fran. I can't live up to those kind of statements anymore."

She changed the subject. "Are your cousins both coming to the funeral?"

"I think so."

"It'll be good to see both of them again," she said. They proceeded to spend the next hour reminiscing about double dating with Ronnie and his many girl friends. They laughed as they remembered steaming up his car windows with their passionate necking. In spite of themselves, they were recalling their past with some gratitude for having been a part of one another's lives.

"You know something, Fran," Lark said during one of the pauses in their conversation. "This is the best talk we've had together in years."

"It's too bad—"

"What? It's too bad what?"

"It's too bad Mom isn't here to share these stories with us," Fran said as a tear gently rolled down her face.

"She is."

They talked of some of the things Mom had done during early years of their marriage. There was the cake she baked without eggs, which came out of the oven almost as dust. There were the numerous flops with meals: the round steak she had boiled, thinking it to be a pot roast; and the excuses for her poor mashed potatoes.

This conversation was lifting both of their spirits, and they knew it. When the mantle replica of a grandfather's clock struck eleven, they decided to call it a night. Fran insisted she sleep on the couch. Lark was so stiff and sore from the night before, he didn't argue. He ambled into the bedroom after going to the bathroom.

Fran called to him from the living room. "Sleep well, Lark."

"Thanks. Good night."

"Good night."

"Fran, I..." Lark started to say as he drifted toward sleep very quickly.

"Yes," she responded dreamily. "What is it?"

No response. He was asleep.

Chapter 38

A WAKE

The viewing was set for seven. By the time Lark and Fran arrived, after spending a rather quiet day of reminiscing while cleaning Mom's apartment, mixed with weeping and consuming a couple of cold sandwiches, many family members were simply standing around, chatting with one another. There was cousin Ronnie and his wife, their three children, and various grandchildren gathered in the reunion circle. There was Aunt Helen (another family altogether) and her two daughters with their children. In another corner stood Ike and his spouse. None of their children had come.

When these three groups of persons saw Lark enter with Fran, their faces revealed a mixture of pleasant surprise cloaked by the appropriate sadness of mourners. Two by two, almost as if rehearsed, they came to greet Lark and Fran. Each said how nice Mom looked and how glad they were that she rested in the arms of the Lord. Lark and Fran politely acknowledged their expressions of sympathy knowing, from long years of practice in the parish, that hardly anyone knew really what to say to a mourner at this time. Most were relieved once this ritual was past and they could return to their neutral corners and continue whatever other conversations consumed them for the time being.

Gradually, old friends came, and the room began to fill with people both familiar and unfamiliar to Lark. As they filed by Lark and Fran, they too would make some attempt to console the couple. Those who did not know Fran would introduce themselves. Those who knew Fran showed no surprise that she now stood beside Lark. Apparently, they had not been told. That was Mom. "Keep it to yourself and don't wash the family's dirty laundry in public," was something she always muttered when a relative would begin to gossip or when she learned some horrible thing had happened to a neighbor or friend. She never passed a story on to another. She possessed enough Irish pride and stubbornness and a multitude of hurts, disappointments, and pain, to keep quiet around all unhappiness.

Finally, two hours had passed and the ordeal was nearing an end. Lark and Fran stood their post throughout the constant hand shaking, well wishes, and sad faces. When the last guest left, there was only Lark, Fran and the family members. They retreated to an anteroom off the funeral chapel, where chairs had been arranged in a tight circle and some light refreshments awaited them. The passing of the threshold between the room where Mom laid in her coffin awaiting tomorrow's funeral and the circle of chairs seemed to change everyone's mood and spirit. The nuclear families now disintegrated, and there was but one gathering of the clan.

"Where's the pastor?" inquired one of Ronnie's grandchildren as Lark poured him a cup of punch.

"He said he'd be here by nine. I guess he got delayed. It's not unusual," Lark said, as he turned to go back to a chair in the circle and rest his weary legs.

When all were gathered and comfortable, it was Ronnie who got the conversation rolling by sharing an old story of the boys from when they were children.

"Remember that time we played army in your house, Lark, and the sink got broken? I can still your face as you looked at me, the water streaming from the pipes and rolling down the walls. You screamed, 'Oh shit.' You ran across the street to the gas station to see if anybody could turn the water off."

370

"Yes," Lark replied, "you had climbed up onto the sink to throw a clothespin through the transom onto your cousin Shorty, and there was a tremendous explosion. The water ran down the dining room walls as we ran over to the gas station."

"How'd you and your brother explain that, when your dad got home from work?" Aunt Helen wanted to know.

"I can answer that one," piped up Ike. "They told their dad that I did it. I wasn't even in town."

Everybody roared with laughter. Many had heard the story before, but this was a great way to start to lighten the mood of the evening. All knew there would be many more stories like this, before the evening ended. This was a favorite one to start with, for it brought back good memories of when all were younger, trying to survive the postwar rigors of putting a country back together and forging families anew following the horrible experiences of the war.

Ike's wife asked, "What did Mom say when she got home from work?"

Lark thought for a moment. He remembered his dad's reaction very well.

He had come home, surveyed the damaged house, and immediately flew into a tirade. When he was done, Lark and Wes were in their beds, their baseball bats and gloves away for the summer, all privileges removed until God knew when, and hoping against hope that they could come up with something which would grant them pardon.

It was Mom who heard the first and only explanation the brothers would ever offer. She listened attentively as they each explained the event to her in words they had spent an hour rehearsing, prior to their dad's arrival home from work.

"We were outside, trying to play ball in the rain. Ike asked to use the bathroom, and there was an explosion. Ike ran out of the house and dashed home as fast as he could go. When we got inside, we saw water and ran to the gas station for help. Mr. Carl stopped the water. When we went upstairs, we saw the sink. Honest."

True to her nature, Mom never repeated a word of this story. Not even to Lark's dad, as far as he ever learned. She simply turned and walked from the bedroom and later brought some soup for supper.

Lark lied, "I don't think we ever talked to Mom about it. I can't remember her having any reaction."

"Then, how did I get blamed?" Ike wanted to know. Lark shot Ronnie a knowing glance. Ronnie had shared that he took care of that part in his own way in his family. Ike was grounded, and Lark's aunt and uncle helped pay for the rebuilding of the bathroom. Case closed.

"I guess you did it," Ronnie replied to uproarious laughter. Even Ike took it in good measure, for this story had been told so many ways and in so many places, no one was sure it wasn't apocryphal.

Once the stories started, it seemed they'd never end. One family story followed another. For the next hour, people laughed and joked together about their past. Each story curiously brought to mind some aspect of Mom's nature, and it was good.

Aunt Helen recalled their trip to Harrisburg, when mom had bowled in the Pennsylvania State Tournament. She relayed how Mom rolled six straight gutter balls in the middle of one set and simply turned and calmly announced, "I am finished practicing. From now on every ball counts!"

Ronnie's wife remembered the time Mom fixed dinner for them, after they moved into their new home. Everything was awry in Mom's kitchen. Nothing had gone right: the scallops had burned; the potatoes were lumpy; and the cake was like rubber!

Tears of joy and laughter were rolling down each person's face as the stories continued. Only a family could touch the simple depths of this woman's life and laugh and rejoice in having known her. Lark felt uplifted in this hour as at no time since his mother's death.

At ten o'clock, just as Ike was beginning to tell about the well known post-war fishing trip, the pastor entered the room.

"Don't let me stop you all," he said, as all conversation ceased and everyone was reminded of why they were having this good time together. "I'm sorry I'm late. Please forgive me."

Lark recalled how often he had to beg forgiveness of the people he served. There never seemed to be enough time in a day.

The pastor talked about the funeral order he would use and, step by step, he rehearsed each passage of Scripture, each poem, and each part to everyone's satisfaction. When he was finished, he asked if anyone wanted him to read or say anything he hadn't mentioned. There was a silence which prevailed while all looked at one another and at the floor.

"You know the song "Alive, Alive Ho?" asked Lark. He doubted this German had ever heard the song, but he knew his Mom loved it, and he thought it might be good to read it at her funeral.

"No, I can't say I'm familiar with it," the pastor said.

"I'll give you the words so you can read them," Lark said, as nearly everyone in the circle began to sing:

> *Crying, Cockles and mussels, alive, alive ho,*
> *Alive, alive ho-oh*
> *Alive, alive ho-oh,*
> *Crying, Mussels and cockles, alive, alive ho.*

The pastor's face revealed some slight recognition, as they finished the refrain of the song. Suddenly, Fran was singing solo while the tears filled many family member's eyes:

> *She caught a bad fayver*
> *And nothing could save her,*
> *And that was the end of poor Molly Malone*

Family members regained their voices and joined Fran as she continued quietly:

But her ghost wheels its barrow
Through the streets broad and narrow,
Crying, Cockles and mussels
Alive, alive ho.

All regained their strength of voice to sing the chorus once more. Even the pastor joined them this time through. When they were finished, he asked, "Are there more verses?"

"Yes," Lark weakly replied. "I'll see you get them."

"I'll be happy to read the song," the pastor assured them.

"Thanks," Lark said, regaining his composure. "My mom would really like that."

"You know, pastor, that one of our Irish ancestors wrote, 'the life of a man is bound to death by way of reproduction, and only relieved by a good story'," spoke Ike, to every family member's amazement. No one had any knowledge that Ike had been researching their family history, and some suspected that he was simply doing what he did so well at social gatherings— talk.

The pastor looked at him with some amusement. Then, he said, "I suppose that's right. There's nothing like a good story to give relief at times like this."

Everyone relaxed. Ronnie then asked the pastor if he'd like to sit a while, have some punch, and get to know the family. He agreed. Aunt Helen got him punch while Ronnie launched into the infamous fishing trip which had been motivated by the Japanese surrender, August 10, 1945. All the men who were back from the war decided they'd go fishing to celebrate the victory in the Pacific and the end, at last, of the war. Lark's dad organized the party, and his mom was recruited to make the sandwiches. Everyone knew there were no fish in danger, and that the sandwiches could have been made of anything, for drinking and card playing was what those vets were really planning to do. What no one knew, but should have suspected, was that Lark's dad and mom were in the process of getting reacquainted with one another following the hiatus war brings to family life.

Nevertheless, Lark's mom fried chicken and fixed potato salad and got everything together for the men. At the agreed time, she appeared at the dock in Williamsport and got help getting everything into the boat for their late-evening fishing excursion, card game, and picnic. By the time she arrived, Lark's dad was half into the bag. But, he managed not to fall from the boat as he assisted her aboard. Soon, the old flatboat converted into a houseboat was chugging lazily down the historic Potomac.

Things went as well as could be expected until the guys decided to take a break from the card game. Nothing much was happening in the river, for everyone had forgotten bait, and the fish just weren't fooled by the naked hooks which raked along behind the sluggish flatboat.

Lark's dad called out, "Those sandwiches ready, darlin'? Me and the boys are getting mighty hungry." He was already well into the bag.

Proudly, Lark's mom came from her solitary perch on the bow of the flatboat and unveiled the evening's repast. Fit for a king, she declared. She couldn't just make sandwiches for these heroes of our nation, she explained. She'd spent the whole day getting this feast ready for them as a grateful surprise, she said.

All of the men sat wide-eyed as she spread the appetizing food before them. It was Lark's dad, who always seemed to have the propensity for saying things aloud that would have best been kept to himself, who spoke.

"Hell, woman," he said, as he stood and nearly tumbled from the boat. "I asked you to fix sandwiches!"

Lark's mom stared him down into his seat, and then she turned, walked to the starboard side of the boat, and jumped overboard. It was a short drop, only a few feet, into the water which was doing its best to hold the old craft afloat in so shallow a river. Once there, she seemed to walk upon the Potomac toward the shore.

"Goddamn, look at that! It's a miracle," Ronnie's dad exclaimed.

Lark's dad staggered to his feet and almost fell into the river as he yelled at her to come back this very minute. She stopped, turned, and walked back to the boat. All hands on board reached out to help bring her aboard a second time.

Once aboard, she stomped to the table while her husband let out a string of profanity that neither could be remembered nor was ever repeated correctly. He told her she was crazy to do what she did. Everyone agreed, afterward, that was the gist of it.

Anyway, she picked up a chicken wing, her favorite part of an old hen's anatomy, put it between her teeth, walked to the starboard side once more, and repeated her earlier version of the miracle.

Mom said nothing and never spoke of it to anyone. Not one of the vets ever brought it up to her again. The stories of her walking across that portion of the Potomac spread throughout the neighborhood, however. Much to her husband's relief, nothing much else was ever repeated about the night the vets went fishing. Although, Ronnie said he did remember a Christmas when his father, after having had one too many egg nogs, nearly precipitated a fist fight in their living room when he asked Lark's dad if he'd gone fishing lately.

The stories continued for another hour. By eleven, most of the family was ready to call it a night. With hugs and fond wishes, they parted company and bade farewell to the pastor until the morrow.

"Mom would have had a great time tonight," Lark said, as he and Fran drove to the apartment.

"She did," Fran replied.

Chapter 39

RESURRECTION

The day started slowly. The children arrived, with Betty Smythe, at the apartment by noon. An uneasy reunion between the children and their father, Lark and Betty, ensued. But, all were sensitive to Lark's need of support. Betty quickly excused herself, promising to be with them at the funeral. The Wilson family, for the first time in over four years, were all going to have lunch out together.

The Waffle Shop was Lark's choice. He had always wanted to take them there, but they never seemed to have the time or money when they came to Hagerstown as a family intact in years prior to 1973. All were intrigued with Lark's story about how his mom had taken him there when he was their age.

They walked into the shop, and nothing seemed to have changed from the way it was in Lark's memory. Even the waitress looked the same: middle aged and dowdy. There was a small crowd of people in the shop when they arrived shortly before noon. Yet, they had beaten the business crowd, a waitress informed them.

The children waited for Lark to order so as to take their cue from him: waffles with chicken gravy for everyone. Nothing in particular sparked any lively conversation between them as they ate. The atmosphere was definitely subdued. Everyone seemed tense.

When all had eaten their fill, the waitress inquired as to their decision about dessert. No one had room for anything more. Their uneasiness with one another had reached the point where space from one another was needed before the funeral.

Hence, they drove to City Park after lunch. They walked around the lake, replete with ducks, swans, and murky-looking water. Fran reminded the children that their dad had worked here the summer they had started dating.

When they came upon the museum, Lark informed the children that his first experience of art took place in this very museum when he was but a first grader. It was a collection of Civil War art that riveted his attention, he explained.

By the time they had begun to climb the hill, the children were lagging behind. Fran turned to the children and suggested, "Why don't you three go back to the refreshment stand and get something to drink. Your father and I will be back in a few minutes."

Walt, Leigh Ann, and Saul were glad to take their leave for a while. Each of them was uncomfortable with grief and unsure how to relate to their father. They jogged down to the snack stand appreciatively.

In the meantime, Lark and Fran had ascended the hill and were standing, looking down onto the ball field below. Lark had experienced some of his most wonderful teenage baseball games on this field. His dad had encouraged him to think of playing baseball for a living. He could hardly wait to brag to the neighbors about Lark's hitting prowess after each game. But his dad had missed, due to his racial prejudice, Lark's finest hour as a hitter. All the folk had heard Ike tell the story the night before, at the wake—how Lark decided to switch hit, batting from the left side, in the annual Jonathon Street game between kids of Lark's neighborhood and the Negroes who lived just beyond the railroad tracks which defined their ghetto on the north. The black pitcher went into his windup, and Lark stepped out of the box. Like Babe

Ruth of Maryland fame before, Lark raised his bat and pointed to the Coca Cola bottling plant across the street from right field. All the black fans loved this sight. They clapped and laughed at this brash white teenager having the pluck to predict where his ball was going when he hit it.

Lark's teammates were mortified. They'd never seen him hit left-handed, even though he first learned to play that way because prior to attending school, he was left handed. Wes wanted to crawl under the dugout, he reported later; his older brother was an embarrassment. But Lark's girlfriend was sitting in the dark sea of faces, and Lark turned to her, tipped his cap, and stepped back up to the plate. What happened next, Ike claimed, was still being talked about whenever baseball is played on Jonathon Street.

Lark swung. It was the sweetest sound and feeling he'd ever experienced in the game of baseball. The ball took off and disappeared deep across the street, after hitting the roof of the bottling plant. Black people and the few white people who saw it, stood upon their feet and roared their approval. The black third baseman said to Lark, as he rounded the hot corner and trotted for home plate, "Hell of a hit, man!" Lark's teammates, including Ronnie and Ike, rolled on the ground with glee at the sight.

Lark went home that night and when his dad inquired about the game, Lark simply said, "We won."

Lark never batted left handed again. Nor did he play first base, like his father wanted him to. From that season on, Lark decided his baseball calling was to pitch. His dad never saw him pitch a game. He missed Lark's game against Al Kaline's team in American Legion baseball. He missed Lark's two no-hitters in high school. He missed Lark's winning home run in the Franklin and Marshall homecoming game his senior year. He missed all of Lark's semi-pro games played in the Blue Ridge Mountain and Dauphin County Twi-Light leagues. Lark's dad never had another word to say about Lark's baseball playing. He lost interest when his son moved from first base to the pitcher's mound. To this day,

Lark regretted that he never told his dad how sweet that hit, one warm night on Jonathon Street, had been.

Remembrances shared, Fran and Lark walked arm in arm down to the refreshment stand where their three progeny awaited. Nothing was said, but the children beamed with pride as their parents walked toward them to gather them for their grandmother's funeral.

The funeral was set for three. Lark drove them to the funeral parlor where they'd spend thirty minutes until the appointed hour. People gathered slowly, including Fran's parents who expressed their sympathy quietly to Lark and then sat with the Wilson children. Each person who came walked by the coffin one more time. It mattered not that most had been to the viewing the night before. They walked past again. Some said the same things: "She looks so nice;" or "She looks just like she's sleeping." The funeral director smiled knowingly.

The hired organist was playing softly when the pastor entered the room and greeted all the mourners. Although Lark had performed this same type of service, himself, many times before, he mused about how deeply he felt the words which were being read.

> *The Lord is my shepherd...*
> *I look to the hills from whence my help comes...*
> *You have sorrow now, but you shall see me again and...*
> *In my Father's house are many rooms. If it were not so...*
> *I saw a new heaven and a new earth and sorrow was no*
>   *more...*

Soon, the pastor was praying, "Support us all the day long of this troublous life," and all were praying in unison; "Our Father..."

As the service progressed, it struck Lark that this man didn't know Mom. He never referred to her by her first name. It was "Mrs. Wilson" this and "Mrs Wilson" that. More words. Lark was growing weary of all the talking. And, suddenly there were the words which moved the lump in his throat into full sobs:

> *"In Dublin's fair city,*
> *Where girls are so pretty,*
> *Sure 'twas there I first met my sweet..."*

Lark cried great tears, as he heard not the pastor's voice, but that of his mother in the midst of the family that began to chant the chorus:

> *"Alive, alive ho-oh*
> *Alive, alive ho-oh,*
> *Crying, Mussels and cockles, alive, alive ho."*

The children glanced at their mother. They'd never seen such a demonstration at a funeral. They'd never seen their father cry, nor heard the mourners sing. She gave them a look which assured them all was well. She reached out to Lark and cradled him in her arms as he cried, and she joined the chorus.

Soon it was ended. The pastor was announcing that the service would be concluded at the grave side, and all were invited back to Ronnie's house afterward for some refreshments. The immediate family members filed out behind the coffin, as the pall bearers guided it down the short funeral parlor aisle and out onto the tarmac to the waiting the hearse. Lark had completely regained his composure by the time he reached the car. They drove the old station wagon to Rose Hill Cemetery in silence. Lark remembered how, as a child, he would stop playing and stare at the cars going out Pennsylvania Avenue in a funeral procession. Now, there were little faces and eyes turning in his direction as they drove to the cemetery.

Grave side services are usually short. Lark often wondered why they were still part of the modern funeral practice. "Everyone's in such a hurry these days, why not drop this part," he had wondered aloud from time to time in clergy gatherings, whenever he was feeling particularly cynical about the ways grief is handled in American society.

He needed no reminder this day of this final ride's importance to those who grieve. When they arrived at the grave site his mom and dad had selected many years before, to place his mom's body next to his dad's, he knew why this was still important to those few who participated. And, for the first time in his life, he appreciated the absence of all but the small family of mourners who lined up beneath the canopy to hear the pastor intone, "Ashes to ashes and dust to dust."

Following the benediction, Lark remained at his mother's grave. Fran reached out and supported him, and he simply stood and looked into the ground which was about to receive his mother's body.

"Goodbye, Mom," he said quietly. "Thanks for everything!"

The children turned to walk to Betty Smythe's car when Ike came up to Fran and Lark to give his farewell.

"Look," he started, "it's really none of my business but, it was good to see the two of you together, even if it did take this dear old woman's death to make it happen."

Neither Fran nor Lark said a word. They simply looked at Ike, as he put his arms around both of them and continued.

"Lark, do you remember that *Harrisburg Patriot* reporter who interviewed you that summer you resigned as pastor at St. Andrew?"

"Yes," Lark replied, wondering what Ike was getting at.

"He was no reporter," Ike said matter-of-factly.

Fran looked at Lark, as he studied what his cousin had just said.

"Look, I gotta run," Ike said. "I'm retiring soon from the company. We'll talk about it then. I've got lots to tell you. I think you'll be interested."

Ike turned and walked briskly to his car where his wife stood, awaiting him. Fran and Lark stood arm in arm and watched him get into his car and drive away.

"Lark," Fran broke the silence between them. "The children and I have talked about South Dakota."

"Yes," Lark responded, taken by surprise yet wary of the rest of the message. "What do you think?"

"We've decided we'd really like South Dakota," she said quietly with a smile.

Lark took her in his arms and whispered, "I'll always love you Fran."

They stood, embracing by his mother's grave, for what seemed an eternity.

Neither said a thing, as they slowly walked to the station wagon. They both thought about what Ike had just said. And, they both knew that there was something they had missed greatly these past few years—each other.